Trapped by deception,
Consumed by desires,
Caught in the act…

Lord, he was half naked!

Merrie choked silently in her hiding place and clamped her hand over her mouth.

"God, Jack, I've missed you—" The lovely woman slid eagerly into his arms, pressing her breasts against his bare chest. She lifted her rosy mouth to him and he claimed it with his own.

That's what this was, Merrie realized dizzily, kissing. It wasn't at all like she'd imagined from the sonnets . . . this was something entirely different; urgent and hungry. She sagged back against the side of the wardrobe, feeling sweat trickling down her neck, between her breasts. Her whole body was hot and steamy . . . and alive in a way she'd never believed it could be.

CAUGHT IN THE ACT

BETINA KRAHN

AVON BOOKS ◆ NEW YORK

The verse on pages 267, 268, and 269 are from *Love Poems of Ovid*, translated by Horace Gregory, copyright © 1963 by Horace Gregory. Reprinted by arrangement with New American Library, a division of Penguin Books USA, Inc., New York, New York.

AVON BOOKS
A division of
The Hearst Corporation
105 Madison Avenue
New York, New York 10016

Copyright © 1990 by Betina M. Krahn
Inside cover painting by Roger Kastel
Inside cover author photograph by Scott Amundson
Published by arrangement with the author
Library of Congress Catalog Card Number: 90-92988
ISBN: 0-380-75778-8

First Avon Books Printing: September 1990

AVON TRADEMARK REG. U.S. PAT. OFF. AND IN OTHER COUNTRIES, MARCA REGISTRADA, HECHO EN U.S.A.

Printed in the U.S.A.

RA 10 9 8 7 6 5 4 3 2 1

for
Don Krahn,
in whose love I am made new, each day

Prologue

"**D**ead."

"As a doornail." The steward of Straffen Manor agreed fully with his goodwife's assessment. The couple, steward and housekeeper, stood by a ponderous oaken bed, staring at their master's mortal shell in the meager candlelight. The ancient Earl of Straffen was a long, lean old man, well into his nineties, and his pale, withered countenance blended into the pristine linen beneath the drapes of his bed. The large bedchamber was darkened, as the old earl liked it, and an evening fire blazed cheerily in the grate of the large stone hearth, warming the room well.

"Took his good time about goin' out. Dem near ten years. Still, if'n he waited this long, he could 'ave took a bit longer." Steward Manley Lombard sighed. There were thought-heavy creases in his broad, plain-featured face.

"Yea, would've been decent of 'im," Goodwife Gert Lombard agreed, crossing herself with reflex piety and clasping her hands at the waist of her long white apron. Thoughts were weighing heavily on her also. "Still, he never was one bit of trouble. Ate his sops and took his powders smartly . . . though he did like a roaring fire." She eyed the crackling blaze, a bit disappointed that it was too far gone now to douse and save the wood. "We did have to spend quite a little bit on wood these last years."

"That we did." He glanced at his wife and nodded.

They stood together for a long moment in silence. The ancient peer of the realm had survived pox and plagues and gout and agues and fevers aplenty in his lifetime, only to be conquered by the divinely designed limitations of the mortal frame. He had literally just worn out. Much as they had understood that this moment must someday come, his steward and his housekeeper could not help thinking it was a bit uncivil of him to die just at this critical time and throw their affairs into such a coil.

Shortly, florid-faced Master Richard Cramden, the old earl's solicitor, was bustled through the bedchamber door by the Lombards' burly son Chester. Frost was still melting on the lawyer's cone-shaped beard and his cheeks were polished from his journey through the icy winter night. He'd taken the trouble to dress fully for this occasion. His somber black woolen doublet was belted securely over his broad expanse of stomach and his hose were properly gartered beneath his voluminous padded breeches. He doffed his flat beaver hat and hurried toward the Lombards' expectant faces.

"Master Lombard, Goodwife Lombard . . . I did hie myself here as fast as I could manage!" He bowed extravagantly in greeting, then craned his fleshy neck toward the figure blending disconcertingly into the bed covers. "It's true, then? That grievous tiding your son brought me of the passing of our most estimable and honorable lord? Saints help us—I can see it with my own eyes! Ahhh—how it afflicts me!"

Cramden halted a foot from the end of the bed and struck a pose and expression of great distress: one toe delicately pointed and his pudgy, beringed fingers splayed over his chest and his jowl in sorrowful horror. In truth, beneath the theatrics common to his profession, he was genuinely distraught at the earl's untimely demise. He, too, had come to count on the old nobleman to live on indefinitely and had managed the old earl's affairs as though they would never be subject to the scrutiny of court officers.

"If only he had held off a bit . . . my youngest and dearest daughter would have been well dowered and set in a fine household. . . ." Cramden halted and reddened beyond his normal rubicund hue, but the glint of recognition in the Lombards' eyes said plainly that they had already seized the worldly sense of his lamentation.

"We be in like distress, Master Cramden. Our eldest, Morris, is at Gray's Inn at Inns of Court in London. . . ." Manley cast a cautious look at his wife and, reading the encouraging gleam in her eye, ventured more of their tale. "He waits the final payment to his master so's he may continue his study at th' law. A right expensive undertakin' is edy-cation." Then, seeing his revelations produce a sympathetic light in the solicitor's countenance, he continued: "Then . . . our eldest daughter be matched to a goodly merchant of St. Albans . . . an' we be pledged to dower. . . ."

Crafty Master Cramden read in these revelations the making of a kinship of need, and his fleshy face creased with a broad smile. "Then we must share our griefs, my good Lombards, and commiserate together." The portly lawyer's stance eased as a bit of guile invaded his mournful mien. "We have been devoted and loyal servants to his lordship; it would certainly be his wish to see us recompensed properly."

The three exchanged brightening grins in the dim candlelight and, as eyes met, so did thoughts and wills. There was a brief silence before Gert stepped to the side of the bed to look down at her departed master with renewed affection.

"Obligin' old cod. The way he was took in stages . . . could sign his name proper, right up to the very last." She smoothed and resettled the folded bedsheet gently over the old man's bony chest and tidied his nightcap against the pillow.

"Was that not purely remarkable?" Cramden responded enthusiastically, holding up one pudgy finger as if recalling something. "The strangest thing . . . upon occasion, my feckless clerk did render to me blank papers and parchment amongst the documents requiring his lordship's signature. I have only just discovered them amongst my papers. Blank parchment . . . with the good earl's most munificent signature. . . ."

It took a moment to settle in on them. There were definite possibilities here.

"Who be th' heir?" Manley inquired, hitting upon their first thorny problem.

"Heir? Good Lord, sir." Cramden was genuinely taken aback. "I . . . don't rightly know. I have never perused that unholy mass of documents my master at the law left me when he died and left the earl's affairs in my hands." He colored hotly under their accusing stares. "Well, it seemed such a task. . . ." Then he scowled, forcing himself to think back. "It comes to me; there was one issue, an aging son. I believe he was gathered into heaven's sweet bosom some years back. Thus, the earl would appear to be *mortuus sine prole.*" He smiled at their puzzlement and translated: " 'Dead without issue.' I cannot even think of a far relation destined for the title. I expect it may expire altogether with the good earl's passing."

"Well, no one visited the old chocker, except'n yerself, sir, fer more'n six years," Gert volunteered eagerly. "Likely he's been fergot even at court."

"Then . . . ain't nobody waitin' about fer dead men's shoes." Manley grinned. Cramden grinned back . . . briefly.

"But wait—in absence of an heir," Cramden suddenly recalled, "it is the crown's right to seize the properties."

"Ye mean . . . after all we done to set th' place arights, they'd scarfle it up?" Manley stared at Cramden, horrified. Poor and obscure to the rest of the world, Straffen Manor had indeed prospered under the Lombards' management and now had several assets of interest . . . and apparently no one to take interest in them.

"It'd be a miser'ble crime, sir, to see such fine estates all broke up by them crown magistrates . . .

dished out like gristles to them slorpy hounds at court,'' Gert declared indignantly.

"A profanation of our magnanimous earl's memory,'' Cramden agreed with a sigh. "If only the juiceless old cod had left some seed—a grandchild, perhaps—then we might be able to continue to benef— . . . administer.'' They all digested that a moment.

"Well . . . then ye mus' search them papers an' records fer an heir, Cramden,'' Gert declared. "Mebee the son spilt a bit o'seed somewheres a'fore he died.''

Cramden sighed, thinking of those monumental piles of parchment and of the hours of labor that such a search would entail. "If we found an heir, there is no assurance that it would solve our problems. We should need time to arrange things properly, and once the old man's rites are reported . . .''

"Rites?'' Manley came to attention and shot a look at Gert.

"Last rites, sir. When the priest records them in his parish books I shall be bounden to send word . . .'' Their blank looks stopped him and it was a long moment before Manley affirmed Cramden's rising hope.

"Do we still do that in th' new religion, Master Cramden?'' Manley winced at the thought of such a dire omission.

"He's not had last rites?'' Cramden's face came alive with unholy glee. "But even in King Henry's and King Edward's new church, a man *cannot* die without last rites!'' He turned to the old earl's silent form, and his slow-building realization of their opportunity came tumbling out. "If the earl has not yet had them, then, *in jure*, he cannot possibly be dead!'' His jowls quivered with excitement. "And we must needs carry on, as the faithful servants we have always been, whilst we search for an heir.''

Gert and Manley looked at each other in amazement, then regarded the silent earl. Incredulity slowly turned to understanding in their faces, and then to crafty determination.

"What a relief it be . . . to 'ave him still with us.''

Gert seized the initiative and patted the old earl's very cold hand. "Give me quite a start, he did. But a body can plainly see . . . he be sleepin' like a babe." With a satisfied sigh, she picked up the candles and ushered her husband and their partner toward the door.

They paused at the foot of the bed for one last look—at the earl, then at each other.

"Sleepin'," Manley observed sagely.

"Like a log," Cramden agreed.

Uncertainty in the affairs of men
Breeds plots, then tends and hatches them.
Wherever chance inscribes an *i*,
Ambition is eager to supply . . .
   a dot.
The greater the uncertainty,
The greater the rewards may be.
Thus, in times of greatest strain,
Sly men watch for chance of gain . . .
   and plot.

Such were the times in England when
King Henry's seed succeeded him:
The people braced, bewildered, awed,
While crown and church fought fang and claw
   . . . over their souls.
Churchmen dreaded the Sabbath day,
For fear of chanting the wrong way.
The pious knew not how to pray
And kept their rosaries tucked away . . .
   beside their Protestant prayerbooks.
Noblemen's sheep grazed peasant crops;
Enclosure went on without stop.
Bread prices soared, inciting riots,
While gentry gobbled gouty diets . . .
   and bewailed their spreading middles.
Farthings and shillings, pounds and pence
Were devalued; worthless recompense.
Farmers starved and martyrs burned

While England for Old Harry yearned . . .
  with perfect hindsight.

It seemed from under every stone,
Sprang a pretender to the throne.
And with each hasty rise to power,
New favorites and new prayerbooks flowered
  . . . briefly.
Then heads would roll or sickness come
And great and lowly were undone.
Edward, Lady Jane, then Mary;
Confusion reigned extraordinary . . .
  in place of wiser heads.
At this foul time, in the English state,
Uncertainty was very great.
Thus it was not so surprising
That servants, masters were despising . . .
  thinking themselves quite as worthy.

Shocking as the notion seems,
Servants through their masters schemed!
The Earl of Straffen was just such;
His servants did not heed him much . . .
  infirm and forgotten as he was.
They used his holdings as their own
Until their fortunes were full grown.
Their schemes and plans became so bold
As Straffen aged and waxed quite cold . . .
  that they bade him die *twice!*
First, under Protestant Edward he went.
And his sly retainers still collected his rents.
Then four years later, without a body to bury,
He died again under Catholic Mary . . .
  and they sent for his heir.

Chapter One

April 1557

Athick-wheeled farm cart jostled down a rutted road north of London, rattling its driver and two occupants like seeds in a dried gourd. It was the third excruciating day in that bone-jarring conveyance for young Meredith Straffen. But unlike the lucky seeds in any gourd, she was forbidden to utter the slightest rattle of protest. Suffering that was not done in silence, her governess had often declared, was unseemly. And since the redoubtable Mistress Overbeake sat across from her in that same cart, bearing the same trials with grim, granitelike fortitude, Meredith clamped her jaw determinedly as her spine was whipped and wrenched and her teeth were rattled in their sockets. The two, mistress and her charge, were a veritable testament to "seemly" misery.

The April air was gray and heavy with a mist that would not rise to form decent clouds nor collect enough to fall as purposeful rain. It wetted their woolen cloaks and hoods, it wilted their linen caps and slowly seeped into their heavy woolen dresses. Merrie shrank further inside her voluminous cloak and tried to avoid all contact with the wooden sides of the cart and with her governess's large, bony knees.

Shifting from one aching buttock to the other, she moaned silently. After three days of this torture, her back, her bottom, her shins, and her tolerance were all badly bruised. Things would have been ever so much easier if only they had made the journey on horseback. But that was out of the question, of course. Mistress

Overbeake despised horses; declared them hideous, smelly, contrary beasts. Merrie sighed and wondered irritably why the governess hated horses so . . . when she and they had so very much in common.

Avoiding her governess's "don't fidget" look, she rearranged herself yet again on the wooden board that formed her seat and tried to fasten her mind on what lay ahead. Soon now, if the Almighty lived up to His reputation for mercy, they would arrive at Straffen Manor, home and seat of the late Earl of Straffen. They must be close; they had already executed the two turns that the innkeeper at their last stop had directed. This rolling green landscape around them, even now, might belong to the estates.

The thought made her study the budding trees, the puddled fields, and the occasional clumps of wattle-and-daub tenant houses with renewed interest. It was a pleasant countryside; a patch-blanket of newly worked fields, woods in the distance, and meandering streams. Dwindling haystacks in the fields caught her eye. For them to be so plentiful and high after a whole winter's feeding, they must have been very large indeed last harvest. Thus, she deduced, it must be a fertile valley, as well.

In truth, Merrie knew almost nothing about the estate where she was commanded to appear. Indeed, she hadn't even known she had a grandfather until almost four years ago. The old Earl of Straffen had somehow discovered her presence in the world and, like a bolt out of the blue, had reached out to exercise his patriarchal prerogative over her. Now that he had died and she was summoned to Straffen, she wondered why she had never been summoned here during the old earl's lifetime. Perhaps it was, as her governess had supposed, that her grandfather was a sickly old man who abhorred the noise and clutter of children. . . .

"How much longer, do you think? Are we on Straffen lands already?"

"We'll arrive when the cart does." Mistress Overbeake settled a dark look on her. Unfortunately Merrie did not see it and thus could not heed it.

''I wonder what Straffen Hall can be like. Do you think it will be timber, or possibly brick . . . goodly kept or ramshackled?'' Merrie's fatigue and preoccupation had made her reckless with her curiosity. The only thing Mistress Overbeake hated more than horses was *questions*.

''It be whatever it is. Cease that infernal questioning, gell! Curiosity in a young gell be most unseemly. I shan't be shamed by your frowardness, gell, ye hear?''

''Yea, Mistress,'' Merrie intoned carefully, lowering her eyes to her hands, which were clasped so tightly that they ached. Her jaw ached, too, from the effort required to keep from uttering something defiant and disastrous.

''Th' earl's executor might have sent a litter and escort, instead of a miserly pouch and a summons to appear with all haste. Not that I complain for myself. . . .'' The mistress's granite jaw had finally been loosened by the pounding and jostling she'd endured. ''But, it be unseemly to treat the granddaughter of an earl so. 'Come hither' . . . like orderin' a hound! Most unseemly—''

The outburst stopped abruptly and Merrie raised widened blue eyes to see what had halted the venting of her governess's ire. And there it was—Straffen Manor. In the mist, the outlines of the buildings were somewhat indistinct, but there was no mistaking the shape of a large hall and the numerous outbuildings that always marked an important seat of residence in the countryside.

Brick and stone, Merrie thought distractedly. Brick formed the wall faces of the manor house and cut stone anchored the corners in pleasing symmetries. Numerous leaded windows, accented by cut stone arches and frames, studded the hall's two floors and attic gables. The roofs were straight and sturdy-looking, made of either tile or slate, and there were numerous chimneys. It was a goodly hall, no question of that. It had a graveled entry court leading right up to the massive front doors, and off to the right, through a small copse of trees, was a large brick building of similar style that Merrie expected would prove to be the buttery and kitchens. The other buildings in the complex, including the stables, were mostly timbered structures with heavy roofs of thatch that made them seem like the heads of children, huddling around the main hall for comfort in the glooming weather.

Merrie's heart thudded strangely in her chest and her fingers grew icy inside her worn gloves. Though modest by noble standards, Straffen Hall was huge and intimidating in comparison to every home she'd known. How could this great place have anything to do with her? Suddenly all those excruciating lessons in etiquette and Mistress Overbeake's interminable lectures on rank and precedence swarmed over her in a rush. Here she might be expected to actually use them, those suffocating rules of place and civility. And just at that moment, every single one of them seemed to have flown out of her head!

Panic gripped her, but her long-standing habit of asking herself silent questions rescued her. What should come first? Greetings, of course.

"And how are superiors to be greeted, gell?" she recalled her mistress's drone in her head.

With a curtsey, she answered mentally. Surely she could manage a curtsey. It never occurred to her that those she would encounter in that august establishment would be anything other than her superiors. So in her head she practiced a small curtsey, a deeper curtsey, and, in case she should need it, a devout, complete obeisance. And hands; gentlewomen extended their hands to gentlemen. She looked down at her damp, worn glove and winced. Was it too much to hope that she'd be greeted only by women?

The hall itself now loomed large, and Merrie's aching eyes were drawn to the entry, with its large arched doors and single stonework step. The front doors swung open and a man and a woman garbed in somber brown emerged, followed by a very portly, red-faced man dressed in the height of fashion. Merrie's eyes fastened in awe on the fat fellow's black velvet doublet with rows of elegant slashings that revealed a gold satin lining. His voluminous breeches matched his doublet and his hose were gold, to match the bright satin of his linings and his hanging sleeves. About his fleshy neck, a standing collar strained to support a small ruff, and a huge golden chain and pendant were draped across his chest. Beside such finery the other man's somber brown doublet and the woman's brown woolen gown looked positively drab. Suddenly Merrie thought of the ill-fitting gown beneath her outsized cloak and felt rather drab and dismal herself.

"Mistress Overbeake, I presume." The brown-clad gentleman with a steward's keys of office about his neck approached and nodded gravely when they had dismounted into the yard. From the black band about his sleeve, it was clear the household was still in mourning for the old earl's passing a fortnight ago. The graying fellow bowed toward Merrie and she panicked briefly and curtseyed back. When he spoke her name, her confusion grew worse. "And Lady Meredith. Welcome, m'lady. I be Manley Lombard, steward of Straffen Manor and his late earlship's estates." He ushered them forward, and Merrie's aching, pinging legs cooperated just enough to move her along. Days in that cramped, jarring cart had managed to loosen every joint in her body and to eradicate every grace of movement she had ever possessed. Just now her discomfort blocked the recognition that she'd been addressed as *Lady* Meredith.

"Might I present Master Richard Cramden, m'lady." Manley Lombard waved to indicate the portly, ostentatiously dressed fellow. "He were the late earl's solicitor and now be exec-utor of the es-tate."

Merrie dropped a curtsey that grew deeper and deeper as her hapless legs refused to counter and reverse it. A glimpse of Mistress Overbeake's hot glare gave her the spurt of strength she needed and she finally managed to straighten.

"My Lady Meredith, welcome." Master Cramden

stepped forward, hand outstretched, and Merrie swallowed and raised her own hand, stepping forward to meet him. But she had forgotten the single step between them and hadn't reckoned on her overlong gown and cloak getting trapped underfoot. . . .

"Master Cr— . . . aaahhh!" She tumbled forward, straight into the solicitor's great, spongy belly. And instead of dropping gracefully to the ground, she suffered an unfortunate, self-protective urge and flailed and clutched at him to keep from going down.

Master Cramden staggered back and sputtered astonishment at the way she launched at him bodily. Belatedly, he realized she was falling, and caught her to lift her and help set her straight upon her feet. Merrie found her fingers had entwined themselves frantically in Master Cramden's fancy doublet slashings and had to extricate them under his incredulous stare. Purpling with humiliation, she just managed to mumble something about it being fine to make his acquaintance.

"And I be Gert Lombard, Housekeeper of Straffen Hall, m'lady." The graying woman with the key-draped girdle about her waist stepped forward into the stunned silence and bobbed a stiff-backed curtsey. Merrie, in catastrophic shock, bobbed back. There was a glint in the housekeeper's keen gray eyes, but otherwise she bore a determinedly pleasant expression on her clean-featured face.

"You mus' be plum exhausted after so long a journ'y, m'lady," Gert said, turning and waving them into the hall. "We prepared chambers for ye and Mistress Overbeake. Mayhap after a rest and a bit of food tonight, ye'll be fit enough to see th' house on th' morrow." Her sidelong glance at the new Lady of Straffen betrayed a certain doubt as to whether Merrie would ever be exactly "fit."

"This be the hall, m'lady." Goodwife Lombard stopped in the midst of an airy, arched vault of a hall that was rimmed with a beautifully carved gallery above their heads on all four sides. A carved staircase soared from the floor of the hall to the gallery on one side and hallways and doors led off the gallery to sleeping chambers above.

The hall below was anchored by a massive cut stone firehearth and mantel, crowned by a massive wooden carving of the heraldic arms of the Straffens. In stately presence in the middle of the hall was a great, carved oaken table surrounded by dignified, lion-claw chairs. The smooth stone floors were covered with fresh reeds that were sprinkled with sweet-smelling herbs. Portraits and tapestries were arranged with pleasing effect along the upper and lower walls and an occasional chest or sideboard nestled beneath them.

Merrie stared, unable to utter a single syllable. When a servant girl appeared at her elbow with an outstretched hand, she started, then realized she was expected to render up her cloak. Soon her overlong gray gown and her wilted linen cap, as well as the womanly young figure beneath them, were exposed. She could feel their eyes on her, assessing her, as she was led forward and seated near the fire.

Meredith Straffen was of middling height and average heft for a woman, but all resemblance to the common run of folk ended there. Her proportions were striking—a slender waist; straight, smooth shoulders; gracefully tapered arms; and delicate hands. Her face was smooth and clear, intriguingly framed on prominent cheekbones. Her skin was given to peachy hues and her straight nose and full-curving lips were exquisitely wrought. Thick fans of silky lashes rimmed large and very blue eyes. She had the marks of true beauty, but just now her grace of movement left rather much to be desired.

The old earl's three agents addressed themselves to the governess, who assured them the journey had been taxing of endurance but otherwise uneventful. Mulled wine was brought and portly Master Cramden explained that Merrie's grandfather had stipulated in his will that she take up residence at Straffen after his death . . . so that she might be properly "advanced" in life.

Merrie drank her wine and tried not to look at her governess as she wondered dimly just what she was expected to "advance" toward. As she listened to Master Lombard's brief history of the hall, her eyelids began to droop in the drowsy warmth.

Oh, Lord . . . it was the wine, she thought distractedly, trying valiantly to stay awake. She had never drunk unwatered wine before; Overbeake never allowed it. Every eye in the hall had taken note of her nodding and shortly she was being trundled up the stairs by her governess and Goodwife Lombard.

She was shown down a hallway to a snug bedchamber with a large, inviting bed and a hearty fire. A fresh-faced young lass named Tess was assigned to assist her and set about unpacking her small leather trunk as Mistress Lombard showed Overbeake down the hall to her chambers.

When the housekeeper withdrew, the governess hurried back to Merrie's room to unleash her irritation.

"Made a full spectacle of yourself, wretched gell! I never been so abased!" she railed. A strangled noise from behind the bed drape silenced her, and when Tess stepped out with a wary expression on her face, Mistress Overbeake stiffened furiously. "That be all, gell. Leave us!" Tess gave Mistress Overbeake a wide berth and slipped out the door with a furtive look at Merrie.

"It will take ages upon ages to undo the calamity of this introduction." Overbeake launched into a detailed list of the wanton incomprehensibility of Merrie's behavior and ended by grasping Merrie's shoulders harshly.

"My legs were weak and I tripped, Mistress." Defiant light flashed in Merrie's blue eyes before she lowered her lashes to hide it. "My gown was too long; you said so yourself. There was no time to hem it properly. . . ." It was a valid excuse, though it bordered on mutiny to blame the garment. The governess stiffened, and Merrie stiffened with expectation. It would not be the first time she had felt the harshness of the governess's hand. But Overbeake released her and stepped back.

"And curtseys to housekeepers and stewards! Ye be *Lady Meredith* now." She shook a harsh finger, but her own reminder of her charge's new status made her pause and withdraw it. "Make no more mis-steps, gell. I shan't be shamed by bumptious and unseemly behavior. Ye hear?"

"Yea, Mistress." Merrie fairly choked on the words but made herself utter them in a level tone. Not quite satisfied, but unable to do more, Overbeake stomped out and slammed the door behind her. Merrie wobbled over to the bench at the foot of the postered bed and sank down on it, taking a handful of the hateful gray woolen in her hand. Her nose curled at the smell that emanated from it in the room's warmth. It was Mistress Overbeake's soured smell . . . because it was Overbeake's gown. She'd had nothing suitable for traveling and the governess had insisted on taking seams up the sides of one of her own sizable gowns for Merrie.

Well, the seams were rudely done, leaving huge ridges down her sides and lumps under her arms, and the gown smelled like the seldom-washed governess herself. The sleeves were too long, the shoulders too wide, and the skirt lay in a pool around her feet. And now she'd tripped over it and fallen into her grandfather's solicitor's stomach and gotten fouled in his clothing and made a perfect booby of herself upon arriving. . . .

What in Heaven's Name was she doing here?

Below, in the cozy small parlor just off the great hall, the Lombards and Master Cramden were engaged in solemn conference. They'd taken the measure of their old earl's granddaughter and now compared their perceptions.

"She be a right comely gell," Manley observed,

pouring them a bit of wine. "Not chitty-faced nor pox-scarred, not pussley-gutted nor sway-backed."

"Indeed. Delightful . . . a sweet, clear oval of a face, with a pert little nose. And most unusual hair," Cramden offered, sipping his grape and recalling wistfully. "Under that modest maiden's cap, I trow I saw summer wheat kissed with the flame of the setting sun. And those lovely eyes . . . blue as a tender robin's egg . . ." He caught himself escaping into poetic muse and sighed, remembering their purpose for her. "A mere waif of a thing, lost in that cloak . . ."

"She be a woman, full-growed." Gert crossed her hands over her waist and cocked a disgusted brow at Cramden's courtly musings. "Her gown were over-large, 'at's all. She be a meek little thing; we be lucky there. A pity she be awkward, though. We shall have to watch the glassware."

"Perhaps we should have announced the earl's death and brought her to Straffen some time ago . . . to see to her upbringing," Cramden said, betraying stirrings of gentlemanly sentiment.

"Tosh, Cramden," Gert chided. "We agreed; it were best to keep her at a distance an' have her reared apart from others, so there wouldn't be no int'rest taken in her. Th' fewer to see her, the better. An' th' less she knows of th' world, the better."

"You're right. Of course," Cramden agreed, shaking off impending misgivings.

"To our little Lady Meredith." Manley's sober face broke into a grin as he raised his pewter wine cup. Satisfied smiles appeared on the others' faces as he continued: "May she live long . . . so we prosper."

Above their heads, Merrie had taken a bit of supper, set her clothes aside, and washed the grime of travel from her. She brushed her full, strawberry blonde hair carefully and climbed up into the postered bed, drawing the drapes. But her mind buzzed too much to permit sleep. She turned, as she so often did, to her own mental dialogue, where all questions were permitted and even encouraged.

What did it mean to be "Lady Meredith"? The steward and housekeeper and solicitor . . . they'd bowed and curtseyed to *her*. Did that mean she was a lady now?

Four years ago, it had been quite a jolt to thirteen-year-old Merrie to learn she was an earl's granddaughter. She had been raised to believe herself an orphan with no surviving blood kin. Her father had died just before she was born and her mother followed him only a year after her birth. All she knew about them was that her father was an older gentleman of good education and that her mother was a very lovely and very young merchant's daughter who had been recently orphaned and was in dire need of protection. The good priest who had arranged the marriage was quite elderly himself and died shortly after pronouncing the vows. Despite the more-than-thirty-years age difference, it had been a marriage in fact, for Meredith was most properly sown, acknowledged, and registered by her father.

But soon there was nothing left to mark what had transpired, except an entry on a parish register and a rosy, robust girl-child. No one thought to search out her prospects and all thought it a fine and decent thing when the old priest's replacement gave Merrie over into the care of a pair of pensioned retainers from the Earl of Essex's household. The aging schoolmaster, Marcus Hale, and his goodwife, Polly, took little Meredith Straffen to both their hearth and their hearts. She became the child they had always desired but never produced in their long years together. They duly watched and guided her growth, comforted her hurts, answered her many questions, and gave her the security of their home and their love.

Marcus, being a scholar of modest renown, insisted that Merrie be given a good and full education. And his standards for what constituted acceptable learning knew no gender. Her first books were in common English, but soon she was required to study Latin and the classics, as had the young noblemen in his charge in earlier days. A great devotee of the Socratic method of teaching, Marcus always answered Merrie's questions with a question.

"Isn't it time for dinner yet, Marcus?" she asked as they worked on their knees in the little garden by their stone-and-timber cottage.

"Where is the sun in the sky, Merrie?" White-haired Marcus paused in his weeding and gave her the somber, expectant look of a teacher.

"Just waning from its zenith, Marcus," she answered.

"And when would you say, according to your experience, does Polly usually make dinner ready?"

"When the sun is just past its zenith."

"And what can you deduce from that?"

"That Polly likely has our dinner ready." Merrie fidgeted and glanced longingly at the cottage.

"Likely it is so. Then, is 'time' the determining factor in partaking of food or is there more required?"

Merrie sighed, trying to think. But when she opened her mouth again, her stomach growled ferociously enough to drown her words. She wailed, "Marcus, I'm starved!"

"Then 'appetite' is also required for partaking of food." Marcus had laughed, pushing to his feet and ruffling her strawberry blonde curls affectionately. "What a scholar you will make, my little Merrie."

By such methodology, Marcus unwittingly sowed in Merrie a trait universally adored in scholars and abhorred in females. She asked questions . . . about everything, from the mundane to the mind-boggling, from the obvious to the obscure. It was the way in which she learned, the manner in which she lived . . . until that day nearly four years ago when, in the name of rank and privilege, her grandfather had laid claim to her and her "welfare."

The Earl of Straffen's first act as her self-appointed master was to pluck her from the Hales' care and install her in a modest house in the town of Witham, under the proper and rigid thumb of Mistress Rebecca Overbeake. Merrie was crushed and bewildered at first, as were Marcus and Polly. But the elderly couple, used to thinking of noble connections as a rare and wonderful privilege, finally convinced her that it was in her best interest to cooperate with the earl's arrangement for her. Much as it broke their aging hearts, they turned their sweet Merrie over to the middle-aged mistress and what became a life of virtual isolation.

Mistress Overbeake, as it happened, loathed questions of any sort, for questions demanded answers and all demands coming from young females were unseemly. The rules of "seemliness," in the stern governess's mind, were no less than a codicil to the Ten Commandments themselves. They were the rules that established the very worthwhileness of life itself. Without that vast body of societal "shalts" and "shalt-nots," Mistress Overbeake was convinced, mankind would dissolve into a mass of slavering, unredeemable animals.

Thus, Merrie had learned to curb her questions, if not her curiosity, for the sake of existence with her stiff-backed mistress. It was a small tyranny, but it denied her a large part of her nature and forced her to measure each word and deed. As the days passed, turning into years, Merrie's longing to escape such dispiriting confinement grew. And now, at nearly eighteen years, she longed desperately for some control over her own life, for a meager bit of freedom in her own thoughts and responses.

In the dim light of the fire's coals, in her soft new bed, she felt a strange expectation building in her. She was an earl's granddaughter, a status that she had already seen made a difference in her governess's eyes. What were ladies' lives like? What were the duties attached to her new life, besides the toilsome "stitchery"? And privileges . . . surely there must be some privileges. Like the freedom to choose her own clothing for the day. Her mind raced and her heart began to thud against her ribs. Freedom . . . the word echoed in her mind and filled her chest with swelling hope. Freedom to speak and think as she pleased? Oh, precious thought! Just imagine: freedom to speak, to ask a question and have it answered, to direct her own time, to answer to no one but herself.

The next afternoon, Mistress Overbeake paused to smooth her gray woolen skirt and tug up her wing collar before she entered the small parlor just off the great hall. The Lombards and Master Cramden had summoned her and she found them waiting with serious faces and clearly evaluative looks. The portly solicitor was seated in a heavy chair and the housekeeper and steward stood on either side of him. The governess took the seat they offered her and held herself erect as she assured them that both she and Lady Meredith had slept well and were recovering from their journey.

"I have been entrusted with the responsibility to carry out the late earl's behests concerning Lady Meredith," Master Cramden intoned smoothly. "It is a grave and awesome responsibility. You must tell me about your young charge, Mistress, so that I may properly execute my duty toward her." Cramden tilted his head back and studied the governess with a sniff. "I don't suppose she can read?"

"Oh . . . sir . . ." Overbeake could not tell whether it would please or displease him to hear it. "The gell does read . . . and write . . . uncommonly well."

At that very moment, "the gell" had descended the stairs from the gallery and was approaching the sound of voices in the parlor. Only the sound of her own name on the governess's lips stopped her from entering the parlor straight away. Overbeake was talking about her. She paused, listening, feeling a bit uncomfortable at the idea of eavesdropping. But the next thing she heard obliterated all her misgivings.

". . . and them miscreants she lived with before the earl placed me over her, they taught her *Latin*," Overbeake was saying. Merrie was stunned to hear her beloved Marcus and Polly slandered so. "And that's not all. . . . Ciphering, too. And not a whit of needle-work—"

"*Latin?*" Cramden choked. "Good God." He glanced with alarm at Gert and Manley and sat forward, all attention now. The gell could read Latin and *cipher?* What an appalling development!

"Pretentious and unwomanly, sir, I know." Overbeake hurried on, truly worried by Cramden's horror. "But I took it upon myself, sir, to remedy such. Wouldn't let her read no Latin, nor anything save Scripture. Saw to it she learnt stitchery and kept her fingers busy. Likely she's forgot it by now."

"Let us all hope so." Cramden tossed a look at Manley and eased back in his chair.

In the hall, Merrie flattened weakly against the wall beside the door, her face flaming. Forget Latin, indeed. She'd sooner forget her own name! And she'd managed to read quite a little bit, thanks to the kindliness of a sickly old neighbor gentleman who had gotten permission for her to visit him in the name of Christian charity. She had read to him from his books each afternoon. It was all that had made her life bearable these last few years.

Cramden's deep frown made Overbeake reconsider revealing her charge's greatest flaw, her penchant for questioning. She concentrated on Merrie's promising accomplishments. "Lady Meredith has a melodious singin' voice, sir, and plays the virginal passably well. She's not one bit grand or given to idle twaddle. It may take her a bit to get used to dealin' with servants, sir, for we had but a cook and a chambergirl. I kept her on prunes an' proverbs, sir, and away from untoward influences. But she's not dull-witted, sir, not one bit. She'll catch on."

"She'll 'catch on' . . ." Master Cramden echoed, casting a meaningful look at Manley Lombard. Heaven forbid the gell ever did that! He became aware of the governess's look of alarm and forced himself to brighten and take charge once more.

"How good to hear she is so . . . malleable. Now let me assure you of his late lordship's concern for her welfare. Lady Meredith is his principal heir, having been his only surviving kin. She has been placed, temporarily, under the guardianship of Sir Edwin Gannulf of Bedford, a dear old friend of the good earl. I say 'temporarily,' for it was the earl's wish that Lady Meredith be wedded as soon as possible. A marriage has been arranged and will be concluded within the fortnight. It is a proper match in all respects and much thought and preparation have gone into it. Once she is wedded, control of Lady Meredith's affairs shall naturally pass to her husband."

"But," he continued with a rueful smile, "Lady Meredith's future husband has business affairs in London, which may require protracted absences." Cramden flicked a glance at the Lombards. "M'lady will have need of advice and . . . companionship. We would naturally wish you to stay on in that capacity, good Mistress Overbeake."

"Indeed?" The governess flushed like a courted maid at the suggestion. "Well, I shall be most honored to continue my duties with Lady Meredith. She still has much to learn of ladycraft, and I shall make it my vocation to see she learns it proper."

Merrie melted against the wall, her eyes huge with shock as the thought hammered into her brain. *Marriage!* The sounds of leavetaking and the scraping of chairs finally penetrated her senses. She started and jolted for the front doors at an unladylike run. She tugged open the doors just in time and hurried frantically out into the warm spring sun. Pausing to collect her outward self, she managed to walk across the graveled court toward what appeared to be a small garden. But by the time she reached it, her legs would barely support her and she dropped onto a stone bench in the shade of a flowering apple tree.

Dearest Heaven—say it wasn't true! She was to be married in only a fortnight . . . to some old man she'd never seen! She'd go from under Overbeake's rigid thumb to under a paunchy old husband's, without so much as a "by your leave"! No, she'd not be just trading thumbs, she'd actually be adding them. They were going to keep Overbeake on as her *companion* in her husband's absences! Good Lord, she was still going to have a governess even after she wedded! She'd be subject to the horse-toothed old governess *and* to a smelly old husband. It was intolerable; she'd positively suffocate! Even now she was having trouble getting her breath.

Merrie's head reeled and she had to hold it between her slender hands to keep from toppling over. How could they do this to her? Just when she thought she might gain some bit of freedom for herself. . . .

Ladies, especially lady-heirs, were expected to marry, she knew. Overbeake had sometimes made reference to it, regarding her future. But somehow she'd never quite connected such expectations with herself. Now that treacherous lot in the parlor spoke of her as though she were some tonnage of a commodity that needed proper storage. Weigh her up and marry her off! It was just too horrible.

"What are the alternatives, Merrie?" She suddenly heard dear old Marcus's voice in her head. It was one of his favorite questions. Marcus saw possibilities everywhere, even in the darkest of situations. And he'd trained Merrie to search them out logically, methodically. Questions slowly began to form in her struggling mind.

What chance was there that the marriage could be prevented? None. It was the old earl's requirement; she was his heir . . . his sole heir.

What would happen if she were to renounce the inheritance? They'd declare her dauncy as a doodle and lock her up, that's what! Nobody renounced a fine inheritance like Straffen.

What about running away . . . taking another name, making another life? As what? Where? With whom?

She sighed, determined that there had to be more. Was there anyone who might lend an ear, then lend weight to her cause? Wait . . . she had a guardian, Sir Edwin Gannulf of Bedford. She knew where Bedford was, sort of; it was north somewhere. What if she went to him and begged him to postpone the marriage a year . . . two years? It was a reasonable request, based on her newness to noble life and custom. She had always been able to set herself forth properly in words. Perhaps she could make him see how wrong it was to force her into such a hasty marriage.

Sir Edwin Gannulf. The name had a wise and noble ring to it. Merrie's determination rose apace with her heartbeat. How would she get there? She would have to have transport, of course. Well, there was a whole stable of horses a few hundred yards away . . . possibly even *her* horses. The thought stopped her. Did she actually own some part of Straffen Manor? Was that what they meant by "principal heir"? She shivered with fear and expectation at the thought. The entire consideration of her future and of the impact of her marriage was borne in on her. Undoubtedly there was property involved, agreements and dowry . . . she knew that much. These were large and important matters indeed. It suddenly seemed a very adult world into which she had been thrust.

She squared her shoulders, fortified by the power of her reasoning and by the tools of thought Marcus had instilled in her. She was not a helpless, ignorant "gell." She'd go to her guardian . . . she'd persuade him, make him see. Bold new determination flooded into her sun-warmed shoulders. Tonight . . . she'd go this very night!

Chapter Two

Had Merrie Straffen been a bit more in the know of things, she likely wouldn't have chosen to run straight to the nearest inn. However, being an innocent, and a very determined one at that, she thought of the considerable wagon and horse traffic she'd witnessed at the Winifred's Noll as they passed it the day before, and counted it a perfect place to find a guide of some sort to lead her to Bedford.

She had played out the evening as though in complete ignorance of their vile plans for her, taking supper in the small parlor with Overbeake and Master Cramden. She spoke as little as possible and afterward asked to retire to her rooms for evening prayers and early sleep. There she prepared for bed with doe-eyed Tess's help and knelt to make especially fervent prayers upon her prie-dieu. Then she climbed into bed and pretended to sleep until the house settled into the night. She rose and dressed, snatching up her cloak and tucking the coins she had secreted from Mistress Overbeake's chamber into her bodice.

Cloaked in shadows, she slipped to the stables and struggled mightily to saddle a gentle-looking mare. She led the horse until she was well away, then shoved her foot into the stirrup and hopped valiantly until she managed to mount. As she struck out along the road, she exulted in her achievement, feeling utterly free.

The Winifred's Noll was awash in lively trade that night; rough wagoneers, traveling gentry, and local farm lads shared the hot, busy taproom of the inn. The air was thick and close when Merrie entered, and she stood fixed in the doorway, squinting against the lantern light for some sign of that fellow the cart driver had spoken to the day before. He was the innkeeper, she knew, and he seemed a goodly enough sort to give her assistance. Two big, staggering rummies came barreling through the door from behind her, shoving her farther into the tavern.

She skittered and shrank back by the door, drawing her cloak closer about her. She'd never seen the inside of a tavern before, nor ever witnessed so many men together in one place. The only other women present were serving wenches, who were laughing and dodging hands, squealing in mock outrage at the bold caresses bestowed upon them. Merrie stared wide-eyed at the pawings and at the wenches' reactions. It gave her an uneasy feeling and made her all the more eager to catch the innkeeper's notice. Making her way past the ale-soaked wooden bar and around the edge of the crude planking tables, she tried to stay as inconspicuous as possible. But just as she neared the innkeeper, an eruption of fists and fury occurred near the door that sent him flying to quell it. She was shoved aside and banged unceremoniously into the wall.

For a few moments all attention was on the disposition of the fight, and Merrie swallowed her heart back into place. Feeling decidedly out of her element now, she became desperate to see the man and started for him again. But she froze in her tracks as a familiar face and bulk appeared in the tavern door and engaged the innkeeper in earnest conversation.

It was a face and form she recognized from Straffen, that big servant fellow—Chester, they called him! Lord, she'd been found out! In a blind panic, she backed away—straight into the newel post of the banister leading upstairs. Without thinking, she turned and grabbed up her skirts to flee upward, into the darkness at the head of the stairs. Standing in the hallway that led to the sleeping rooms, she watched with horror as Chester Lombard's burly strength advanced toward the stairs with the innkeeper.

She staggered back, feeling her way along the dim

walls, passing door after door. And as she approached the end of the hallway, two male figures appeared in the gloom at the head of the steps. Trapped now, she found her hand on a door latch and lifted it, escaping into a dimly lit chamber.

Through the pounding of her heart in her ears, she could still make out the sound of footsteps on the creaking boards outside. Desperate, she groaned and scoured the chamber for a place to hide. A huge, battered wooden wardrobe stood to one side of the door and at the urging of those ominous footsteps and male voices, she jerked it open and climbed inside. She just managed to pull the tail of her cloak in after her as the chamber door was flung open and a deep, resonant male voice issued from the doorway.

"See if the innkeeper has brandy, Seabury, then keep watch for my lady."

"Brandy?" came a response. "Even if he has it, it'll be outrageously expensive—"

There was a muffled reply of some sort and two deep male laughs with a knowing edge to them that unnerved Merrie. Then came the sound of the door closing, and through the generous gap between the warped wardrobe doors she saw the room's occupant stroll into view.

It was most certainly not Chester from Straffen. It was a tall, powerful-looking man with raven hair and no beard. He was dressed in an expensive dark green velvet doublet, with ivory satin linings visible through fashionable slashes, and breeches that matched. He wore hose of the same green and tall riding boots that glowed dully in the candlelight. From hiding, Merrie watched him cross the room and light the other candles in the holder.

He began to hum some rather melodious nonny-nonny and brought the candelabra to the small table beside the draped bed. He pulled back the quilt to check the freshness of the bed linen, then sent his hands to work the top buttons of his doublet. He certainly didn't seem in any hurry to be gone. Merrie moaned silently.

A rap came on the door and he exited her view, to return a moment later with a tray laden with a flagon and two pewter wine goblets. He grinned to himself as he sampled the brew, then leisurely tossed back the rest of the goblet. His face was fully visible now, a smooth, muscular face with strong bones and a straight, noble nose. Merrie's eyes fastened on his mouth, his full, well-defined lips that now glistened from the "brandy." He was, she realized helplessly, a very handsome man. This time, his fingers went to his buttons in earnest and right before Merrie's horrified eyes, he removed his ruff and his padded doublet, baring a soft, collarless shirt with voluminous sleeves.

But her horror was destined to grow worse. He untied the shirt to reveal a broad, well-muscled chest, shadowed by a thatch of black hair, then paused to eye both the wardrobe and the doublet over his arm.

God please—Merrie prayed in hot desperation—*let him be a slovenly wretch who never hangs his clothes!* Whether in answer of her prayer or not, the gentleman—for he could be nothing else with such fine raiment—turned aside and hung the doublet over the back of the wooden chair nearby. Her wilting relief was short-lived. He proceeded to strip the shirt completely from his wide, smooth shoulders.

Lord, he was half naked! Merrie choked silently in her hiding place and clamped her hand over her mouth. She'd never seen a man's unclothed body in her life. She was entranced by the pure horror of it. Broad, smooth bands rippled under the glowing skin of his back and caps of well-defined muscle formed the crest of his shoulders. Then he turned and Merrie saw the hard, prominent mounds of his chest and that black hair that seemed like lace against his skin from this distance. She was a little shocked to see brown blotches on his chest, right where bubbies were on her. Her arms crossed and pressed her breasts as she tried in vain to swallow. His body tapered to a much narrower waist and there were ridges of muscle over his ribs. He was fascinating—and terrifying.

The air in the sour-smelling wardrobe was suddenly suffocating. Pushing her hood back from her head, she tried to loosen her cloak and shrug it from her shoulders. It was hopeless in the cramped quarters. Lord—what was she going to do? She'd be roasted alive.

A soft rapping came on the door and the gentleman hurried to answer it with one boot on, one off. There was a flurry and the thud of the door in its frame and suddenly there were two figures in the chamber. The man drew a cloaked woman into Merrie's line of sight. But the cloak was soon abandoned to the floor. Beneath it was a gown of stunning crimson reembroidered brocade and in the gown was a very beautiful dark-haired woman.

"God, Jack, I've missed you. . . ." The lovely woman slid eagerly into his arms, pressing her breasts against his bare chest and shivering as though the contact brought her some physical purge of ecstasy. Jack laughed a queer, animal sort of a laugh, and sent his hands to rub her slender, brocaded waist. She lifted her rosy mouth to him and he claimed it hungrily with his own, pressing, slanting, rubbing it over her lips. She moaned and clasped his broad back with possessive fingers.

They stood entwined for some time, kissing. That's what this was, Merrie realized dizzily, kissing. Her fingers ventured to her own lips and her throat constricted strangely. It wasn't at all like she'd imagined from the sonnets . . . which made it sound quite noble and divine and glorious. This was something entirely different; urgent and hungry. And as they turned just slightly, their lips parted for an instant and Merrie realized that their mouths were fully opened, that their tongues—

Now she really should faint, if there was a single drop of decency in her! But instead her eyes began to burn and she felt a strange hollowness, which mimicked hunger, in her stomach. Now it felt like her body was being roasted from the inside out!

"I couldn't resist sending for you, you haughty vixen. I was afraid you wouldn't be able to come." Jack raised his head, nibbling and sucking on her lips in shocking and tantalizing ways. Merrie licked, then chewed her own itching, tingling lips in unblinking response.

"My husband is in London till next week," the haughty vixen moaned between voluptuous bites of his kisses. "I'd come to you anywhere, anytime. Undo me, I want to feel you against my breasts. God, Jack I'm so hungry—"

His hands withdrew and Merrie gasped when she saw them working the tiny pearl buttons on the front of the vixen's gown. But some perverse and distractable part of her admired his obvious skill with the fastenings; she always had such trouble with her own. . . . Lord, what was she thinking? She tried closing her eyes, but it was no good. The throaty groaning coming from the pair compelled her to apply her eye to that wretched slit of light again. She *had* to see what was happening, even if it did send her straight to perdition.

Jack was peeling the vixen's elegant gown from her, kissing—no, devouring—her skin as it was revealed. He licked and nipped and nuzzled her bare nape, her shoulders, her elbows. Soon the elegant gown lay in a heap about her feet and Jack took her in his arms and consumed her with another open-mouthed kiss. Only this time their bodies pressed and rubbed, especially their lower halves. Soon Jack's breeches were falling, leaving him clad only in form-fitting hose. Then the vixen's petticoats dropped in a flurry of hands and lips and the pair worked their way, kissing, toward the edge of the bed nearest Merrie.

Jack's hands worked at the vixen's steely corset, half tearing it from her trembling body in eagerness. And her chemise—he did rip ribbons on that as his hands pushed it aside to take her small, cool breasts into his big hands. His kisses lowered down her throat as she wriggled her pelvis against his lower parts. And as Merrie's horrified eyes widened to the maximum, his mouth lowered toward the dark little nipples the vixen was thrusting insistently at him. . . .

The banging on the chamber door startled Merrie and she thumped her head against the side of the wardrobe. Fortunately the other banging was so loud that her own thump went unnoticed. She bit her lip and set her eye to the crack again as she heard Jack's soft curses and the lady's groan of frustration.

"I'll be right back, lovey." He teased one nipple between his fingers and the vixen squirmed and gasped as though he were torturing her.

"Get rid of them, Jack—I'm too hot to share you," she rasped commandingly. He murmured something in her ear and she gave a very naughty laugh. When he turned to the door, Merrie gasped audibly, then clamped her hand over her mouth again. The front of his hose, below his waist, was bulging hugely. Instinct, and her few observations of farm animals in various states of rut, helped her deduce what it was. She sagged back against the side of the wardrobe, feeling sweat trickling down her neck, down her back, between her breasts. She could hardly breathe. Her whole body was hot and steamy . . . and alive in a way she'd never imagined it could be.

There was a long silence in the room, though muffled men's voices were discernable outside. Merrie opened her eyes and saw that the vixen was fully naked now, except for her stockings and garters, and she was drinking a bit of the brandy Jack had ordered earlier.

"Damme, Jack"—the vixen savored the taste and licked her lips with a seductive smile—"you never forget what a gell likes, do you? Well, I haven't forgotten either." She dipped her fingers in the brandy and dribbled it over both her taut nipples, rubbing it about and closing her eyes as though she enjoyed it.

Merrie watched, thunderstruck, making the connection in her fertile mind like a good little scholar; brandy and bubbies . . . both for drinking. . . . Oh, Lord— surely not!

Please . . . no more . . . she didn't want to see any more! And, *please, God,* if she lived to get out of here, she'd ride straight back to Straffen and be a good little bride and *never* run away again!

The door opened partway; the voices from the hall became quite clear.

"Been here ever night fer a week, waitin' for ye, sarr, an' I ain't goin' on wi'out ye. I'll not budge me from th' spot til yer ridin' wi' me!" came an irritable voice.

"Hell's hump, man, have you no decency—I've told you I'll be along presently!" Jack was obviously quite irritated himself. "All right, then stand there like a bloody great stump—grow roots, for all I care!" He slammed the door and strode across the room to take the vixen in his arms again. He kissed her quite forcefully and Merrie's beleaguered brain deduced weakly that there must be quite a few ways of kissing . . . depending on the mood of those so engaged.

Then before Merrie's burning eyes, Jack's mouth lowered to capture one of those brandied nipples and he laughed, a ragged, desirous laugh of surprise. "You little witch. You're well prepared, aren't you?"

Then he released her with a dark, almost predatory look on his handsome face. He untied his hose and rolled them down, shucking them off. And Merrie was suddenly privy to manhood's last great secret from her: the sight of a male member, engorged . . . erect.

Something momentous was about to happen; Merrie could feel it. Her whole body was weak, her stomach was churning and she couldn't seem to drag her eyes from the splendid horror of his manly shape. Then the vixen climbed up into the middle of the bed, bracing on her hands and knees, and wriggled her bare bottom at him, groaning.

"Come get me, Jack. . . . I'm so hot for you! Come take me."

Jack stalked slowly around the end of the bed, his face dark and dusky, his eyes fixed on her wriggling invitation.

Oh, please—Merrie prayed desperately—*not that!* Especially not *that!*

He climbed up over the end of the bed and bit—*bit!*—the vixen on one buttock! Merrie went utterly limp and slid down against the side of the wardrobe; everything was going dark. But she didn't have to see it to know what would happen. When she lived with Marcus and Polly in the country, she'd seen horses and cattle in the fields . . . and this was exactly like it. He was going to—

A harsh pounding came on the door again and Merrie jolted, clamping her hands over her mouth. She trembled, squeezing her eyes shut tightly. Her heart thudded wildly in her throat. She heard muffled epithets of anger, both male and female.

"What are you doing?" the vixen called with an edge of irritation in her voice. "Jack! Don't answer it. . . . They'll go away. Who the hell is it, anyway? Ja-ack!"

But there was a rustling and a muffled voice through the door. It was pure mortal sinfulness that made her put her eye to the crack again, Merrie knew. But she did it anyway. The vixen was alone on the bed, scrambling to pull a quilt up over her bareness, and she looked positively furious. Merrie could hear the door being opened.

"Ye come wi' me now, sarr," came that indignant voice, "or don' bother comin' a'tall!"

"Dammit, man, you can see I'm busy. . . ." Jack sounded like he spoke through his teeth. There was a creak of the hinges as he stepped farther outside to keep the fellow from seeing exactly who he was busy with.

"I see yer busy, sarr." The voice was barely audible now. "But ye kept us waitin' a whole week, a'ready. It be now or *never.*"

"Dammit." There was a coil of conflicting interests in Jack's voice. Someone else was apparently as eager for his company as the haughty vixen. There was a prickly moment of silence in which he made his unhappy choice. "Let me get my clothes. I'll be with you shortly."

The door closed sharply and Jack strode back inside, shedding the breeches he'd donned hurriedly. He reached for his hose and leaned a broad shoulder against the bedpost to pull them up his long, muscular legs.

"What's happening?" The vixen slid to the edge of the bed, clearly affronted by Jack's actions. "Just what do you think you are doing?"

"I have to go out, lovey, for a little while. A pressing business matter; it won't take long. I'll be back before you have a chance to cool off." He shot a wickedly charming grin at her . . . which didn't work.

"The hell you are!" she stiffened imperially. "I came here to meet you at some risk, Gentleman Jack, and I shan't be left in a cold bed while you chase about—"

"Of course not, lovey," he uttered soothingly, abandoning the ties of his breeches to take her in his arms and kiss her thoroughly. "I'll be back in an hour—and I'll heat you up properly. All over. This is an important business settlement . . . a small fortune involved. Nothing less could tear me from your side."

Under his stunning, possessive kisses, the vixen seemed to melt physically and soon she was reclining on the bed, watching him don the rest of his clothes. When he was ready, he turned to her for a last, lusty kiss and a grasp of her alluringly draped buttocks.

"I won't be long." He extricated himself from her clasping arms and exited to the petulant wail of his name.

"Ja-ack!"

Merrie swooned in her airless hiding place, wondering weakly what they would think when they found a suffocated virgin in "Gentleman Jack's" wardrobe. But the sound of stirring in the room roused her and she raised her wobbly head to see the vixen striding irritably about the chamber, collecting her clothes.

"How dare he leave me . . . primed and un-stretched. The handsome swine—business settlement indeed!" she railed, hauling on her corset and straining viciously at the lacings. "Gone off to make a 'settlement in tail' elsewhere, I trow. I'll not stand for it!" She settled her petticoats about her waist and tied them with jerky movements.

"If he thinks he can do this to me . . . to *me*—" She choked, her fury rising to turn her face as crimson as the gown she was donning. Soon she raised her skirts and shoved her feet into her slippers, scouring the chamber visually for anything she might have forgotten. Then she snatched up her cloak and furled it about her shoulders, storming out.

The chamber was empty. It took a while to register on Merrie's shock-numbed brain. She roused herself and shook her head, feeling as if she were moving in a fog. Her first thought was to clamber out of that wretched wardrobe into breathable air, but her second thought stayed her. What if one of them came back? She groaned, remembering the misery her impetuosity had already bought her, and made herself wait a few more interminable minutes before she stirred herself and thrust open the doors.

Peeling herself from the walls of her hiding place, she slid her cramped, sweaty body out of the wardrobe and gasped lungsful of decent air. Her legs were barely strong enough to support her as she clomped forward, bracing her hands on her knees to drag in breath after cleansing breath.

When her heart slowed its pounding and her head seemed to be clearing, she remembered her cloak and retrieved it from the floor of the wardrobe. She pulled it about her shoulders, teetering a bit so that she bumped into the table where Jack and his vixen had left the brandy. Recoiling as if bitten, Merrie stared at the jiggling goblets and then turned her gaze to the rumpled bed.

A pure wave of anxiety coursed through her. She squeezed her eyes shut, trying desperately to blot out all she'd seen. But the impact of it was all too clear in her mind. She'd never imagined such things went on. It suddenly occurred to her that there might be a great deal in the wide world that she had no notion of.

She was a maid . . . a mere gell, with little experience in the world. On a clandestine journey to Bedford she could be prey to any one of several vile and hideous fates. The foolhardiness of her flight from Straffen was now eminently clear. She might have been discovered in this "Gentleman Jack's" chamber and sent home in utter disgrace, or—her eyes widened further— she might *not* have been sent home at all.

Lord help her! The promises she'd made in the wardrobe suddenly came back to her and she pulled her hood up and over her cap so that none of her burning face could be seen. Collecting the cloak firmly about her, she stalked stiffly to the door and listened. There was only quiet outside and she lifted the latch and escaped into the hallway. She was going home, to Straffen. And if heaven was merciful, she would find another way to reach Sir Edwin.

As she slipped down the rickety back stairs of the inn, she searched the back lot for her mount and nearly melted with relief to find the mare still tied where she had left her. She repeated her hopping mount into the saddle and reined off quickly in the direction from which she'd come. It was a much wiser "innocent" who now retraced that narrow road by moonlight.

Riding far ahead of Merrie on that same moonlit road were the tenacious Chester Lombard and the reluctant John "Gentleman Jack" Huntington. They rode quickly through the night, unspeaking, resigned to the necessity of each other's company. It was only when they came within sight of Straffen Hall that hulking Chester broke the silence.

"We go 'round th' back." He motioned, veering off the main road and drawing Jack with him. Jack sensed a certain stealth in burly Chester's manner and his self-protective instincts, honed by years of living on the edge of bedchamber discovery, came alive. He followed cautiously as Chester wended his way far around the hall and dismounted near a side entrance.

Chester led him through a maze of darkened hallways to a cozy chamber and left him in the doorway, fading back into the darkened house. It was a goodly, well-furnished chamber, like a London parlor, Jack recognized with an evaluative sweep of his tawny eyes. He added the impression to those he'd already collected about the hall itself. It was larger than he'd expected, no mere country hovel.

From near the stone hearth, a very portly man garbed in extravagant crimson velvet turned to acknowledge his presence with a chilly expression.

"John Huntington, I presume . . . at last. You were to have been here a week past." The fat fellow appraised Jack's dashing form openly.

"I was . . . detained by affairs of some importance." Jack lifted his square chin, untroubled by any comment on his behavior, past or present.

"Just so. . . ." Master Cramden stroked his chin speculatively. *Affairs, indeed.* "I am Richard Cramden, solicitor to the recently deceased Earl of Straffen and executor of his bequests." He finally advanced on Jack with an outstretched hand. After a telling pause, Jack accepted it and allowed himself to be waved into a seat across from the one Cramden was settling in.

"I understood I was called here on a matter of finance. The gentleman who contacted me in London said there was a matter of *five hundred* a year." Jack sat back, only now catching sight of two figures looming in the doorway on the far side of the chamber.

Cramden caught his searching look and followed it to where the Lombards stood. He waved them forward and introduced them as the Lombards, Straffen's other agents, steward and housekeeper. They settled stiffly on a padded bench at the solicitor's left, their gazes combing Jack's broad-shouldered form.

"It is the execution of his late lordship's will for

which you have been summoned here,'' Cramden intoned with a glint in his eyes.

"To my knowledge, I never made the late earl's acquaintance, sir.'' Jack felt their eyes strongly on him now and shifted slightly in his chair. He thought himself impervious to scrutiny of virtually any kind, but this searching expectation, this cool analysis of his entire frame, was something new to him. Prickles of anticipation played up his muscular neck. To counter these unaccustomed feelings, he stretched his long legs before him and casually laid one booted foot over the other.

"Nay, you never met our late lord, but that is of no importance. The opportunity is to be yours, providing you are found suitable, sir. A few questions and answers should establish your case. You are not presently entailed in marriage or betrothal? And you have no other . . . *a-hem* . . . entangling 'associations'?''

"Certainly not.''

"And are you of sound body and seemly habits and godly disposition?'' Cramden lifted a document from the table on his right and perused it pointedly, waiting for Jack's response.

"Of indisputably sound frame, sir.'' Jack settled back into his chair with a wry cant to his sensual mouth. "As to my character, you must inquire elsewhere. *In propria causa nemo judex* . . . a man is never a fair judge unto his own case.''

Cramden returned his smile with slightly narrowed eyes, very aware that Huntington had just proved himself to be a man of education. "We already have, sir. And we have found your repute to be . . . perfectly in keeping with the late earl's expectations.''

Now that *did* surprise Jack. He was seldom considered "perfectly in keeping'' with others' expectations, especially noble ones. He was known all over London as a high-living rake who, in earlier days, had been sent down from Cambridge no less than four times. The thing that made his record for such bootings so remarkable was that the officialdom had seen fit, despite his perfidies, to reinstate him three times! It was his innate charm and the true potential of his mind that had kept hope for him alive at Cambridge, and even in the bosom of his family, long after his record should have discredited it.

"I perceive someone has done me a great service in recommending me," Jack observed dryly, tilting his head slowly to eye the threesome, rubbing his lower lip.

"Your family, sir. There was certain commerce between ourselves and your brothers. They are interested in seeing you settled . . . though, regrettably, not near them in Kent." Cramden smiled distractingly. The steward cleared his throat and Cramden turned to him. While he whispered into Cramden's ear, Jack's mouth quirked up on one end.

Cramden was lying. It was a smooth lie, but a lie, nonetheless. His three brothers had all threatened to run him through upon sight, some years back. And he had no reason to believe they'd changed their attitude toward him. He was the wayward son of the late Baron Huntington, who had never quite given him up for lost. But with his father dead, his eldest brother, Henry, had had no qualms about trouncing him straight out the door. Cut loose from all legitimate family connections, he was then free to pursue his own way in the world, unencumbered by normal expectations. His living from that time on had been secured exclusively by his charm, his surprising range of knowledge, and his fine and worthy luck at gambling. No, it was not his family connections that had brought him to the attention of the Earl of Straffen, he was sure of that. A swell of something akin to an alarming urge to ask questions rose in his chest and he squelched it, harshly. He hadn't sought this plummy opportunity, it had sought him. And he intended to leave it at that.

"A few clarifying . . . personal . . . matters, sir." Cramden lifted his jowls to appraise Jack. "Given the nature of our charge, we are duty-bound to inquire: you are not afflicted with the Frenchman's disease, nor given to perverse and untoward tastes in matters of the flesh?''

Jack's jaw slackened. God's Teeth. They actually expected him to answer. And for some reason he felt a perverse urge to do just that. ''I am clean wheat, sir, with regard to the first. And as to the second''—his body tightened visibly—''I am amenable to a variety of pleasures. If you would care to enumerate those practices you find offensive, I shall answer them yea or nay, so that you may judge for yourself.''

Cramden reddened and pulled his chins back sharply. There was another throat clearing and he leaned toward the steward and housekeeper again. Both whispered this time, while the woman cast telling looks Jack's way. Cramden sighed, but they scowled with determination and he gave in.

''There is a bit more. Your personal habits . . . You are not given to frequent bouts of drunkenness, are you, sir?''

''I would say not,'' Jack pronounced levelly, inching a bit straighter in his chair. Both he and the situation were losing some of their humor.

''You're not tanglesome . . . given to tankerous fits of temper?'' Cramden shook his own head as if trying to induce a negative response.

''Nay.''

''And you do keep clean linen . . . and decent bathing habits?'' Cramden nodded slightly, begging an affirmative answer.

''To the best of my ability.'' Jack's tone was now clipped. There was, indeed, a small fortune involved here, he reminded himself forcefully. This was no time for manly sensibilities.

There was a slight hiss and Cramden turned to the housekeeper with a ''what now'' expression. But he leaned closer and when she'd whispered, he gave her a dark look. She seemed adamant and after a moment Cramden relented yet again.

''You''—the solicitor cleared his throat—''you have no bantling bastards, do you, sir?''

"Not one," Jack growled, flicking a glance at the woman, who lifted her chin.

Cramden's throat cleared and he shook his head entreatingly again. "And yet one more thing . . . you do not slorp your food when you eat?"

"Saint Edgar's balls—I've had enough of this!" Jack sat forward in his chair, appearing admirably cool even while irritated. "Perhaps you wish me to strip buck naked, sir, so that you may examine me fully! What perverse creatures you are to question *my* peculiarities!"

Cramden sputtered and glanced furiously at the Lombards. "Forgive the intimate nature of our inquiry, sir. You are brought here, Master Huntington, to speak of marriage. And we have been charged by the gell's guardian to ascertain all possible about you before sealing the marriage contracts. It is incumbent upon me to offer the hand of Lady Meredith Straffen to you in marriage . . . subject to certain conditional agreements." Seeing Jack's shock, he clarified. "Lady Meredith is the late earl's granddaughter, now of marriageable age."

"An offer of marriage . . . me to the earl's granddaughter," Jack echoed, sitting forward. His angular face became a study in incredulity.

"I am empowered to offer you the match, subject to certain conditions. To wit . . ." Cramden lifted a sheaf of official-looking documents and held them at arm's length to read and pronounce. "The marriage shall take place two weeks from this date, in the hall of Straffen Manor, to be conducted by the Bishop of Malden. You will consummate the marriage in meet and seemly fashion, then shall remove yourself to your own abode in London on the very next day. Thereafter, you shall return to Straffen for a week each year at Christmas and shall otherwise lead a quiet, private existence in London, on the generous stipend of five hundred pounds per year." Cramden lowered the paper and looked at him expectantly, gauging his reaction. "Shall I read the conditions again, sir?"

"I believe I already have the sense of them, sir,"

Jack said through well-cloaked shock. What it baldly came down to, he quickly calculated, was five hundred pounds a year for a name and a night's work between the sheets. Perfectly amazing. "Let me be sure I understand you properly." He leaned his broad shoulders forward a bit, scrutinizing the three before him with the same intensity they had used on him moments before. "I am to marry the earl's granddaughter, bed her one night, then hie myself off to London and live in grand style on a fine stipend. Then I return yearly for a duty visit." At Cramden's nod, Jack sat back with a wary look in his eye. "Then surely something must be expected of me in London. . . ."

"You are to do . . . whatever you ordinarily do, sir." Cramden seemed a bit uncomfortable with the topic. "As long as it avoids the shabby, the notorious, and the illegal. There is the lady's reputation to consider." After a long silence the lawyer spoke again. "What say you, sir?"

It was a marriage of convenience they proposed, Jack realized, a very lucrative one. And it couldn't have come at a more opportune time.

"I *say* the old earl was quite mad. But his madness appears to be my fortune. And I am not a man to question fortune."

"We thought perhaps you were not, sir." Cramden relaxed, flicking a pleased glance at the Lombards. "You do understand, there shall be but one night with the gell . . . then you are to go?"

"I believe I understand that most clearly, sir." A knowing grin spread over Jack's rakish features. Suddenly an undiscussed aspect of the arrangment occurred to him. "One night and once a year thereafter. . . . I cannot be sure of making a babe on the gell."

"Oh, well . . ." Cramden glanced at the Lombards. "We'd rather you didn't, actually. It might complicate the arrangement enormously."

"I do have certain . . . financial obligations that need attending," Jack informed him pointedly. Cramden flicked a glance at the Lombards and nodded, as if he had been expecting it.

Jack's sensual grin was reborn as he shrugged his acceptance of the offer and its attendant conditions. "Then show me what I must sign, sir. I am perfectly agreeable to your arrangement."

A quarter of an hour later, Jack Huntington was shown out of the house by the side door. A leather pouch jingled in his pocket, funds for proper wedding attire and for the settlement of his several gaming debts in London. With a jaunty air, he mounted his horse and reined off, passing directly below the dimly lit window of Merrie Straffen's bedchamber.

Meanwhile, in the small parlor, Manley poured out three cups of good claret with a very pleased expression. He handed one each to Cramden and his wife and raised his own cup to propose, "To the weddin' of Lady Meredith and Gentleman Jack." He drank deeply, as did Gert. But Cramden just stared into his cup, as if searching the ruby liquid for something.

"Come, Cramden. Ye bro't it off, man. Take yer credit," Manley urged him, grinning.

"Did you not think it odd . . . he asked not a single question about his wife-to-be?" Cramden mused with a knitted brow.

Gert lowered her wine cup and huffed. "He weren't s'posed to ask no questions, that were the point in choosin' him. He be a high-liver and a fast-goer. He be jus' what we need."

"Still . . ." Cramden apparently harbored some gentlemanly doubt and the Lombards looked at each other irritably. "He's so . . . worldly."

"As well he should be. Caught right on to the lay of things. Knowed enough to not ask no more'n he needs to know," Manley asserted.

"But the gell is so tender, so young. . . ." Cramden persisted, pulling out his handkerchief to mop his fleshy neck and brow.

"An' he be as handsome as mortal man can be,"

Gert declared. "It was yerself insisted he be manly-lookin' an' smooth with th' women . . . an' well practiced, for her first night. What be botherin' ye, Cramden? Be ye gettin' fishy-livered on us?"

"Indeed not!" the solicitor asserted. "I just never quite reckoned on the persons of those involved. Four years ago, when we learned of Lady Meredith's existence, she was just a faceless cipher, a blot upon the page of fortune. And when we planned this marriage, it seemed a perfect solution to the problem of how to remain in control of both the gell and the old man's estates."

"An' it still be th' perfect so-lution, Cramden," Gert declared stoutly. "Jus' remember how we paid yer daughter's dower, an' tossed a proper weddin' fete. An' recall how our Morris be set solid in the law now, a secretary in the Court of Wards. He's been immeasurable helpful in gettin' things arranged. A lot o'good has come from our work here—an' we got bigger irons yet in th' fire."

Her earnest talk heartened him considerably and he brightened. "Of course. You're perfectly right, Goodwife Gert. The gell would have had nothing at all had we not sought her out to assure her inheritance and extend our benevolent arms about her. And he is devilish handsome, all a young gell could ask in a strong, comely husband. And just think—we have even saved her the trouble of later contracting wifely megrims at night."

"Here, here!" Gert agreed heartily. Manley's sudden frown made her subdue her enthusiasm a bit.

"Then let's drink to this delightful marriage," Cramden crowed with renewed humor and raised his cup. "He'll wed and bed the gell, then be gone . . . and we'll have Lady Meredith to comfort and to watch over . . . in her dear husband's stead."

Jack Huntington reentered the Winifred's Noll by the back door, flushed hot with success and taking the stairs two at a time. But his chamber was empty and in the light of the guttering candles he scowled irritably and banged on the wall, summoning his man by that prearranged signal. Seabury arrived in Jack's chamber, pulling on his shirt and blinking sleep from his eyes.

"What is it, Jack?" he asked, raking his brown hair back and staring blearily at his master, though, in truth, they were usually more friends and companions than master and servant.

"Why didn't you stop her?" Jack demanded. Seabury stared at him, then, realizing whom he meant, scoured the chamber visually.

"I didn't even know she'd gone." Seabury took a deep breath. "I don't pretend to omniscience where your amorous pursuits are concerned. I don't have the endurance for it. Did you quarrel?"

"Not exactly. That great oaf from Straffen made an unholy racket in the hall and insisted I go with him, just as we were about to . . . engage. But I thought she'd wait for me, the haughty piece. Her blessed pride outstrips even her passions. I expect she's peeved aplenty." Jack sat down on the edge of the bed and began to remove his boots with a thought-weighty expression. In truth, he was more annoyed by his own error in judgment than disappointed by the countess's absence. Preoccupation with his dire financial condition had interfered with his usually accurate assessment of feminine inclination. It was a troubling "first," misreading a woman, having her leave his bed angry and unsatisfied.

Jack Huntington prided himself on knowing the female sex: it had been the study of his life since he sprouted his first beard and his scholarship in the mystifying discipline was impeccable. He knew how women dreamed and schemed and worried and loved . . . and especially what they wanted in their deepest heart of hearts. And women, intuiting his special and intriguing knowledge of them, admitted him to their society, their beds, and their confidences with special eagerness for the range of the satisfactions he afforded them. Their weakness for Jack's companionship and irresistible loving made them vulnerable at times. But Jack's genuine affection for women and his tenacious male pride had kept him from exploiting them financially. It was that regrettable gallantry that had led him to such dire financial straits.

However, an advantageous marriage of convenience was another matter altogether, to his way of thinking. Foremostly, it was a financial and legal agreement, an arrangement of mutual benefit that would allow him to sustain the comforts of a life he had become accustomed to in recent years. But the idea of a casual marriage of convenience appealed to his nature as well as his purse. With his general love of women and his varied taste for pleasure, he would never have considered any other kind.

Perhaps Deirdre's abrupt departure wasn't such ill luck after all, he consoled himself, since he was soon to be a married man in the same county. The haughty countess did have a way of complicating things wherever she was.

"Well, as long as you've awakened me, what happened at Straffen? What was this five-hundred-a-year opportunity you were summoned to investigate?"

"As of this night we are no longer *in forma pauperis.* Nor am I in further danger of having Roscoe Swather, Esquire, extract a hundred pounds for gaming debts from the marrow of my bones. I'm to be married, it seems, to an earl's granddaughter." Jack's mood improved as he thought of it and of the bizarre interview that had brought it about.

"You? Married? And to the Earl of Straffen's granddaughter?" Seabury's laughter produced a rather sheepish grin on Jack's face. "This is actually worth getting waked up for. Good Lord—married!" He laughed again. "And what about this five hundred a year?"

Jack pulled the leather coin pouch from his doublet and tossed it to Seabury, who weighed it with a respectful hand and widening eyes. "I believe the five hundred is for bedding her on the wedding night and once a year thereafter. After which we shall go back to our pleasantly debauched life in London, so much the richer." It sounded better all the time. His striking eyes crinkled at the corners as he savored the full impact of his fortune and worked the fastenings of his doublet.

"Well, what is she like, this bride of yours?" Seabury settled on the end of the bed, wondering at Jack's uncanny knack for landing in a pot of jam.

Jack paused as he pulled off his ruff and shucked his fashionable doublet. "It never occurred to me to ask." He flashed a beguiling, devil-may-care grin that had proved the downfall of many a lass . . . and just as many gamblers, thugs, and noblemen. "You know I'm not a man to—"

"Ask questions," Seabury finished for him in genuine amazement. It was true; Jack Huntington never asked questions of any kind. He had perfected the art of accepting the world at face value, asking nothing, expecting nothing. And, as though intrigued by his very casualness and bidding for his attentions, the world usually saw fit to provide him a comfortable, if not always entirely respectable, living. Seabury had been with Jack for several years now as he'd cut a rakish swath through London's fleshier precincts, and even through the edges of the royal court itself. He thought he'd seen it all, until now.

"Lord, you are a piece of work, Jack Huntington. Have you not the least bit of curiosity about her?"

"Not the least." The glint in Jack's tawny eyes was pure deviltry. "They're having to buy her a husband at five hundred a year. I'll let you draw your own conclusions."

Chapter Three

"Wed. I see." Merrie choked on the words, staring up into Master Cramden's fleshy, resolute face on her right side, then into Mistress Overbeake's tight-lipped look of warning on the left. She sat in the small parlor, the very day after her misadventure at the inn, hearing the fate she already dreaded announced to her as though it were the grand honor of a lifetime. Wedged between the two formidable figures looming over her chair, she was thinking that now she knew exactly what the psalmist meant by "the valley of the shadow of death."

"It may be my duty to marry, I suppose." She paused, lowering her sky-blue eyes, realizing she trod dangerous ground. "But why now . . . so soon? Shouldn't I be permitted some time for adjustment? I am hardly even accustomed to life in this great house. How can I make a proper lady-wife?" She was unable to keep the heat from her tone and it came out more like a complaint than was entirely prudent.

"Ye shall be a proper lady-wife, gell, simply by the takin' of vows," Overbeake said, dismissing her concern while sending her a shriveling glare that dared her to continue her insolence. "No more be required. As to preparation, ye mus'n't fret. I am asked to stay on . . . to guide you."

Merrie groaned internally and hoped her special loathing for that prospect wasn't too obvious.

"An' we got Mistress Darstow comin' to sew fer ye, m'lady." Gert Lombard, who had been standing to one side, now stepped before her. "Ye'll have fine new garments fer the weddin' an' after." She spoke as though she expected the thought of new garments to dispel all of Merrie's concerns and misgivings. The thought rankled. Dandle a scrap of fancy cloth before her eyes and she was expected to abandon all pride and good sense.

"An' we got ye a fine weddin' feast laid on." Manley Lombard's voice came from behind and a glance over her shoulder told her he'd blocked her last possible exit. "Frenchie wines, roast pig, stuffed pheasant . . . an' Cook'll be swarpin' up them fancy almon' cakes an' jam tarts. We be sendin' all the way t' London fer them Spanish or'nges an' figs."

Now they stood over her, the four of them . . . the north, east, south, and west of doom. She could scarcely breathe. Figs and frippery . . . they expected them to pacify her. They really did think her a ninny. And why shouldn't they? she wondered in despair. She'd certainly acted the part since her arrival!

"But I have not even met the gentleman to whom I am given." She stiffened and clutched the edge of the chair with white fingers, trying to remain calm. A quick, shocking vision of that haughty vixen's posture in the midst of that bed revisited itself on the backs of her eyes. Unless something were done, she'd have to place herself in the same unthinkable position, submitting to some old man's . . . Oh, Lord. She suddenly felt dizzy and a little sick. She could hardly mind Master Cramden's words.

". . . thoughtless of me. Of course you would want to know. The gentleman that was chosen by the old earl and your guardian is Master John Huntington. He is the son of the late Baron Huntington of Kent. A fine, upstanding family, the Huntingtons. It may please you to know he is an educated man of younger years. . . ."

"Six and twenty," Manley helpfully supplied.

"Indeed, my lady, a suitable husband in every sense." Cramden nodded, beaming. "And you will have the entirety of the betrothal day to become acquainted before the bishop pronounces the vows."

"The entire betrothal day?" The sense of that

dawned on Merrie. "Do you mean we're to be betrothed one day and wedded the very next? But what of the banns?" All color had drained from her face and her blood had chilled so that it pumped sluggishly through her veins. She didn't wait for the answer; she already knew it. Trembling, she thrust up from her seat, surprising Gert Lombard into skittering back. She bolted for the door before anyone could think to lay a hand on her.

"M'lady!" and "Lady Meredith!" and "See here, gell—" Their utterances fell at her back as she tugged open the rear door of the hall and escaped into the yard.

"Well, she didn't take to it straight off," Manley said, casting a wary glance at Cramden and Gert.

"I shall speak to her at once!" Overbeake lifted her skirts and meant to sail out the door after Merrie, but Cramden turned to block her with an upraised hand. The acrid look on her coarse features gave him a fair idea of just what means the overbearing governess planned to use on her charge, and for some reason it rankled him.

"There's no need to trouble yourself, Mistress. As you have observed, she is not dull-witted. Let us give her a time alone; she will see it is best and reconcile to the notion."

Overbeake stiffened, thwarted in her desire to take her charge to heel immediately. She nodded and withdrew, still simmering, and the Lombards exchanged looks before turning to Cramden.

"Ye must let the woman see to th' gell, Cramden." Gert's eyebrows drew together atop her narrow nose. "Likely we'll need 'er, later."

"I do so despise the use of brute force." Cramden drew his chin in so that it split into three distinct rings, and defended himself petulantly. "Imagine presenting a bruised bride to the most excellent Bishop of Malden in a fortnight. I have no stomach for such stuff."

Gert looked pointedly down at Cramden's broad

belly and her mouth quirked wickedly on one end. "Tosh, Cramden. Ye gots plenty o' stomach."

Merrie's fingers were knotted into icy balls on her skirts and her blood was pounding in her head as she strode past the women churning outside the buttery door and the scullery maids sweeping and carrying ashes out of the cook house. Young boys were feeding the birds in the wooden dovecote as she passed, and housemaids were beating the dust out of window hangings that had been trundled out into the yard for spring airing. Straffen Manor's servants paused to watch their young lady striding by with a tight, unhappy expression and a determined set to her back. She was dimly aware of their nods to her and of their whispers to each other as she passed. Though the sun was bright and the breeze was gentle on her heated face, her thoughts were awash with the merciless gloom of her constricting future.

Then her unswerving path ended abruptly at the door of the brick-and-timbered stables, bringing her up short. That small, exhilarating taste of freedom last night, when she'd mounted and ridden off to the inn, revisited her vividly. It was exactly what she needed just now, a breath of sweet freedom . . . a *ride*. Good Marcus had insisted she balance her mental pursuits with healthy exertions, and riding was both an acceptable and accessible exercise for young girls in the country. But from the day she came under Overbeake's thumb until last night, she had not been permitted even to sit a horse. Rebellions boiled up hot and urgent within her.

Striding angrily inside, she came to a halt in the straw-littered alley of the stable, beside the dappled mare on which she'd purloined a bit of freedom mere hours ago. A voice beside her startled her and she turned to find hulking Chester staring down at her.

"What be ye doin' here, m'lady? These be th' stables." Chester had a positive gift for the obvious.

"I want a mount." She made herself face up to him,

trying on an air of angry command that she borrowed from the overbearing Overbeake. "I want to go for a ride."

Chester scratched his thickly thatched head and regarded her dubiously. "Wull, I ain't rightly sure, m'lady. . . ."

"Answer me this, Chester, if you can. To whom do these horses belong?" It was a point she had yet to make clear for herself. She didn't expect Chester to know either, but she did hope the question might confuse him into cooperating. Relief surged through her when he slowly scratched his chin, then scratched his belly and shrugged.

"I ketch yer meanin', m'lady."

"Good. Then shall you saddle her up or shall I?" The irritable question quite horrified sturdy Chester.

"Wull, I will, I reckon." He scratched again. Either it helped him think or Chester had fleas. "Ma would murther me if she learnt ye lifted a hand twyrd saddlin' a horse."

"Well, then. Saddle her up, Chester." Merrie gave him a compelling look that also came straight from Overbeake's repertoire. As he hurried to obey, she eased to a simmer and asked: "Does your mother live on Straffen, too?"

"Yea, m'lady." Chester seemed a bit surprised as he lifted the saddle. "Me ma's housekeeper here."

"Mistress Lombard is your mother?" Merrie's ire was dimmed briefly by surprise. But why should she be so surprised to find the Lombards had a son living and working on Straffen? Servant families were certainly the norm in households great and small. It was just that he resembled them none at all. And he seemed an unlikely son for two such capable retainers.

Shortly, she was cantering determinedly across the pastures, skirting the fields that spread along the floor of the valley. The little mare was eager for a good run herself and responded readily to Merrie's returning skills with the reins. She sped past clumps of tenant cottages with their small garden plots, past hedgerows and farmers in the fields with coarse-woven bags slung over their shoulders sowing barley and wheat. Her frustration was drained by the rush of wind past her burning cheeks and overshadowed temporarily by the glory of sheer motion.

Spotting a small woods, she rode for it, seeking the shelter and solace of the stirring trees. As she threaded her way through the venerable trunks and tender saplings, the burning in her lungs and the panting of the animal beneath her warned against pushing too far. In a small clearing, she slid to the ground, finding her knees a bit unsteady. Something dangled about her head and she reached up to retrieve her linen cap just as it threatened to fall completely. She stared at it irritably, reading in its folds, stiff wires, and measured stitches the cramped and tortured dimensions of her future. Her ire rose afresh, mingled with deep hurt.

How could they do his to her . . . force her to marry a stranger, some man she'd never set eyes upon? And after only one day's betrothal!

She'd heard enough talk of noble marriages to realize that few were entered into with regard for anything but economic arrangement or the begetting of legitimate heirs. Her own father, an earl's son who had been fast leaving fifty behind, had been persuaded to a match for fear of dying heirless—and before his own father did. And her poor, lovely young mother was certainly wedded and bedded out of sheer economic necessity. But where, her fertile mind screamed, was the necessity of her own match? It seemed dictated solely by the caprices of an ancient man determined to meddle in earthly affairs even after he could no longer participate in them.

"It's not fair," she moaned, crumpling her cap furiously, mashing its wires and pleated border. "I never asked to be a lady, to be an earl's granddaughter! I just wanted to live with Marcus and Polly and ride horses and ask questions and . . . and . . ." And what?

"And anything but *this!*" she shouted, tossing her cap against the nearest tree trunk. The thrill of release that small defiance gave her made her search for something else to toss. A stick, a clod of dirt, and a small branch—she picked them up and hurled them at that stoic trunk, feeling a small burst of satisfaction with each thwack. The blood pounded in her ears and surged through her vision, blotting out all but the heady fury of long-repressed urges. And when she could find no more suitable missiles, she seized a substantial fallen branch in both hands and smacked it repeatedly against that trunk, unaware of the tears burning paths down her cheeks.

The snort and movement of horses behind her finally penetrated her fog of misery and she whirled to confront a veritable wall of horseflesh. She froze, chest heaving and eyes burning, at the sight of a mixed riding party arrayed behind a slender, stately young woman garbed in somber black. Merrie's robin's-egg eyes lifted to meet piercing brown ones set behind lashes so pale they all but disappeared, giving the face around them a rather surprised appearance.

"What grievance have you against my tree, madam, that you abuse it so?" came a thin but commanding voice.

Merrie stiffened, jolting back to reality, and hastily swiped at her eyes and wet cheeks. Crimson with mortification, she backed away a step, then two. "Nothing really. . . . I just . . ." Then the sense of the young woman's words saved her. "These are your trees?" She looked frantically about her, then at the party of grooms and huntsmen and a waiting lady that accompanied her regal inquisitor. "But I thought . . . I'm not on Straffen land still?"

"Straffen? The old Earl of Straffen's estate? I should say not. You crossed the border onto Hatfield lands some ways back." A barely perceptible motion of the elegant lady's hand sent a groom bounding onto the ground to assist her in dismounting.

Even on the ground, the woman was still intimidating, Merrie realized. She was slightly taller than Merrie and more slender of frame, with pale, delicate skin and a rim of vibrant red-gold hair visible beneath her flat beaver hat with its stark white plumes. Her fitted gown was fine black velvet, rimmed with gold cording and fastened with buttons of black mother-of-pearl. Her features were both fine and commanding and her dark eyes had a remarkable life-force in them. "I collect now; it was old Straffen's trees you intended to attack."

"I . . ." Merrie washed hot crimson with humiliation, but made herself answer as sensibly as possible. "I did not mean to attack any trees, ma'am. I had quite lost myself. Please . . . there is no great damage, I think." She glanced at the stoic old trunk and wondered if beating trees was punishable by the same standards as poaching. Then the name the young woman had spoken settled fully on her beleaguered brain: Hatfield. Overbeake had mentioned it on the last day of their journey: "We be nearin' Hatfield soon, the Princess Elizabeth's principal seat. How fine that the earl has such exalted neighbors." Merrie was suddenly sick.

"Oh please, Your Grace, I meant your tree no harm. I was just unseemly angry." She swayed and dropped immediately into a deep curtsey.

"Indeed, you were." The Princess Elizabeth stared down at the top of Merrie's bare, strawberry blonde head and had difficulty suppressing a smile. "Who are you, gell?"

Merrie groaned inside, wishing she didn't have to answer. "I am Meredith Straffen, the late earl's granddaughter." She looked up at the princess, wondering if she should rise yet. Sensing her difficulty, Elizabeth waved her up. For a moment they stood face-to-face and all present were struck by the similarities in their appearances. Both had long, red-gold hair, fair skin, and comely proportions. But it was impossible not to note the differences as well. Merrie's frame was softer, more rounded; her eyes were thickly lashed and her features had more girlish prettiness about them, while Elizabeth was taller, assured, with piercing eyes and regal elegance of carriage and movement.

"I might be prevailed upon to forget this attack upon

my holdings, gell, if I were to know what incited it. Walk with me a pace." Elizabeth turned and strolled forward into the sunlit meadow. Merrie swallowed hard and made another furtive swipe at her wet lashes as she joined the queen's half sister. Elizabeth turned an expectant look on Merrie.

"I am to be wedded . . . in less than a fortnight." Merrie glanced at the princess uncomfortably, expecting swift censure. When none was forthcoming, she ventured more. "I've only just arrived at Straffen; I'm new to such a noble life. And . . . I don't want to wed, at least not now, not yet."

"How old are you, Lady Meredith?" Elizabeth cocked her head, searching Merrie openly.

"Seventeen years; eighteen soon, Your Grace."

"Old enough for marriage, then. And who is the gentleman in question? Is he so objectionable that you must flee him and flay my poor trees?" She waved toward a great old log lying nearby and they strolled toward it. "Some paunchy old croat with gouty legs and rotted teeth, perhaps?"

"I cannot say how objectionable he may be, for I have never set eyes upon him. He is a baron's son, John Huntington by name. We're to be betrothed one day and wedded the very next."

"A special license, then. A baron's son . . . not an unseemly match for you." Elizabeth settled herself on the log and waved Merrie down beside her. She was searching her astonishingly keen memory for some trace of that name, Huntington. For now, it was just beyond the reach of recollection. Her brow creased with her private thoughts and she released a rare sigh. "It is a sad fact of noble life that few of our marriages are made in joy, Lady Meredith. It is the cost of privilege and power to have many obligations."

"But I have no power, Your Grace, nor any privileges to speak of. I cannot ride a horse or even choose my own clothes for the day without defying some dread authority." Merrie's eyes were wide with anguish of spirit. "And it will be twice as bad to have to obey yet another force—a husband."

– "Nor do many young gells have privileges at your age; they come with time." Elizabeth rebuked her mildly, adding, "I was reared in similar manner, Lady Meredith. All young gells from worthy houses are brought up in close and strict disciplines. It is to prepare them for the rigors of their obligations. You cannot fault your protectors for seeking to prepare you thus. Nor do they deserve rebuke for finding you a husband to protect and defend you and your interests. God knows, there is much in this world to prey upon a young gell, and precious little to afford her protection."

There was silence as Merrie struggled with the princess's revelations. It seemed as though the princess spoke from deep personal experience, sharing a hard-won lesson. And, indeed, she did. Elizabeth mused separately on the treacherous shoals of romance, which had sent her hurtling into the jaws of disaster some years ago. Her first close brush with treasonable death was the result of Thomas Seymour's reckless bid to marry her without the Privy Council's permission or knowledge.

"It has been my observation that more women are brought low by marriage than are built up by it," the princess mused moodily, seeing her own experience only added to that of a veritable parade of hapless noblewomen in recent history, including five of her own father's poor, wretched wives. "And it is my conclusion that a woman must find some advantage for herself in marriage and seize it; make it work toward something she desires. It is woman's holy duty before the Almighty to marry and bear children, but there is no dictum in Scripture that says we may not benefit from our duty, as men are wont to do."

Merrie turned a surprised look on the princess and found her fine jaw set and her lips compressed into a determined line. A glint entered Elizabeth's eye as she contemplated something, and just at that moment she looked every bit the regal, strong-willed daughter of lusty old Henry Tudor.

"I shall have to marry someday, myself, to please the royal offices of the crown." Her voice carried the gravity of destiny. "By Heaven's Knees, when I do marry, I shall wring every bit of benefit from it I can, for it shall certainly exact its duty from me." There was a melancholy air of acceptance of that royal and inexorable fate in the Princess Elizabeth's mien. It was devastating to witness.

Merrie dropped her eyes and her shoulders rounded. Her own troubles paled to insignificance beside the princess's destiny, for royal marriages decided the fates of nations. All she worried about was a bit of personal freedom; it suddenly seemed petty and selfish of her.

In that quiet moment her view of Straffen and her role in its life underwent a drastic enlargement. When Overbeake spoke of her having much to learn, she had thought the governess meant more interminable lessons in etiquette and such. But Overbeake had likely been speaking of far more important things, of the running of the great house and estates. If that were the case, then she truly did have much to learn, and important obligations to discharge. How could she ever learn enough to do it properly?

Master Cramden's words to Overbeake came back to her: her affairs would pass into her husband's hands after the marriage. Was that the reason for the quick nuptials? To assure the estates a lord and master, someone to take charge of things and to see to the welfare of the estates? Elizabeth's words echoed in her ears: young gells had little enough protection in the world. She thought of the worldly dangers her headstrong behavior had exposed her to in the night just past. Perhaps she did need to be protected from the forces of the world . . . betimes, even from her own foolishness.

"Well, Lady Meredith." The princess roused herself and stood with an aura of command. "Where is your duty now?" Merrie rose with every bit of grace she could muster, feeling awkward beside Elizabeth's queenly poise.

"At home, Your Grace." Merrie flushed and lowered her eyes. "I do thank Your Grace for sharing your excellent wisdom and helping me to see my duty more clearly."

"And opportunity," Elizabeth added, searching Merrie again with those piercing brown eyes. "You must also search for the opportunity of your heart's desire in duty, else life is too difficult to be borne." Merrie nodded and sank into a curtsey that would have made Overbeake proud indeed. "And if things go too awry . . ." Merrie lifted her gaze to witness a wry smile on the princess's mouth. ". . . you have my permission to come flay yonder tree as you like."

Merrie could not help but smile back and soon they were walking toward the princess's party. The groom knelt and assisted Elizabeth to mount, then at her silent command, performed the same service for Merrie.

"God preserve Your Grace," Merrie called, holding her mount in check as the princess's small party moved off. Then she turned her own horse and jolted back through the woods in the direction she had come.

Elizabeth cast a glance over her shoulder to see the banner of Merrie's burnished hair flying behind her and she grew thoughtful. She turned to her waiting lady with a scowl of concentration.

"Huntington . . . Where have we heard that name? A baron's son, I believe. . . ." She turned it over in her mind. At first she met with a shake of head and a frown of puzzlement.

"Oh, Your Grace." The plump, brown-haired matron's eyes flew wide after a minute. "At court . . . over a year back. That awful debacle over the Countess Whittington and that gentleman in the queen's ladies' apartments."

"Good Lord, yes!" Elizabeth groaned, now placing both the name and her own reason for not recalling it. She'd been ill at the time and her bitter, suspicious sister, the queen, had held her in utter isolation in

Hampton Court. They had had only snippets of news trundled in by servants to make out what was happening in the palace, and half of that was gossip of the scandals abounding amongst the courtiers.

"Yes, I recall something about his being passed from ladies' chamber to ladies' chamber to avoid discovery, protected by a covey of skirts. . . ."

"Gentleman Jack—that's what they called him." The waiting lady remembered, laughing and shaking her head. "Some fancy bit of manhood to inspire such devotion in so many proper ladies."

"Good Lord." Elizabeth cast a look back over her shoulder at the spot where Merrie had disappeared into the trees. "I believe I've just been party to the seduction of a terrible innocent. I shall have to remember to light candles for the gell."

Merrie reined to a walk as she reentered Straffen's huddled complex. The flurry near the rear door of the hall made it clear she'd been watched for and spotted. She halted outside the stable doors and Chester came hurtling out, a baleful look on his broad, blocky face and a suspicious red swelling on one of his ears. From the corner of her eye, she saw Overbeake and the Lombards bearing down on her across the yard like the dreaded Horsemen of the Apocalypse. She swallowed hard and muttered to her reluctant accomplice in freedom: "I collect, Chester, we've been found out."

She was duly impounded by the grim threesome and escorted into the house and into the small parlor, where she was given an extended lecture on the dangers and indecorum of young gells riding out by themselves, without permission and in unknown territory. Her surprisingly composed response was a question: "Then in future, to whom must I apply for permission to ride?"

The question had the predictable effect. Overbeake was sufficiently outraged by her insolence to rail on for another full hour, and Merrie was emphatically prohibited from sitting a horse again in the foreseeable future. Somewhere in the ravings her question was answered:

everybody on the place, with the possible exception of
Chester, apparently had the power to disallow her actions.

Afterward, all afternoon and evening, she was required to keep to her chamber, stitching and praying
for deliverance from her own wayward impulses. In
defiance, she stitched halfheartedly and prayed earnestly . . . for the wretched governess's removal. But
the isolation did give her time to think on the strange
events of her first two days of noble life. If nothing
else, it certainly hadn't been dull.

She sighed and rose from her chair to stare out the
open window at the blossoming countryside she'd enjoyed so briefly. What a noddy she'd been these last
days, she thought. Not at all like her eminently reasonable and logical self! It was high time she took
herself in hand and used her head a bit.

The questions began to come. Did being heir to Straffen Manor really mean owning it? Well, what else could
it mean? She, Meredith Straffen, *owned* Straffen Manor.
She sighed heavily. Then why did she feel like the
Lombards' unwanted guest? And why was she still to
be Overbeake's unwilling thrall?

Because, she reasoned anew, they saw her as a silly,
headstrong gell who was as yet unfit for managing and
controlling her own affairs. They undoubtedly sub-
scribed to the views Princess Elizabeth had remarked
upon, that young gells should have few privileges until
they earned them by marriage and age and responsible
behavior. Not so strangely, marriage seemed a bit less
oppressive when thought of as the gateway to new
status and greater privilege.

That thought conjured the princess's other words in
her head. She must find opportunity in her marriage
for the fulfillment of her heart's desire, whatever that
might be. And just what did her heart desire? That was
easy . . . freedom. But even as she said it, she realized
how naïve it sounded. She now had a place to take in
the world, responsibilities to assume, a life to make

with a husband. But, in the doing of her duty, might she find a modicum of personal freedom as well?

It was as though someone had lit a hundred candles in her head at once. Marriage might just prove the remedy for her difficulties after all! If she seemed a sober and godly young woman, accepted her husband with mature grace and goodwill, and if she applied herself to learning how to manage the estates wisely, how could any reasonable man refuse his lady-wife's request to be shed of her governess? Her heart beat faster just thinking on it. It would mean ingratiating herself with her new husband. And just how did one endear oneself to a husband?

For the first time, she let herself think on what this John Huntington might be like. He was a baron's son, well used to noble life and undoubtedly chosen with an eye to his responsibility and industry in administering estates. A younger man, six and twenty. Yet enough years older than herself to have a level and sensible head, she supposed. She tried to picture him in her mind and came up with a broad, unsettling pair of male shoulders and a strong, rakish face and raven hair. Certainly not! Most likely he would be . . . shorter than that, with sensible brown hair and a grave and godly bearing. And he would probably be impressed by curtseys and stitchery. . . .

In the days that followed, amidst the flurry of wedding preparations, Merrie made a grave and determined effort to learn about Straffen Manor, quietly exploring the house and requesting escort about the immediate grounds so that she might meet some of the folk who peopled her new home.

Investigating the buttery and kitchens, she met Edythe, the chief cook, and her retinue of fetch-it lads and scullery gells. Next she encountered Bennie the pig man, Ellie the goose gell, Hollis the carpenter, and May the head of the weaver's house. Each warmed to their earnest little mistress with the sweet smile and the great blue eyes that lighted visibly with the discovery of each new part of Straffen. Ranging further afield, she met Arthur, the overseer of her plowmen, and his sturdy crew, including the gargantuan workhorses that bore names drawn from the oddities of their personalities: Nipper, Straight Ahead, Lagfoot. . . .

Sweet-natured Tess introduced the housewomen: plump Maude, haughty Julia, graying Bevis, and slow-moving Jean. When Merrie noted the striking similarity between Julia and Jean, she was told they were twins, and cousins to the others.

"An' Tessie, here, too." Bevis gestured to pink-cheeked Tess. "We be blooded kin frum way back at ol' Harold Lombard. Ye'see, him 'ad four wifes and his second give birth to my old pa, whilst Maudie here she come frum the first brither. Tessie, here, an' her pa, Manley, come frum the last'un."

"Wait." Merrie blinked and shook her head to clear it. "You mean to say you're all Lombards?"

"Wull, all 'cept'n Maudie here," Bevis explained earnestly. "She were married oncest and took 'er man's name."

"Does that mean you're Manley and Gert's daughter?" Merrie turned to a now wary Tess, who nodded. "Then, that means Chester . . ."

"Be my brother, m'lady," Tess admitted ever so reluctantly.

"Wull, at least on 'er mother's side." Bevis cackled a bit wickedly. Tess shot a furious look at her elder cousin and quickly ushered Merrie outside again.

Merrie thought briefly on the revelation and realized the implication of Bevis's jibe. Chester was thought to be a tare in the Lombard oats. Well, he didn't resemble Tess or her mother or father. Poor Chester.

Shortly she was caught up in a gaggle of lads who kept the dovecote and privies, and was being introduced to the motley crew of hounds who sometimes haunted the underside of the table in the main hall. The hounds had been banished from their rightful place, the lads informed her somberly, by the arrival of herself and the other august personages yet to come.

She found a place in the hearts of both lads and hounds when she let the friendly pack lick and nuzzle her enthusiastically and promised to see them restored to their rights in the near future.

Thus, Merrie Straffen completed the conquest of her holdings and claimed sovereignty over the affections of many who dwelt therein.

Mistress Darstow, the seamstress imported from London to clothe the bride, arrived and set to her labors with vigor. She examined Merrie's coloring and figure and seemed pleased to have so pleasant a foundation for her creations. She chose an array of blues and greens to complement Merrie's unusual coloring, some in velvets, some in brocades, and some in fine, polished woolens. The gowns were of similar design: long, tight-fitting bodices with broadly flared skirts and long fitted sleeves joined to the bodice by padded epaulets sewn into the seams. Necklines varied: some bore winged collars, others standing collars to which detachable ruffs could be added; still others had square, low bodices that were to be worn over gauzy underbodices gathered to a band and small ruff about the neck. Some skirts were widely split and meant to be worn over decorative satin petticoats; some were pleated; some were graced with a short, rufflelike peplum at the bottom of an elongated bodice.

It was all complicated clothing, meant to be worn over steel-ribbed corsets that insured a lady's posture and prevented her from doing anything even moderately active. The corsets were the one place Merrie chose to assert a judicious resistance. She would not wear the torturous contraptions and, despite Overbeake's snarling and lecturing, she remained fast. She would wear her usual body stitchets or none at all. In the end, Mistress Darstow came to her aid, agreeing that her waist was already passably small. It was only her unfashionable breasts that needed restraining. Small corsets would do.

There were wired caps and French hoods, two rimmed with small pearls, and several pairs of gloves.

There were girdles to hang about her hips for both decoration and use: one with a new pair of ladies' scissors attached, one with an elegant white feather fan. Merrie watched the growing accumulation of apparel and felt conflicting emotions rising and sinking in her chest. The clothing was purely luxurious and would likely make it impossible for her to dress herself properly without assistance. But she was set firmly on a course toward a liberating marriage and this was no time or place to give in to petty grievances.

It was only in her maiden's bed at night that the old Merrie Straffen emerged, and the tensions of her vigilant restraint melted into bodily aches and sleepless hours. Somewhere in the long night that unthinkable episode at the inn always intruded into her restlessness. She closed her eyes and again saw Gentleman Jack's naked shoulders and those long, muscular legs . . . and felt a queer tingling in her lips and a shocking warming in her breasts and lower, in places she didn't want to think about. Oddly, the "vixen" had faded in her remembrance and only Gentleman Jack remained on the stage of her mind, strutting, swaggering, laughing that wicked, carnal sound that sent waves of hot confusion through her. And inevitably she recalled watching those stunning kisses and feeling her lips itching and burning strangely. Sliding deeper into mingled memory and imagination, she saw that bed and herself now on all fours, waiting for . . .

She twisted and flopped and pounded the feather bolsters, trying to banish such unholy and unsettling thoughts. But it was a part of her approaching marriage that was coming to weigh more and more on her mind. She was to be a woman . . . to a man. And now that she had a clear idea of just what that involved, she wished with all her heart that she could be purely ignorant of it again until the hour of necessity. Then, when she finally tumbled into sleep, she dreamed of tawny, catlike eyes and full, sensual lips approaching hers or lowering on the skin of her breast.

Chapter Four

The first day of May, Merrie Straffen's betrothal day, dawned bright and balmy, auguring an auspicious start to her new life. Birds were singing in the trees outside her open window and she could hear the dim flurry of servants back and forth outside her door as she finished her breakfast tray. They were scurrying to prepare chambers for John Huntington, for the good Bishop of Malden and his party, and for the representative of her guardian, Sir Edwin Gannulf, who was unable to attend the festivities himself, owing to an attack of the gout.

The bishop arrived first that morning and with some ceremony, blessing the house, the fields, the bards, and most especially, the busy kitchens and buttery. He proved a round-faced man of considerable girth and pleasantly pious mien. Merrie curtseyed and kissed the good prelate's ring, welcoming him demurely and receiving his blessing. Shortly, however, she was bundled off to her chamber to dress and had to depend on Tess's reported observations of the comings and goings in the hall below.

Sir Edwin's solicitor, Master Makepiece, arrived from Bedford. He was another soss-bellied fellow who sweated profusely and talked unceasingly, according to Tess's irreverent summary. A lot like Master Cramden, Merrie thought, laughing conspiratorially; perhaps such a constitution was required for admission to the law.

Then a few noteworthies from the local gentry arrived on horseback, among them Sir Daniel Wycoff, a staunch Catholic and a local official, known to be strong in the Catholic queen's good graces . . . primarily because he kept her well informed of the doings and intrigues in the area surrounding her half sister, Princess Elizabeth's estate of Hatfield.

Then at last Tess brought word that Merrie's future husband had arrived. When Merrie groaned nervously and pressed her for a description, Tess merely rolled her eyes impishly and declared her mistress would be very well pleased indeed. Before there was time for more, Overbeake appeared at the door, instructing Merrie to present herself in the hall for the short ceremony.

The moment had come. Merrie made a quick prayer on her prie-dieu and sat with cold-fingered fidgets on the bench at the foot of her bed while Tess gave her long, burnished golden hair a last brush and pinned her heart-shaped cap on the crown of her head. She stood and let Tess smooth her sky-blue brocade skirts and fluff the lace edging about her wing collar. Clasping her icy hands together frantically, she rounded the gallery and descended the staircase.

She searched the small gathering at the far end of the hall, near the hearth, trying to match identities with Tess's colorful descriptions of those in attendance. The bishop and his assistants stood in front of the cold hearth with Master Cramden and another corpulent and well-garbed fellow. Probably the other solicitor, Merrie mused distractedly . . . birds of a feather . . . But her eyes fell immediately to the prelate's right and there he was, her husband-to-be.

Relief washed over her. He was exactly what she had hoped . . . exactly! On the tall side of middle height, with trimmed brown hair and a neat little beard, sensible but stylish in a brown velvet doublet and breeches, with clean features and kindly eyes. She lowered her gaze and flushed becomingly as Master Cramden claimed her hand and led her forward.

"And may I present to this august assembly"—he led her before the good bishop—"Lady Meredith." A dozen pairs of eyes searched her form openly and she felt every one of them. Her scarlet face raised to the good prelate when he took her hand from Cramden. She had to battle her own wayward impulses to keep her eyes from seeking her husband with unseemly interest.

"What a lovely bride you make, my lady. 'Pon my honor, you are breathtaking—is she not, gentlemen?" Merrie flushed with fresh heat at the hearty agreement that comment produced, and she murmured a well-rehearsed thanks for his kindliness in presiding at her vows. "And now, of course, you would greet Master John Edward Huntington, your husband on the morrow."

Her curiosity freed at last, Merrie turned toward John in anticipation. But there was a moment's confusion as the bishop turned the other way, pulling her hand with him. Her face came up, filled with consternation, and she allowed herself to be turned well about in the other direction. The bishop placed her hand in another's and Merrie found herself confronting a broad, dark wall of a chest; a black velvet doublet, rimmed with crimson satin and bearing dagged hanging sleeves of that same sleek crimson.

She raised helpless eyes to a perfect sculpture of a face with the strong square chin and seductively carved features . . . that she'd seen every night in her dreams for the last fortnight! It was the same raven hair and generous lips and he was smiling a courtly, measured smile that revealed straight white teeth. Those same tawny eyes were lighted with surprise as they strayed over her with gentlemanly interest, touching her, taking her in. Then he was bowing, speaking her name in a deep, male rumble, and bestowing a chaste, reverent kiss on her icy hand.

Lord—no! It was *Jack!* This was Gentleman Jack, not John Huntington! How could Gentleman Jack be *her husband?* This just couldn't be! She reeled, unable to peel her horrified eyes from his manly frame, or to halt the panicky thudding of her heart or the ringing and spiraling that had begun in her head. When he straightened to gaze down at her with those glowing, black-rimmed eyes, every bit of her blood drained from her head—trying to escape proximity to him. He was speaking, for verily his lips were moving. But she heard only a dim rumble as everything constricted into a narrow cordon of light, which was quickly snuffed. Merrie sank into utter darkness.

The goodly bishop was making nervous talk about the delights of such a handsome and propitious match while watching the blanching of Merrie's delicate face. She weaved a moment, then, without warning, collapsed to the floor in a dead faint.

Only Jack's hold on her hand and his belated grab of her other wrist kept her from smacking the floor with some force. There were gasps and a rush of both bodies and concern as the bishop knelt at her head and Master Cramden and Mistress Overbeake hurried to crowd close, horrified by Merrie's untoward reaction.

"What's happened to her?" Master Cramden patted her cheek delicately while scowling Overbeake snatched up the hand Jack had just relinquished and gave it several sound pats, which sounded more like swats.

The bishop looked grave, indeed, as he pronounced: "She's fainted . . . likely from the excitement," adding mentally: "or the shock." He slanted a look at the large and roguishly handsome bridegroom, then at the young and virginal girl by his knees, and knew immediately what had happened. He'd seen this sort of thing before, in his years of officiating at the nobility's weddings. The gell had looked into the conjugal duty inscribed in the bridegroom's worldly, sensual face and been frightened into insensibility. Oh, how it made his clerical blood roar with displeasure!

"She mus'n't jus' lay here," Gert said, hovering frantically about the edges of the knot of persons collected over Merrie's limp form. "Ye mus' take 'er up to chamber, straightaway so's she can be tended proper."

Jack watched incredulously as Cramden rose, excusing himself from carrying her owing to a quirky back, and the bishop staggered up and back, with his hand over his heart, panting a bit and drawing a flurry of attention from his assistants. Then Manley eyed her as if he thought it not quite proper for him to be so familiar. Good Lord, Jack realized, they were abandoning her on the damned floor!

He knelt beside her and scooped her up into his arms, struggling briefly with collecting all of her very limp form he could manage within the bounds of propriety. "Show me the way to her chamber," he ordered Gert, who nodded and hurriedly led him toward the stairs and gallery.

Jack Huntington looked at the limp, blanched form of the young gell in his arms, feeling slightly bemused. He'd produced some rather strong reactions in women before, but none quite so strong as this—upon a mere introduction. It was disconcerting, to say the least, especially considering what was at stake here.

His manly stride slowed around the corner of the gallery as he took the covert opportunity to scrutinize his bride. The feel of her in his arms was soft, feminine, and she seemed to be nicely curved in some places and delicately tapered in others. It took a moment for him to realize that she was the complete antithesis of all he had expected. She was certainly younger than he would have thought, given the unusual circumstances and conditions of their marriage of convenience, and she was surprisingly lovely. She had smooth, fair skin and large eyes that he had managed to realize, just before she fainted, were the exact hue of the dress she wore. Her lips were pale just now, but he could imagine a lovely warm flush in them when she smiled, and judged their gently formed bow to be eminently kissworthy.

At Gert's direction, Jack carried her into the modest bedchamber and deposited her gently on her bed. There was throat clearing and a feminine flurry that gradually insinuated itself between him and his bride-to-be. He was a bit chagrined to find himself standing, staring at her still figure, while the housekeeper, the

gell's companion, and some serving maids stared at
him, evidently impatient for him to withdraw.

He came to himself and mumbled something half ar-
ticulate about leaving her in their capable hands, and
made his way back downstairs to the hall. Cramden,
Manley Lombard, the bishop, and brown-clad Seabury
crowded close for some word as to her condition. Jack
could only shrug a gentlemanly disclaimer and offer an
expression of concern, which to his surprise was utterly genuine.

Cramden, who was designated to act as host for the
occasion, called nervously for refreshment, and soon a
fruited wine and buns and cakes, which had been
planned for after the formalities, were being trundled
around. The bishop caught Master Cramden's eye and
frowned fiercely, beckoning him aside to demand a
conference with the principals of the "situation" in the
small parlor immediately upon receiving word of the
girl's condition. Cramden could do nothing but agree
graciously and send Manley upstairs to fetch Gert and
Overbeake as soon as possible. Then he ushered the
bishop and the bridegroom into the small parlor.

They had not long to wait. Manley soon appeared
with his wife and the governess, bearing word that the
gell's color was returning and she now seemed to be
merely sleeping. The bishop invited them, somewhat
forcefully, to be seated and proceeded to fix each in-
dividual present with a searching, irritable look before
coming straight to his point.

"I have presided over numerous unions during my
years in the priesthood," he began, "and I have seen
some strange and wondrous things. But never have I
seen the need for the full observance of published
banns so clearly demonstrated as I have this day. It is
obvious that the gell is far too young and tender to be
wedded to—" he paused and gestured to Jack with a
hint of disapproval—"a gentleman she has had no opportunity to know."

The bishop, a lifelong student of human nature, had
fluently read Jack's too-handsome-for-his-own-good

frame and carnally inspired confidence. The glint in those tawny eyes and the sinuous, catlike movement of that big body bespoke a full and polished education in the pleasures of the flesh. And how utterly astute of the gell, the bishop mused with a certain wonder, to have seen it, too . . . and at very first glance.

"Thus, I have decided, and cannot be dissuaded, that the full fortnight of the banns shall be observed. Only at the end of that time, when Lady Meredith has made a better adjustment, shall I speak binding vows between the couple." He crossed his arms over his chest and braced determinedly to withstand the expected storm of protest.

"B-but . . . the guests!" Cramden labored up from his chair. "We have promised them a wedding. . . ."

"I shall speak to them myself and send them home this very hour." The bishop waved a hand, dismissing such a temporal concern.

"But—the gell would never wish to cause such commotion," Overbeake intoned. "She'd be purely mortified to think th' arrangements was cancelled on her account, Your Worship."

"Nonsense." The bishop batted that suggestion away as well. "Serves only her own best interest, and the interest of a proper start to her wedded life. I shall not be moved on this point, madam."

Manley opened his mouth twice, moved it soundlessly, and closed it again, realizing that if the wordy solicitor and the proper governess had made no headway, then he probably had no chance. He turned to Gert and found her staring meaningfully at the bridegroom, as if urging him to protest this unthinkable delay in their plans. Manley added the weight of his stare to his wife's impelling frown and shortly Cramden realized what was afoot and threw his considerable glare behind it, too.

Jack felt the ill-disguised heat of their looks in the silence and knew what they wanted. But he also had the bishop fully in view and sensed, astutely, that the bishop would never be culled by a smitten-swain appeal . . . not from him. The unexpected nature of his bride-to-be and the gell's violent reaction to him had both taken him by surprise, and until he had time to take stock of the situation, he was determined to do nothing that would jeopardize the rosy future he had planned. So he sat, rather coolly, looking at the bishop and saying absolutely nothing.

"Then the couple shall have a fortnight to become acquainted," the bishop said. "Surely by that time Lady Meredith . . ." He did not finish his discomforting thought; there was no need. "So be it." The bishop took a deep, authoritative breath and strode out to disperse the guests to their various homes. Overbeake followed him, declaring she must see to her charge, leaving the Lombards, Cramden, and Jack in the parlor.

"Well, ye coulda said somethin'." Manley leveled a scowl at Jack.

"And made myself appear indecently eager for the gell?" Jack raised one rakish eyebrow. "Or a mercenary bastard who would inflict himself on a swooning innocent? No thank you, sir."

"What's done is done." Cramden moaned unhappily. "There will be no vows on the morrow, nor for a fortnight. Such a great mischance!"

"Now he 'as to stay th' fortnight," Gert observed, and crossed her arms over her chest, glaring at Jack with thorough disgust.

"And . . ." Cramden seemed to get hold of himself at the thought, "he shall have to make himself amenable to Lady Meredith, enough so that the bishop will have no qualms about finishing the job when he returns in two weeks' time. We simply cannot countenance a repeat . . ." He turned on Jack in earnest. "You can make yourself amenable to a young, inexperienced gell, can you not?"

Jack merely narrowed his eyes, refusing to dignify the question with any other response.

"O' course he can." Manley spoke with a hint of arrogance at Cramden's apparent naïveté, then proceeded to display his own as he turned to Jack. "Ye'll have to go slow wi' 'er. She be a timid little thing."

"We didn't count on ye havin' to court th' gell." Gert rubbed her hands together as she began to ruminate on the possible problems and ramifications of this unexpected development. One prospect occurred to her, and she pulled Manley and Cramden off a pace to discuss it in whispers.

Jack watched the threesome, feeling a strange annoyance at their secretive behavior. But he reminded himself that he was there to make the most of a very lucrative opportunity, and if it took a bit longer than originally planned, then so be it. As he watched their consultation and felt their sidelong glances, he pondered Gert's words. He'd have to court the gell a bit.

It had been a while since Jack Huntington was reduced to flattering and seducing young things into cooperation. The women he'd associated with in recent years had been fully aware of his worldly designs and amorous intent from the moment they detected his interest in them. Very little courtship had been required. But then, courtship was not something a man like himself had to work very hard at. Flattery, a few songs, worshipful glances, and longing sighs . . . followed by secretive touches and sweet, stolen kisses that became longer and sweeter . . . It all came naturally to him and he had no reason to believe his practiced charm would not work on a "timid little thing" like Lady Meredith.

His mind was just turning back to consideration of his unexpected bride when the threesome broke ranks and approached him, with Cramden as reluctant spokesman.

"We are agreed, you must stay and court the gell. We must count on your discretion, sir, in the matter of . . . the conditions of your marriage. We would not have Lady Meredith troubled with . . . the details."

Jack studied their tense faces and caught their meaning full well. He nodded casually. "As you wish."

But as they left the small parlor, a still, small voice

that had lain long-dormant inside Jack Huntington whispered: "The gell knows nothing at all about her own marriage. . . ."

Merrie soon awakened to Overbeake's shrill, strident voice, working itself into a full, lathering fury near the bed. From the corner of a mostly closed eye, she could see Tess wincing and blanching, and realized the little maid stood as proxy for herself under Overbeake's towering wrath.

". . . nearly ruint it all, with her lily-livered swooning, she has. Th' guests has all been sent home an' the bishop leaves at the crack of dawn, not to return for a whole fortnight to speak th' vows!" Burning with the frustrated need to both blame and punish, Overbeake gave Tess a vicious pinch on the upper arm. "Like as not ye laced her up too tight, chit!"

"Ow-w-w!" Tess scuttled back, rubbing her arm. Then seeing Overbeake turning on her sleeping mistress, she rushed to the bedside ahead of her. "Oh, Mistress, it be purely dang'rous to wake a body up from a swoon. Folks get addled that way."

Overbeake halted, not quite willing to defy common medical wisdom and risk addling the gell's mind further. "Then bring word th' very instant she wakens, ye hear?"

Merrie heard the door slam and wilted into the soft bedding beneath her. She took a deep, steadying breath, but it caught, half in, half out. A broad, black-clad chest and well-sculptured, angular features crowded everything else from her mind. It was the last awful vision of *him*, as he'd held her hand and kissed it and raised his rakishly handsome face to hers. And in those tawny, black-rimmed eyes, she'd seen the awful certainty of her own terrifying conjugal fate. Suddenly she recalled it all. . . . Good Lord—she was to *marry* Gentleman Jack!

The hot, humiliating details of her one-sided encounter with him at the inn came flooding back to her with a vengeance. The sight of his big, naked body, of his long muscular legs, of his passion-darkened face and glowing catlike eyes was scored deep into her mind by a fortnight of shameless rememberings. Helplessly, she recalled the sight of his shocking, open-mouthed kisses and the heady horror of seeing his strong male hands and fascinating lips mastering a woman's body. She was once again in the full thrall of the powerful, raw terrors and titillations she'd experienced while watching him. She was trembling, just recalling it.

How could she marry a man who sent icy, tingling shivers of fear through her entire body? A man who met women at country inns while their husbands were off in Lon—Oh, Lord. It wasn't just the shocking act of procreation she had almost witnessed . . . it was *adultery!* He'd been at that inn to meet a married woman. Awful insight flooded her. Those strange, sliddery feelings and confusions she'd felt in her body—likely she'd felt them because she'd sensed that what she was witnessing was wrong . . . sinful. Now they were going to make her marry a man she'd caught in the act of adultery! She bolted upright in bed, her eyes wide and her heart pounding.

"M'lady?" Tess hopped up from her nearby chair, searching her with a squint of concern. "Be you all right?"

"Y-yes . . . I think so," Merrie managed to say, cradling her head in one hand and trying to hold her heart in her chest with the other. How could she possibly be all right—promised to a lecherous, venial beast of a man . . . an adulterer! "Please, Tess, don't go for Mistress Overbeake just yet. I must have a time to recover first."

"Oh, yes, m'lady." Tess nodded in perfect sympathy. "Rest be what ye need. Th' bishop sent th' guests home an' declared that the vows must wait th' full fortnight. But Master Huntington's goin' to stay, I heard. So's ye get a chance to know him some." She braved her status to give Merrie's hand a reassuring pat. "I'll jus' slip down to the kitchen to see if them almon' cakes be goin' wantin'."

Merrie watched her go, then slid from the bed, her

head spinning as she stood. Her sluggish brain began to engage and questions began to form. They were going to marry her off to an adulterer in a fortnight. What was she going to do? Who could she tell—

Tell? No one, that's who. What basis would she have for her charges unless she explained how she knew of his dissolute character? That she'd run off to the inn in the dead of night, nearly been caught, and been forced to hide in a wardrobe where . . . She sagged, feeling utterly trapped by her own shameful knowledge. She had counted herself lucky indeed to have escaped the potential consequences of her own willful rebellion that night. But perhaps this was to be her punishment, long delayed: to know the base nature of the man to whom she was given and to be completely unable to do a thing about it. Even if she braved the consequences and told what she knew, how likely were they to believe her? Probably Overbeake would punish her severely for ''conjuring up poisonous falsehoods'' and they'd make her wed him anyway. And *he'd* be properly furious with her, and when she faced him in their marriage bed he would . . .

Both of her cold fists came up to press against her mouth as a chill coursed through her. Once they were married, she'd have to submit to his . . .

Oh, please! she prayed silently. *Not that!* There had to be some way. . . . But try as she might, think as hard as she could, only one slender possibility presented any hope at all. She had virtually no hope of escaping the marriage herself, being a young and powerless gell. But if *he* decided to cry off, refused to marry her . . . The thought kept coming 'round in her mind and finally seized her full concentration. If *he* refused . . .

What would it take for a man to renounce a woman in marriage? The wheels in her efficient mind began to turn faster. What would it take to make a woman objectionable to a man, especially a man whose tastes, from what she had been able to observe, ran to the finest and most elegant in women?

What, indeed? Inspiration flared, hot and brilliant. Her eyes fluttered shut and her lips curled into a smile of discovery as she savored her sudden insight. Overbeake had tirelessly drummed a list of womanly virtues and graces into her head: meekness, sobriety, grace of movement, mildness of temper, quietness, tidiness, agreeableness. . . . All were things a man would especially wish to see in his wife.

A fortnight. She had two weeks to make Gentleman Jack Huntington abhor the very idea of wedding her!

Chapter Five

That same evening, Merrie sat on the bench at the foot of her bed and endured Overbeake's furious threats and denouncements with surprising equanimity.

"I—I was just overwhelmed at the sight of him, Mistress," she murmured contritely. "I promise, I'll have myself much better in hand when next we meet."

"Indeed you shall, gell, or suffer the consequences," Overbeake snapped irritably. "You'll dine wi' Master Huntington and Master Cramden and His Worship in the hall, shortly. Remember yerself, gell, for I shan't be there to o'ersee you. Now change your gown and set that one aside for the speakin' of the vows. They'll be awaitin' you." Overbeake clomped out and, with a glint in her eye, Merrie gave Tess her back lacings to undo.

"B-but, m'lady, it ain't fittin'. Ye gots to have a corset, m'lady, else yer gown don't fit proper." Tess shook her head in horror at Merrie's shift-clad form.

"It's miserable and uncomfortable. I'm convinced it caused my swoon earlier. I shan't wear it." Merrie was the picture of determination, standing with her hands on her curvy hips and her stockinged legs spread. "Now help me on with my petticoat and gown, Tess."

Tess reluctantly obliged, and when Merrie was laced into the dress, she saw from the curl of distaste on the little maid's nose that she'd achieved the desired effect—unfashionable lumpiness. She looked down and sighed pleasantly at the bulging bodice of her gown and started for the door.

"Oh, m'lady!" Tess hurried after her with a brush

in one hand and a new linen cap in the other. ''Ye mus' come, let me fix yer hair proper 'neath a cap.''

''Oh.'' Merrie paused with a faint shake of her head and a swish of her flowing red-golden hair. ''I don't think so. . . . Not tonight.'' And she glided out.

Pausing at the end of the hall, near the gallery, she dragged her fingers through her hair, rumpling it, and shook her head vigorously, setting her long tresses washing over her shoulders in thick, careless waves. Tidiness. Gentlemen wanted their wives to be tidy. She smiled craftily. Remembering, she rounded her shoulders and struck a comfortably slouched posture. Graceful. Gentlemen wanted their wives to be graceful. And she turned her toes inward and clumped around the gallery and down the stairs.

''Here is Lady Meredith now.'' Master Cramden shoved to his feet from a chair near the hearth, bringing Jack Huntington and the others up with him. He tugged at his straining doublet and bustled over to the bottom of the stairs to extend an arm to assist her. ''I do hope you're feeling much better, my lady.''

''Ever so much,'' Merrie murmured, feeling every eye in the hall turned upon her in full scrutiny as she rested her hand on the solicitor's voluminous slashed sleeve. ''It was purely the excitement, Master Cramden. Being fresh from the nursery, I have not encountered so many august personages in one place before. It was quite overwhelming.''

Cramden observed her ruffled and unadorned hair, and a flicker of consternation crossed his face. As they traversed the rush-covered stone of the floor, he noted a certain hitch in the gell's gait, as though she tried to keep from tredding on her skirts.

Merrie felt Jack Huntington's bone-melting smile trained on her and a trill went up her spine. Lord, he was so big and dark . . . and so very male. A quick, heated vision of his bare chest flashed before her eyes. *Stop that!* She squinted and blinked to banish that unholy sight and screwed up her determination, clutching Cramden's sleeve a bit harder.

"Your Worship." She nodded to the bishop, then offered her hand to Jack as he stepped down from the broad hearth step to greet her. "Master Huntington." She eased her squint as she stared up at him and managed what she hoped would pass for suitable maidenly interest. The warmth of his hand was a stark contrast to her own icy fingers and she wished she could break that disturbing contact.

"My lady Meredith," Jack intoned, lingering over the *m*'s so that he seemed to be physically savoring the sound of her name. "I trust you are better rested."

"I am." She had to swallow in order to speak.

"Then, I am emboldened to say, your ordeal of the afternoon has left you undiminished. You are very like . . . a summer meadow."

Merrie stiffened at the warmth radiating up her arm from his touch. She scowled slightly, seeming confused. "All gone to seed and crawly with vermin?"

Jack huffed a short laugh, caught aback by her question. "Nay, my lady. I meant"—he waved a hand to indicate her thick, glowing hair and then her eyes—"alike in the sun-kissed glory of your fragrant hair and the delightful cornflower blue of your eyes."

"You can smell my hair from there?" She seemed genuinely alarmed and caught a lock of it to hold to her nose, sniffing vigorously.

Jack's jaw loosened, but his gallantry remained unshakable. Lord, what a literal mind the wench had! "It is a poor comparison, I see that now. I shall endeavor to please you better with my next effort at poetry, my lady."

Cramden rescued Jack from his unraveling courtship by waving them to seats at the great table, draped with cloth and set with good silverplate. Merrie clumped along at Jack's side in an admirable slouch, still twirling that lock of her hair about her finger.

Taking the host's seat at the head of the table, Cramden risked offending the bishop by appointing Merrie

to sit on his right. After that worrisome start between
the engaged couple, he thought it was best to keep an
eye on her. Fortunately, the bishop accepted the seat
beside her with good grace. Across from Merrie, Jack
settled into his chair, watching his bride, who was
craning her neck to peruse the oncoming platters of
food with great interest. The serving began immediately, under Manley Lombard's watchful supervision.
And each time she was served, Merrie halted the serving lad by the arm and proceeded to help herself to
several more of what had already been placed before
her. Gentlemen, she repeated in her head like a charm,
wanted their wives to have dainty manners.

Slabs of fried fish and cold meat pie, heaps of boiled
turnips and carrots grew on her trencher. She took a
deep breath and dug in to the repast with astonishing
relish, slicing and spearing and spooning so that her
cheeks soon were stuffed like a squirrel's. She chewed
determinedly, stuffing another hunk of bread or bit of
kidney pie into her mouth as soon as the meagerest
room for more had been cleared. And when Manley
himself brought around the flagon of wine, she
snatched up her goblet and held it for him, as if eager
to wet her massive mouthfuls of food. She stared
darkly into the small amount he'd poured and snatched
him back by the sleeve with a silent demand for more.
Under her expectant gaze, he filled the large goblet to
the rim and, with an emphatic ''do something'' look
at Cramden, he went on to fill the bishop's cup.

All around the table, consumption was slowing as
Lady Meredith's conspicuous stuffing and swilling and
munching continued. She felt Cramden's questioning
eyes on her and lifted a guileless, foody grin to him.
Then she turned to her husband-to-be to collect his reaction and found him staring between her mouth and
her trencher with a very controlled expression that hid
most of his thoughts. But it was clear he'd noticed, and
she was quite sure it wasn't delight he was suppressing so vigorously. The thought warmed her consider-

ably . . . either that or it was the wine that spread this new warmth in her middle.

Looking forlornly at his own scarcely touched plate, Cramden determined to engage them in conversation as a means of halting her shocking indulgence. "It is most excellent food, is it not? How I always enjoy a stay at Straffen Hall. Edythe Lombard is a perfect master of the art of seasoning."

"Edy-tthe th' cook iss-s a Lom-bard?" Merrie looked up at Cramden's tight face and was dimly aware that a particle of food had launched from her stuffed mouth when she broached the *b* in Lombard. She managed to seem totally oblivious to the fact that it had come to rest on poor Cramden's fancy quilted sleeve.

"Manley Lombard's elder sister, I believe," Cramden uttered, lowering his arm and giving it a shake to remove the offending glob.

"I didnn' know tthat." Merrie turned her gaze back to her trencher, swallowed, and stuffed more fish into her mouth.

"Truly, a most excellent kitchen," the bishop added, taking up the flagging effort.

It had better be, Jack mused privately, watching Merrie's ravenous indulgence. He had honestly never seen a woman eat like this in his life. From beneath lowered lids, his gaze slid over her petite but nicely curved figure. She had such a dainty, gell-ish look about her. His eyes came to rest on the straining fabric of her bodice. Well, perhaps not altogether gell-ish. . . .

In a valiant effort to slow her down, Cramden turned to Manley and motioned for him to clear the trenchers and bring on the next course. Merrie managed to stuff her cheeks before they removed her trencher so that she continued munching for a while yet.

"And how are things in the church, Your Worship?" Cramden asked, mounting yet another valiant conversational sortie.

"As fine as may be expected, I suppose. It is a trying time . . . so many devisive elements. This constant threat of Protestant resurgence is most wearing. Our good Queen Mary is a vigilant defender of the true Catholic faith, but every new rumor of her ill health foments another wave of unrest amongst those 'Protestant' dissidents.''

''I have often wondered, Your Worship . . .'' Merrie finally swallowed her last mouthful and drew deeply from her goblet. She was starting to feel rather full and a bit tingly all over. ''What did they do with all the Protestant prayerbooks that were confiscated?''

The bishop looked rather surprised as he turned toward her. ''Well, they were burned, I am quite sure. I saw quite a little bit of it, myself.''

''I do wonder, and perhaps you can enlighten me . . .'' She drew again from her goblet. ''What do you get when you burn prayerbooks?'' She blinked expectantly. ''Holy smoke, do you suppose?''

While the bishop sat back with a slack jaw and Cramden blinked and blustered at her unthinkable remark, she turned to find the glazed pheasant and roast pig being ferried in on large platters, and her face lit with glee. ''Oh, stuffed pheasant, my favorite!''

Jack chewed his lip and his shoulders gave two convulsive twitches as he squelched an involuntary laugh. God's Teeth, she was an impudent little glutton! But as he scoured her delicate, guileless features he was forced to reconsider his assessment. Perhaps she didn't realize the near-treasonous irreverence she had just perpetrated. Perhaps it was just a thoughtless whimsy from an empty, childish head. He watched her serving herself generously from the pheasant and the pork, and bade his face to remain utterly calm and polite.

Merrie had felt his gaze on her, but refused to return his look. She was making a bloody spectacle of herself for his benefit and prayed he was getting the point.

In an effort to maintain some modicum of civility, and to draw attention from Merrie's vigorous noshing and swilling, Cramden turned desperately to Jack. ''Master Huntington, you might wish to tell Lady Meredith about your home . . . in Kent,'' he prodded, gray-faced.

"In truth." Jack took the hint and tried, half successfully, to engage Merrie's attention. She was drinking at the moment and had to raise her head from her trencher to accomplish it. "I am seldom at my family home in Kent. My firstborn brother, Henry, is Baron Huntington now and I make my home in London. I have three brothers, all married and with families. I am lastborn."

"Truly?" she managed to say through a mouthful of pheasant. "Then who is bestborn?"

"Bestborn?" He flashed his most beguiling smile full into her cornflower blue eyes and had the disconcerting experience of wondering whether his most infamous expression of charm had made any impact on her at all. "Another must be judge of that, sweet lady."

But his look had found its mark. Some great bass string at the very bottom of her being was set vibrating by that blatant visual caress. She shivered inside, feeling a queer warmth puddling like liquid in her loins. Suddenly the lurid sight of his lean, naked hip and thigh flashed into her beleaguered mind. *Cease that! This instant!*

Shaking her head, she flushed hotly and refocused her eyes on her trencher, just in time to see it being whisked off the table. She managed to retrieve a plump piece of pheasant breast before it got totally away and attacked the meat with thorough abandon, willing herself not to look at Jack again . . . ever, if she could help it. It was utterly dangerous. Maybe she should say something, show some interest in the proceedings, so as to keep from rousing his suspicions.

She tossed the empty rack of ribs over her shoulder with a flourish and proceeded to wipe her greasy fingers on the heavily embroidered estate cloth that covered the table. From the corner of her eye, she saw Manley toss his head in a silent groan and witnessed Cramden flinching noticeably at the sight.

She licked her fingers daintily and sent a suitably delighted smile toward the bishop as she seemed to suddenly discover her napkin. She wiped her chin vigorously with the linen and sucked air noisily through her teeth on one side, trying to dislodge a stuck bit of meat. Failing that, she stuck her finger in her mouth to remove it. Satisfied with her dental hygiene, she licked her lips broadly and reached for her empty goblet, turning it up to drain the very last drop.

"Kent." She mused on the bare bottom of her goblet, seeming disappointed it was emptied. Then she lifted a quixotic look to Jack. "And what do the Huntingtons grow in Kent, sir? I perceive that bishops grow wise . . ." She waved one floppy hand toward the good prelate, who was now staring at her in round disbelief, and the other at purple-faced Cramden. ". . . and solicitors grow fat. Then, what do Huntingtons grow?"

Before Jack could frame an answer to her stunningly pithy question, she beamed a guileless smile and offered: "Do the Huntingtons, perchance, grow wicked?"

She could see the genuine shock in Gentleman Jack's handsome, worldly face and the self inside herself hugged itself with impish, wine-warmed glee.

"Surely *prosperous!* They surely grow p-prosperous," Cramden sputtered, trying to pour oil on the already turbulent waters she was churning.

"Or pious," the bishop added emphatically.

"Or sheep." Merrie sank back in her chair with an overstuffed sigh. "Perhaps Huntingtons grow sheep."

Jack's jaw loosened fully as he stared at her. For one brief instant he'd seen a bold glint of fire in her big, amber-rimmed eyes. It was a glimpse of wit and spirit so quixotic that he wasn't entirely sure he hadn't imagined it. But she'd called him *wicked*. No mistaking that. The chit had posed a multifaceted question worthy of a damned philosopher and used it to set him up for an unparalleled goad. Jack Huntington grows *wicked*, she had proposed, then she had sunk blithely back into the morass of gell-hood and that infernal air of innocence.

And bestborn—she had wanted to know who in his family was bestborn. A strangely wizened question from a young gell with the table manners of a sow. He stared at her as she snatched a second jam-and-custard tart and a glazed almond cake from the serving tray as it was withdrawn. He watched the light in her strawberry blonde hair and the working of that ripe little bow of a jam-covered mouth and realized he was gripping the arms of his chair, trying to penetrate her visually, to make out what was inside her. She stuffed another mammoth bite of tart into her mouth, and he heard what seemed to be a groan of pure animal satisfaction in relishment of the sticky treat. Her eyes closed briefly and her pink tongue came out to lick her jammy lips. Jack's eyes fastened on that darting softness, and he unconsciously conjured the feel of it stroking his own, felt his lips melting over her jam-covered ones . . . tasted the raspberry. . . .

He stiffened all over. Lord, he was going dotty as a doodle. Look at her, a mere whisp of a thing, a slovenly child. And his entire body had just sprung to life from watching her eat a jam tart! Debauched as a sybarite. Maybe he *was* growing wicked.

Jack downed his rich wine and found it did little to alleviate his heated discomfort. In the volatile silence came the soft lapping sound of Merrie Straffen licking her fingers again . . . like a good little cat.

"Lady Meredith does play the virginal most passably well." Cramden leveled a grim look at Overbeake as they settled in chairs near the hearth in the hall after supper.

"Oh, indeed, she does, sir," Overbeake put in, seating herself beside her disreputable-looking charge with a face like tight white plaster. She'd answered a panicky summons from Gert Lombard to come to the hall immediately and had arrived just in time to witness Merrie's gluttonous consumption of sweets at the end of the meal. Now, seeing Merrie's mussed hair, her puckered and rumpled gown, and the smear of jam on her cheek, the mistress was quivering with suppressed rage. "Lady Meredith, you must play a spell for Master Huntington."

Merrie lifted drowsy eyes to her governess and tried to protest. But even through her painfully stuffed and wine-woozied state, she could make out the strength of that command and knew that she'd best obey. She rose to make her way to the virginal cabinet, and opened the lid and front doors. Manley hurried to provide her a straight chair and she took a moment to settle herself. Lord, she was starting to feel perfectly awful.

She thought of a suitable piece and began a series of scales and trills to loosen her fingers. Then she began to play, and the tinny, melodious plinging of the strings came together in a marvelously complex piece that built slowly in feeling and intensity. The melody lilted, in intricate, enticing runs, then lifted urgently toward some beckoning completion . . . until she misplayed and produced a discordant run and stopped utterly, leaving her audience hanging, hungering for a proper finish. She turned to Overbeake and then to Jack, who was seated close by.

"I am sorry. I do seem to stumble there sometimes. Let me do it over." And she turned back, taking a deep, miserable breath and doing it again. The same lilting melody issued, the same complex play of tones that deepened and began to build to the same promising conclusion, carrying all ears and minds with it . . . only to fall afoul of those same grating discords. And so she tried yet again.

The third time she played, building to that same promised climax, displaying what bordered on pure virtuosity, every hand in the room gripped a chair arm in anticipation. Their collective tension was focused on her now, following every phrase, willing her to get it right, aching for that well-deserved conclusion. When her fingers went awry this third time, her audience, quite understandably, was roused to furious heights of frustration. But Jack took it especially to heart, for his ear for music was highly refined and his surprise at her skill was some part relief that she owned accomplishment at anything.

He sat, enduring the dying discords of those final, misplayed notes, his hands clenched upon the chair arms. Dammit, he swore mentally, it was as if she did it a'purpose! A musical tease . . . getting him primed, allowing him the pleasure, plying him with anticipation, then denying him that full, satisfying musical *climax!* He was quivering with frustration, roused in a way he didn't understand and certainly didn't like. When Merrie turned to him again with that blue-eyed innocence of hers, he had an urge to throttle her!

"I have not played for some time, Master Huntington," she demured. "Perhaps if I tried one last time—"

"No!" Jack sat forward quickly, then checked himself. As he caught Master Cramden's surprised look of warning, he gentled his speech. "It was lovely, Lady Meredith. Most enjoyable. You shall have to play again for us . . . sometime."

Merrie nodded, watching the tightness around his eyes and in his flexed jaw, which belied his complimentary words. Her playing displeased him, she could tell. She nodded with duplicitous pleasure. The horrendous mass of food congealing in her stomach was becoming downright painful and she rose, somewhat unsteadily, and yawned broadly. The gentlemen all came to their feet with her.

"I am fatigued. If it would not vex you overmuch, I should like to retire for the night." She made a decent curtsey to the bishop and nodded to Cramden, then paused to extend her hand to Jack. He took it with a convincing display of gallantry, bestowing a kiss upon it and bidding her restful sleep and pleasant dreams.

She remembered herself just in time to alter her gait convincingly and then pulled herself up the stairs. It wasn't until she was around the gallery that Overbeake sprang into action and followed.

Merrie felt miserable. Lord, she'd overdone it a bit with the food. Her stomach was stretched to near bursting and her head pounded from the wine. Soon Overbeake was there, giving her a nasty pinch on the arm and railing on and on about her ingratitude and her unforgivable behavior. It wasn't so bad, actually; the misery inside kept her from worrying too much about Overbeake's noise and bluster. She promised to behave much better on the morrow and then collapsed on the bed in dreaded illness, while Tess fussed and flothered over her. All that comforted her during her gluttony-induced sickness in the night ahead was the hope that Jack Huntington now found her perfectly revolting.

Merrie would have been gravely disappointed to know Jack's thoughts as he strode through the twilight in the small gardens near the entry court of Straffen Hall. In the darkening azures and night-driven purples of evening, his mind turned inescapably to the cornflower blue of Meredith Straffen's eyes. It was a velvety blue, a deep, caressing, engulfing blue. And he found himself standing on the weedy cobblestone path, his body braced and intent as he squinted, trying to make out just what was behind those very memorable eyes.

He shook himself physically and continued his evening stroll, ordering himself not to dwell on the mercurial and incomprehensible nature of his bride-to-be. It was a marriage of convenience, after all, nothing to involve himself in overmuch. After the inauspicious start of their first meeting, he had actually entertained a fleeting worry about whether the delicacy of her constitution would withstand the intensity of his usual courtship. But this evening's supper had certainly eliminated all such concern. She was about as delicate as a cow . . . and likely had four stomachs to match! At least the mystery of why they were having to buy her a husband was solved.

He paused by a French lilac in full bloom and ran his lean fingers over the blossoms and heartlike leaves. Still, her appearance was pleasing, when she wasn't slouched or distorting her face with food. Without quite realizing it, he was back to the person of Lady Meredith Straffen again. She had the most unusual hair color he'd ever seen . . . like living flame, the way it shone and danced about her shoulders. Gold teased with lights of red . . . which looked like a birch-broom in a fit, he reminded himself sourly. And then, there were those eyes, those huge blue eyes, which seemed perfectly guileless and yet somehow closed to him with the same look. And the things she said: one minute literal-minded and childish and the next minute complicated and bordering on the sardonic. He found himself poised on the verge of asking a question and stiffened, battling back that horrifying urge. Get hold of yourself, Jack!

He filled his head and lungs with the scent of lilacs and turned to carry it back to the house with him. Fourteen days. He had fourteen days to make little Meredith Straffen simply adore the very idea of marrying him.

Manley met him in the hall with a candelabrum and showed him up the stairs to the old earl's bedchamber, murmuring a perfunctory wish that he would find the accommodations satisfactory. Jack found Seabury standing in the midst of the large, well-furnished chamber, his arms crossed, leaning his shoulder against a post of an imperially draped bed. The servant cum companion wore a pleased expression.

"Look at this place." Seabury waved a hand about him, indicating the tapestries, the massive carved furnishings, the snowy, inviting bed linen. "And you should see the chamber they've given me. . . . It connects out that side door and down a short hall. In the servants' hall they eat like bloody kings. Damme, Jack, I don't know how you do it. This is the master's chamber, you know; you shall be lying in the stead of earls."

"Only for a fortnight." Jack made a leisurely circuit of the chamber with a devilish grin, feathering an appreciative touch over the heavy crimson velvet and tapestry that covered the chair pillows near the vaulting marble hearth. "Enjoy it while you can, Seabury. After I've bedded her, it will only be a place to visit once a year." Seabury noted an unusual, pensive tone in Jack's voice and slanted a look at him.

"She's something of a beauty, your bride," Seabury observed. "I stood near the bishop when she was presented."

"First impressions, Seabury. Notoriously untrustworthy. She leaves quite a lot to be desired." Jack turned a searching look on the stately bed where he'd seal the bargain of their marriage in a fortnight and spoke to himself as much as to his man: "But then, desire has damned little to do with it."

Chapter Six

The sun was midway through its course the next day, and the good bishop had long since departed by the time Merrie was fit enough to venture from her chamber. She appeared, at Overbeake's insistence and under her stern escort, wearing the stiffest corset she owned and a suitably ashen color. The reasons for including gluttony among the Seven Deadly Sins had been made appallingly clear to her in the night just past. Henceforth, she would have to content herself with slightly less "deadly" affronts to Gentleman Jack's sensibilities. Fortunately, that still left a heartening range of disillusioning possibilities and a night of suffering had only deepened her determination to make Gentleman Jack cry off from the marriage.

Merrie was greatly relieved to find him absent from the hall when she arrived. At Overbeake's direction, she deposited herself in a chair, in a shaft of early afternoon sunlight, and took up her needlework. She applied herself vigorously to the toilsome poking, drawing, and stitching, and received a tight nod of approval from her mistress for her determined ladycraft. "Noblemen wish their ladies t' wield a fair needle," Overbeake reminded her, and for once, Merrie was actually grateful for the mistress's incessant promptings. With each stitch and snarl and knot she produced, her grim little smile and her slump in the chair deepened.

Jack appeared shortly, entering through the door leading from the rear yard, accompanied by Master Cramden and Manley Lombard. They had apparently been for a look at the stables, for they were discussing the lineages of Straffen's better horseflesh. Merrie felt

Gentleman Jack's deep, resonant tones lapping about her like warm milk and fidgeted in her chair. Determined not to look at him, she lowered her head a fraction more and raised her needlework so that it was mere inches from her nose.

Upon Master Cramden's meaningful nod in her direction, Gentleman Jack tugged down his splendid velvet doublet and strode toward his capricious bride-to-be and her stump-solid mistress. He paused by Merrie's chair, scrutinizing her slumped shoulders and the way her nose was buried in her needlery.

She blinked and pulled her hoop even closer to her face, squinting as though she had difficulty seeing it properly in the light that had suddenly dimmed. Casting a confused glance about her, she came nose-to-nose with his enormous green velvet codpiece. She started and her face flamed, jerking upward to encounter his dark outline leaning over her chair, blocking the light.

"Oh, sir!" She blinked and winced and brought a hand up to shield her eyes against the bright light . . . and against his unholy assault on her senses. "It is you blocking the light. Faith, I thought for a moment the sun was dying." She turned back to her stitchery, poking and pulling at the threads with a single-mindedness that completely dismissed his manly presence.

Blocking her light? Jack's eyes narrowed briefly and he sank with determined gallantry onto one knee beside her chair to remove his dread offense. "A good day to you, Lady Meredith . . . and to you, Good Mistress." He nodded to Overbeake, who gave him a weening smile. "I am pleased to see you in such fine fettle, my fair lady." He placed his arm on the arm of Merrie's chair, nudging visually into her notice.

But she seemed to ignore both his presence and his compliment and doggedly continued her stitching. He drew a quiet breath and tried again to snag her attentions. "Tell me what it is you labor so diligently to produce, Lady Meredith." He leaned toward her, lowering his head to catch a glimpse of her handiwork, but she promptly tilted it away from him.

"Stitchery, of course." She cast a frown at him as if he were daft, then turned straight back to her work.

"Indeed." He managed a gentlemanly smile. "But there is surely a pattern or some fair scene that you seek to capture in your work."

Merrie swallowed hard. For the last minute she'd been sun-dazzled, seeing the glowing outline of his head and shoulders on the light-colored fabric before her. Now he was mere inches away and his sleeve was insinuating itself into her awareness. Deep, forest green with braided cording and ivory satin linings in fashionable slashes . . . He was wearing the same clothes he'd worn that night at the inn! A hot memory of naked, mounded chest and a dark flat nipple streaked through her mind. *Ohhhh!*

She started and looked up. Everything about him swarmed at her at once: his shining raven hair and the sultry ease of his long-lashed eyes, the wideness of his shoulders and the sun-warmed smell of his clothes. . . . She just managed to unfocus her eyes, blunting the stunning effect of the sight of him, though not the warmth. When he reached for her birch hoop, she was strangely unable to resist him.

He dragged it over to look at it, giving her a glance of admiration that he had found universally effective on women. When he looked down, that approval congealed in his handsome features. It looked as though someone had shot yarn through canvas with a blunderbuss: thick, unwieldy stitches in utterly random directions, knots and coils of yarn upon messy, gaping backgrounds.

"Ah . . ." He recovered quickly, making what sense of it he could. "Flowers." He saw a sag of disappointment in her shoulders and corrected himself. "Or, perhaps a basket of fruit." She lowered her eyes to the tortured canvas he now rested across his arm, set her jaw as if mightily insulted, and began to stitch determinedly. "Or perhaps some illumined homily to adorn these fair walls."

"It be the crest o' Straffen, sir," Overbeake supplied, staring darkly at her charge's uncongenial reaction to her future husband. The gell was acting strangely. It would be just like her to queer th' wedding arrangements wi' her wretched ninnynooking!

"But of course; it certainly is that. I see it now." Jack's worldly eyes widened on the mess. A pure assault upon the senses, he was thinking. Perhaps the Straffen blood was somehow tainted. . . .

Merrie squinted harder, counting some imaginary thing in the canvas weave with her finger and abandoning the hoop to Jack's grip altogether as she applied her needle with two-handed abandon, pinching and pulling. Alarmed now, Overbeake set her own work aside and came to look over Merrie's shoulder.

"L-lady Meredith!" Overbeake sputtered and hovered, her hands convulsing with the urge to give Merrie a sound pinch. What had the chit done to her needlepiece?

Jack's eyes narrowed on the delicate little cap, mere inches from his face, and drifted down the lush fall of shining strawberry-golden hair beneath it. However lumpish or full of crotchets, that maidenly coif reminded him, she was still a young gell. And there were ways of bringing a young gell around. . . .

"Such meticulous work must be exhausting, indeed, my lady," he offered with dogged courtliness. "Perhaps a walk in the garden would prove refreshing."

"But of course." Overbeake pounced on the suggestion like a hunting hawk. "A walk in the garden. . . . We could certainly do with one, Lady Meredith." It was a scarcely cloaked command, and both Merrie and Jack responded by straightening. Merrie relinquished her needle with a loud sigh of compliance and rose, starting for the front door of the hall, remembering to hunch her shoulders and clump a bit. She was chewing down the curl at the corners of her mouth.

Jack pushed to his feet and put her needlework on her chair. It left his hand, only to cling tenaciously to his other arm, the one on which it had been resting.

"Wha—?" He tugged at the hoop, his eyes widening, his face reddening under the formidable mistress's horrified stare. Lifting his arm, he peered beneath the thing and discovered scarlet yarn, dug like claws into his padded green velvet and ivory satin. God's Toenails! She'd stitched the bloody thing to his sleeve!

It was a few minutes before Gentleman Jack and Overbeake emerged from the front door, striding purposefully for the gardens, both flame-faced. Merrie swallowed back a giggle, wishing with all her heart she could have seen his face when he found himself wearing her catastrophic needlework. She turned as they approached, intent on leading him further down the garden path.

As they strolled along the overgrown walkways, scarcely wide enough for two, Jack found himself pushed ahead or trailing behind, for Overbeake entrenched herself at Merrie's side, determined to see her charge behave in more seemly fashion.

Jack turned to cast a purposefully fonden eye on Merrie and found her stopped, examining the faded blossoms and borning fruit on an apple bough overhanging the path. He strolled back, examining the alluring curve of her cheek and the gentle flutter of her hands over the young leaves . . . and the smallness of her waist. . . . He cleared his throat as if to banish those thoughts. She looked up with enormous, velvety blue eyes that stopped him in his tracks.

"Was it not Sophocles who said: 'Ugly deeds are taught by ugly deeds'? And does not natural philosophy teach that ugly apples must come from ugly seeds? Where, then, do ugly men come from, Master Huntington?" That fiery glimpse of wizened wit, that strange light of learning, glowed unexpectedly in her gaze again. "From ugly seeds inside or from others' ugly deeds?"

Jack Huntington stood transfixed on the path before her, staring into those fathomless eyes, feeling confusion welling hotly in him. The echoes of her quote—spoken in Greek!—and her question thundered through him like a spring storm. She posed him a

question—by geck and by galfry!—one that had eluded
sages since the dawn of man. Does wickedness come
from within a man or is it learnt? she wanted to know.
He suddenly felt opened, exposed to that strangely
probing gaze. It was as though she saw into the
worldly, hedonistic core of him and demanded to know
how he came to be so!

"Surely one or t'other, my lady . . . or both, perhaps," he managed to say, ripping his eyes from hers
and feeling thoroughly rattled by his wildly conflicting
reactions to her. He pivoted as gracefully as possible
and ambled farther down the path, looking at the gil-
liflowers and budding woodbine and seeing nothing
but patches of soft, entrancing blue. He blinked and
blinked again to retrieve his vision and took a deep,
steadying breath.

A moment later, he turned and found her wincing
and rubbing the top of her arm, as Overbeake's hand
jerked away. He saw the reddening of Merrie's fair
cheeks and the way her remarkable eyes would not
leave the paving stones. And he didn't know whether
to feel incensed at the old harridan's badgering of the
gell or grateful for it. The rest of the walk was endured
in deep silence.

That night at supper, Overbeake joined Master
Cramden and Merrie and Jack at the table, posting herself beside Merrie. Merrie seemed perfectly oblivious
to the implied threat of the governess's presence, as
well as to the sensibilities of her fellow diners. She held
up a tender piece of roast rabbit, commenting, "Do
you not think bunnies look ever so much better with
their skins on? But fein, imagine what we should look
like without our skins—all squaddy, red, and squishy,
I should think."

With that thought queasy on their minds, she sank
her teeth gleefully into the haunch she was holding.
Moments later, she truly horrified them with another
observation: "Is it not a wonder how much better food
looks going in than it ever does coming out?"

Not another morsel passed another gullet at the table. Overbeake quivered with rage and rose to insist Merrie retire, since she obviously was not feeling herself.

"I *am* feeling rather oddly." Merrie rose with a wrist pressed to her temple, drawing the men to their feet as she bade them good eve. She cast a sidelong glance at Jack, and the turmoil evident in his handsome face heartened her enough to withstand Overbeake's upcoming tirade. She clumped as lumpishly as she dared to the stairs.

Jack watched his unnerving bride lurch out of sight, then flexed his broad shoulders to dispel their tension. By th' Eternal—she was a tangled coil inside! Mauping over skinned bunnies one minute, then sinking her teeth into them the next, like a little cannibal! She not only thought the unthinkable; she dared speak it as well. One minute it was the highest, most elevated of mankind's contemplations; the next, it was some bald irreverence or some gruesome crudity! He excused himself from the table and nodded absently as Cramden suggested they repair to the smaller parlor for a bit of Straffen's good claret.

Mercurial, inscrutable Meredith Straffen was coming to occupy every blessed corner of Jack's mind, while he had the disconcerting feeling that he hadn't even entered hers! Every time her gaze fell his way, he suffered the dread suspicion that she was somehow looking straight through him. She'd ignored him so completely that afternoon that she'd stitched right through him . . . as if he and his wretched sleeve were nonexistent! Saint Patrick's pizzle! Not in his life . . . not in his whole bloody life had he met a female who *ignored* him!

And she spoke to him only through pithy, philosophical questions that had a faintly unearthly and rebuking tone, like a blessed schoolmaster . . . or a priest! He was a man who prided himself in his thorough understanding of women, and in his ease in mastering and pleasing them. How infuriating that he was finding his fortunes inextricably linked to the one female in his entire life who proved a profound puzzlement to him!

Merrie rose early the next morning and dressed herself, omitting both her corset and her gathered shift under her embroidered, scooped-neck bodice. She intended to be "slovenly" with a vengeance today, adding that quality to Gentleman Jack's graceless, unaccomplished, and ill-mannered bride. From what she could see in the silvered glass, she was nicely lumpy and excellently unkempt. She hurried downstairs before Overbeake appeared and was halfway through breaking her fast when her mistress discovered her there. She took one look at Merrie's bare chest, bulging bodice, and uncovered hair and staggered in apoplectic shock. Just as she recovered enough to lace into Merrie, Jack and his manservant appeared on the stairs with Master Cramden in tow.

"Good morn, my sweet lady," Jack called, his deep tones prolonged in the echo-prone hall. He strode to take her hand and lavish a courtly kiss upon it. As he bent over her, his gaze dropped unexpectedly into the crevice between her shockingly exposed breasts.

For an instant he froze, staring and unable to straighten. *Lord, look at them . . . deliciously full . . . smooth, like risen cream. . . .* He shoved upright, unnerved by his spontaneous warming, and made his way around the table with Cramden, greeting the stern mistress and introducing his servant and companion, Thomas Seabury. Ordinarily servants did not come to table with their masters, but since Overbeake was there . . . He motioned Seabury to a seat and settled across the table from Merrie with an entrancing smile.

In spite of her resolve not to look at him, she had followed his gaze around the table and now held it as the warmth of his smile poured through her. She swallowed hard and tore her eyes away. He was wearing a wine-red doublet with black cording trim and looked very dashing indeed. Black hair perfectly groomed, strong chin fresh-shaven . . .

While she worked at ignoring him, he was fully oc-
cupied with scrutinizing her. Her tousled hair was a
glowing mane in the morning light; her skin was like
translucent satin; her lashes were thick amber fans
spread over velvety pools of sky blue; and her lips . . .
He forced himself to stop at her lips. She was biting
off a ferocious hunk of a hot breakfast bun that was
smothered in melted butter and dripped honey. He
watched, enrapt, as those fine white teeth sank into
the crusty bun, and he saw the unheeded bulge of
honey on the edge grow and break off and drop . . .
straight onto the creamy skin of her succulent breasts.
Then he watched, tantalized, as it slid slowly toward
the erotic crevice between those soft mounds, just as
his gaze had moments before.

With a thoughtless finger, she scooped up the drip
and licked it, unaware that she sent a wild wave of
heat through her bridegroom in the process. It was exactly, he realized desperately, what *he* wanted to do!
He scowled and attacked his food with an appetite that
fully matched his quirksome bride's.

As the food was cleared away, Jack asked Merrie to
escort him about the grounds on a walk. She paused,
then nodded, finishing licking honey from her fingers
and wiping them on the linen Overbeake shoved forcefully into her hands. When Overbeake rose to accompany them, Jack set her back on her heels with, "You
mustn't trouble yourself, Mistress; I'll see to my lady.
Seabury will require your assistance this morning in
learning the routine of the house and hall." And he
grasped Merrie's hand and planted it firmly on his arm
to lead her out the rear door into the warm spring sun.

The sight of Overbeake's ill-disguised indignation as
the door closed behind them lingered in Merrie's racing mind and she dared a surprised glance up at Gentleman Jack. Apparently he found Overbeake's
company every bit as loathsome as she did . . . and *he*
was in the enviable position of being able to dispense
with it. The thought brought a grateful smile to her

face, which she managed to turn elsewhere so he wouldn't see.

Merrie just remembered her halting gait in time and let his long stride carry him past her altogether. He paused and she looked up, blinking and squinting in the bright morning sun. "Oh, sir. I fear you must temper your great stride if you would have me for company. My . . . legs are not so very long or strong as I might like, sir."

Jack winced a smile, having that discomforting feeling that she was looking through him again. But, in truth, it was hard to say where she looked, with the way she screwed up her face by squinting; bright sunlight apparently bothered her eyes. He reached for her hand, which had slid from his sleeve to dangle by her side, and plopped it firmly on his sleeve again, covering it firmly with his own hand. He led her off toward the grainery and the barns in stiff silence. He ventured a few polite comments and was answered with "Verily, sir," when he was answered at all. She hunched and clumped along beside him and occasionally paused and breathed hard, as though the exertion of mere walking overcame her.

They drew odd stares from Straffen's folk, who watched their sweet, gracious little mistress in bemusement. They'd never seen her walk or look quite like this. But there was one group to whom their Lady Merrie would always be the same, in looks, in loving nature, and in accessibility. Without thought to propriety or consequences, Straffen's full contingent of young servant boys and a host of wildly excited hounds descended on them.

"Ohhh—" Merrie saw the yawping pack of hounds streaking toward her, halted, and stumbled back a step. When the hounds reached her and lunged, Jack tried half successfully to thrust her behind him and take on himself the brunt of what seemed a vicious attack. He kicked at them, sending two yelping back, but the others surged in, barking and jumping and shoving, swirling around their feet like a storm of fur and flesh. It took a moment to realize that they weren't snapping—they were licking!

"Nooo—no!" Merrie saw that their raw enthusiasm was grossly misinterpreted and managed to shove in front of Jack to bat some of them down and scold. "Nay! Down, you naughty beasts—have you no manners a'tall!" A breath later, they were inundated by a second wave—of rag-tailed bodies and bowl-cropped heads about chest high. The second invasion, boys calling her name with glee and jumping and trying to sort barking hounds, was every bit as boisterous as the first.

Jack watched in combined horror and astonishment as the hounds trammeled Merrie's rose brocade skirts with dirty paws, drooled from lolling tongues on the exquisite fabric, and fairly knocked her down as they jumped on her and invaded her skirts to frisk about her ankles. And all the time she was smiling and laughing, even while struggling to stay upright. "Fie and forget my promise! You'll not sit under my table for a time yet!" she threatened with good nature. As she struggled against their raw enthusiasm to give all the hounds' and boys' heads a pet, one overzealous beast dashed under her skirts and between her feet, all but sweeping them from under her. She flailed and twisted to keep her balance and fell facefirst, with a squeal, against Gentleman Jack's wide chest.

Jack caught her and found himself holding her, looking down into those big sky-blue eyes that sparkled with life and mischief. A hundred separate perceptions clamored for attention: the soft feel of her in his hands, the tantalizing sight of her ripe breasts near to spilling from her gown, the swirling cloud of dazzling tresses turned to fiery gold in the sun. He felt the breathless pace of life pulsing in her and experienced a strange swirl of warmth spiraling downward through him. But as he stared into that quixotic face, the limits of his own long-standing habits with women began to filter and focus his perceptions into more carnal realms.

Then all he could see was her lips, those full, coral lips. . . .

"Oh, sir!" Merrie tore her gaze from his, feeling weak and rattled. "These are my friends!" She seized the most outrageous explanation she could imagine. She pulled free of Jack's dangerously potent touch and stooped into their midst, laughing and patting and letting the hounds lick her, even her face, as they buffeted her. Any gentleman would be properly horrified by such an abandoned display. The thought sent her arms around boys and hounds alike, in buoyant hugs.

She finally staggered up, feeling ripely disheveled, and sent them off with a wheeze and a sigh. Then she turned to witness Gentleman Jack's loathing for her and instead found him looking at her with an intensity that was like a physical touch. It made her feel very hot and fluttery inside . . . and wobbly in the knees. She lowered her eyes hurriedly and made a messy swipe at her long, wind-ruffled hair and wet face. Did she disgust him now or not? There was a long, expectant pause between them in which she stared down at her dirtied gown and he stared at the top of her head, wishing vehemently that he could pry it open and peer inside.

"Shall we continue?" he asked, giving her his arm.

Merrie squinted up at him, confused by his dismissal of the incident. A quick, shocking vision of his lips parting and descending toward hers flashed in her mind and she stiffened. *Stop that!*

He escorted her slowly around the manor house, toward the front garden, measuring his stride to match her graceless gait. He stole heated glances at her, frustrated entirely in his compulsion to make out what was inside her. At the moment she was that frail, awkward chit who never looked at him, who scarcely knew he existed, while only minutes earlier she'd been pressed against him, her eyes and spirit alight with excitement, her body soft and alluring. God's Teeth! Were there two creatures inhabiting that frame? He looked again at her slovenly slouch. Perhaps there were two mortal frames as well! He was utterly bumfuzzled . . . be-witched!

By the time they reached the garden paths, he was determined to confront her with her own contradictions and learn the true nature of his bride. "Those lads, they called you Lady Merrie," he observed.

"A shameful liberty, sir, I know." She managed to sound miles away.

"I wish you would call me John, my lady." He stroked her hand as it lay on his elegant arm. "And that you would permit me the liberty you grant your urchins, to address you as Lady Merrie."

Merrie swallowed hard and nodded permission, shocked by the ripples of excitement flowing up her arm. She spotted the stone bench past the first bend in the path and seized the chance to demonstrate a very unsuitable weakness.

"Sir, if you would not mind, I would sit for a while. The exertions of walking . . ." She pulled her hand from his sleeve and lurched over to the bench. With a palm clasped over her thumping heart, she sank onto the stone with an awkward plop and emitted what sounded for all the world like a tortured wheeze.

"Are you quite all right, Lady Merrie?" He frowned, watching her suck and expel breath raggedly.

"Yea, sir." She heaved one last time, relieved that her "suffering" hadn't gone unnoticed. But her pleasure dimmed as he strode over and eased himself onto the bench beside her.

"I have noted, you are surprisingly well lettered for a young gentlewoman, Lady Merrie. I believe you quoted Sophocles in flawless Greek yesterday."

"Oh, sir." She shrank toward the far end of the bench and confessed: " 'Tis true. I am grossly and foully lettered, sir. You may as well hear it, since you have guessed." She recalled Overbeake's deep convictions against teaching young women to read and prayed he shared them. "My old foster father was once a schoolmaster in the service of the Earl of Essex and he taught me unseemly and unmaidenly things, sir.

Latin, Greek, the classicals, sir. Mistress says all that learning sits ill upon my mind, makes my head buzz with strange thoughts, betimes."

It was the most she had ever spoken to him at once and the shyly regretful tone of her confession captured him utterly. He stared at her, letting the soft, melodic tones float in his head and seep into his chest. A moment later the sense of what she'd said stung him. She'd been taught to apologize for her learning, for the "shocking" accomplishments of her mind.

"You mean, you read Latin . . . Horace and Cicero, Seneca and Pliny. . . ."

He sounded a bit choked and Merrie imagined the horror with which he would receive this next: "I double translate, sir."

"Dearest God." He watched her shrink so far that she teetered upon the edge of the bench.

"Oh, I promise never to do it in your presence, sir." Her voice quivered nicely as her fingers tied themselves in knots in her lap. "Around you I shall strive to be *magis mutus quam piscis.*"

He jolted and his mind scrambled, frantic to translate it . . . "silent as the grave"! His jaw loosened and worked as he watched her obvious dread of his reaction. He suddenly recalled the stern old mistress's reaction to her use of Greek yesterday and realized that she probably expected *him* to pinch her, too. A wild jumble of anger and protectiveness surged into his broad chest and through his muscular arms to curl his hands into impotent fists. The thought of anybody abusing this odd, unpredictable being suddenly enraged him!

"Lady Merrie . . ."

His voice was full of righteous anger and Merrie was sure she'd pushed him too far this time. She looked up into his raven-framed features and saw the fierce glow of his unusual eyes, and was genuinely frightened by the power she glimpsed there. She managed to stand, paling. "Oh, sir, I never meant to—"

"Merrie—" He was on his feet in a trice, catching

her arm to keep her from bolting. In those wide, depth-less blue eyes he read her fear and deeply regretted his part in it. "Sweet Merrie, I've frightened you—" He grabbed her other arm and turned her to him. "I won't hurt you, little Merrie."

Her heart thudded wildly as she looked up into his handsome face and watched the angry sparks muting to other lights, to a knowing, manly glow. He was so big and strong, towering over her, the wine-colored fabric that covered his chest filling her vision as his sandalwood scent filled her head. Her blood came tumbling and crashing back into her cheeks . . . and into a strange collection of other bodily parts: her lips and bubbies and womanly parts below. Warm, swirling sensations invaded her head and her middle as his hands dragged her closer and closer to the hard, dangerous wall of his body. She was reeling, unable to resist. His face took on that sultry, lidded look she'd seen that night at the inn and his lips were parting. Ohhh—She was feeling that same choking in her throat—she couldn't swallow!

Jack absorbed the sweet confusion of her reaction and the irresistible allure of her large eyes. He visually claimed the luscious curve of her lips and felt the seductive pull of her disheveled gown and hair. He was seized by the urge to tousle and mousle her further, to kiss those lips, to slide his fingers inside that tight bodice. . . . A quick vision of those hounds, licking her, pawing her, flashed in his mind, eroticized now by his rising desires. He wanted to lick her himself, wanted to put his paws on her, too—all over her! He wanted to fill her with that same sensual joy, then to absorb her laughter with his mouth, with his very being—

His lips came down over hers softly as he pulled her fully against him. The hard-soft wonder of his lips wrapped around her senses, encompassing every aching, tingling expectation in her. It was her first kiss, and yet it was reassuringly familiar, for she had lived it in dreams each night. His mouth slid over hers, caressing, massaging, coaxing her response in ways she couldn't have imagined. And as in those shocking dreams, she softened in his arms and tilted her head to receive him, molding her mouth beneath his in pliant, changing patterns that produced one heavenly and unexpected sensation after another.

Her hands came up against his broad, hard chest as she sagged against him and felt his arm glide around her waist, cradling and supporting her. Then his other hand came to touch her face and trail down her throat onto her shoulder. Rivulets of fire followed his fingers, sinking deep into the marrow of her weakening bones. She was dizzy, her head was spiralling, and her heart was pounding wildly. Her lips parted breathlessly and his tongue began to explore that tantalizing crevice, slipping inside to find its honeyed inner borders.

Hot—she was flushing hot and tingling all over, and the only places on her body that weren't burning were the places that were pressed firmly against him. And those places were aching in an oddly pleasurable way.

Jack's hand trailed down her bare chest to that beleaguered bodice and, with practiced ease, inched inside, touching, covering, claiming one hard-tipped breast. His fingers closed around it, exploring its silky form, luxuriating in the cool feel of it against his palm. Then his fingers brushed her nipple and drew a violent shiver from her. Her wild response echoed through his passion-sealed senses, and of habit he responded, closing his fingers over that hard, nubbly point, rolling that sensitive spout back and forth between them.

She gasped and shuddered wildly with each shocking tug and roll of her bubbie's burning tip. The fiery bolts of pleasure shot through the steamy mists of pleasure that had beguiled her virgin senses. In a blink, she realized where she was and what he was doing to her. Panic enveloped her, for she knew just where such sinful toyings led. And already he was leaving her lips, trailing his hot kisses down her throat, bending her back over his arm, working the edge of her bodice down. . . . Merciful Heaven—not that!

She went utterly limp in his arms, and in his passion-fogged state, he nearly dropped her. He stared at her fainting form with pure disbelief, staggering aright. Swooned? God's Very Bones! She'd swooned when he touched her! Desire congealed in his throat and he had to swallow it.

He wrapped both arms around her and dragged her to the bench. He patted her flushed cheek and her hand . . . and got no response. A second later, his entire being flushed beet red, draining strength from his arousal. Ye gods! What a lecherous oaf he was, inflicting himself upon the gell, a raving innocent if he'd ever experienced one! It was likely her first kiss from a man . . . and he'd unleashed his full, roiling desire on her. He'd assured her he wouldn't hurt her and then proceeded to frighten her to pure insensibility!

Jack gathered his limp little bride into his arms and carried her into the hall . . . and into a storm of outraged concern. Her disheveled condition appalled Cramden and Overbeake and the Lombards: her dirty, spotted gown; her half-bare breasts; her tousled hair and bee-stung lips. He saw their horrified looks as they followed him upstairs with her and realized they held him entirely responsible for her unconscious and disreputable-looking state. Lord, if there was ever any doubt about his marrying her, it would be dispensed with now. He'd be forced to marry the wench—to set her right!

He deposited her on her bed, and as the housekeeper and governess edged him aside, he managed to collect how small and delicate she seemed against the large draped bed. He was ushered downstairs under the glare of a very distressed Master Cramden, who ventured a sharp comment on the drastic consequence of his wooing. And as he stalked out to clear his head with a brisk walk, he saw even Seabury wagging his head in shock.

Upstairs, Merrie felt them loosening her bodice and wiping her face with a cool cloth, and heard their gasps and tsk's and clucks. When the door finally closed behind them, she opened her eyes.

It had worked! Thank the merciful heavens! She sat up and found her loosened bodice gaping open, baring her bubbies. Her eyes squeezed shut and she shuddered as the sensation of his fingers tugging on one nipple recurred in both bubbies. She clasped her arms over her tingling mounds, pressing hard to dispel those shocking, sliddery sensations. But the alarming feelings only seemed to migrate down through her to tumble about in the tender flesh between her legs. Wicked feelings—they must be!

She swallowed hard. It was her first kiss from a man. Lord Above, it was exciting and powerful and pleasurable and all manner of things she hadn't expected! She'd gone all weak and muzzy-headed, and her body had caught fire. She was mildly surprised to find her clothes unscorched. It was an experience, all right, her first kiss. . . .

And if she had anything to say about it—she harshly staunched these wayward sensations—it would be her last!

Chapter Seven

Doe-eyed Tess Lombard found her mother and father in the oak-paneled parlor the next morning, deep in conference with a moist-faced Master Cramden. She'd been summoned for a report on her lady's condition and drew herself up before the three of them with a thudding heart and a brave countenance, intent on pleading her mistress's case.

"She be frightened sick of 'im, ma'am," she uttered gravely.

"I knew it!" Cramden mopped himself with a linen handkerchief and turned an outraged look on Manley and Gert. "One has only to observe the gell a moment to see it. She can scarcely walk in his presence . . . and is given to strange crotchets of behavior and great trembles of clumsiness—"

"The gell were alwus awkward, Cramden." Gert glowered at her waffling partner, then turned back to her daughter. "Go on, Tessie."

"She walkt the floor half th' night, ma'am, starin' off into th' darkness. Then she come to her sense and give a great shiver . . . like someone stepped on 'er grave. An' she ain't hardly touched the tray I bro't her this mornin'." Tess's fingers began to wring themselves white with worry. "I be fearful for 'er, ma'am. She be so young an' tender . . . and he be so big an' so . . . so . . ."

The exact word to describe Jack Huntington eluded poor Tess, but all present knew exactly what she meant. Gentleman Jack Huntington was big and powerful and sensual and very worldly . . . and more. Just how much more, none of them wanted to think. The three conspirators looked at one another uneasily.

"She . . . said naught of what sent her swooning yesterday?" Cramden shifted in his chair and mopped his face again.

"Nay, sir." Tess bobbed, eyes wide, as she shoved her hands into the pockets tied over her skirts. "She has yet to shed a tear. But 'er look, sir. Bereft and sorrowful, sir. Deep of gloom." In her linen pockets, her fingers raked a bit of stiff parchment, a letter Lady Merrie had given her in confidence two days before. Beside it was the silver coin that was to be used to buy the letter swift and secret passage to Bedford. For the twelfth time, goodly Tess wondered what to do with it.

"You're a fine gell, Tess." Master Cramden rocked to his feet and came to lay a fleshly hand gently on Tess's arm. "Loyal to your mistress's welfare, as are we all. It tries us all, meeting her grandsire's requirements for her. We must lend her our strength and see our little lady through it."

The wistful, tortured look of his face brought mist to Tess's eyes. Master Cramden was a man of tender sensibilities, she knew. She must trust him and her mother and father to do what was right for their little mistress. She squared her shoulders and pulled the letter and coin from her pocket.

"Milady give me this letter, sir, to see it sent quick to Bedford town. I didn' know whether it be right or no. . . . So, I trust it to your care, sir. You will know best how to send it forth." Her big brown eyes drilled into Cramden, who received the parchment with a shocked nod.

"See to yer lady, Tessie." Gert collected her daughter and sent her on her way with a pat. When she closed the door and turned back, Cramden and Manley were staring at the letter in horror. There, in a clear feminine hand, was the name of Sir Edwin Gannulf, Merrie's "guardian." Good Lord—they looked at each other—the gell was writing her guardian!

At Gert's insistence, Cramden tore open the seal and read the letter aloud. It was a clear and plaintive cry for clemency from the horror of an untimely and ill-conceived marriage. It was so beautifully written that Cramden mopped his watery eyes as well as his jowls and stumbled back into a sturdy chair, shaking his head.

"Ahhh—" His beringed fingers splayed over his corpulent chest. "How it lays upon my heart! That great, licentious beast set upon the poor little thing. . . ."

"Tosh, Cramden." Gert came to take the parchment from his hand and gave it an unhappy look. "We knowed she weren't anxious to wed." Then she thought again of Lady Merrie's blanched face and rumpled state and of sweet Tess's fears, and felt her own concern for the little mistress pique unexpectedly. "Like as not, it's *him* what's at fault. Used to tougher hens, that one. I tho't he'd be smoother wi' the gell. Ye mus' talk wi' him, Cramden. Get 'im to understand." Cramden made to protest, but their compelling glares staunched it.

"None o' us wish to see th' little thing abused." Manley voiced their common sentiment soberly. "We only wish t'control her life . . . an' her for-tune."

Merrie finally appeared that evening at supper, looking demure in dark violet silk and seeming as pale as the heart-shaped cap that nestled over her well-groomed tresses. She managed a timid look at Jack and a wan smile at Master Cramden and otherwise kept her eyes lowered. When the food was served, she ate with less than her customary abandon.

Jack watched her and was baffled by her anew. He'd been swarmed by unaccountable guilt at first . . . having unleashed his manly passions so that he'd sent the child into a full swoon. But when Cramden had presumed to deliver him a sweaty lecture that afternoon on the "unseemly vigor" of his courtship, he had felt his own defenses rising. He had begun to think on the situation in a more objective light.

All modesty aside, if any man in Christendom could read a woman's amorous response, it was himself. And with each recollection of the events that afternoon, he became more convinced that she had participated in that kiss willingly—enthusiastically, it might even be said. Little Merrie Straffen had *enjoyed* sharing her mouth with him, and likely had enjoyed the other things he'd done to her as well. He'd merely proceeded too quickly for her delicate constitution.

He managed a polite mien through supper and later made his way to his grand and elegant chamber. Ignoring Seabury's inquisitive silence, he stripped off his doublet and small, wire ruff and threw the leaded window open wide to stand in the cool night air and moonlight.

His mind stubbornly conjured a kaleidoscope of images of his bride: delivering a Latin phrase, lurching along beside him, turning those velvety blue orbs on his. . . . Today he'd learned she was educated like a bloody "philosopher-king," that she let mongrels lick her and counted ragged urchins amongst her friends. He had learned that she kissed like a sweet little wanton and fainted afterward like the greenest of virgins. And he still felt as if he knew absolutely nothing about her!

He had learned some things about himself, however. He was still capable of feeling carnal guilt, which he had thought long-purged from his worldly being. And there was a streak of mawkish sentiment in him, which extended a strange rush of protective anger around her. And he was coming to want Merrie Straffen's appallingly delectable flesh with something akin to physical burning. Unthinkable, every bit of it, he chided himself. This marriage of convenience was turning out to be damnably involved and inconvenient, and he didn't like it at all.

The next morning, the fourth day of her engagement to Gentleman Jack, Merrie rose early and stood by her window, watching Straffen awaken at her feet and thinking hard on her quandary. She'd been a grace-less, gluttonous, unaccomplished, unthinkably edu-cated, and slovenly bride . . . thus far. Then she'd added insult to injury by enduring the estate's hounds' affections and then fainting rather than endure *his*. And he seemed utterly unmoved by her unsuitability. He was unflaggingly gallant and gracious in the face of her outrageous behavior. It had to stop!

Well, there was one thing no man could accept in a bride—ill health. It was the trickiest of her gam-bits. . . .

"What, milady?" Tess stared at her in disbelief some time later.

"Peppercorns. Oh, Tessie, I must have them, thirty-seven of them. Their strength is said to lend strength to a body, laid under the pillow at night. And t' Al-mighty knows I can use . . . strengthening." Merrie gave dutiful Tess her most doleful look, and the little maid soon agreed.

An hour later, Tess carefully counted them out into Merrie's handkerchief, recounting the difficulty she'd had in secreting them from the spice wardery, under her Aunt Edythe's nose. Merrie gave her a quick hug and dismissed her. As soon as Tess was gone, she pulled them from under her pillow and put several of them in her handkerchief. Then with a purposeful glint in her eye, she took off her slipper and bashed the black, pea-sized balls soundly.

Replacing her shoe, she straightened and took a deep breath of the flakes of black pepper in her handker-chief. She sneezed several times in succession.

If anyone noted her reddened nose and watery eyes at the table that morning, they said nothing. It was a bit of a disappointment to her. She declined Gentle-man Jack's invitation for a ride with a glance at Mis-tress Overbeake and a comment that she never applied herself to such overwhelming rigors. But she could scarcely refuse him a morning stroll. Overbeake, heed-less of Jack's pointed suggestions that she must have more pressing obligations, insisted on accompanying them about the grounds.

Thus, they walked; Merrie wedged between her overpowering governess and her overwhelming bridegroom. It was such a daunting spectacle that Gert Lombard was forced to agree with Master Cramden that it was likely too much for the gell. They watched the way her slouch deepened, and winced at the way she paused with her handkerchief from time to time, giving vent to fits of sneezes and snuffling. Her health would suffer, they feared, if such a strain continued.

That very afternoon, Overbeake was asked to advise Goodwife Lombard with the assessment of the household linen, while Lady Meredith and Gentleman Jack kept company in the hall. Merrie and Jack went a long time saying little, then out of the blue, Merrie erupted with:

"Are you a religious man, sir?"

"I am not known as a pious man, my lady," he answered with surprised candor.

"In such turbulent times, what duty is there in devotion?" she asked in a far-off tone. "And in London, it is said, fires of conscience have become pyres of conscience. I should hate to be St. Peter, called upon to sort it all out at Heaven's gate. When saints as oft as sinners burn, where's the point of virtue?"

They seemed very personal questions, yet fully abstract in their theology. It was another of those queries that seemed aimed at the very center of him. Jack stared at her, his confusion plain on his face. God's Nightshirt! She was a puzzle! Merrie looked up and started at the intensity of his glowing tawny eyes.

"I am sorry, sir." She shrank as if expecting a pinch. "Mistress Overbeake says I ask unseemly many questions. I cannot seem to stop myself; my mind buzzes so. Have you ever had a question roil up in your belly, shove into your breast, and then clog up your throat until you have to give in and ask it—no matter who it offends?" She gripped the edges of her chair with whitened fingers and raised an anguished face to him.

"Nay, Lady Merrie." He shook his head. "I confess, I am not given to questions. . . ." His voice trailed to a whisper. "Not of any kind."

"Oh." She seemed unhappy to be so unique in her affliction.

"But I am not offended by your queries. Lord, no! Put them to me in torrents, fair lady." He sat forward, aiming an irresistible smile at her humped little person.

She flushed hotly, fumbled for her handkerchief, and wiped her nose vigorously. Three violent sneezes, a cough, and a swipe of teary eyes later, she righted herself and apologized. "I fear I am given to attacks of the snurle. Are you afflicted bodily, sir?"

Jack's eyes narrowed briefly. *Only with raging lusts.* "Nay, Lady Merrie, I am sound of wind and limb."

She nodded and sighed, making a show of feeling her forehead and cheeks for signs of fever.

He was proving a devil of a man to disenchant!

The next day, as was becoming their wont, Jack escorted her on a morning walk in the front garden. She sighed and slouched, ripely annoyed and sick of her pretense and aggravated with his endless good graces toward her. Had the man no pride, no impatience, no indignation in him? Why would a handsome, educated, accomplished man such as himself continue to court and cosset a gell so utterly unacceptable . . . and even infirm? Why?

Five hundred a year, he was thinking, walking at a snail's pace beside her. It would scarcely compensate him for the turmoil she was generating in his mind and body. He tried not to look at her, tried valiantly not to let his mind run in those torturous paths again . . . to those bizarre glimpses of spirit, of life, of passion that had seized him unawares and sunk themselves into his very core. Over and over, he'd told himself that he imagined such things. But he still found himself scrutinizing her, longing for some sign that he was wrong, and itching for a taste of that warm, scintillant creature. . . .

He avoided looking at her, even clamped his hands behind his back to prevent even accidental contact with her person. He was going depraved. He was sure of it; for, even as she shuffled and snorted and wheezed beside him, he was roundly tempted to take her in his arms and kiss her senseless again. Even sickly, red-nosed, and shriveling, something about the quirksome little chit roused him . . . dammit!

When they reached the stone bench, she sank onto it gratefully, sneezing and wiping her nose diligently. He watched her, raking her with his eyes, furious with frustration. He'd never met a woman in his life that he couldn't discern and conquer, one who was completely beyond understanding. His eyes dragged down her long hair, down her rounded shoulders, to those slender little hands clenched around her handkerchief in her lap. And he gritted his teeth and sank onto the bench beside her.

"I am so sorry, sir," she said, beginning yet another carefully crafted apology, "that I am so ill-knitted together. I fear you have made a poor bargain for your life, to be saddled with a wife so delicate and infirm." She rounded her shoulders a bit more and prayed that she looked as pitiful as she felt. Her nose was on fire from all the pepper, and all this slouching was giving her cramps.

"Nay, my lady," he managed to say through tight jaws. " 'Tis but a passing blight upon your health, surely. You will soon be right as rain and embracing the joys of wedded life with me." Embracing? He shot a cutty-eyed look at her knotted form and wondered if he was going mad.

"I think not, sir. I do not wish you to be tied to a bargain so . . . unsuitable." Merrie was desperate enough to use strong terms indeed. "Your patience and gallantry are like hot coals upon my head, sir." She squinted at him. "My sight grows dimmer with each passing month. I fear they have not told you that." She saw him straighten and watched his surprise as it sank in. Hope welled within her. "And I have the asthma and the snurle, especially at night, when Mistress Overbeake straps me to—'' She bit it off, shooting him a horrified look and fumbling to rise. He was on his feet in a flash, taking hold of her, making her look up at him.

"She straps you to something?"

"Oh, sir . . . i-into my . . . Do not make me speak of it, sir, I beg you." She turned her face away in apparent anguish.

Jack felt as if he'd been impaled. "Something terrible afflicts you?" He gently turned her face back to him. "You must tell me, Lady Merrie. Please God, you must unburden yourself—"

"My spine is . . . melting. I am getting a hump," she whispered.

His eyes flew with alarm to her rounded shoulders, searching frantically for some trace of the anomaly. God's Teeth! She was getting a *hump!*

"Have you not noticed my ungainly walk, sir? Have you not truly noticed that I am lacking in the usual maidenly grace?" *Heaven's Haunch!* she thought. *He'd better have noticed!* "Faith, sir, be honest." She made herself squint up into his face and sniff loudly. "It is a creeping affliction . . . and by night, my old mistress must lace me against iron poles—" She bit it off and looked away, feeling the first delirious twinges of victory at seeing the blanched horror in his handsome face. She'd at last found the very thing that would make him take to his heels! She was breathless to collect and savor his reaction.

The absolute injustice of it rampaged through Gentleman Jack with a vengeance. She was afflicted with a wasting disease. Dearest Lord! He took her chin in his hand and plunged into the hazy pools of her eyes, assuming that it was the shame of this revelation that clouded them. This bright, mercurial child was suffering in untold ways, yet she would reveal her private calamity to spare him. In the grip of a totally foreign impulse of pure compassion, he drew her into his strong arms and took her to his chest, holding her gently.

Wrapped in Jack's arms, Merrie was overcome by confusion. Fully ten different emotions had trailed across his handsome features before he pulled her into his arms. And now he simply held her, comforted her. A moment later the feel of his arms began to burn . . . into her body and into her conscience.

"Please, sir." She shoved away, feeling dizzy and confused inside and not daring to look at him. "I have no need of pity. And I gladly release you from your promise to wed me." She turned on her heel and made her way to the hall as quickly as she could go, at a convincing clomp.

Jack watched her go, feeling utterly stunned.

Merrie went straight to her chamber and, daring not to appear for supper in the hall, used the excuse of her falsified symptoms to have a tray sent up to her. Then Tess wrung her hands and fussed and flothered so that Merrie was forced to climb into bed and pretend to sleep to get her to leave as well.

She lay there, bare-skinned beneath the soft sheets trying to relish her victory and to imagine what Gentleman Jack would say to Master Cramden when he ended the betrothal. But the sweet success was tainted with encroaching misgivings. She began to feel Gentleman Jack's arms around her, as they had been earlier that day, comforting . . . and so very strong . . . like great steel bands. A vision of those arms and of those broad, muscular shoulders—bare and flexing in amorous endeavor—flashed unexpectedly through her mind. *No! Not that—never!* But as soon as she had banished his body, his face appeared. His tawny green-gold eyes glowed beneath that smooth, noble brow that was knitted in concern for her.

His reaction to her "infirmity" was not what she had expected, not at all. Instead of recoiling in disgust and fear, he'd looked as though her revelations somehow wounded him. Then he'd sheltered her against his body, as if offering her his comfort, his strength. He'd been so big and warm. . . .

Dangerous thinking, indeed! She sprang from the bed to don a light shift and pace. What if she'd misread him? What if he didn't cry off after all? Good Lord— what if he stayed and married her out of pity, thinking her a hopeless invalid?

Then a truly horrifying thought occurred to her. What if he married her *hoping* she would sicken further and die . . . so he could go back to his haughty vixen . . . and perhaps other sloys and hoydens as well? If Jack Huntington were half the sinful wretch she considered him to be, that was probably the first thing that would cross his mind! Oh, Lord. He might just see her infirmities as an opportunity rather than a calamity!

And if he did . . . She had to do something! Who could she . . . ? It had been nearly a full week since she'd written to her guardian. Why hadn't he responded? Surely he'd had time, gout or not. She had to contact him, had to plead her case again! Only this time, she must do so in person!

It was a much wiser Merrie Straffen who plotted and executed a second escape from Straffen Manor. She arranged to remain in her bed all the next day as well, owing to the dread onslaught of illness that all had observed coming on in her. Then she planted bolsters beneath the covers, with her nightcap at the head, to make it appear she was, indeed, abed and asleep.

She waited for the house to empty and for the usual sounds of midday chores and clatter, then garbed herself in her sturdiest brown velvet gown. Without Tess's assistance with the lacings, she was forced to forgo her corset and to wrestle desperately with the fastenings at her back, but she persevered. She then crept from her chamber and slipped from doorway to doorway, making her way to the narrow servants' stairs at the back. She held her breath and flattened herself against the wall several times as she made her way out a little-used side door and through the bushes to the far corner of the kitchens.

From there, it was a quick dart to the end of the stables. She slid around the door of the harness well, giving thanks for her earlier study of Straffen's outbuildings and resources. Once through the room where harness was stored and repaired, she closed the planking door softly and turned . . . to find herself face-to-face with stolid Chester Lombard.

She straightened and swallowed hard. "I need a horse, Chester."

"Aw, m'lady . . ." He wagged his thickly thatched head, pulling his neck into his shoulders. His dark look said he was recalling all too clearly the last time he'd allowed her to talk him into such. Merrie was just desperate enough to tell him the truth.

"Chester, this is my last hope. I have to get to Hatfield to see the Princess Elizabeth. It may be a matter of life and death. *Please,* Chester!" When she turned those great blue eyes on him so beseechingly, solid Chester dissolved into puddles.

Merrie got her swift little mare . . . and a bit of advice on the best way to proceed toward the cover of the woods and through them, to reach the seat of Hatfield. She startled Chester with a grateful hug and seized the reins to lead her mount out the rear of the stables and along the hedgerows between fields that Chester had indicated would shelter her.

As luck would have it, Jack Huntington and his man Seabury were walking solemnly up the cart path that ran parallel with those very hedgerows. They had strolled in silence for some time; all between them had been said. Jack had revealed what he knew of Lady Meredith's pitiful condition to trusted Seabury, and now both men's hands were clasped behind them and their brows were furrowed in thought.

In Jack's mind's eyes, he kept seeing Meredith Straffen's slumped shoulders and her oddly unfocused gaze and the way she dabbed at her nose and sneezed and wheezed. It had completely escaped him that his initial

impressions of her had been that she had the constitution and appetite of an ox. Her recent woebegone
attitude and her consistent shuffling and worsening
posture had convinced him she was as frail and ill as
she claimed. For no woman . . . *ever* . . . had resisted
Jack Huntington's company as little Merrie Straffen
had. Even Seabury agreed; there must be some drastic
reason for it.

Her illness certainly explained this wretched marriage of convenience to a notorious rakehell. With characteristic rake's pride, he assumed they had meant to
find her a husband who would please her, if any man
could, and who would take the money and ask no
questions . . . and carry no tales.

For one brief instant, in the darkest hour of the very
long night just past, he had considered crying off,
walking away from this tragic scheme. Then he recalled Merrie's anguished eyes and battled back that
cowardly impulse. For some unfathomable reason, it
was important to him that he fulfill his obligation here.
And he might be able to give little Merrie Straffen a bit
of pleasure on her wedding night. A bit of pleasure
might somehow comfort her in the painful days that
undoubtedly lay ahead for her. The very thought of his
once-lecherous impulses toward her now baffled and
shamed him to his marrow. He had had a surfeit of
pleasure in his life. He reasoned that now fate was calling upon him to even the score a bit, to give something
back. It was a startling new idea for him, owing something, giving something. . . .

A flash, a movement—something along the hedgerow off to the left caught his eye. "Look there!" he
pointed, shading his gaze against the sun to see better.
He made out a flicker of flame. "Fire—" He breathed
as it burst on his mind. "The hedgerow is afire!"

But as they scoured the brambles for the extent of it,
Seabury declared, "It's not fire—there's no smoke!"

Jack's entire body came to attention, focused on the
breaks in that hedgerow. There it was again, a dance
of red-gold flame through the opening.

He squinted. That wasn't flame—it was *hair!* The realization galvanized him. It was . . . Merrie Straffen's fiery hair! As his gaze anticipated her linear movement and flew to the next break in the hedges, his hands curled into fists at his sides. There she was, and the movement with her—she was leading a mount! But that was impossible! She was ailing . . . abed all day! Confusion roiled up in him. Then what in . . . *Bloody hell!*

Hot chagrin burst in his face, bronzing his features. *Sick little Lady Merrie* . . . He'd been duped, choused royally, defrauded! "It's *her*, dammit! And she's got a damned horse with her!"

A heartbeat later he was in motion, running straight for the stables with Seabury at his heels. It didn't take much, given the towering state of Jack's rage, to make Chester produce his mount and divulge the avowed destination of Lady Merrie Straffen.

Hatfield! Jack groaned. Dammit—nobody went to *Hatfield!*

He bounded into the saddle and dug in his heels, charging off down the cart path to intercept her. Shortly, she emerged from the hedgerow, made an energetic, hopping mount into the saddle, and began skirting the open fields. The noise of his approach reached her and she looked up to behold him racing toward her. She kicked her mount and slapped it with the reins, bolting across the soft, new-sown fields toward the path leading through the woods.

Through the blood in his eyes, he watched her modest brown cap come undone and saw her hair lick the wind behind her like a hungry flame. Through the pounding of his mount and the pounding of the blood in his head, he collected that poor, pitiful little Merrie with her habitual "snurles" and her "melting spine" made one bold-as-brass horsewoman! She went streaking straight toward a low stone fence, and he ground his teeth with both fury and relief as he watched her gather, jump, and clear it. Dammit! he swore mentally. Just wait until he got his hands on her!

They raced wildly, their intentions converging on the

opening of the cart path through the woods. She was determined to flee down it; he was determined to stop her. Merrie reached the entrance to the path first, but the mare skittered in the turn, costing her precious seconds. They righted and lunged off the narrow, weedy path just ahead of Jack's long-legged beast.

It was madness—sheer folly to race breakneck into a half-overgrown path, a pure peril to life and limb—not to mention valuable horseflesh. Merrie bit her lip and eased the reins back. But with her ahead of him, picking out the safe path, Jack was free to concentrate on speed. In mere seconds he was at her heels and trying to nudge beside her on the trail.

She dodged and maneuvered, but suddenly the path widened and he was beside her, leaning, snatching at her reins, nudging his mount ahead of hers to slow it. The raw heat in his big frame, the fire in his eyes, sent panic through her and she tried vainly to turn her mount. But Jack had seen the covert dart of those beguiling eyes and grabbed her reins to halt her.

"Stop—dammit!" He reached for her arm, but she shrank and threw her legs across to make a wild, sliding dismount down the mare's far side. She hit the ground in a tangle of herby growth, and in a breath she gathered up her skirts and began to run. Jack pounded to the ground and charged after her, finding to his aching dismay that "sickly" little Merrie ran like a cornered doe.

But she couldn't run far. Weighed down by heavy velvet skirts and unaccustomed to such exertion, she soon began to slow. The sight of an open clearing just ahead heartened her briefly and with Jack's long legs still making up ground behind her, she surged into it . . . and tripped on a hidden branch. She went flailing onto her knees, tangling in her skirts, and by the time she made her feet again, Jack was upon her. She barely had time to scramble up and put an old hewn stump between them.

He was fiery-eyed and furious, she realized as she panted, trying to contain her thrashing heart. He knew her illness was a sham—and likely that the rest was deceit as well. Lord! He was so huge . . . and heaving . . . and hot, very hot. And from the looks of him, he was of a mood to trounce her bodily. When he darted to one side, she darted the opposite way, to keep the stump between them. For a long moment, each struggled to regain wind and senses, glaring at the other.

Chapter Eight

"You . . . clevershins!" he growled, punching an accusing finger at her as his voice dredged the bottom of its register. He was recovering unholy fast, stalking her about the stump. She could see he was regrouping for another lunge. "You sly, dishonest little . . . Thought you had me culled, eh? Snurles and asthmatics," he snarled. "You conniving little glutton! You're about as sickly as a damned brood sow!"

"That's . . . not true!" she cried, stalling as she eyed the grassy clearing for some avenue of escape. "I was ill. I felt horrible. Then I started to feel better . . . and decided to . . ." It was no good; she read the certainty in his face. She was only digging herself in deeper.

Sweat trickled down Jack's neck like cold fingers. One hot rake of his eyes down her curvy, unslouched body, and his padded crimson doublet became like an oven, baking his resolve. She'd done it all a'purpose—pretended and feigned illness and Lord knew how much more—to avoid him. God's Liver! To keep from having to marry and bed him! The idea sank through him like a hailstorm of burning brands. She'd generously "released" him from their betrothal. No woman had ever resisted—much less rejected—Jack Huntington!

"Dammit!" he snarled, getting a very dangerous carnal gleam in his eye and crouching by ominous degrees. "If you don't have a hump, Lady Merrie Straffen, you'd damn well better grow one before I strip that fancy gown from your shoulders." His voice dropped to a menacing rasp. "Because if you don't have one, if I find you're as hale and hearty as I think you are . . ." He laughed a very wicked, chest-deep laugh and left the rest to her fertile imagination. The sensual set of his handsome features left no doubt of his meaning.

He was going to make her submit to him . . . there . . . on the spot! "Oh, Lord!" She sucked in a panicky breath and made a frantic lunge for freedom. But Jack was quick and strong, and he was becoming cursedly adept at reading her intentions. He snatched her back so sharply that her squeal was half strangled, then wrestled her with practiced ease until her back was pressed against his front so that the threat of her dangerous, flailing arms was mostly nullified.

"Well, well, my contrary Merrie," he rasped, clamping one arm about her waist and sending the other to the lacings at the top of her back. "Let us see what you have beneath this proper little gown, sweeting—"

"Wretch! Plundering oaf!" Merrie swung fists from her sides and tried to kick backwards, to no avail. He handled her with such mastery that she couldn't help but think he'd done this very vile thing to women before. Stripped their clothes from their backs, then assaulted them— "Don't you touch me! I demand you let me go, you slavering brute! This is the true John Huntington, at last! I knew it! Sick with sinful lusts—"

Jack paused with her lacings half undone to laugh at the painful accuracy of her taunt. "True, sweeting . . . sick with desire for your delectable flesh. But depraved as I am, I was bounden to treat you honorably, to spare you my 'sinful' and 'degraded' lusts. Until I found my decency mocked and my honor spurned." And his rake's pride in his own irresistibility bruised!

"Stop—*no!*" she wailed, pulling frantically at the arm crushed around her waist. Then she felt her velvet bodice being peeled down her shoulders and knew it was too late. She felt him pause, felt his gaze burning into her bare shoulders . . . her straight, unblemished, naked shoulders. Fear clogged her throat. She could feel the subtle tightening of his arm around her, the anger rising in him.

In truth, his eyes were burning as they laid across the sleek, perfect skin of her shoulders. And his bulging arm was contracting like a cinch around her small waist. But it certainly was not anger that was rising, freed and molten, within him. It was desire. Up out of his loins it came, scalding his nerves, setting his chest afire, and searing up the back of his throat to burst in his brain. Feeling her shapely little bottom pressed against his hardening shaft, aware of the rounded firmness of her body under his hands, seeing the sweet-cream skin of her shoulders and the half-bare nape of her neck, he was suddenly burning for her.

His mouth came down hungrily on the slope of her bare shoulder as his other hand went around her middle to help lift her. Soon he was nibbling, kissing, devouring the lush satin of her back and shoulders.

His mouth was like a hot brand that burned all the way to her core, cauterizing her resistance. A maelstrom of feelings raged inside her: fear, excitement, horror at what she knew would come next. But they were all being overwhelmed by the raw pleasure sweeping through her, engulfing her senses, drowning her will, forbidding all responses but one.

He felt her melting, sensed her rising response, and his entire being vibrated with primal male exultation. For the moment, his redeemed pride in his amorous power was all that mattered. He released her wobbling form enough to turn her around, then he tightened his arms around her again, clamping her against his taut body.

"No hump." His tawny eyes glowed from under crescents of lashes so long that they seemed to weight his lids. His handsome, sculptured features tightened visibly, sharpened by need and accusation. "You've as sweet a back as I've ever tasted, my lady."

Merrie's head was spiralling. Her body was tingling, burning. And some great hand squeezed her throat so that she could barely speak. A hot, horrifying vision of him biting that haughty vixen's buttock flash-burned through her mind and she charged weakly: "You've tasted quite a few, I trow."

"Enough to claim gourmanderie of the female form." His deep, vibrating tones seemed to penetrate her from all sides, entrancing her. "And if your front is as well crafted as your back . . . and if your sweet bottom matches what I've felt of your top . . . then you are a dish to be relished indeed, my little glutton. And it will be an investigation worthy of my talents to see if your appetite for loving matches your ravenous ways with food."

Merrie's jaw dropped, her mind all but emptied from the shock. He spoke of *her* desires, of *her* lusts. Oh, Lord. Those strange hot and sliddery feelings beneath her skin, in her bubbies and womanly cleft—It was probably true; she had them too!

Then his mouth closed over hers and she ceased thinking altogether. She opened helplessly to his kiss, drank in the liquid heat of his tongue invading her mouth. Of their own will, her arms came up to clasp his waist, to curl hesitantly around his big, hardened body. His hands flowed beneath the opened back of her bodice, exploring her uncorseted waist then working up to her bare shoulders, stroking, claiming.

Then he spread and braced his legs, pulling her fully against his aching manhood, flexing against her tantalizing softness. Their kisses deepened, taking Merrie's breath, making her head waffle strangely. His hand left her back to clasp her buttocks through her skirts, discovering their shape, their erotic firmness. She wriggled against him, feeling the bulge of his hardness through his breeches, and suddenly the remembered sight of his organ, roused and fully engorged, burst on her mind.

That was what was happening. Somehow this was linked to *that!* And *that* was what he intended for them to do . . . now . . . here! Fear wadded into her throat as that burning thought torched the rest of her mind. Lord—what could she do? And it burst on her fevered brain . . . the most effective gambit she had.

Merrie went completely limp in his arms and was halfway to the ground before he came to his passion-steamed senses and caught her. "Lady Merrie," he croaked, hoarse with disbelief. He grappled to collect and lift her back into his arms. She'd fainted on him . . . *again!* Ye gods! This happened every time he kissed her!

He took a deep, tortured breath and scooped her up, giving thanks that she was halfway manageable. He looked around for some clue as to direction toward the horses and struck off toward the path. But with Merrie in his arms he didn't see the root sticking up and couldn't avoid it.

He stumbled and miraculously recovered, but in that threatened fall, Merrie instinctively tensed in his arms. When he righted himself, the implications of that perception became clear to him. He stopped, staring down at her rosy face and love-swollen lips, suspicion welling in him. His eyes narrowed as he searched her form and realized it was not quite so limp as it should be. But then, damned little about Merrie Straffen was as it should be . . . or even as it *seemed* to be.

He took two more steps and weaved sharply, slackening his arms as if he might drop her, and there it was again, that protective stiffening reflex. Dammit! She was culling him again! Well, he was the very man born to best little Merrie Straffen at her own game. This was indeed a game between them, a very old game, and one at which he was a past master. His tawny eyes crinkled wickedly as they searched the grassy clearing for a suitable spot. In the shelter of a broad-girthed old oak, he laid her down in the sweet spring grasses and stretched out beside her, scrutinizing her supposedly unconscious form. Lord, she was a handful, in more ways than one.

"Dear, delicate little glutton," he said, wagging his head. "You don't honestly expect me to believe you're dead afaint." He watched her silent, motionless form and turned his gaze away, taking a deep, deadly patient breath. "You are a trial. This is what I've always loathed about virgins . . . the damnable fuss. And you are a virgin, sweeting—the greenest, most inexperienced chit I've ever set hands to. Albeit, you do prove godawful entertaining in other ways."

He paused and reached for a stem of grass, popping the end of it into his mouth, leaning back on braced arms and pushing his legs out before him. He bade his body be quiet and closed his eyes a moment, considering his course while he savored the feel of the sun on his face.

"What to do with her. . . ." He spoke his thoughts to the air, knowing she was listening. "She dreads losing her maidenhead so much that it drives her senseless every time I take her against me. Perhaps I should just dispense with it now, while she can't feel it. A few clean thrusts . . . and it's all over." He watched the pace of her breathing escalate in spite of her and noted a brief, panicky flare of her nostrils. He grinned, leaned closer, and lifted her arm and dropped it. It plopped like a soggy dumpling. He had to admire her determination.

"But if I take her now, while she sleeps, there'll be none of those delicious screams that pierced virgins always produce. And damme, I do love the screams. . . ." He leaned near her face, watching her color deepening and imagining the turmoil going on inside her. An irresistibly wicked grin spread over his face.

"Merrie. Sweeting," he murmured, testing, leaning nearer still. She was silent as the grave. There was more than one way to revive a reluctant female! He flashed a vengeful smile and began to peel her bodice around her shoulders and down her front. Soon her shoulders and her gauzy thin shift were bare. He trailed fingertips across her chest and down over one temptingly veiled mound. He felt her shiver all the way into his own loins. His grin broadened and his caresses became more earnest.

"Merrie, lovely, if you're determined to play at sleep, then you must endure it while I play at other things."

His supple hands closed on her breasts, touching, kneading. Then he leaned down on one elbow and brushed her warm lips, her nose, her chin with kisses. He buried his nose in the hollow of her throat, kissing, nibbling, licking. She stiffened and he grinned as he blazed a downward trail straight to her delectable breasts.

Merrie felt his mouth on her like a liquid fire, pouring over he skin, sinking into her. With her eyes closed, her tactile senses were magnified and throbbing. It was all she could do to keep from squirming at that torturous mousling. But when his hands closed over her roused, aching bubbies, she clenched her jaw to stifle a moan. She was being tortured . . . Lord! . . . with her own responses! Then she felt him peeling her shift down and flew into a full panic. He actually meant to do it! He'd strip her naked and mount her on the spot!

Jack bared her breasts and watched the scarlet flush of her face and chest. His eyes warmed on the rousing sight of her taut, dark-hued nipples. They were long, luscious little spouts, with a rosy ring of flesh drawn up protectively about each. He'd never seen such erotic nipples in his life! He explored them first with his hands, rubbing his palms over their sharp tips in lazy circles. He groaned silently, wondering how she could bear it when he scarcely could. "You have delicious-looking little ducks, Merrie." He leaned near her ear and whispered, "I trow they'll taste as sweet. . . ."

He kissed her ear and left it humming. Her whole body was vibrating, purely quivering. Then she felt the moist heat of his mouth close over one aching, burning nipple and jolted involuntarily. She stiffened, going rigid all over as she battled this wicked seduction. But next there came wild tuggings and swarmy hot swirlings. He was suckling her! Oh . . . Ohhhh! It felt so . . .

Her eyes fluttered partway open—she had to look, even if it sent her straight to perdition! Saint Catherine the Virgin! The sight of his dark head at her breasts, the motion of his mouth on her, flexing, caressing,

suckling . . . coupled with her own wild sensations . . .
She almost swooned in earnest! But her body's instinct
overrode her maiden's modesty and in spite of herself
she moaned. His head came up and she met his scorch-
ing gaze, was snared and soon lost in it.

"Merrie," he uttered hoarsely, plunging deep into
those velvety, encompassing eyes that had the power
to turn him inside out. Mysteries, he realized—there
were whole worlds to be discovered in those eyes. And,
God help him, he was determined to brave and claim
them. He spread himself on the grass beside her and
sank into the yielding, responsive treasure of her
mouth.

Merrie opened helplessly to him, having the frightening yet exhilarating feeling that, from this time on,
she would always open to him . . . would always yield
to him the pleasures he took from her. Her hands,
cumbered by her bodice, came up to clasp the side of
his doublet, pushing and then *not* pushing.

She gasped as his hand lifted her skirts and found
the silk of her bared thigh and he lifted his head to
look at her. Tension and fear lingered in the passion-
darkened depths of her eyes. It would take little more,
he knew; his fingers rested so near her woman's heat.
Another soul-deep kiss, another nibble of her luscious
nipples . . .

She was quivering, wanting him yet afraid of him
and of her own wanting. The conflict was so clear in
her eyes that Jack was certain it had to be the cause of
her resistance to him. Twice she had "fainted" just as
their passions reached the point of carnal commitment
and she looked for all the world as though she might
swoon again, any moment. He withdrew from her
skirts to stroke her cheek with his fingers, then ran his
hand through the soft jumble of her glorious
strawberry-gold hair. And he made himself swallow
the desire that filled his throat.

This was not the time nor the place to initiate Merrie
Straffen into the arts of loving, he decided with the carnal calculation of a true rake and the tenderer instinct

of a true gentleman. He wanted a whole night to make love to her, to tease and prepare her, to produce and luxuriate in her awakening. He was a man who had learned that pleasures were best when slowly spent and had perfected the subtlest arts of spending. And with a possessiveness that was utterly foreign to his unencumbered personal creed, he realized that he craved the undisputed rights to her in the old earl's bed, the proper place for the spilling of her virgin blood.

It was not the first time Jack Huntington had forgone carnal pleasures for the sake of a greater gain, but it certainly seemed the costliest abstinence of his life. His entire being was howling with need and he had to console himself with hot promises of greater pleasures yet to come. When he raised above her and drew her shift up with trembling hands, he saw both the shock and the relief in her face and grudgingly congratulated himself on his knowledge of women's passions. But as he dragged her bodice back up her arms to settle it on her shoulders, the heart-melting gratitude in her luminous eyes stung his self-serving gallantry sharply.

He got to his knees and stood, pulling her to her feet and turning her brusquely to relace her bodice. Trembling like a reed, she lifted her hair aside and as his practiced fingers pulled and tugged the cords, twigs snapped and branches swished nearby. They froze.

Horses burst into the far edge of the clearing, four very fine horses bearing horrifyingly memorable riders. Merrie and Jack found themselves looking up into the piercing brown gaze of the black-clad royal princess, who was flanked by a waiting lady, a groom, and a huntsman. From their ruffled appearance, they had been riding fast until they entered the woods . . . probably riding to hounds. Merrie flushed crimson and prayed desperately that they hadn't witnessed what had occurred between herself and Jack.

"Your Most Excellent Grace." Jack swallowed his shock and clamped a hand on Merrie's wrist as he made his finest leg to Princess Elizabeth. The motion pulled Merrie down and she sank into a deep, if somewhat unsteady, curtsey.

"Your Grace," she murmured, head bowed so that she had a horrifying view of her own rumpled and littered skirts.

"Lady Meredith." Elizabeth observed the tousled pair with a stern expression. "Straying from Straffen lands yet again, I see. And who is this fellow who knows little better than to lure innocent gells into trysts in my woods?"

"John Huntington, Your Grace." Jack bowed his head with ceremony, then had the temerity to lift a dazzling smile straight into the princess's flushed face. "I am Lady Meredith's betrothed husband . . . and next week her husband in fact. We did not realize we had strayed onto your lands. We do beg your pardon, ma'am, and can only plead . . . distraction."

Elizabeth canted a look over this fancy piece of manhood, with fresh appreciation for how he had cut so deep a swath through the queen's own ladies more than a year past. Dark, fine-limbed, and handsome as Lucifer; he was temptation incarnate. Then her gaze drifted to Lady Meredith's disarranged clothing and love-stung lips. The gell was ill-equipped to handle such a one as he, that was plain enough. But they were to be wedded in a week. She lifted her chin and leveled a regal glare on Jack Huntington that communicated far more than mere words could.

"Take care, Master Huntington, how you let *distractions* rule you. You have your lady to think of now."

Jack took the chiding, and its hidden thrust, with a perfectly calibrated smile. "I assure you, I shall think of my lady Meredith first, in all things."

Elizabeth forced a smile. Liar, she thought. Men are all such liars. "Felicitations on your marriage, then"— she nodded—"and good day to you. And Lady Meredith," she could not resist adding, "my tree is ever at your disposal."

Merrie nodded shakily and the princess led her party

off into the woods again. When they were out of sight, Jack turned Merrie and finished her lacings.

"I collect, you and the princess have met before," he observed tightly.

"We have. The princess often rides here."

Jack twitched as he put the pieces together. "Damme—the Princess Elizabeth . . . You were going to see Elizabeth herself!" When she didn't deny it, he ran a hand through his raven hair in exasperation. "God's Teeth! You have no more sense than a turnip! Setting foot on Hatfield is tantamount to an admission of conspiracy against the queen. Mary has spies everywhere. Faith! You need a keeper!"

Stinging with fresh irritation, he suddenly recalled his volcanic ire and was chagrined by how easily his passion for her had supplanted it. He snatched her wrist and pulled her along the rough path toward their horses, scarcely slowing when she stumbled on her skirts.

Neither had spoken when they reached the horses; both were breathing hard and mentally searching the ramifications of their encounter. Jack prevented her from mounting and took both sets of reins in one hand and her wrist in the other.

They strode the weedy cart path beneath a canopy of dappled spring green and flirtatious sunlight. Merrie darted glances at him from time to time; his rigid posture, his square-set jaw, the firm line of his sensual mouth spoke his anger and determination. She finally could bear it no longer and planted her heels, jerking him to a halt with her.

"You—Are you so determined to marry me?" She suppressed a shiver when he came to spread his legs solidly and tower above her. His tawny eyes glowed in the flickering light.

"I am." He watched the barely perceptible droop of her shoulders. "And if you are still so determined to dissuade me"—there was vengeful amusement in his voice—"then the next week will prove entertaining indeed." When she lowered her eyes in confusion, his tone tempered to a sultry taunt. ''I wonder what more you have in store for me, my inventive little fambler. Perhaps you will suddenly grow three heads and a serpent's tail, or take to walking on all fours and barking like your hounds. Or perchance you'll get full-to-the-bung with brandy and prance mother-naked in moonbeams.'' Her face came up, blushing, her eyes big and artless. ''I intend to marry you, Merrie Straffen, whoever . . . whatever you are.''

She was becoming the single maddening riddle of his life, a consummate puzzle that the jaded fates had thrown in his path. She was the surprise of ten mortal lifetimes. And he wanted her. In that moment, Jack Huntington realized he'd never wanted anything, anyone, quite like he wanted little Merrie Straffen.

For a long moment Merrie stared into his determined face, searching it, trying to understand this jumble of feelings inside her and utterly horrified by her perverse delight in his persistence.

''Then I suppose I shall just have to live through it. *Vulneratus non victus.*''

Jack started. ''Wounded, not conquered,'' he translated mentally. And he threw back his handsome head and laughed.

Half of Straffen's inhabitants stopped at their chores and came to their cottage doors to witness their mistress and her betrothed husband strolling down the cart path, side by side and seemingly hand in hand. Word had flown through Straffen's tightly knit family: Lady Merrie, who wasn't supposed to ride, had taken a horse and ridden out. And Master John Huntington, who was all a'lather over something, had ridden out after her. And as the Straffen folk awaited their return, all noted that he was taking a precious long time in fetching her back.

Now they appeared; Lady Merrie with her gown dusty and littered and her uncapped hair atangle, and Master Huntington with his hose stained and bits of old leaves stuck in the fancy slashings of his breeches.

They'd had a roll in the meadow somewheres, it was plain to see; Ellie, the goose gell, remarked such to May, the head weaver, who passed it on to Edythe, the cook, who ran straight to Gert Lombard, who rushed into the house to gather her husband and Cramden and the gell's outraged governess.

Thus when Jack and Merrie arrived at the stable door to hand poor Chester their horses, they found him nursing another swollen ear and themselves facing a veritable wall of indignation. Cramden, the Lombards, and Mistress Overbeake stood shoulder to shoulder, of one mind and one purpose, like staves in the barrel of righteousness. Merrie stopped dead, reading the cloaked anger in Overbeake's gaze and knowing she was in for it. Jack flicked a glance at the ferocious foursome, then at Merrie's paling face, and pulled her tight against his side, to confront them.

"I collect you were concerned for our absence," he said, radiating irresistible, tawny-eyed charm. "I confess, when I saw my sweet lady on horseback, I was likewise concerned, especially in light of her recent illness. But as you see"—he swept a gallant hand down Merrie's disheveled form—"she is hale and fit . . . a small miracle, I daresay. Perhaps she was only wanting *a good ride.* . . ." He smiled with roguish duplicity, laid Merrie's hand on his sleeve, and led her stunned form off to the house.

Cramden's face blanched like lard as Gert and Manley turned to glower at him and Mistress Overbeake gasped and sputtered. "Master Cramden," Gert said prodding him with their united opinion, "ye mus' do somethin'."

"Do what?" Cramden produced his handkerchief and patted himself anxiously. "It would appear the damage is already done." They turned and followed his gaze to the sensual prowl of Jack's manly stride and the graceful new sway of Merrie's skirts . . . and had to agree; he was probably right.

Jack led Merrie up the stairs to the gallery and proceeded with her to her chamber. But he didn't stop at the doorway; he escorted her inside and stood with legs spread, surveying her modest chamber. Tess arrived out of breath from having run to see to her lady, and Jack thrust a pitcher in her hands and bade her fetch Merrie some water. The maid looked up at his dark, overwhelming countenance, nodded dumbly, and exited.

Merrie found herself facing him alone, feeling discomfitted by his blatant assessment of her. She stared down at her rumpled gown. "I . . . expect Mistress is purely outraged."

Jack nodded. "Pitchin' furious." Then with a wicked glint he corrected it: "Pinchin' furious. Like as not, I got you out of a sound pinching just now. You see, even 'foul, slavering brutes' have their uses." Merrie blushed hotly, and he added, "As do conniving virgins." He laughed and the deep, rich vibrations set her fingertips atingle.

"S-sir—"

"John," he chided. "Call me John." The room grew very still around them as he watched the flicker of nervousness in her eyes as she lowered them. His gaze drifted over her straight shoulders and small waist and came to rest on her demurely covered breasts. The velvet feel and the sun-warmed taste of their nubbly tips suddenly recurred on his tongue and in a phantom touch against his lips.

"I intend to have you, Merrie Straffen," he warned with deep, passion-roused promise. "Make no mistake about it." He caught the spark in her eyes before she veiled it and realized he'd seen that light before and not recognized it. It was defiance, well disguised.

He tore himself from the sight of her, backed out the door, and made his way to his own chambers with a grin on his roguish face. What a stubborn little virgin she was . . . still set to resist him even after he'd boldly pleasured her. Well, he was going to convince her, persuade her, make her want him . . . and admit wanting him. And in the process, he was going to unravel the mystery of Merrie Straffen . . . and dispel her potent and unsettling effects on him once and for all.

Seabury was waiting with a brush for his clothes, a basin of water, and an expectant stare. Jack watched the question working its way out of his friend and paused with his hands on the ties of his hose.

"Well?" Seabury had to know the outcome or die.

"I can say with authority, she has no 'hump,' " Jack answered with an insolent curl at the corner of his mouth. "Albeit she does sport two 'bumps' that are perfectly spectacular."

Chapter Nine

The next morning, Jack rolled over in the polished oaken temple of Straffen's great bed and allowed himself the luxury of anticipating the feel of Merrie Straffen's satiny curves tangled in the bedclothes with him. The strength of his instantaneous arousal was mildly shocking. He threw back the sheets, donned his shirt and hose, and began a scrupulous shave. This morning he would mount a campaign to uncover the true Merrie Straffen.

Jack first determined to rid them both of that sour, horse-faced old trot of a governess. After breaking fast in the hall, he intervened with Mistress Overbeake, who shot an outraged look at Cramden. Cramden shrugged wanly. What good did it do to chaperone them, that woeful gesture imparted, when the little thing was likely "had for a morsel" already? Merrie watched the stern mistress stiffen and stalk back to her tedious needlery, and she cast a relieved look at her betrothed husband. Then he asked her to accompany him on a morning stroll in the garden and her gratitude evaporated.

She had no desire to find herself assailed by his venial impulses and her own sinful desires, and was convinced that even a short spell in his private company would bring on both with a vengeance. She cast a wary glance at Overbeake and realized why Jack had so handily dispensed with the mistress's company. Distasteful though Merrie's sphere of safety seemed, she declined his offer of a walk and planted herself in an oaken chair across the way from her old mistress, taking up her needlework.

Jack watched her ploy with narrowed eyes and, undaunted, dragged a chair beside hers and posted himself in it. Then he leaned on the arm of her chair and began to make a gallant nuisance of himself.

"My sweet lady"—he sent a smile sliding down the front of her gown—"I do admire your . . . tenacity at this ladycraft. Especially in light of the difficulty it gives you." When she paused mid-stitch to frown at him, he lifted her hand and handled her fingers gently, examining them and bestowing a chaste kiss on each one. Those chaste kisses, as intended, sent hot trills of excitement up her arm. She jerked her hand away to jab her needle through the canvas irritably.

"But do take heart," he continued. "Not all ladies' fingers may produce measured, even stitches and not all ladies have the delicate eye required for capturing scenes artfully. Perhaps you will find other, more suitable, occupations for your fingers. . . ." His voice dropped to a sensual rumble near her ear. He left little doubt of what sort of occupations he had in mind.

How dare he disparage her ladycraft . . . and in the same breath insinuate that her "talents" lay only in fleshier pursuits? Her eyes flashed with ire and she fled to the far side of her chair, plunging into her needlework with a vengeance. And it seemed that every stitch she made called forth some sort of response from him: "Is that one quite long enough?" or "Perhaps if you had better light . . ." and "Yes, yes, you do seem to be getting the flow of it there. . . ." After a full hour of his taunting "encouragements" she was ready to poke him in the nose with her needle!

Jack watched her jaw, set like fine marble, and felt angry heat welling in her. He ventured one last comment, intended to push her over the edge of her pretense. "I swear you do seem to have improved. Perhaps with my assistance, you will make a needlewoman yet, my lady!"

"Sir!" She jabbed the needle into her beleaguered piece and faced him. Confusion boiled up in her, just as she feared it would. His eyes were lazy with amusement, taunting in their sensual ease. "I have no need of anything you might teach me," she choked, extending her meaning with the burning look she gave him. She fumbled for the tapestry bag by her feet and produced a piece of completed needlework, thrusting it into his hands. "This, sir, is the companion piece."

She pushed up and strode for the stairs and the quiet of her chamber. Jack watched her go with a wry grin, wondering if he'd won or lost. Then he looked down at the work in his hands, a veritable masterpiece of the art of crewelwork embroidery, with the crest of his own House of Huntington as its subject. It was startlingly lovely, strong of design yet delicately wrought. Oak leaves so realistic that he had to run his fingertips over them to luxuriate in their captured texture. Then he knew . . . he'd won. He'd made her want to show her accomplishment, to prove her talent to him. He smiled dazzlingly at dour Overbeake and sauntered out for a breath of fresh air.

By dinner, Merrie still hadn't emerged from her chamber, and he braved her door to escort her to the table, where he planted himself beside her, instead of taking his usual place across from her. Ignoring Cramden's glowering and Overbeake's gray indignation, he proceeded to sample the capon, the boiled beef, the pasties, and the breads, taking one bite of each and declaring each dish somehow "off."

The capon was dry; he plopped the piece he had tasted onto Merrie's plate. The beef was tough; it joined the disparaged fowl on her trencher. The pasties were undercooked—too doughy for his taste; they added to the mounds growing before Merrie. Then the breads needed more salt and the soup had too much onion and pepper. He plunked the slabs of bread onto her heaping trencher and shoved his bowl before her with a guileless flourish.

"I do so loathe the wastage of food." He sighed, staring pointedly at Merrie's vulgarly heaped plate. " 'Tis a mercy on mankind that th' Almighty chooses to mate finicky palates with those having no discrimination at all."

Merrie sat looking at the heaps of food before her, and her bile rose. How dare he taunt her with her own gluttony! She seized the leg of capon and tore into it vengefully, pretending it was *his* flank instead. But the bird was indeed dry and when she swallowed hard and reached for her wine goblet, he shoved his own into her hand.

"Oh, do take mine, my lady. I fear I found the sack a bit too watery."

She stiffened and shoved it away, rising from the table with silver sparks in her eyes. "I believe I've had quite enough."

Jack felt the others' eyes on him as she stomped out and he leaned back in his chair with a satisfied smile. She was uncommonly skilled with a needle . . . and she was no true glutton. Yes, his wholehearted acceptance of her "deficiencies" might help him learn quite a little bit about his bride.

Later that evening, as the sun was setting through the leaded panes in the hall windows, Merrie reappeared and settled herself between Cramden and Overbeake in the hall. She'd spent the better part of three hours pacing and fuming. She had to face him, to show him he couldn't best her.

Seabury hurried through the hall and shortly Jack appeared, entering from the rear yard, flushed and obviously fresh from horseback. He removed his gloves and flat, plumed hat, handing them to Seabury, and strolled over to greet his bride and her protectors.

"Nothing like a good hard ride to stir the blood," Jack observed, leaning over the back of her chair so that he sent his next words sliding down the back of her neck. "Good for the posture and the lungs. You might try it, Lady Merrie . . . as an improving discipline for the spine." Merrie was stung perfectly straight in her chair and he smiled and seated himself beside her.

Cramden sweated profusely, watching Jack's veiled taunting, wondering at the rake's conceit. He must think highly of his amorous prowess indeed to treat a young gell so, after only a single tryst! Determined to civilize the proceedings, Cramden tried valiantly to raise a bit of conversation. But none of his offerings produced a spark of animation in Lady Merrie. She seemed determined to ignore them all until Jack mentioned how fine it would be to have some music on such a balmy spring evening.

"But Lady Meredith plays," Overbeake offered pointedly. "My lady would certainly—"

"Nay." Jack sat forward quickly, catching Merrie's wrist. "Do not trouble yourself, sweet lady." He stroked her fingers gently and raised a sultry gaze to her. "I can but imagine how fatigued these dear little fingers must be after such toilsome stitchery. I would not ask the impossible of them, to make coherent melody. . . ."

It was a challenge, an out-and-out taunt! But Merrie felt the heat of his gaze sinking through her, belying his words. He meant to prick her, yet on another level he was stroking her visually and coaxing: "Play for me, Merrie. Play and enchant me. Please me." And something deep within her began to respond to that enticement, to resonate with it.

The defiant flush of her cheeks signaled her decision and she rose and made her way to the virginal cabinet. Soon she was seated and her supple fingers limbered themselves over the keys. Then she conquered meter and executed the keyings smoothly, and a lilting, complex melody began to flow . . . seemingly from her very frame. Jack watched the shadings and subtle language of her body as she played, roused by her expressiveness, savoring her with a true connoisseur's eye.

Merrie felt his gaze on her like a bold, searching caress and tried desperately to ignore it. He was nearly as great a puzzle to her as she was to him. What kind of man was he, to suffer her hoaxes with such grace . . . and then turn them back on her so effectively? He was making her recant them one by one by one!

She finished the piece and launched into another,

and by the time a third was finished there was no disputing her virtuosity. And there was no mistaking for whom it was intended. She played for Gentleman Jack.

She rose to find him standing behind her, watching her with a strange intensity in his insolent eyes. She collected his bow of tribute and went silently back to her seat . . . on wobbly knees.

The next morning, Merrie stationed herself in the hall, beside her old mistress, at her irksome stitchery. Jack stood, leaning his shoulder against the parlor doorway, watching her. She was such a mystery, tough and tenacious . . . tender and tenuous. And he intended to pry her mercurial little person from that seat once and for all. He slipped to the door to the rear yard and returned some quarter of an hour later to find her still seemingly engrossed in yarns and hoops.

"My lady Meredith," he called from the doorway, and succeeded in snagging her attention. "A promise made should be paid promptly. Methinks you have one in arrears." He pulled the door open, throwing it wide, and in came a bounding, yawping, exuberant wave of houndflesh. Every mutt and mongrel on the place came streaking into the hall, tripping and hurtling over each other, leaping and racing and barking! In the racket and chaos, they spotted their friend and quickly engulfed her chair in a heaving, howling tide from which there was no escape. They leaped and licked and mouthed her as she held them off with shocked gasps that turned to exasperated chiding, then to stern commands.

The mayhem subsided into mere turmoil and the hounds began to cavort and nose about in the rushes beneath the great table for fallen morsels. With a perfectly beguiling expression Jack waded through them to reach her.

"I have always thought this hall lacking, somehow." He folded his arms over his chest and traced a lean finger across his bottom lip as he regarded the confusion he'd unleashed. "Too sober, by half. And then it came to me . . . the hounds! And I recalled hearing of your promise to restore them, my lady.''

Merrie read the mischief in his eyes and followed them to where Overbeake was shrunk back into her chair, snarling ''Filthy beasts!'' and thunking the hounds that were climbing her skirts and nosing through her needle basket on the head with her hoop of needlework. But her abuse only drew their attention and swelled the number milling about her.

Then they caught her scent and began yapping and mousling her enthusiastically. Apparently something about the horsey old mistress's smell fascinated and excited them, for they were soon leaping and pawing her with wild abandon, invading her skirts. One particularly dense bit of dogflesh became so utterly enamored of her shank that he threw himself upon it in a blind, amorous frenzy . . . determined to perpetuate his kind upon it! Overbeake began to shriek and howl, shaking her leg and thrashing at that poor, doomed bit of dogmeat . . . to the accompanying lunges and barks of his fellows.

Merrie stared, suspended between horror and hilarity, clamping her hands tightly over her mouth, her blue eyes bulging. She looked around wildly and found herself caught in Jack's grin. ''Laugh, Merrie—'' that warm caramel gaze impelled. ''I did it for you.'' And in spite of herself, Merrie burst into gales of laughter.

She laughed in great, releasing gulps and hoarse, throaty rasps. She laughed until she crumpled and ached and until tears filled her eyes and she could only feel Jack's hand on her arm. He pulled her to her feet and pulled her into a run with him through the hall . . . and out into the smiling spring sun.

When they slowed, she wiped her eyes with her hands and found herself in the gardens. She wobbled toward the first stone bench, her shoulders still shaking with convulsive bursts of mirth, and sank upon it. She took several deep breaths to calm herself and finally managed to raise her face to Jack, who stood nearby, looking at her. His marvelous eyes were still glowing with mischievous lights, and she went off in yet another round of helpless giggles.

Several deep breaths later she got hold of herself again and turned a look of strained sobriety on him.

"You fiend."

"I am, indeed." He took a deep, cleansing breath and came to sit on the bench beside her, drinking in the new softness of her, the laughter-purged clarity of her essence. Her eyes sparkled like perfect sapphires; her face glowed with health and life.

"I cannot remember ever laughing so." She rubbed her sternly corseted ribs with a rueful smile. "Overbeake will be incensed."

"No doubt."

One last quiet rumble of amusement went through them, sealing off Overbeake and the entire rest of Straffen. Suddenly there was only Merrie and Jack . . . in the whole world.

Merrie began to tense with expectation and her eyes sought his hands. They lay quietly on his muscular thighs and she made herself calm down. She could tell he was staring at her, but was strangely unannoyed.

"You are a puzzlement, Merrie Straffen," he said, finally breaking the silence. She looked up to witness a new, thoughtful look on his handsome face and blushed prettily.

"Verily, I am that. Sometimes I quite puzzle myself." She lowered her eyes and in the same instant lowered her guard. "But as Heraclitus said, 'You cannot step twice in the same river, for other waters are continually flowing in.' Then, does it follow that I am never quite the same as I was? From one moment to the next, am I always changing? If so, then what a trial it is to be me." She sighed and clasped her hands together in her lap, feeling as if she was rattling on and not daring to look at him again.

If she had looked, she would have seen wonderment in his worldly face. He watched the ageless wisdom in her youthful countenance and felt touched by something profound . . . and very rare. It might prove easier to capture the wind itself, he suddenly realized, than to ever really know Merrie Straffen.

"My mind does race," she admitted into the soft silence that surrounded them. "And I do ask unseemly many questions for a young gell; that much of me is true, sir. But it is so frustrating to have a question burning inside you and to want to know with all your soul . . . and to always have to wait until you are older and have earned the privilege of asking questions."

Questions again, he thought. Twice now she'd lamented her unsavory bend toward asking questions. It seemed a peculiar trait to count so grievous a flaw. "The privilege of asking . . . ?" He frowned. She believed curiosity was a privilege that must be earned? Sour Overbeake flashed in his mind and he realized where Merrie had gotten such a hideous idea. The ignorant old bloat, like her viciously upright counterparts throughout proper society, considered intellectual curiosity un-Christian and corrupting!

"By design, young gells have few privileges in this life, sir. I understand it, I supp—"

"God's Teeth!" he snarled, and took her face in his hands and made her look into his eyes. "Ask me questions, Merrie," he demanded. "Ask me any question you wish!"

A dazed, almost sensual expression invaded her luminous eyes and he realized with some shock that he'd unwittingly stumbled across one key to the puzzle of Merrie Straffen . . . her unthinkably curious mind. A trill of elation went through him, followed hard by the physical urge to take her into his arms and kiss her thoroughly. And to keep the temptation at bay, he released her chin and took her hands in his.

Did he really mean it? she wondered. Did her questions and her learning not disgust, nor even annoy him? She found herself drawn into the center of his warm caramel gaze and read an unexpected and utterly undeserved acceptance in it. A pang of conscience suddenly quivered through her at the way she'd flammed and fambled him . . . and at the gentle skill of his revenge. He'd been gentlemanly beyond thinking, and he'd not denounced her. And though he'd had cause and opportunity, he'd not even performed the act of procreation on her . . . yet. There was apparently more to Gentleman Jack than venery, licentiousness, and adultery. And what a ninny she'd been not to have realized that he must have some very fine qualities, indeed, for the old earl to deem him the proper husband for her. In her mind's eye, she could see old Marcus shaking his head in disappointment at her. She bit her lip uncertainly as a question bubbled and trickled its way up through her.

"What business is it you pursue in London, sir?" And a second whispered close behind it: "And does the queen really go to privy in a gold closestool?"

Jack twitched at the wild juxtaposition of her curiosities and a smile warmed the fierceness of his look. "I am . . . a partner in schemes of 'finance,' " he offered smoothly. "And as to the queen's privy . . . you must trust me, for I do have firsthand knowledge of this; it is most assuredly not gold. I trow the queen would trade you yours in a wink." He saw the light bloom in her eyes and felt an unnerving twinge of something akin to guilt at the wistful gratitude in her face.

An instant later, he froze with the realization that guilt was but one of several discomfitting feelings he'd experienced during this improbable conversation. He'd felt surprise and awe, rebellious urges against society's absurd strictures, protective anger, delight, desire. . . . Good Lord! She had him reeling from feeling to feeling like a drunken fool.

"Walk with me, Merrie." He pulled her to her feet and found himself staring down into those dangerously engulfing blue eyes, being lured into their spell again. He countered desperately with his most infamous smile. "And you may ask me more. . . ."

He placed her hand on his sleeve and led her along blossom-lined paths. She began, shyly at first, to ask the questions she'd wondered about him and about

London and the court . . . and about life. He had no difficulty with the court and London, but on the subjects of himself and "life" he found himself on uneasy ground, for it had not been his wont to examine either too closely. He revealed that he was well read in the classicals, though he confided he'd been sent down from Cambridge for "casualness" toward his studies. He credited his learning to travel, his varied associations, and his true delight in reading. He had a love of horses that had begun on his family estate in Kent and a genuine appreciation of music and the visual arts, and he revealed that he and Seabury fenced regularly and with some skill.

Merrie was greatly relieved that he seemed unoffended by the range and content of her questions, or by the Latin that occasionally seasoned her speech. It puzzled her how they managed to wander from her inquiries into revelations of her own background . . . her life with Marcus and Polly, her surprise at learning she was an earl's granddaughter, and her own recent arrival at Straffen. And she learned yet another surprising thing about Gentleman Jack's character, a trait which the many ladies in his life had come to cherish with all their hearts. Smooth and sensual Gentleman Jack was a consummate listener.

She was astounded later, as they approached the manor house, that in more than two hours together he had answered nearly every question and not once kissed or advanced himself upon her physically. Beside her, Jack was recognizing the same phenomenon and feeling a bit unnerved by it. It wasn't that he hadn't wanted or intended to seduce her. With all her questions and with coping with his own confusing reactions to her, he just never quite got around to it. It was another dismaying first for him, letting a perfect opportunity for amorous indulgence get by him. He consoled himself with all he'd learned about her and renewed his determination to make her want him . . . and to make her admit it.

Over dinner they talked quietly, astounding both

Cramden and the pride-sore Overbeake. And when their new congeniality extended into the evening hours and Merrie graciously played the virginal at Jack's request, Cramden and Manley Lombard exchanged slack-jawed looks of wonder. The rake's unorthodox mode of courtship had apparently proved itself, for the gell did appear to suffer his companionship willingly. It was a great relief to them the way she occasioned a maidenly smile at Gentleman Jack and the courtly and confident way he returned it.

Over the next three days, Jack mounted a campaign worthy of a master. He took Merrie riding, and on long walks, and on a picnic where young Tess and capable Seabury accompanied them as chaperones. He listened to her remarkable questions on the marvelous and the mundane, the lofty and the lowly, and unwittingly allowed them to invade and invigorate him. Being with her, experiencing her, was like being given a tutoring in the very fullness of the human gift of thought. And occasionally he would feel those startling blue eyes turn on him with questions too deep for asking and found himself reeling, grasping, and groping for the solid, the sure. At such times, he resorted to kissing her. And he usually had a devil of a time stopping with mere kisses. His entire body sprang to life with the slightest prompting from her sweet flesh.

Gradually, Merrie grew accustomed to the sight of his big, raven-haired frame above her. The arc of his stride, the angle of his shoulders, and the swing of his arm as he walked were a geometry of unending wonder to her. But, as enthralling as his physical presence was, it was the permissiveness of his nature and his wry indulgence of her curious spirit that warmed her to him. In his presence, she felt freer, lighter. In his presence, the prohibitions and proscriptions that bound her life seemed to melt away. The adulterous knave she'd loathed and feared was fading in her mind, replaced by this man of warmth and wit and patience. She never tired of being near him; she began to positively hunger for it. And her looks began to tell of that hunger.

Cramden and the Lombards noted the warming of their charge's gazes and began to feel a little alarmed, especially when they turned to the handsome rake they'd bought her and saw those potent looks encouraged! They began to watch closer and witnessed the dreamy exchanges of eye and the chaste but lingering touches of sleeve that betrayed a ripening of true feeling. They set themselves to ward off the development of any such untoward attachment by interrupting and inserting themselves into the couple's presence at every possible turn. Thus, they were properly horrified to have Gentleman Jack withdraw pointedly from company of an evening, taking Merrie into the small parlor, *alone*. And they were aghast to realize he was reading to her from one of the old earl's three books . . . and allowing her to read to him!

There were other signs as well, the three conspirators realized as they commiserated in the parlor after the rest of the house was asleep. She laughed at his tart witticisms, and sent him glowing gazes of admiration. And he shamelessly begged those looks with sparkling repartee and courtly manners and indulgence of her quirks and questions. And rather than pressing her physically, he seemed to handle her increasingly as though she were made of delicate, carved ivory.

The rake's talents in seduction were truly beyond anything they'd imagined, so smooth and convincing was he. Sure signs of disaster, they realized. He was a man with a vast carnal reputation, obviously well earned. And innocent Lady Merrie was falling hopelessly under his opportunistic spell. They hadn't counted on that. And there seemed precious little they could do about it . . . until after the vows were spoken and duly consummated.

On an afternoon ride, three days before the bishop was to return to speak the vows, Merrie and Jack came upon Arthur, Straffen's overseer, and his plowmen engaged in hot dispute with Squire Avery Millingham's men over a far-flung hedgerow that separated Straffen from Millingham's neighboring lands. The squire's men were trying to pull the hedge out by the roots and Arthur's lads were trying to prevent them, claiming they stood on Straffen land and daring them to grub up one more bush. Millingham's plowmen squared off against Straffen's lads, spoiling for a row, and not even Jack and Merrie's intrusion produced any noticeable change in their hostility. Merrie grew alarmed and turned to Jack with a pleading gaze.

Jack was startled, realizing she expected him to do something about it. Good Lord—he knew nothing about farming or hedgerows . . . and it certainly wasn't *his* fight.

"You must do something before they come to blows!" Merrie whispered frantically.

"But I—" He stared at the ripening row and recoiled. Then Merrie's expectation was joined by Arthur's, as the overseer looked desperately to Jack to lend some authority to Straffen's cause. It came as a minor shock: they actually expected him to act like the new master of Straffen! He swallowed hard, stung by Merrie's confusion at his reluctance to become involved. And in a moment, he was swinging down from his saddle and making his way to the center of the volatile dispute.

Merrie watched, fascinated by the instant authority his tall, handsome frame commanded. Both sides eased enough to listen as he raised his deep voice to proclaim that both sides would have a say. After an airing of each case and complaint, he declared that the hedgerows would stay, in the interest of sound management, until the exact boundary might be established. The hedgerows would surely wait a week, he proclaimed, then he would call on the good squire soon after his marriage to settle the matter.

Both sides shuffled their feet and dragged their caps and hats from their heads to acknowledge his decision, and Straffen's men exchanged covert looks of approval at their new master's appreciation of the value of good hedgerows. Shortly, Jack mounted again, and as the sides reluctantly decamped, he led Merrie off to finish their ride.

She looked very sober when he stole a glimpse at her, and he tried to recall what he'd said back there . . . to see if it made the least bit of sense.

Beside him, Merrie was remembering what he'd said, too, and it made a great deal of sense to her. With his striking manly presence and his reasonable, Solomon-like solution, he had just proven the "why" of her marriage to him. Whatever his fleshly flaws, it was clear that Gentleman Jack was a prudent manager of men and resources. Likely, he knew a great deal about estate management and finance and that was why he was chosen to husband her. It made perfect sense. And it was senseless to fight it anymore—she flicked a glance at his handsome frame—especially when she didn't want to.

They paused later, on a tree-covered hilltop overlooking all of Straffen, and dismounted for a rest. Jack came to stand close behind Merrie as she leaned her shoulder against a great old tree and looked out over the valley.

"Marry me, Merrie," he whispered. When she stiffened, he leaned even closer so that she felt his breath on her hair.

"You know we are to wed in three days' time, sir." She had to swallow to say it and her heart lurched queerly in her chest.

"And you still call me 'sir,' " he chided softly. "Say you would wed me willingly, Merrie Straffen." It was both a command and a coaxing.

"I . . . would wed you willingly . . . John."

Her shy glance at him from beneath a lush fringe of lashes sent a pleasurable swell of triumph rising through him. When he turned her to face him, his handsome features glowed with satisfaction . . . and perhaps something more.

"And what of you, John? Do you wed me willingly?"

"I?" He laughed, caught off guard by her question and the odd look in her depthless eyes. "I believe I declared my intention to wed you from the start."

"Your determination," she replied, amending his answer. "You have known other women. Is there not another you would rather wed?" After a long absence, Jack's "haughty vixen" chose this moment to reappear in Merrie's mind.

"Of course I have known other women—" he began defensively, wondering how she could know . . . Then he realized it was not pleasures she spoke of, it was *hearts*. He looked into her lovely face and was unnerved by what he read there. Why hadn't he seen it earlier? Saint Edgar's— He truly was losing his touch!

He knew what women wanted . . . what all women craved in their deepest heart-of-hearts. They all wanted to be *queen*. The kingdoms they ruled needn't necessarily be grand, nor populated by more than just one heart. But in her kingdom, each woman wanted to rule utterly . . . to hold exclusive sway over the love and devotion of her subjects. Now Merrie Straffen wanted to know what woman had ascended to the throne of *his* heart. There had been many pretenders to that worldly domain, but until this moment, none had claimed it.

"I would wed no one, sweet Merrie, but you."

He stroked her cheek and felt that odd, discerning gaze of hers peering into the worldly core of him again. She knew things about him, that look said; perhaps things that he himself didn't even know. And for the first time, he wondered just what it was she saw when she looked at him . . . and into him. In spite of the warm day and the pleasant heat welling in his loins, a shiver ran through his broad shoulders. And he closed his eyes firmly and kissed her.

Chapter Ten

The most excellent Bishop of Malden and his two faithful assistants arrived promptly at ten o'clock on the ides of May. This time they found a startlingly hale and willing bride. The rakish bridegroom had obviously put the fortnight's delay to good use; any fool could see little Lady Meredith was perfectly bedazzled by him. Sighing and donning his stole and straightening his robes, the good cleric set about the task of uniting the twosome.

The audience for their vows was exceedingly small. Sir Daniel Wycoff, Queen Mary's local agent, had returned to scrutinize the proceedings, and Sir Edwin Gannulf's soss-bellied lawyer, Master Makepiece, again represented him. The rest of those in attendance were Mistress Overbeake; Straffen's principal agents, Cramden and the Lombards; and the house servants, who exchanged looks and sniffles and eyed the bridegroom with thoughts of the night ahead.

". . . *habendum et tenendem* . . ." the bishop droned and chanted. "To have and to hold," Merrie translated mentally. She looked up into Jack's glowing eyes and read the promise of the future and perhaps someday . . . a love. And as she promised "*fideles*," to be faithful, "*in secula seculorum*," forever and ever, she looked up into Jack's glowing eyes and privately vowed to find some way to please him as a wife so that he wouldn't need his haughty vixens ever again.

Master Cramden had arranged for a bit of music at the wedding feast, mostly to cheer himself, and Edythe, the cook, had managed to save the Spanish figs for a whole fortnight and had again labored over her special almond cakes. The food was plentiful and delicious, and after the great meal the bishop and guests tottered to benches and chairs to recuperate and enjoy the music of the hired minstrels.

Sir Daniel Wycoff posted himself by Jack to investigate the political leanings of the new master of Straffen Manor and was greatly pleased to find him completely inured to both politics and his royal neighbor, Princess Elizabeth. Cramden and the Lombards watched their exchanges with baited breath, but sighed relief when Sir Daniel climbed aboard his horse and departed, his duty satisfied. Soon after, Sir Edwin's lawyer summoned his litter and began the journey back to Bedford and the house became quiet . . . very quiet indeed.

The old earl's bedchamber was grand and elegant. From the polished floors to the Persian rugs and marble hearth and mantel, to the great polished oaken bed and the intricately carved chests, it was an intimidating vault of a chamber. Merrie stood between Mistress Overbeake and Goodwife Lombard, surveying her new residence as the servants trundled in the last of her things from her old chamber. She bit her lower lip as she fought the way her eyes were drawn to the bed linen that had been turned back, now exposed and waiting. It reminded her of her coming fate. . . .

Overbeake and Gert Lombard solemnly pulled her blue satin gown and her petticoats and corset from her, brushed her hair, and pinched her cheeks. She knelt on her prie-dieu and made her evening prayers with special fervor. Then they removed her smock and installed her in the cavernous bed. Overbeake remained behind an extra second with a tight-lipped frown and a bit of advice: "Endure it, gell, whate'er he does to ye. Let us hear no craven-ninny shrieking."

No shrieks. Merrie lay like an icy board in the bed as they left her, thinking she wasn't even to be permitted the usual scream that pierced virgins always produced. A stifled noise by the door proved to be Tess, seated on a stool, trembling, left to keep the vigil with her mistress until the bridegroom came.

"Tess," Merrie said, bolting up in the bed, "I've got to have brandy . . . a whole flagon of it. Go—"

"B-brandy?" Tess blanched. Lady Merrie must be purely sick with fright! Well, if her mistress wanted brandy, she would get it. Tess nodded, scurrying out the door as if relieved to escape. Merrie bounded from the bed to pace, mother-naked, in the golden candle-light.

She wasn't going to cower or flinch or shriek or dissolve into tears; she rang her hands. She knew what was expected of her and she was going to do it properly . . . *with th' Almighty's help!* She fell on her prie-dieu for a last desperate prayer that she wouldn't disgrace herself when he climbed on the bed. . . .

When the door opened, she looked up, expecting Tess. Her heart folded and slid straight to her knees, which were the lowest point on her body as she knelt on the prayer bench. It was Jack, carrying a small tray holding a silver flagon and a silver goblet. He'd apparently intercepted Tess as she returned and had sent her on her way. Now he stood stock-still, staring at Merrie with an expression that defied description.

There she was. He absorbed her with his eyes, her sweet little body selectively, seductively, veiled by her hip-length hair. Naked . . . on her prayer bench. It was so like her: an absurd innocent, an unwitting bawd. He didn't know whether to laugh or to ache at the sight. Something in his chest began to swell as he read the tension in her great blue eyes and knew instantly the content of her white-knuckled prayers. And just behind that beguiling fullness in him came a blast of dry heat. She was his.

Desire, possession, discovery, tenderness, amusement . . . they were all part of the look he wore as he placed the tray on the table before the cold hearth and turned to her. His movement broke her trance and she pushed up from the kneeler with her entire body ablush. Then she turned to face him, and he smacked into a wall of pure desire and stopped.

She was perfect. Every feature, every curve, every

mound . . . Dear God, he'd never seen a body so beautifully proportioned, so exquisitely crafted for loving. Full satiny breasts peered through that river of flame that flowed over her body; they were rounded, smooth, with a tantalizing hint of weight that made a man want to reach out . . . lift them, luxuriate in their feel against his palms. Those long, velvety nipples . . . he was captured by the remembrance of their firm sweetness against his tongue. Her waist was dainty indeed and her hips curved with a divinely proscribed arc . . . a full but gentle flare framing a flat belly and a fiery bush below, that made him want to warm his hands on its visual heat. Her legs were perfectly tapered, shaped to be seen, worshiped. . . .

Merrie felt his eyes on each successive part of her and burned with tension, embarrassment . . . and another, hot, fluid feeling she dared not acknowledge. Bareness itself did not trouble her; she'd slept bareskinned most of her life and had been seen regularly by Overbeake and by their old chambergirl and, of course, Tess. But until now, she had never known what it was to feel naked. Under Jack's bold, possessive stare she felt hot and muzzy-headed, and her heart was racing like a cornered rabbit's. She wanted to cover herself, but she wanted even more to please him.

"You . . . ordered brandy." The very fact was proof of her lingering fears. He managed to tear his eyes from her to toss a glance toward the tray. She nodded and slid warily past him to pour the brandy and offer him some with averted eyes and trembling hands.

"I won't hurt you, my little Merrie." He made no move to accept the cup.

Her eyes came up. The bronzed heat of desire in his face gentled into a dazzlingly reassuring smile. She swallowed hard. Of course. This was *Gentleman* Jack. . . . She lowered her face and took one swallow of the potent medicament, gasping and twitching as it burned down the back of her throat and into her lungs. Then like an earnest little hoyden, she dipped her fingertips in the brandy, as she had seen the haughty vixen do, and rubbed them over one taut nipple. Then she wetted them again and swirled them over her other little spout. She stared at them, surprised by how cold then warm and tingly they felt as the liquid dried . . . and how her rosy nipple rings drew up into a proud pout.

Jack's jaw loosened. His worldly eyes widened. He stared at her . . . applying brandy to her succulent nipples like a well-practiced courtesan. God's Teeth! He couldn't imagine where she had gotten such an idea! One minute she was a frightened, trembling little waif of a thing, the next she was parading about naked and drizzling her delicious little ducks with brandy for him to . . .

Flame exploded in his loins and raced up the walls of his body. His blood was suddenly roaring in his ears, pounding through his limbs, pouring into his male parts. He froze, half afraid he'd erupt if he so much as moved, and he closed his eyes briefly. When he opened them, she was moving toward the bed . . . like a naughty whisper . . . soft, rousing, and irresistible. His hands went to his doublet buttons, dispatching them recklessly. He slid the doublet from his broad shoulders and paused. She was standing by the bed, watching him, her eyes as big and blue as morning glories. Waiting . . . She was waiting for him. . . .

"Are you . . ." Her voice was a tight whisper and she swallowed and began again. "Are you going to . . . kiss me?"

Jack's eyes closed as a wave of foreign and oddly delicious pain swept through him. It was desire . . . so keen, so powerful that it was like a hurt. "Yes, sweeting." There was the low crackle of flame in his voice. "I am going to kiss you."

When his eyes opened, they fell on the prie-dieu nearby. With a wry wince of apology, he hung his doublet over it gently, then turned. He watched the widening dark centers of her eyes as he came to claim her and he smiled his seductive best. He was going to kiss away every bit of doubt, every bit of fear in that delectable little frame . . . if it took him all night.

She felt his glowing gaze sliding over her like warm honey and then his hands touched her hair and lifted her chin. His head bent slowly and he kissed her, absorbing her hesitation, initiating a slow, seductive dance of tongues and a long, conquering caress of her bare shoulders, breasts, and waist. The familiar warmth of his hands on her and the foreign feel of his clothes against her naked skin were powerful charms against her anxieties. A rosy glow spread beneath her skin, flowing from their joined mouths, downward into her breasts, then into her loins and limbs. The knots in her stomach began loosening and tingles of desire began stirring in her womanflesh.

His arms tightened full around her and his mouth began to migrate downward as he lifted her hard against him. Then he found one of the nipples she'd so generously prepared for his consumption and jagged bolts of lightning shot through her as he fastened his mouth on it and sucked gently. She gasped and wriggled briefly before surrendering to it. Some dim wisp of reason lingered; she'd expected this—Heaven, she'd prepared for it! And when his head finally lifted, she flexed and arched against him, offering him the other brandied delight and moaning soundlessly when he claimed it.

When he finally set her back on her feet, she swayed and had difficulty getting her breath and righting her vision. Everything was swirling in a warm, vaporous mass of enthralling sensation. It took a full minute to realize he was releasing her, stepping back, jerking the ties of his shirtfront and the band of his breeches.

The sight of his bare, muscular chest jolted the pleasant haze from Merrie's senses and she knew the time had come. She swallowed hard and turned to climb up into the great, feather-plumped bed, into the midst of that soft, snowy linen. And she braced on her hands and knees.

In the midst of kicking off his shoes and ripping open

the ties of his hose, Jack looked up . . . and stopped dead. He stared and blinked at her braced, rigid pose— on all fours in the middle of his bed. He had no earthly idea . . . When she didn't move, his eyes widened with unthinkable speculation that slid into recognition, then raw disbelief. Rubbing brandy on her nipples and now . . . Surely not! But the sight of her voluptuous little buttocks, so temptingly bared and rounded—and *waiting*—drilled its way into his very heated mind. His throat clogged and his engorged shaft throbbed wildly at the provocative curve of her back and the tantalizing dangle and jiggle of her lush breasts. God's Nightshirt! She expected him to mount her like—to take her like—

He stood in broad shock, staring at her determined and utterly unmistakable posture. She was without a doubt the most dissolute and depraved little virgin he'd ever encountered in his life!

A faint thud vibrated up her arms to let her know he'd reached the edge of the bed. A craven impulse seized her and she choked out, "Please don't bite . . . too hard. . . ."

Bite? Jack staggered to one side, incredulous, peering around the drape of her hair at her tightly shut eyes and the way she was mangling her lip. Not only did she expect him to do his plowing from behind, she apparently also expected to hate it! The sight of her, rigid and waiting, expecting God-knew-what barbarisms and perversities, struck him with gale force in his sense of irony. He, Gentleman Jack Huntington, who had known and pleasured countless women from Barstow to Calais, from Gibralter to Copenhagen, was at last closeted with his own bride . . . only to find that she dreaded his manly service and expected to be used in unspeakable ways. Don't *bite* too hard, she begged!

The sweet absurdity of it seized him, quaking his shoulders, rattling through his lungs, then rumbling up his throat. Loud, uncontrollable bursts of laughter exploded from him to shower through the quiet chamber.

His laughter hit Merrie in fistlike waves, startling her,

bringing her head up with a gasp. He was laughing— *laughing!*—at her. Her whole body burst crimson with humiliation and she scrambled madly for the covers, burying herself completely in the bedclothes, pulling them tightly over her head and curling into a burning ball of shame. The violent heat of her embarrassment temporarily blanked her mind. She was mortified past all mortal limits!

Jack watched her desperate dive beneath the covers and tried valiantly to staunch his untimely mirth. It was his own tension, he understood too well, that made him laugh so. It had been a long time since any pleasure had been this important to him. As he fought to control himself, he watched the motionless lump in the bedclothes and felt a strange, hurting fullness in his chest again. Delicious, unpredictable little Merrie . . .

He climbed onto the bed beside his virgin lump and began to forcibly peel the bedclothes back, against her vehement attempts to prevent him. He persisted and finally uncovered her tousled hair and burning face . . . and her shamed and luminous eyes.

She wriggled briefly, trying to escape him, but he quickly spread his big body over hers to hold her in place. When he forced her chin up she slammed her eyes shut against his reaction.

"Sweet little Merrie." His deep voice was now gentle with its amusement. "You honestly believe it is done that way?" His fingers on her jaw eased and her eyes opened, filled with defensive sparks.

"It *is* done that way," she declared around the lump of humiliation in her throat. "I saw it!"

"*Saw* it—" he started. When in Heaven could she have seen such a th—Then he realized, with the desperate deduction of a man who asks no questions, that she'd been raised in the country. Relief washed through him, followed by a wave of understanding. She'd undoubtedly seen animals rutting in the fields, horses and cattle, stallions mounting mares, nipping at them. . . . He had no way of knowing that the animal she'd seen mating thus was none other than himself.

"Merrie, sweeting," he said, his voice invading her heated form from all sides as he entreated, "look at me." When she finally obeyed that compelling command, she found his eyes glowing and his smile tender. "You are a quick little thing, Merrie Straffen. But people—" He corrected himself: "*Husbands and wives* go about it . . . in a different way."

Her look of stubborn doubt broadened his smile to a raffish grin. "I can see you need convincing." He rolled from the bed and quickly peeled his hose from him.

The sight of his powerful, naked form was both stunning and oddly familiar. *Husbands and wives*, echoed inside her. Could it really be so different within wedlock? she wondered. Her cold fingers relinquished the covers when he returned and slipped beneath the soft linen with practiced grace. She gasped silently as his body slid down hers and tensed as he pulled her into his arms. He only smiled into her clouded gaze and kissed the end of her nose . . . then her cheeks and eyelids . . . and finally her trembling lips. His mouth was warm and winey; sleek wet satin lined his cheeks and his tongue was rough, rousing velvet. Warmth spread from the familiar intimacy of their joined mouths and she began to ease.

His hands stroked her bare back, finding ticklish spots that took her breath and other spots that made her arch and quiver with flashes of new pleasure. And as she melted slowly against him, his hands ventured further, edging onto her breasts, twirling and teasing her nipples to eager, aching attention. Then his kisses lowered down her throat and chest, and his mouth gently claimed those proud little spouts, suckling, licking, swirling. She was swarmed by sensations, engulfed in a breathtaking cloud of feeling as his hands and mouth caressed and excited every part of her. A vague sense of expectation, an undefined wanting, opened in her belly as her womanflesh warmed and tingled in strange ways.

"Put your arms around me, sweeting," he murmured against her mouth, and as he shifted slightly, she obeyed. Then her tapered hands began to move shyly over his body, exploring the broad pillars up the middle of his back and the smooth, hard layerings of muscle over them. And as his hand ventured lower, to the curve of her waist and the flair of her hip, he urged her hands lower on him as well. "Touch me, Merrie," he said, moving her hand down his flat belly toward the swollen lance of his male desire. "Learn me. Don't be afraid."

She held her breath as her fingers brushed him. His huge shaft quivered at the brief touch and she melted physically. It was warm, like his flesh, not like a cold iron rod at all! Her fingers feathered shyly against him again. . . . He was soft, so sleek and satiny. Then he groaned and his body flexed, sending his shaft full against her hand, and she learned the hardness, the strength of his manhood as well. When her hand closed around him, he shuddered and plunged hungrily into her waiting mouth. And his fingers sought the tender flesh of her woman's cleft, to return those pleasures.

She gasped and started as he found a spot in the very heart of her secret flesh that produced quivering vibrations all through her. His fingers circled that little button of pleasure over and over, sending her senses spiralling, making her shiver and wriggle with response. And when the time was right, he nudged her knees apart with his and slid between her thighs, spreading them as he wedged his shaft against her. He felt her sudden tension at the unaccustomed position and cradled her head in his hands, kissing her anxiety away with generous leisure.

"A-are you quite s-sure it's done this way?" She swallowed hard, flushing hotly as she gazed up into his hungry, black-centered eyes. "Breast-to-breast . . . belly-to-belly?"

"I'm certain, Merrie," he rasped, nuzzling her ear, pulling her closer to his chest. "Trust me."

"But . . . it's so intimate, so personal, face-to-face. . . ."

"It's supposed to be personal, sweeting. It's as personal as humans may ever be to one another." His desire-bronzed features sharpened into a beguiling mask as he rubbed another knowing circle around the sensitive hub of her sexual response and watched her beautiful curves arch and shiver beneath him. His fingers stirred her body even as his dark, glowing eyes stirred her deepest womanly feelings, relentlessly, inescapably.

"B-but . . ." Every thread of logic she possessed was unraveling. "It doesn't seem . . . quite seemly."

"Seemly—Lord!" His eyes closed as a white-hot spear of need burned through his loins and seared into his throbbing shaft. "This is as 'seemly' as it gets, little love!" His entire body rippled against hers with convulsive need. Then he sank his arms beneath her, cradling her, adoring her with kisses, and he began the slow, maddening dance of commitment and withdrawal that prepared her for what was to come.

Somewhere in the undulating caresses of his body and the gentle but insistent thrusts of his manhood against her tingling flesh, she realized what he intended and realized that it was probably just the thing to soothe the aching emptiness, the hot, quivering trembles of her body. When he felt her hands sliding onto his taut buttocks and felt her body reaching, opening for him, he kissed her deeply and thrust full inside her, rending her maidenhead in one strong, silky stroke.

Stinging discomfort caught her by surprise, and she gasped and stiffened. At her resistance, he lay quietly within her, straining to tame his need, stroking her face, calling her his little love, his angel, his heart of hearts. The stinging subsided and under his loving caresses she began to feel the fullness of him as the steamy fulfillment she'd sought.

"The worst is over," he whispered softly. And he looked full into those misty blue eyes and promised,

"From now on there will only be pleasure." And when he felt the subtle easing, the trusting of her body against him, he began to make good that promise with small liquid motions, like playful waves lapping at her tension, eroding it.

Soon she was meeting his motions with her hips, arching to receive him, absorbing his rod deeper within her. And with the care and flawless skill of a great master, he began to lift her onto startling new planes of sensation, undoing her inhibitions one by one, coaxing her joyful response.

Higher, faster, she rode a tightening spiral of pleasure that soared to breathless heights. Strange fluid pressures built within her loins and limbs so that she quivered and shuddered with each thrust and strained to get closer to him . . . closer. . . . Then abruptly the wild spiralling ended and she was flung violently aloft, launched free of mortal confines as passion exploded within her. Her senses dissolved, seared by wild torrents of pure molten feeling.

Jack felt her response deep within his own sinews and stunning satisfaction coursed through him even before he found his own volcanic release.

It was a long time before he recovered enough to move aside to keep from crushing her. And it was even longer before Merrie righted her shattered senses and realized that he'd withdrawn and now cradled her gently against his body. He touched her cheek and called her name softly, watching her shallow breathing anxiously and fearing she'd truly fainted this time. When she finally opened her eyes, they were dark-centered, dazed with discovery, and smoky with spent desire. He relaxed into a smile. He'd never seen such a combination of sensual awakening and satisfaction in his life.

"Ohhh . . ." she sighed weakly.

"Oh, indeed," he agreed, watching wonder in her face and realizing he shared it.

"Is it always so between husbands and wives?"

He took a ragged breath. "I am as new to husbanding as you are to wifery.'' A crooked, distracting grin broadened over his love-softened features. He refused to admit former partners and pleasures to their bed even to appease her delectable curiosity. ''Perhaps it will always be so between us, little heart.'' The thought made something deep in his chest quiver.

''You—you've done it before,'' she murmured, struggling to keep her eyes open. ''It's done the other way, too, is it not?''

''It is. Though I believe that particular way is . . .'' He searched for a way to satisfy her. ''. . . an acquired taste.''

''Oh.'' Merrie looked drowsily into his love-weighted eyes and realized dimly that it was probably one of *his* acquired tastes. But for some inexplicable reason, he preferred to be belly-to-belly and face-to-face with her. And as embarrassing as it was, it was also *wonderful* to be so close to him, so personal with him. She managed an exhausted smile of adoration, nuzzled his hard chest, and sank into the sweet oblivion of sleep.

Below, in the small parlor off the great hall, Master Cramden and the Lombards were keeping an unhappy vigil, with the comfort of Straffen's best claret. The great house was so quiet they could hear mice scurrying in the walls, but there was no discernable noise from the master chamber to either reassure or outrage them.

''Tessie swears it be 'er first,'' Gert mused, propping her bleary head up with her hands.

''Ahhh. The veriest thought of it assails me. The little thing . . . prey to his wicked and carnal nature for the entire night. . . .'' Cramden shook his head and took a long pull from his goblet for consolation.

''Wull, if any man could do 'er proper, it be him.'' Manley tried to inject a woozy note of reason into their gloomings. ''He be a smooth one, all right. An' she be soft on 'im, it be plain to see.'' He sighed and took another stout drink. ''Ain't heared no shrieks ner pitiful sobbin'. . . .''

Cramden's eyes widened in horror at those drastic possibilities and he massaged his portly chest with stubby fingers. "Such a great mischance, having the gell beguiled and then used by one so unworthy."

" 'E has to be unworthy, Cramden." Gert glowered unsteadily. "We need 'im unworthy." She paused to listen for some sign of what was taking place above them. "Recall—we gots anoth'r iron in th' fire. We mus' be shed of 'im, come the morrow. And th' gell needn't suffer 'im again fer a long while. . . ." The others nodded bleak agreement.

Meanwhile, below in the servants' hall, Tess was sitting, wide-eyed, amongst the snoring, wine-soused forms of the other house servants, who were curled on their benches around the walls. Master John had dismissed her to return to her own bed on one of those benches, saying she wouldn't be needed till morning. But in the gloom, she kept seeing Lady Merrie's pale face and frightened eyes. Her little mistress had been so sick with dread that she'd sent her for brandy. Thank the heavens they kept a little store of it for use in emergencies.

Unable to sleep, her heart weighted with dread, Tess slipped from the servants' hall and up the back stairs. She paused in the passage, lowering her lashes as she passed Thomas Seabury's small chamber, then hurried on toward the master chamber. But as she neared the door, the passage brightened and she jerked to a halt. There on a narrow bench, outside the chamber door sat Thomas Seabury, his head laid back against the wall and his legs braced straight in front of him to keep him upright.

Her muffled sound of surprise brought him bolt upright, blinking. He wondered if this was simply a continuation of his dream . . . seeing curvy, brown-eyed little Tess standing there.

"I-I . . ." She realized she was staring and stammered, blushing. "I . . . come to see . . . I tho't me-bee . . ." She gave it up and spoke the truth to those earnest gray eyes. ''I couldn' sleep. I was . . . afeared for m'lady.''

Seabury's tension melted and he smiled a slightly sheepish smile. He didn't even have that excuse. How many times he'd kept this very vigil for Jack as a watch against untimely discovery. Such was not a threat tonight, but old habits were hard to break. ''I simply . . . wanted to be here in the event they needed anything,'' he said.

She nodded and rubbed her hands down her skirt, turning to go. At the last second, her eyes fluttered back to him, shyly, inescapably. He felt the brush of her interest physically and came alive. For days now, he'd gone out of his way to speak to her, to carry things for her, to just watch her. But that subtly alluring look was the first true evidence he'd had of her interest in him.

''Tess . . .'' He lurched foward on his narrow seat and she halted. ''Would it ease your mind to keep the vigil here, with me?'' She bit her lip and nodded. He moved to one side on the bench to make room for her and she settled beside him, clasping her hands together in her lap. He found himself clamping his hands together, too.

''She'll be all right . . . your lady. You needn't fear.'' He turned slightly toward her.''Master Ja—John is a very . . . kindly . . . man. He would never hurt Lady Merrie.''

''But Mister Seabury . . . she was so afeared.'' Seabury's warmth and concern melted her discretion altogether. ''She sent me fer *brandy*. Sick wi' fright, sir. If ye coulda seen 'er eyes. . . .''

''Brandy?'' Seabury's smile was very endearing. In the country, the potent drink was still considered a medicament, something to be used with both prudence and righteous suspicion. But in decadent London, and especially at court, it had come into frequent use as a drink of pleasure, and was indulged in quite openly for its powerful intoxicating and ''liberating'' effects. ''If she was truly frightened sick,'' Seabury observed with a wry expession, "then a dram of brandy was surely just the thing to cure it."

"Ye think so?" Tess looked up into his soft gray eyes and eased visibly. Her bowlike lips were cherry red and lusciously moist from her biting them. Seabury felt his own tingling.

"I'm sure of it." He gave up his internal struggle and slid a hand over her smaller ones, startling her. "Your lady will be fine, Tess. I think it's wonderful that Lady Merrie has someone so devoted to her. You're . . . a splendid lady's maid."

"Oh, sir." She swallowed hard and blushed again, looking down at his hand on hers.

"And a very pretty one." The intimacy of the moment overwhelmed his usual sense of decorum. His hand tightened on hers and he watched her tense. Was it fear that made her eyes glisten so and brought such color to her smooth cheeks?

Before he could stop himself, he was leaning close, pressing his lips to hers. She responded by leaning closer to him, increasing the pressure of his mouth on hers, parting her lips so naturally. But when he deepened the kiss and made to take her into his arms, she broke away and turned to rise. Seabury caught her, halfway up, by the wrist and held her.

"Don't go, Tess."

"M-mister Seabury—" It was half plea, half exclamation.

"I'll not kiss you again—I promise." He would have been gratified to know the conflict that assurance generated in her. "Just sit and talk with me. Please. It will be a long night. . . ." She sat down slowly, warily, and Seabury released the breath he'd been holding.

"I would like it very much if you would call me by my Christian name, Thomas. No one else uses it, not even Jack."

"Thomas . . ." Tess blushed at the liberty he offered her. Had he seen the longing she'd been unable to suppress when she looked at him? She glanced down at his hand, still wrapped around her wrist, and felt a startlingly physical wave of warmth through her. When she lifted a tenuous smile to him, he felt as if he had just stepped out of fog into sunshine and he smiled back.

Through the next hour they talked, shyly at first, but then more easily. Tess asked about his family, his travels, and the wide world outside Straffen. By the wee hours of the morning her eyes had drifted shut under the lulling comfort of his gentlemanly words and presence, and she didn't protest as he pulled her drooping head against his shoulder. As minutes passed, she grew pliant and sagged fully against him. Seabury opened his eyes and raised his head from the wall to look at her.

"Tess?" He looked down at her, nestled against him. He should probably carry her back to the hall, to her own sleeping place. But he couldn't make himself relinquish this sweet contact between them. He laid a chaste kiss on the top of her hair, then collected her shoulders against him and cradled her across his lap.

He smiled ruefully at his predicament: holding the gell he wanted, just the way he wanted . . . and still being so far from the paradise he craved. Jack would certainly never have such trouble. Some men were just meant to be conquerers . . . while others, he sighed, were born to be comforters.

Much later, by the dim light of guttering candles, Merrie slipped from Jack's arms as he slept and crept from the soft bed to wash and collect herself. Her knees were wobbly and her womanflesh felt very thick and sensitive, but she felt strangely alive in a fascinating new way. When she turned back to the bed, she found Jack coming toward her and she flushed from head to toe as he paused in naked, manly splendor before her. The dusky glow of his features and the heat of his eyes on her body burned his rising desire into her awareness. Then his fingers touched her cheek and trailed down her jaw to her shoulder and one irresistible nip-

ple. She read in that fonden touch a promise of renewed pleasures.

"D-do we . . . are we supposed to . . . do it again?"
she whispered softly, feeling sinuous vibrations in her
tender parts at the very thought.

"We can, my little heart," he said, his voice a constricted rasp, "if . . . you want." His body was making
his wants quite plain.

Merrie swallowed and surrendered her gaze to his
hot, enveloping look. Melting new warmth washed
through her and she nodded. He bent to pick her up
in his arms, but she stumbled back to elude him, jarred
to remembrance by his movement. "Wait—"

He watched, eyes burning, while she moved to the
table, picked up a goblet, and rubbed that potent
brandy over her tight, tempting nipples again.

"Overbeake did not teach you that," he declared
hoarsely, pointing at her busy fingers and giving his
suddenly parched lips an unconscious lick. When she
turned to him with her eyes and nipples glistening in
the dim, golden light, his loins caught fire. Heat fanned
up through him, turning his voice to a smoky growl.
"And it most certainly was not your little green Tess
. . . nor sober Goodwife Lombard. . . ."

"Nay, none of them," she agreed, volunteering
nothing. When she came toward him there was wan-
tonness in her sway and uncertainty in her chin. "Does
it please you?"

He pulled her into his arms, shuddering at the feel
of her softness against his hardness. "It pleases me—
Lord, how it pleases me." He took her mouth in a
long, sensual epic of a kiss that contained all past and
all future joys. When he lifted her and carried her to
the bed, she was well past shyness and determined to
return him pleasure for pleasure.

"This time," she whispered as he laid her on the
bed, "we'll do it my way."

His eyes widened and he halted, watching her turn
sinuously onto her stomach, then push up onto her
hands and knees. She faced him with eyes like steamy

pools and lush, brandy-tipped breasts dangling inso-lently. Her fiery hair caressed her body in one glorious, clinging tangle. She arched and wriggled, catlike, purr-ing, "Take me, Jack. Show me. . . ."

He was incapable of uttering a sound. Desire con-sumed him. His entire existence focused on the need that rampaged through him. He'd meant to rein his desires, to consider her fears, her innocent sensibilities on this night . . . only to find some of her sensibilities anything but innocent! God's Nightshirt—how *she* shocked *him!* He closed his eyes, muttering the closest thing he could recall to a prayer of repentance, then climbed onto the bed to give her exactly what she was asking for.

He collected her against him, sending trembling hands over the pliant curves of her body and devour-ing her skin with greedy kisses. Each caress, each throaty endearment, pushed her desires higher, until she was panting softly, wriggling closer, craving ful-fillment. And when the time was right, he raised her to her knees and fitted himself gently into the tight sheath of her womanflesh. She gasped and moaned softly as he touched and stroked her intimately, heightening her arousal as he began to move.

The erotic roundness of her bottom, pressed tightly and then jogging softly against his loins, was nearly too much. He gritted his teeth in a pleasurable agony of denial and held her still against him until he eased. Then a slow, senuous rhythm built between them as he clasped her waist and trailed possessive hands over her back and down over her breasts. When his need for release could not be checked any longer, he moaned her name and clasped her tightly, bursting inside her. Panting wildly, he withdrew and turned her over, cra-dling her, sinking into her again to complete her re-sponse. And soon she joined him in a sweet spiralling release that was somewhat gentler and somehow deeper than the first.

Merrie lay on the hard pillow of his flexed arm, with a sheen of satisfaction on her skin and in her luminous eyes. She was floating, transformed into pure light, suffused with sensual joy. She'd never imagined such wild, tumultuous feelings existed! She managed to look at him and found him watching her with smiling eyes that were saturated with pleasure.

"I never guessed it would feel like this," she murmured, savoring the love-bronzed perfection of his face and the aura of shared passion that held them enrapt. "Why didn't anyone ever tell me about it? It's so wonderful, you'd think people would talk of nothing else. And write about it—" She rambled on, "Though I've never heard of such writings. . . ."

Then it struck her that perhaps people *did* write and speak about it, and she'd just never been exposed to it. A frown dented her brow briefly. She'd never have been exposed to anything but the working end of a needle if Mistress Overbeake had had her way. "People do write of it, don't they?"

He chuckled soundlessly, seeing the wheels of curiosity turning in her mind again. "Not nearly as often as they should. It's a very powerful force, Merrie, one powerful enough to create a life." A disconcerting knot began to form in his gut as he realized what he'd said. He hadn't considered the sexual act in such terms in years . . . not since he escaped the oppressive thrall of his rigid, pietistic family. It was another of those weighty and unnerving ideas that were occurring to him with disturbing frequency.

Merrie watched emotions cross his face and reached up to trace his cheek with gentle fingers. It was powerful, she thought to herself, powerful enough to join a man and a woman into one flesh *in secula seculorum* . . . "forever and ever."

"And it is because it is so powerful that young gells are sheltered from it . . . to protect them from misuse and harm." Jack found himself trying to explain, feeling like the wolf explaining the need for the fence to the sheep! "Thus, it is largely left to their husbands to introduce them to it." The natural question followed.

"Then . . . who introduces husbands to it?"

Jack laughed and hugged her tightly. The knowing, worldly tone of his mirth told Merrie all she needed to know. Vixens, of course.

He read the dismay in her face and guessed where her decidedly sophisticated logic had led her. And he didn't want her to think of wickedness and sin and corruption when she thought of sexual pleasure . . . or of him.

"Nature, my little heart," he said, providing a reassuring alternative. "It is sweet Nature herself who introduces husbands to it."

Merrie absorbed the adoring glow from his eyes into her hungry heart and melted again under his masterful charm. She snuggled closer and feathered her fingertips over the hard, smooth skin of his chest. Her eyes drifted shut as sated languor overtook her.

"Jack?"

"Ummmm. . . ." He was drifting, too.

"I think I like your way better."

Jack laughed and hugged her, ever so softly.

Chapter Eleven

Late the next morning, Jack rose from their bed to summon Seabury from down the connecting hallway. He ordered a hot soaking tub for Merrie and a light repast for them both. To Seabury's inquiring look, he responded with an indolent and hugely satisfied grin. "And fetch the lady's maid, Seabury. I trow you've marked where the wench sleeps." Seabury flushed and went off to see to the duties he had performed so many times on a morning after. A warm, scented bath and honey-smothered buns with cream, Seabury recalled; Jack certainly knew what a woman wanted after a night of loving.

Jack stood over Merrie, watching her sleep, enjoying the cozy, kittenish sigh she made, tangled in the bed-clothes and in the glorious masses of her hair. Every part of her seemed uncannily mated to his standard of the "ideal" in womanly appearance, except perhaps for her hair. He'd always preferred dark tresses that flowed in sinuous rivers over pale, naked skin. Now he could only believe that he had preferred such because he'd never seen hair like Merrie's before . . . so vibrant and seductive . . . a living flame that was the outward blazon of the fiery passions secreted inside an oddly demure little being.

Merrie wakened to the feel of his hand on her hair and looked up into his glowing eyes, thinking he must be more glorious than Michael or Gabriel or any of the other angels. He was sitting on the bed beside her, looking so large and manly and yet so beautiful. There was an assured calm to his gaze that bespoke the tenderness of his touch and the generosity of his nature. In the night just past, she'd learned the depths of his gentlemanliness as well as his passions and she counted herself a fortunate young woman indeed.

"Stir yourself, lazybones." He trailed a knuckle down her cheek, her bare shoulder, and over the half-covered swell of one breast. "Else I shall be tempted to stir you myself. . . ." Her skin flushed with maidenly modesty, but a wanton flicker lighted the backs of her eyes. Struck by the contrast, he laughed and pulled her up to a sitting position. "Hoyden, don't tempt me so. I've ordered you a bath and a bit of nourishment. Imagine what your little Tess would think if she discovered us . . . *stirring* . . . when she arrived."

Merrie colored hotly as a soft rapping came at the gallery door. Soon Tess was bustling about the chamber preparing a tub and toweling, her cheeks aflame and her eyes fixed to the floor. Then Seabury appeared with a tray of food and housemaids Bevis and Jean in tow, bearing kettles of hot water.

Merrie shrank back against the bolsters, pulling the covers high about her chin as they cast curious looks her way. Jack, half clad in hose and breeches, came to settle on the bed and bolsters beside her. The traipsing in and out and the commotion continued as a great wooden tub was filled and the tray of food was prepared. Oblivious to Merrie's stiffness, he pulled her against his side and nuzzled her love-rumpled locks.

"A bath . . . in a tub?" she choked. "What must they think?"

"Don't be embarrassed, sweeting," he whispered into her ear. "Behave as though it is the most usual thing in the world, then so must they. You are mistress of this house . . . their mistress." She looked up into his face and absorbed his words as he brushed her lips reassuringly. "Trust me; the warm water will help . . . the soreness." Merrie blushed as she realized what he meant.

"But . . . they'll know . . ."

"They already know what's happened to you, love." Jack smiled softly. "It's expected on a wedding night. It's writ in the very linen."

Startled, Merrie realized what he meant: the small stains that they would see when they stripped the bed for proof of consummation later that morning. She stared at the covers, mortified.

"They know *what* happened," he murmured with a wry expression, "but they cannot know the pleasures we shared. Those are yours and mine alone. Our secret treasures."

Merrie searched the certainty in his face and her tension eased as she gratefully borrowed his smooth, sensual confidence. When Bevis and Jean and Seabury withdrew, Merrie made herself slide from the bedclothes and step into the steeping bath under both Jack's and Tess's eyes. By the time she'd soaked away her soreness and dried and dressed, she was feeling that confidence all through her in a new, womanly way.

It was midday before the newly wedded couple emerged from their chamber into the household's unblinking scrutiny. All witnessed Merrie's rosy glow and Jack's raffish half-smile and took note of the way he never let her out of his reach. They went for a walk to their tree on the hill overlooking Straffen, then spent time watching the mares and foals at pasture. As they went about, they accepted the felicitations and honors paid them by Straffen's varied inhabitants with a mannerly absence of attention. It was clear, they had eyes only for each other on the day after their marriage.

Cramden and the Lombards watched through strain-reddened eyes, relieved to have their charge emerge unscathed from her long, perilous night. But their relief soon changed to indignation. To them, Jack's sensual stride and his possessive manner with Merrie bespoke an unseemly carnal pride in the job he'd done. And the rake's smugness made Lady Merrie's open adoration of her husband all the more alarming to witness. They grew determined to have the next part of their scheme done quickly.

Late in the afternoon, as Merrie and Jack reentered

the hall, they were met by Gert and Manley Lombard, bearing a sealed parchment. Manley nodded and shoved the missive at Jack with a hint of impatience.

"This come fer ye, sir." His look pinned Jack full-square.

Jack frowned a bit and stared at the elegant lettering on the packet in his hand. It bemused him briefly that someone would send him messages here at Straf— When he raised his eyes, Gert's meaning-filled look made the sense of it clear to him. The terms of his lucrative marriage agreement suddenly flitted through his head: he was to bed Merrie Straffen and be off to London. Then, this was an arranged communiqué . . . the device by which he was to take leave. It stunned him momentarily.

Merrie stared up at the immobile sculpture of his features and grew concerned. "What is it, Jack? Can it be bad news?"

"Nay." He came to his senses and forced a winning smile as he slowly folded the unopened letter in half. "I know the contents . . . and it is of little consequence. I marvel that my partners in London should bother me with so trivial a matter on the day after my vows." He stuffed the parchment into his doublet, took a deep breath, and turned to Manley. "Master Lombard, some of that most excellent claret in the small parlor, if you please."

Manley and Gert stood gaping with indignation as they watched Gentleman Jack lead Lady Merrie off toward the parlor. How dare the varlet just crumple and stuff the summons! They hurried up the stairs to Master Cramden's chamber, where they shared Jack's unthinkable reaction with their partner.

Cramden winced and tugged at the beleaguered ruff about his portly neck. "Perchance he did not understand."

"He knowed what it were, all right," Gert declared sourly. "Elsewise, he'd 'ave looked. Jus' folded it up and tucked it straight away, bold as brass. Ye mus' do

somethin', Cramden. Speak to 'im at table. Make 'im
know an' agreement's an agreement.''

Cramden looked a bit queasy at the prospect, but
Gert's and Manley's steeley expressions persuaded him.
For the remainder of the afternoon he paced and re-
hearsed what he would say to Gentleman Jack. And it
all went for naught when Jack bypassed the table and
whisked Merrie upstairs just at sunset, ordering them
a light repast on a tray.

Infuriated now, Gert and Manley took things into
their own hands. They delivered the food and wine to
the master chamber themselves and pointedly asked
after Jack's ''London news.'' Jack waved them aside
with a roguish hand and assured them it was nothing
of importance. He thanked them for troubling to bring
the food themselves and insisted with equal pointed-
ness they not trouble themselves further . . . for the
rest of the night. They soon found themselves on the
far side of the door, livid and sputtering impotently.
The knave! He obviously intended to have a second
night on the gell—in flagrant violation of the prenuptial
agreement!

Jack stood looking at the great oaken door he had
shut firmly behind them, seeing the Lombards' horrified faces outlined on it. There was to be one night
with his bride, those faces reminded him. One night; a
meet and seemly consummation of the vows was all
that was required of him. Then he was to hie himself
back to London and his own life, a richer man. But, he
reasoned, that had been before he'd seen and gotten
to know and bedded his tantalizing little bride.

He turned to find Merrie arranging the food on the
table. She had removed her cap with its new silk matron's hood and had unbuttoned the top few buttons
of her gown in the chamber's lingering warmth. Her
hair swished about her narrow waist and her hands
moved with unstudied grace as she poured wine into
goblets. The curve of her cheek and the thoughtful pout
of her lips as she concentrated sent a fierce heat
through him.

When he agreed to this bizarre arrangement, he certainly hadn't reckoned on being mated with someone as rousing and appealing as Merrie Straffen. He'd never imagined he could possibly desire one woman, a specific woman, like this. Wanting her was like being immersed in honey-taffy; it was so damnably sweet and pleasurable . . . and purely inescapable.

Through their quiet meal, Merrie felt his eyes warming her and tried to quell her trembles of anticipation. All day, by his side, she'd suffered delicious flushes of remembered pleasure and had to suppress the physical shivers they caused. She now looked up from her goblet into his warming gaze and let the shivers come. He saw her reaction and reached for her hand to pull her around the table and onto his lap.

"This, sweet wench, is why young gells are sternly prohibited from sitting on gentlemen's knees." His roguish eyes crinkled as his hand slid silkily under her skirts without the slightest outward sign of the encroachment. Merrie gasped and stiffened as she felt his fingers on the back of her bare knees and creeping up her thigh. Jack's most licentious grin appeared. "Kiss me, sweeting, and I'll show you more. . . ."

More. Merrie's heart was thudding and warm eddies of fluid sensation twirled through her womanly parts. She put her hands on Jack's broad shoulders and obediently applied her lips to his. Then her arms wrapped about his neck and her tongue darted into his mouth as his hand rose higher beneath her proper skirts. She squirmed wantonly toward that hand, only to have it still on her inner thigh.

"Young gells must also be cautious of gentlemen's whispers," Jack rasped when she ended the deep kiss. His other hand came up behind her to nudge her head closer and turn it so that he could nuzzle her ear. "For whispers often contain naughty things. . . ." And he tongued the delicate sworl and channel of her ear and nibbled her earlobe. Tiny lightning flashes of pleasure rained through her and she moaned softly, melting against him.

"Gentlemen have numerous distracting ways . . . that can lead a gell astray before she notices," he whispered raggedly. And suddenly the last of Merrie's skirts were slid from beneath her, so that her bare bottom rested on his bulging codpiece.

Her eyes widened helplessly. How had he managed to do that without her feeling it? His catlike eyes answered her wordlessly: distractions. He nuzzled her ear meaningfully again. Then she felt a movement beneath her and in a moment his naked, throbbing shaft rested against her bare buttock. A shocked chill coursed through her. A blink later, she realized that they were mere inches from heated marital indulgence and that her outer skirts were not disarranged in the least! She swallowed hard and stared at him with awed discovery.

"Gentlemen are treacherous indeed," she murmured. With such devious skills, he could have taken her at any time in the last week, she realized. "Why didn't you ply gentlemanly wiles to 'distract' me before?"

"Because . . . I'm no gentleman," he observed with wry, double-edged honesty.

She laughed and kissed him saucily. Then a mischievous glow entered her eyes and she felt through her skirts for the hand that rested on her naked thigh. She grasped it boldly and with his help she drew it up her thigh to her hip. Her eyes closed as he caressed her all the way along.

"I wondered what that would feel like." She sighed, not caring that her curiosity was immodest. Then she urged his hand to more sensitive and private realms and held her breath as he began to stroke her. Her voice came low and full. "And I wondered if I'd only dreamt this."

Through the raging fire in his blood, Jack managed the beleaguered thought that her body seemed every bit as curious as her mind. It was the second key to the puzzle of Merrie Straffen. She wanted to be touched—was absolutely hungry for it. She yearned to be taught the fullness of her woman's role and to experience these heady new pleasures. Surfacing from the throes of a wild, careening kiss, she verified his discovery with yet another question.

"Jack . . . we could do it here, too, couldn't we? I mean . . . we're . . . so close . . ." He laughed and removed his hands from her skirts to clasp her waist and run his hands possessively up her ribs.

"Yes, it can be done this way." He watched the sultry flutter of her lashes as she absorbed the knowledge and her fertile logic carried it a step further. She shivered and wriggled delectably on his lap as her eyes became starry nightpools of wonder.

"Then there must be . . . other ways as well." Her pink tongue flicked out to moisten her sensitive lips and she felt his body flex and arch against her.

"There are," he rasped, holding her tightly against his lap, and rubbing his hot member against her bare hip. He was roused and charmed and utterly in her thrall. "And I'll show you every one I know, little love . . . one at a time."

Jack Huntington honestly did not think of the consequences of his reckless refusal to withdraw from Straffen. He did not want to go, and in the manner characteristic of rakes, he chose to ignore that which he could not either charm or seduce. Thus he stole a second enchanting night in Merrie's arms, teaching her the joys of pleasure and claiming the true reward of all teaching . . . the delight of learning from his pupil.

But as the gray dawn spread over Straffen, stony determination spread through Straffen's agents. After a second sleepless night, they were frantic to be shed of their cursedly persistent bridegroom. His very presence in the house drew attention and curiosity toward Straffen, and people would surely follow. And with people came notoriety. And with notoriety came trouble of a sort the Lombards and Cramden could ill afford. Not the least of their worries was the unthinkable attachment Lady Merrie seemed to be forming for the cunning Gentleman Jack.

They waited through the long morning, watching the chamber door and chaffing mightily as Jack ordered food and heated water again, as if he truly were the new master of Straffen. It was near to midday when the newlyweds appeared, walking arm in arm and seeming the very personification of nuptial satisfaction. Cramden moaned, Gert curled one side of her nose and looked away, and Manley winced at the sight. The rake had clearly beguiled the little thing into serving his jaded appetites. The idea sat harshly upon their rather selective sense of morality.

It was mid-afternoon before Master Cramden was able to pry Jack from Merrie's side by saying, "A matter of supreme urgency, sir. A correspondence that simply will not wait." Jack rose from his chair with a disarming smile at Merrie and followed the portly lawyer into the parlor. Gert Lombard, and then Manley, slipped into the parlor with them and Jack realized what "supreme urgency" they were about to discuss. He braced himself.

"You have willfully and maliciously breached your marital agreement, sir," Cramden said, coming straight to the point, furiously waving a sheaf of parchment at him. "And we demand you withdraw to London forthwith . . . or forfeit the entirety of your fortune."

Forfeit? The entirety? Jack stood, confusion descending upon him. He was a man unused to heeding society's dire warnings and stern rubrics. He'd lived in recent years as though tomorrow would never come and it was a nasty surprise to suddenly find that tomorrow actually did come . . . and indeed was here.

"You cannot possibly mean that one night's . . ." But the looks on their faces, from dour disgust to pious outrage, convinced him they were serious indeed. They meant it! A vow, a brisk jig between the sheets, and a quick fare-thee-well! It strained Jack's most callous and self-serving impulses. They insisted he bed his own delicious little wife one night and then abandon her! "Good galfrey, man, I've *wedded* the gell!"

"Subject to conditions," Cramden declared, purpling like a turnip and dragging a large handkerchief out to mop his beaded brow. "Your marriage is subject to the conditions set forth in the old earl's last testament. And *in jure*—by law—you must abide by such or forfeit the lot. Begone to London, sir, this very afternoon, or find your stipend withdrawn for good!" Cramden put his considerable weight behind the statement and appeared most immovable.

"You cannot honestly expect me to leave—" Jack stepped forward, fists clenched, glowering at Cramden in disbelief. The lawyer's uncharacteristic gravity stunned Jack, and in that moment of confusion, his disbelief enlarged to admit his own anger and resentment. He was trembling at the thought of leaving her. His chest was squeezing, hurting at the prospect.

And that unthinkable ache suddenly shocked him. It bespoke his growing attachment to Merrie Straffen . . . a true deepening of affection that was neither prudent nor desirable. With dismay, he realized that his weakness for her was but one of a mounting number of dangerous lapses in his worldly nature and habits of late. By th' Eternal—he was in real trouble here!

"If th' agreements be breached, th' vows mus' be annulled . . . by law," Gert proclaimed with a sharp, silencing glance at Cramden. "Then ye'll 'ave naught. No bride, no livin'."

"Yea," Manley added, throwing his weight behind it. "Don' be a clevershins, sir. 'Twill only end in grief. And five hundert a year be a fine livin'."

Five hundred a year pounded through him. Jack swallowed hard and his eyes widened in horror as they fell on the documents in Cramden's grip. He must be going dauncy—risking such a plummy future. But when Merrie's sparkling eyes and perfect body wriggled into his mind and onto the other end of the balance, he was vascillating wildly again. God's Blood! He'd never faced such a dilemma. He *hated* dilemmas!

"Be not misled by sentiment, sir." Cramden sweated profusely as he watched the conflict in Jack's face and frantically sought a lever to use with the rake. "You may think you wish to stay now, for the bloom is quite on the rose. But it is well known that you are a man who requires a certain . . . freedom. The varied and unencumbered life you require awaits you in London, sir . . . along with certain 'associations' which, no doubt, have given you much pleasure."

Jack blanched, stung by Cramden's unmistakable reference to his paramours and the regularity with which they'd always changed. They knew about him, he realized, *all* about him! And they expected that a rakehell like himself should have no difficulty fulfilling their hideous agreement: one night . . . a quick kiss and cuddle and *begone!* The impact of it now crashed in on him, sending him reeling. Only one night with Merrie . . . and he'd already taken two. He had to leave Straffen this very day . . . or forfeit all. . . .

Jack strode from the parlor, face dusky, eyes hard behind a façade of practiced charm. He bellowed for Seabury, then came to rest on one knee before Merrie's chair in the hall.

"Whatever is it, Jack?" She looked up into his face with wide-eyed concern.

"A matter of the utmost urgency, sweeting." He groaned extravagantly and laid a hand over his heart. "I am called to London in all haste. One of my adventures has gone sour and my . . . partners declare I am the only hope of fixing it. The message I spurned yesterday—Ah, the relentless beast of commerce! How monstrous of them to tear me from your side after only two days' bliss!" He cupped her surprised face in his hands and gave her a hot, mind-numbing kiss. "Come. Savor every last moment with me, my little heart." He dragged the needlehoop from her stunned fingers and pulled her up and toward the stairs with him.

Seabury came at a run and, after a few terse orders from Jack, was soon bustling about the master chamber, gathering clothes and boots from the great chests and shaving things from the washstand. Merrie's eyes followed Seabury disbelievingly as Jack pulled her to a seat on the bed and took masterful control of her senses. Between potent, mind-glazing kisses and mesmeric touches, he explained that he might be gone a while and that she mustn't be sad. Her bewildered gaze kept drifting to Seabury and the chest he'd just emptied of all Jack's doublets and breeches.

"We needn't take all that, Seabury," he instructed with an easy wave of the hand. "Just two or three suits of clothes will do." Seabury paused with a puzzled frown and Jack shot him an emphatic look above Merrie's head that spoke volumes. The perceptive manservant nodded and dutifully returned a few of Jack's lesser garments to the chest. Soon the small leather-clad trunk was ready for travel and Seabury was helping Jack on with his riding boots and spurs and was changing off his doublet for a plainer one. It all happened so quickly, around Jack's charming banter about the journey and time passing quickly, that Merrie scarcely had time to think.

"Long for me, sweetness." Jack swept her into his arms as soon as Seabury and Chester Lombard trundled the trunk out and down the stairs. "God knows . . . I'll miss you, wench." He kissed her forehead, her nose, and then captured her lips in a sultry, open-mouthed ravishment of a kiss that contained all the compressed desire he was feeling for her. His hands wandered over her waist and breasts and bottom, absorbing her charms, committing her to memory.

The desperate heat of his need jarred Merrie to life against him. She clasped him tightly, breathlessly molding her pliant young body against his lean hardness. By instinct her hands sought him as his did her; caressing feverishly, ruffling hair, claiming all that could be held. When that kiss ended, both were dark-eyed with desire and trembling, struggling to remain upright. He stared at the flush of passion in her cheeks, the cherry redness of her swollen lips, and was seized by need.

"The horses are ready, Jack."

Seabury's timely interruption startled Jack back to his senses. He stiffened, clamping his jaw against the raging maelstrom of emotion in him and forcing his arms to loosen about her. Lord—something about the wench took possession of him!

"Coming, Seabury," he called hoarsely, collecting her wobbly form against his side and smiling his most dazzling smile into her dazed face. "Come see me off, sweeting."

The horses waited in the front court and an astonishing number of Straffen's folk had assembled to say farewells. Cramden and the Lombards and Mistress Overbeake looked on tersely as bobs and nods were made to Jack. When it was their turn, they made their respects with eyes narrowed in disapproval on Merrie's dismay and on the way Jack held her tight against his side.

Something in the sight of the horses penetrated Merrie's shock and she finally understood: he was leaving . . . really leaving her! "Jack!" She pulled back as he led her toward the horses and they came to a halt, facing each other. "Why now? Can it not wait even a few—"

"I've told you, sweeting." He smiled his rakish best, but it was stiff and felt wrong, like the lie it was. "I must go. A fortune rides upon my presence in London within two days." That much, at least, was true. But it did not help the guilty, hollow feeling inside him.

"Then—let me come with you!" She stepped closer, quivering with anxiety. The loss of him was too huge to comprehend all at once and when he stroked her cheek with his fingertips, she focused on them. His hands—she wouldn't be able to slip her hand inside his or to feel the ever-changing wonder of his touch on her skin. "I-I could make ready quickly—"

"Nay, Merrie." The bewildered hurt in her face tied his belly in knots. "I'd not have time for you with this cursed business tangle. And London is no place to be in summer, filled with foul airs and humors and desperate street roughs. I'd have not a minute's peace thinking I'd exposed you to such risks.''

''But, Jack, we've had no time. I promise I won't be any trouble to you!''

''But you're needed here.'' Peeling her fingers from his sleeve, he kissed them desperately. ''I need you to see to the house and holdings for me. I'll return as quickly as I can.'' He took her by the shoulders and kissed her fiercely, and then again with an aching gentleness that called forth an undeniable response in her. She swayed as he released her and she felt that last stroke of his fingers across her cheek, upon her very heart.

Jack had moved to his horse and was mounted by the time Merrie broke free of the web he'd spun about her with that last kiss. ''Jack?'' She lurched forward, her eyes huge and luminous with tears. ''Please—don't go.''

He flashed that shopworn rake's smile and blew her a kiss as he reined off. ''I'll send you word from London, my love.'' The ''my love'' was lost on the breeze, as he was already turned and giving his mount the spur.

''Jack!'' She took one step after him, then another and another. ''Ja-ack—''

The next moment she was jolted to a stop and found her arm captive in Overbeake's tight grip. ''Stop this, gell! Makin' a spectacle of yerself! Cease straightaway!''

''Nooo . . . stop!'' Merrie struggled against Overbeake's hold on her and managed to bring them to a straining halt. She watched Jack and Seabury growing smaller and smaller along the road and felt a terrible, wrenching pull in her breast, as though he were dragging her heart with him. Great hot tears began to burn down her cheeks and her breaths came in ragged gasps. She bit her kiss-reddened lips to keep her grief seemly and silent, while her eyes, her face, and her straining body cried out for him . . . praying he would turn back.

But his dashing figure grew steadily more indistinct and her desperate hope faltered. She shuddered a silent sob and sagged. And Overbeake seized that opportunity to trundle her, bodily, back into the hall.

Jack halted near the crest of the rise and turned in his saddle to stare back at Straffen. He could make out Merrie's pretty, lace-rimmed lilac gown and the insufferable Overbeake dragging her back into the house.

He set his handsome jaw like granite and closed his aching eyes. He wanted to thrash the old harridan, wanted to turn around and ride back and— His hands were fists about the reins and there was a strange, sour constriction in his throat.

Cramden loomed in his mind with fresh taunts about his past and the sort of man he was. Cramden was right about him, he realized with a painful squeezing in his chest. And it was probably better this way. Merrie would have a safe and secure life . . . and he would have his blessed freedom. In time, she would come to see him through wiser eyes, and her hurting would stop. And it was probably just as well that he wouldn't be around when that happened.

He turned and drew himself up straight in the saddle, feeling Seabury's troubled eyes searching him. "To London, Seabury," he ordered thickly. "We have to find someplace to live."

In the great bed of Straffen's lord, Merrie lay, tear-spent and motionless. Night shadows were falling across the great chamber and in the deep quiet she caught an occasional whisper or murmur of passion that seemed to linger in the confines of her marriage bed. Whispers were all there would be . . . for how long to come?

He was gone. She sniffed and wiped her cheeks with the soft sheet yet again. He had climbed on his horse and ridden off, back to London, leaving her stumbling after him with the taste of his kiss on her lips, calling his name like . . . The realization hit her like a fist in the belly, taking her breath: like his haughty vixen!

He'd kissed and caressed her, and left her longing for more, just as he'd left his paramour that night at the inn. Now she understood the vixen's frustration, for a smoky ache of desire coiled through Merrie as she lay in their bed, longing for him. She wanted to feel him against her and to lie naked in the shelter of his arms. She wanted to kiss him and touch his bristled chin of a morning and feel the sultry penetration of his kisses. She wanted to be with him, to talk with him and to listen to his naughty whispers . . . to ask him her questions. . . .

She sniffed again. She still had all sorts of questions to ask him, multitudes of questions. How long would it be before she saw him again? A fortnight? A month? Longer? She squeezed her eyes shut and forced another pair of teardrops onto her cheeks. What had she done, or not done? Again and again she conjured the events of the morning and steamy pleasures of the night before, sifting them for errors or omissions, for reasons that would make him leave her.

There was so much left unsaid, undone, between them. . . . She'd never even had the chance to broach the subject of getting rid of Overbeake. Now that he was gone, she was again in the irritable old mistress's thrall. It was twice as unbearable now, since she'd tasted a brief bit of freedom under his protection and had it ripped from her the very instant he left. Her whole life seemed to be blossoming . . . and now it lay under a layer of cruel frost.

Some time later, Tess slipped into the darkened chamber to check on her mistress. Merrie declined the offer of food; she wasn't hungry. But she did allow Tess to remove her good lilac silk gown and was grateful for assistance with her hair.

"He'll be back soon, milady, don' you fret." Goodly Tess's voice was choked as she paused mid-stroke with the brush and laid a comforting hand on her mistress's shoulder. Merrie nodded wordlessly and gave Tess's hand a trembling squeeze.

Sleep did not come easily that night. She tossed and turned until her hair was a damp tangle and her body ached. Finally, she rose and donned a loose, shirtlike shift and slipped along the darkened gallery and downstairs, to sit in the cool hall in the moonlight. But as she rounded the bottom of the stairs, near the door to the small parlor, an eerie, glowing visage loomed out of the hallway beside the small parlor and she squealed and stumbled back, banging into the well behind her. The face cried out in equal surprise and there was a muffled scuffling in the darkness nearby. Merrie clutched frantically at her throat, then recognized Gert Lombard's face, shadowed strangely by the light of a dim tallow lamp.

"Milady!" Gert righted herself on her feet, then cast a furtive look over her shoulder into the pitch-black hall. "Ye give me a rare fright.' "

"I am truly sorry, Goodwife. I-I could not sleep and thought it would be cooler in the hall." She felt Goodwife Gert's scrutiny of her thin linen garment and crossed her arms over her chest. A moment later she realized the housekeeper was fully dressed and capped at this odd hour. "Has something happened to bring you up and about in the dead of night?"

"I . . . we . . . ahh . . ." Gert stammered.

"We wus called late to th' stables . . . fer a foalin'." Manley Lombard stepped out of the darkness behind them, startling both Merrie and Gert. "That fancy mare . . . Chester callt us t' help."

"Yea," Gert agreed hastily. "Now, th' thing's done. . . . Ohh, ye cannot sit in this drafty hall, milady. Night humors be foul an' grievous under a full moon. I'll see ye up wi' the light."

Merrie nodded, relieved to be over her fright, and turned toward the stairs. Behind her back Gert flashed Manley a scowl and jerked her head emphatically toward the darkness behind him, then toward the rear door of the hall. Gert hurried after Merrie and as they rounded the gallery, carrying the meager light with them, shadows in the hall below began to move.

Merrie climbed once more into the midst of the great, glooming bed and slid beneath the covers. Jack's faint but unmistakable scent clung to the bolsters. She buried her face in them and relived the deep tenderness of his eyes and the pleasurable fury of his loving . . . as she clung tenaciously to his vow to return.

Straffen quickly settled back into the comfortable routine it had observed before the coming of Gentleman Jack and the courtship and marriage of Lady Merrie. Master Cramden was finally free to pack his things and return to his own home in the nearby town. And, with great relief, the Lombards focused their attentions on the efficient ordering and running of the business of Straffen Manor . . . and their other "irons in the fire." There were quite a little number of things that needed attending. Now that Gentleman Jack was removed and Lady Merrie was once again in their capable hands, they were free to pursue their ever-enlarging ambitions once again.

The redoubtable Mistress Overbeake resumed her close "companioning" of the Lady of Straffen, ordaining and ordering Merrie's activities and measuring out seemliness from her own cramped cup. Fortunately for Merrie, Overbeake had made certain modifications in her tactics with her lady-charge. Sensing Master Cramden's disapproval and cognizant of Merrie's new status as a wife, she gave up pinching in favor of merely grabbing Merrie's wrist. It worked every bit as well, even if it didn't afford quite the same satisfaction. Stitchery was again next to godliness, and books and curiosity were both forbidden. The hounds were once more exiled from the hall and a stiffling sobriety descended upon Straffen Manor.

The only relief from such tyrannical "seemliness" came in the evenings, when Merrie was permitted a solitary stroll in the garden. She felt close to Jack there, amongst the lupines and fragrant spikenards and wild roses. And night after night, under the Lombards' ever-watchful eyes, she would pause by the road, watching for him, wanting him. Then she would turn back to the house with heavy steps and mount the stairs to her lonely bed.

Chapter Twelve

The days dragged by in ponderous succession, May rains giving way to seeping June dampness. One afternoon, when Merrie could stand the maddening confinement no longer, she slipped out to walk about the grounds. She recalled her vow to learn the work of managing Straffen's people and resources and determined to put this interminable waiting to some purpose. She visited with cook Edythe and her minions in the kitchens and buttery, and then went on to the weaver's house, where the other women's work was done. The afternoon was so enjoyable, so free of terror of misstep and misspoken word, that Merrie quite forgot the time.

Overbeake came on the stalk and was outraged to find her there, trying her hand at the loom's shuttle. "Unbefittin', m'lady—puttin' yer hand to such! Present yerself back in th' hall at once!"

The women glanced at each other furiously as Merrie stood, red-faced and shame-choked, before the old mistress. And as she struggled with anger that was rising perilously close to the surface, May, the head weaver, stepped forward to take the brunt of the disagreeable mistress's ire.

"I begt Lady Merrie to come, Mistruss, an' help th' young gells with their stitchin'."

Overbeake could scarcely argue with the desire to improve Straffen's needlecraft and, at length, she was forced to withdraw. Merrie smiled wanly at sturdy May, who nodded conspiratorially and offered her a loom bobbin for winding.

The incident stayed on Merrie's mind the rest of the day and into the long night. She tossed and turned in the warmth of her bed, thinking of Jack, yearning for him. If only he had been there that afternoon he would have intervened, maybe even sent Overbeake packing!

But Jack wasn't there and as she let her mind drift back into the memories of their time together, she recalled his comment that she was mistress here now. She began to think on that. If she was old enough to wed and to wife a man, then why wasn't she old enough to direct her own time? And if she was the rightful heir and the Lady of Straffen, why did everybody on the place seem to have more say in things than she? And if she was really mistress here, shouldn't she be speaking up for her servants, instead of having them stand up for her? Shame colored her cheeks. Was there some heinous deficit in her she could not see? She curled around a bolster, hugging it as proxy for her missing mate. If only Jack were here. Warm, loving, permissive Jack. Strong, wise, and capable Jack. Around him she felt stronger, more capable, too. If he were here, he'd take things in hand. . . .

By nightfall of his third day in London, Jack Huntingdon was indeed taking things in hand, quantities of good wine, playing cards, and other gentlemen's money, to be exact. He and Seabury had spent the better part of two days seeking out suitable lodgings, something in keeping with their new prosperity and yet something that would permit them some "freedom of association." Unfortunately, Jack's reputation in both flesh and finance had preceded him and there was some reluctance amongst landlords in respectable London precincts to make him their tenant.

Just as they were about to abandon all aspirations to respectability, they came upon word of a house owned by an ailing and charitable old widow in London's twin city of Westminster. She was anxious to quit the noise and bustle of the city, with her aging retainers, and was reluctant to leave her town residence unoccupied. Jack's courtly manner and his sincere-eyed promise to be a worthy steward of her property carried the day.

By the next nightfall, they were the sole occupants of a solid and pleasantly furnished house that nestled between the Strand and Covent Gardens.

Now, deep into that same night, Jack sat at the crimson-clad gaming tables at Lady Antonia's, London's most lavish palace of pleasure. His face was dusky with drink, though not enough drink to fill his head, and his hands were filled with a royal flush . . . and still he felt somehow empty. Around him, his peers and betters reveled noisily, drinking, gambling, and enjoying the charms of scantily clad wenches that Lady Antonia termed her "naughtie nieces." Lord Carlton Ferrar, Earl of Wolden, sat across from him with a cheery red face, a lap filled with a shapely young "niece," and a hand full of losing cards.

"Damme, Huntington," the pudgy, good-natured lordship said, shivering as the giggling wench devoured his ear and wriggled distractingly against him, "you've napped the devil's own luck tonight. I'm dem near cleaned!"

Jack grinned wryly and spread his winning hand to a noisy ragging from his fellow players. It was astounding good luck; he couldn't seem to lose. Taking a deep pull from his brandy-laced drink, he shrugged. "Lucky at cards . . . unlucky in love."

"Pish!" Ferrar laughed. "Old Scratch hisself pines for your luck wi' women. Go away again, Huntington! Give us mere mortals a sporting chance for a bit of seduction—" There was raucous agreement at that. "Where the hell did you disappear, anyway? Not Kent, I trow."

"Nay. Hertford." His drink-reddened grin faded a shade. "I . . . was married . . . a week past."

Exclamations of "Married!" and "Wedded—*you?*" accompanied hoots of astonished glee from around the table.

"Well, Hell's Hump, man, who is she?" Ferrar demanded, laughing.

"The Earl of Straffen's granddaughter, Lady Meredith." Jack took a deep breath and buried his nose in his goblet, feeling strangely empty and cursedly sober, though he knew himself to be neither. He was wondering what had possessed him to mention his marriage here, now.

"The Earl of Straffen." Ferrar squinted, trying to recall, as the wench on his knees invaded his doublet with eager fingers. "Lord, there's an old name. Haven't heard it since I was a stripling."

"Huntington—married!" The randy young Baron Bosworth, seated nearest Jack, roared, "This calls for a damned fine debauch!" He pounded the table and rose to call to the mistress for more drink and for her ablest "nieces" to companion the bridegroom. None of the rowdy company asked further after his bride. They all understood, as far as their woolly heads allowed, that it would be bad-mannered in the extreme to discuss a wife, even Gentleman Jack's wife, here. And Jack's presence in London's costliest flesh palace a mere week after the nuptials already said quite a bit about her.

They resolved to salve his nuptial disappointments with the finest feminine balm available. Jack soon found himself inundated by heated and perfumed bodies with rouged lips and nipples, some of the more noteworthy of which were already familiar to him. He graciously endured their toyings and rubbings and purrings and, like the gallant he was amongst women, he kissed their busy fingers and sent them on their way, one by one.

When only two were left, one of them, a voluptuous little blonde, snuggled her way onto his lap and at the drunken encouragement of his fellows began to undulate hungrily against him, to kiss him and nibble his ear. She was determined to sample the delights she had heard Gentleman Jack Huntington afforded, and so placed his supple hands on her scantily clad hip and artfully exposed breasts to encourage him. Of habit he began those motions, those caresses that were as natural as breathing to him. With a curious sense of detachment, he analyzed her eager enjoyment and his own mild arousal.

Mild? Alarm bloomed and spread through him. He coiled inside, making himself concentrate on her considerable charms and the dark promises of satisfaction imbedded in her eyes. A moment later he seized her pretty head between his hands and kissed her with all the raw sensuality at his command, demanding, exploring every combination of their mouths, pressing harder, devouring her bit by bit. And at each deepening level of physical sensation he found disappointment waiting. Her scent, the practiced tilt of her head, the textures of her mouth . . . all lacking. Something in his chest went soft and began to sink, opening a painful void in the middle of him.

He ended that stunning oral assault, his chest heaving, his lips bruised, and his head reeling. He looked at the wench's lustrous eyes, now black with desire, and was appalled to find no answering passion in his own frame. He swallowed hard, forcing what he hoped was a suitably lusty expression to satisfy the ribald urgings of his fellow revelers. But privately, he shivered with the awful realization of what was happening to him. He knew now . . . he was seeking the liquid satin of Merrie's mouth, Merrie's tempting little moans and wriggles, her startling blue eyes. It was Merrie's cuddles and kisses he wanted, and it confounded him that even his wretched loins seemed to know the difference between hers and someone else's. Nothing like this had ever happened to him before!

"Tend my winnings, milord!" He flashed a dazzling rascal's grin at Ferrar, braced and rose, lifting the wench up into his arms. He exited toward the stairs with a raucous chorus of laughter and bawdy advice lapping at his back. Mounting the steps determinedly, he followed the wench's breathless directions to an elegant chamber, where he deposited her at the door, placed two shining sovereigns in her questing hands, and bade her have a restful night. Then he reeled off, down the back steps, to roust bleary-eyed Seabury from a drinking bout in the less pricey establishment that was provided for gentlemen of lesser means on the floor below.

As they made the long, sobering trek back to Westminster, Jack felt a frightening, long-dormant urge uncoiling in his belly and shoving forcefully upward, trying to invade his chest. In full terror, he battled it . . . heaving, wrestling it to a standstill. By the time they reached their new home, beads of sweat lined his brow and his face was a shield of strain, but he had conquered the urge to *question* . . . once again.

By the time they located the small cache of wines and liquors the old widow had left behind in their new home, they were both horrifyingly sober. And they had to start over . . . to get roaring drunk.

A month after Jack Huntington's departure from Straffen, a rider came pounding down the road, aimed straight for Straffen's front doors. From his plain woolens and sturdy boots it was plain to see he was a groom, and his breakneck pace made the urgency of his errand clear. The lad pounced to the ground before the doors of the hall, just as Gert and Manley arrived. He bore greetings from a riding party of nobles who were coming Straffen's way with the intent of calling upon the newly wedded master and mistress.

Gert and Manley exchanged dark looks as they sent the breathless lad off with a houseboy to water his mount. It was just like a bunch of idle, feckless nobility, those looks said, to go riding aimlessly about the countryside all day and then descend on an honest, hardworking house just as the dinner hour neared. They'd expect hospitality, of course, food and drink and plenty of it, the slorpy hounds. And they'd expect to be received graciously by the master of the manor. The Lombards stared uneasily at each other. This was precisely the sort of thing they'd hoped to avoid. There was nothing for it but to receive the brood, stuff them with food, and be shed of them as quickly as possible.

Manley hurried off to warn Edythe and to trundle

quantities of ale, cider, and respectable sack up from the cellars. Gert took a steadying breath and hurried to the small parlor to inform Overbeake and Lady Merrie of the impending invasion.

"Guests?" Merrie pushed up from her seat, her eyes widening as the idea bloomed to unexpected excitement within her. She was so steeped in her solitary life that the notion that they might have callers had not even occurred to her until this moment. "But who are they? And what could they want?"

"They'll be wantin' to meet th' new master o' Straffen," Overbeake announced before Gert could reply. With a smug squint, she set her needlework aside and rose. "Ye'll have to host 'em in his stead. They be payin' respects, gell, and ye must prove worthy, like I taught ye." She turned on Goodwife Gert with an imperial air. "They'll be needin' refreshment, I trow. See to it, Goodwife, as I see to my lady."

Overbeake snatched Merrie's arm and dragged her past cutty-eyed Gert Lombard and up to the master chamber, to prepare her. Tess hurried to help change Merrie's gown and to brush her hair and replace her cap with a fashionable French hood. Sounds of arrival, hooves on stone and hounds yapping and voices clamoring above the din, drifted up to the gallery and into the master chamber. Merrie could scarcely mind Overbeake's shrill promptings on place and deference and who took precedence over whom.

Overbeake launched Merrie's stiff form toward the door to the gallery, hissing last-minute reminders of proper conversation. Merrie halted at the top of the stairs, part in seemly restraint, part in anxiety. The noise in the hall dropped precipitously as the riding party turned from scrutinizing the hall itself to searching the person of the hall's young mistress.

Word of the death of the reclusive earl and of the heirship and marriage of his unknown granddaughter had passed slowly through the countryside. But when the identity of the bridegroom was recently uncovered, interest in Gentleman Jack Huntington's bride had become positively feverish. And none were disappointed by the object of their curiosities.

She made a stunning picture, standing above them, swathed in a scoop-necked gown of luxuriant violet silk and a white heart-framed hood that echoed the heart-shape of her face. The translucent silk of her chemise, banded at her neck into a delicate ruff, hinted at the fullness of the breasts beneath, and a braided chain girdled and emphasized the smallness of her waist. Her fair skin and delicate features were flushed a becoming pink and her large, luminous eyes rivaled princely sapphires in color. She seemed to float down the stairs toward them, an unexpected vision of loveliness, with a stunning air of innocence.

Merrie's first impression was of an unruly rainbow; she'd never seen such a palate of hues and textures. And each lively blot of color contained a face that was trained on her in open assessment. She paused at the bottom of the steps and was surprised to find her voice quite steady as she announced:

"I bid you welcome to Straffen Hall, good lords and ladies. I am Meredith Straffen Huntington, newly come to my grandfather's house. My husband, John Huntington, is away in London for a time. In his stead, I extend warmest greetings to you and bid you sample our hospitality."

"Ah, lovely Lady Meredith!" An older gentleman in brilliant blue raiment and fashionably gartered boots stepped forward and took her hand with great ceremony. "You are as gracious as you are beautiful—is she not, gentlemen?" There was an outpouring of agreement that bordered on jovial rowdiness. "Since I outrank these hungry hounds," the fellow went on genially, still holding her hand captive in his, "I shall make the introductions. I am Edmund Layton, Earl of Epping, at your service." He made a courtly bow and turned to search the gathering for someone. "And my wife is here . . . somewheres. . . . No matter, you'll meet her later. And this fellow, with the peculiar taste in clothing"—the earl turned to gesture with mock severity to a fellow in a shocking lime-green doublet shot through with slashes lined in crimson and purple brocade—"is Lord Terrence Steverage—Baron Steverage."

The baron stepped forward to kiss her hand with a sly, suggestive look that lowered and lingered well below her face. "The old croat is jealous green," he intoned. "He knows that within the year the entire court will be wearing the fashion I set."

Merrie murmured a greeting, made a circumspect dip, and was reclaimed by the amicable earl for further introductions. An earl, a baron, a baroness, three squires, a Knight of the Garter, a dowager countess . . . It was overwhelming, being drawn into the midst of such an exalted company.

The names and faces and the powerful scents of horse, leather, sweat, and clashing perfumes began to run together in an overpowering fume. But Merrie's attention was riveted on the way the graying, robust earl bandied his rank about like a bludgeon and had a verbal skewer of some sort for each member of the party. They took his badgering and thrusts with able parries or good-humored ripostes that made it clear they took no real offense.

Such behavior was a direct contradiction of all she'd been taught about proper society and she scrambled to understand it. After few quick mental questions, she made a major discovery: she'd been taught awe of the nobility, not what the nobility were truly like. She caught a glimpse of Overbeake standing at the edge of the group, looking discomfitted and more pinch-mouthed than usual. The horsey old mistress was as shocked by their behavior as she was, Merrie realized. Then . . . all those wretched lectures on place and precedence and manners . . . all the instilled terror of the misstep and the gaffe in society was—

"Ah, here is my wife now." The earl was craning his neck toward the door where a lady in exquisite riding velvets was entering on the arm of none other than Sir Daniel Wycoff. Merrie's thoughts were interrupted as the twosome approached and separated to a slightly less scandalous distance. She glanced at the earl and found his eyes narrowed and his smile turned to carved stone. A moment later she extended her hand to Sir Daniel, who she had already met twice, and then to a beautiful, dark-haired woman who was years younger than her noble husband. The countess turned from baldly inspecting the hall to nod at Merrie. And Merrie froze.

That alabaster skin, that dark hair, those vivid exquisite features . . . It was Jack's vixen! Here, in the flesh, standing in her house, taking her hand. . . . She somehow managed a word of greeting and felt through their joined hand the countess's corresponding surprise. The countess uttered something cryptic about the joy of being a bride and continued her heated scrutiny of Gentleman Jack's wife behind a queenly and condescending smile.

At that moment, Manley entered with a noisy retinue of house servants bearing trays of food and trenchers and flagons. The interruption brought Merrie to her senses and she blushed and invited them to refresh themselves and to partake of food and drink as they desired. With the instant of awkwardness past, the group dispersed, some to wander about the great hall, admiring tapestries and furnishings and architecture, some to eat and drink, and some of the ladies to avail themselves of the offer of a cool bedchamber and the use of the necessary.

Merrie moved among her guests in mild shock, her mind beset by images of Jack and the countess together. A countess . . . Jack's vixen was a *countess* . . . the Earl of Epping's lady-wife! Over the last weeks, she'd purged the memory of what she'd witnessed at the inn. She didn't want to think of Jack like that, didn't want to recall that he'd been passion-roused and pleasuring another woman the first time she'd ever laid eyes on him. And now the vixen's presence at Straffen's table, abiding in Straffen's hospitality, brought it all back with a vengeance. The touches, the kisses, the nibbles and caresses . . . Merrie could scarcely breathe, much less attend the conversation going on around her.

Her preoccupation lent a demure air to her countenance, and among the guests the assessment was passed from eye to eye: Jack Huntington's wife was an angelic young thing. Behind veiled gazes, pictures were conjured of the two of them together, and heads shook covertly at the woeful mismatch.

Merrie endured one hour, then another. She found herself wedged between the earl and the foppish baron, whether walking about the grounds or seated in the hall. She managed an occasional word of wit and suffered their delighted laughter on grating nerves. It was something of a relief that the Countess Deirdre absented herself from both her husband's company and her hostess. But that small comfort was ruined by Merrie's sense that the rest of the group were just as unseemly eager to inspect both herself and Straffen Manor.

At length, she excused herself to see to her lady guests' comfort and, instead, slipped out the servants' door to the front gardens. She intended to stay just a few minutes, to collect herself. But as she rounded the first crook in the overgrown path, nearing the first secluded bench, she stopped in her tracks—just short of barging into the niche where two figures were embracing. She clamped a hand over her mouth to muffle her gasp of dismay and would have turned to go, except that the dim outline of the figures and a throaty, feminine murmur rooted her to the spot. It was . . .

". . . Deirdre, lovey, what a cat you are." It was Sir Daniel Wycoff, the queen's own agent, entwined with the haughty countess this time.

"It's true, Daniel," she murmured, wresting backward so that she coquettishly broke his light embrace. "She's a child, for God's sake, an insipid little squeak. All huge, ridiculous eyes and hideous red hair. Small wonder he's gone back in London a mere month after the vows. There's nothing to keep him here."

"Sheath your claws, lovey"—he caught her around the waist again—"and let's not waste breath—"

"Really, Daniel." She stiffened and he relented, releasing her and sinking onto the bench while she aired her stinging pride. "It's plain to see why he's married her. It's the hall, the manor." She gestured broadly around her. "Edmund said this place was probably derelict and a shambles; the old earl was such a miserly recluse. I couldn't imagine what would possess a known rake and gambler like Jack to suddenly *marry* and install himself in a decrepit old country house. I should have known; the handsome bastard has too grand a taste for elegance, and for women, to be mired away in some absurd, penniless marriage. Just look at the place. Ripe for the picking. The knave always did have an uncanny knack for getting the most out of a woman." Her naughty laugh drove home her double meaning and Wycoff laughed.

"I must credit the stud; he's feathered a fine nest here."

"If he doesn't mind scouring his shins on that green stick by night," she snapped.

"But, as you say, he's not 'scouring his shins,' lovey," Wycoff reminded her tauntingly.

"True." The countess took vengeful delight in the thought. "He's back in London, probably plowing a deep furrow through several lucky chits. I trow, he couldn't wait to escape. He was never one to go too long without a good jogging, and I believe he only requires a quarter of an hour between 'occasions' . . . or between women."

She arched a challenging look at Wycoff, who snorted at the thinly veiled goad. In a flash, he was on his feet and pulling her forcefully into her arms. She turned her face at the last minute and his kiss landed on her ear and slid greedily down her neck. Her sharp laugh was meant to goad him to greater amorous effort, but its greatest impact was on their unseen audience.

"Perhaps I'll find excuse to go to London in a few

days," she crooned breathily, "and help him spend the chit's money."

"Witch!" Wycoff clamped her savagely against his body and from beneath his bruising kiss, the haughty vixen moaned with sensual triumph.

Merrie stumbled from the gardens in a haze of misery and disbelief. The scathing derision of herself as a woman, the revelation of Jack's past, and the cruel conjecture on his present were crushing. Standing there, naive in the ways of feminine manipulation and reeling from the way her world seemed to be shifting beneath her feet, she had drunk those poisonous barbs into her heart. Now they did their deadly work. Jack, her Jack, in London with other vixens . . . pleasuring them.

Somehow, despite the lead in her limbs and through a blinding blur of tears, she made it to the house, up the servant stairs, and into the master chamber. Her legs buckled beneath her and she sank to the floor beside a chair.

Her whole world was turned upsidedown. Jack, her loving, warm, permissive Jack . . . they'd called him a gambler and a rake who had married her to have her inheritance. They said he had other vixens—one every quarter of an hour!—and likely couldn't wait to escape *her* to get back to them! And as those awful jibes rumbled in her ears, the memory of him in the countess's arms and of his haste to be away after the wedding lent credence to that awful possibility. He wouldn't have time for her, he had said. In her heart now, she gave those words new interpretation: no time for her . . . with all his vixens to pleasure.

The mystery of why he was so intent on marrying her, in spite of her resistance and unsuitability, was finally solved. It was money, land, a solid living he wanted, and he saw Straffen as a goodly prize. Despair welled in her. She was a mere child, a "green stick" with eyes that were too big and hair that was a hideous, brazen color, and who fainted when he so much

as kissed her. How she must have taxed his worldly
tastes. The sound of his laughter on their wedding
night echoed cruelly in her empty heart, and her humiliation boiled over into great scalding tears. She buried her head in her arms and sobbed.

Tess found her there, on the floor, crying her heart
out into the seat pillow of the chair. Tess could get no
explanation for her mistress's tears, beyond a shake of
the head to the question of whether she was ill. When
Tess helped her to the bed, Merrie swiped at her wet
face and reddened eyes and implored: "I can't go back
to them. Oh, Tess, you must tell them I'm . . . taken
ill . . . with a terrible megrim! Beg Master Lombard to
see them on their way, in all haste!" Tess looked into
the misery in Merrie's face and nodded.

Within minutes, the news was whispered to Goodwife Gert, who whispered it to Manley. Manley
scowled and stiffened and strode through the hall to
find the leader of the noble pack, the Earl of Epping.
He cannily informed the lord of his lady's indisposal
and assured him, "She give orders ye was to enjoy th'
hall and hospitality fer as long as it pleases ye."

With the delightful little lady of Straffen removed,
the earl was pleased to stay no longer and rousted his
companions to depart Straffen. One by one, they expressed concern for the little mistress's health and
mounted their horses, ignoring Overbeake's gray-faced
assurances that they needn't leave.

Chapter Thirteen

The chamber door slammed back minutes later and a purple-face typhoon surged into the dusky master chamber. Young Tess was hot on the old mistress's heels, begging her to wait, pleading Merrie's illness. But Overbeake advanced on Merrie in a terrible rage, demanding to know what madness had possessed her to abandon her noble guests so. In a blink she was snatching Merrie from the bed and dragging her to the middle of the floor.

The sight of Merrie's reddened eyes and swollen nose infuriated her. "Of all th' feckless, senseless . . . shamin' the repute of Straffen with yer lilly-livered shrinkin'! How dare ye withdraw and leave a belted earl coolin' his heels in th' hall in want of ye? What have ye got to say fer yerself, chit?"

Merrie was dumb with grief. How could she explain what she'd learned from their "noble" guests—or the pain it had brought her? Her husband was a known rake and gambler who had married her fortune, not herself. He had found her so lacking as a woman and a wife that he left her after two days of marriage. How could she say that the thought that he craved the pleasures of other women left her feeling small and worthless, or that the thought of him joined in deepest passion to one of his London vixens—perhaps even the haughty Deirdre, soon—was like a knife turning in her? What kind of excuse was a breaking heart to a mistress who'd never had a heart?

"I s-say—" She choked and began struggling frantically to break away. "I say—let go!"

Surprise at her sudden resistance loosened Overbeake's grip just long enough for Merrie to wrench free.

She caught herself as she stumbled and then backed toward the door, staring at Overbeake through angry tears. When she reched the door and bolted past Tess into the gallery, the outraged mistress was not far behind, determined to bring her charge to heel.

Merrie had cleared the stairs and was halfway to the front doors before Overbeake overtook her and jerked her to a halt by the arm, hissing furious orders for her to stop this nonsense or face dire consequences. Gert and Manley Lombard had heard the row and rushed into the hall, just as Tess came flying down the steps. Together, they jostled their way through the other house servants, who were collecting into an anxious ring nearby.

Merrie strained away and wrested her arm in Overbeake's grip, looking desperately about for help. "Please—" But there was no one to intervene on her behalf; the Lombards stood in proper shock, and Tess and the other servants stared in helpless horror. *If only Jack—*

Jack. White-hot pain shot through her already savaged spirit. Jack wasn't here. And he wasn't coming; she knew that now. The great emptiness inside her was cavernous. There was only her. . . .

In that moment's harsh impasse, Overbeake seemed to realize the spectacle they were making before the entire household. "Get to yer chamber—this instant!" When Merrie made no move to obey, Overbeake jerked Merrie's arm and snarled the order again, punctuating it with her long-standing coercion, a vicious pinch.

Pain lashed through Merrie and the day's overwhelming anguish rose in her on a rush of anger. Her arm was back before she could think and her hand slammed forward, smashing into the old harridan's cheek with all the force she could muster. Overbeake staggered back, clutching her face in disbelief, and Merrie swayed briefly herself, suspended between exultant fury and bald shock.

"I-I . . . I won't be pinched and bullied."

"How dare ye—" Overbeake quivered with stunned fury.

"How dare *you?*" Merrie had finally sounded the depths of her hurt, and now rose, splintering the cramped and dutiful shell of submission that had bound her for four long years. The despair of her heart had set spark to the tinder of a blazing defiance a long time in the making.

"I am mistress here, am I not?" Her pain-luminous eyes fixed on the Lombards, half in anguished appeal, half in demand. She dodged Overbeake's punishing grasp, then stopped and braced, refusing to flee again. "And if I am old enough to be a wife, and to receive nobles in this hall, then surely I am old enough to choose my own clothing and order my own time. I'm lettered beyond most men and I know at least as much about the nobility and proper behavior as Mistress Overbeake—and *more* about womanhood and wifery! She's never even been married! I'm no idler who must be prodded and cuffed; I've been diligent in learning my duties toward Straffen."

It was true, every word of it. The Lombards exchanged horrified looks at the raging pain in Merrie's countenance. They'd seen too much of Merrie's earnestness and too much of her wrenching loneliness of late; it had begun to work on them.

"I've learned the lessons of gell-hood. I don't need a governess anymore," Merrie declared desperately, giving her swelling anger free rein. It was too late to turn back—she didn't ever want to turn back—no matter what happened. "And if I must have a companion, then . . . then I should have the right to choose one for myself. And it would never be *her!*" She flung a furious finger at her erstwhile governess.

Shocked silence reigned as Overbeake choked with fury and glared at the Lombards, demanding their support. But she was very much mistaken if she expected them to endorse her tyranny this time. They'd seen too much of her puff-adder temper and her inflated estimate of herself. With something akin to guilt at the hurt their charge had suffered, Manley reluctantly ratified her bid for freedom.

"Wull . . . who *would* ye choose fer compan-yun?" As he cast a cutty-eyed look at Overbeake, the old mistress began to sputter and protest in decidedly less than Christian terms.

Merrie reeled, unable to believe her ears. Were they actually listening to her? "Why . . . I—I'd choose . . ." She spotted Tess's pale face and earnest brown eyes trained on her and she pointed at the little maid. "Tess! I'd choose Tess. And I'd see Mistress Overbeake *sacked* and packed off within the hour!"

Sweet, dutiful Tess. It was a splendidly convenient choice, to the Lombard's minds. They exchanged borning looks of relief, and Overbeake snarled and started for Merrie with her fingers twitching. Merrie held her ground, bracing for the worst, when Gert Lombard stepped between them.

"It appears, Mistress Overbeake, ye been sacked."

Granite-jawed Overbeake was indeed sacked and packed and deposited in the back of a horse cart bound for the town of Witham, before an hour was past. Merrie stood on the gallery, watching her leave through a window overlooking the courtyard. With every turn of the cart's wheels, Merrie felt some of the burden of her heart lifting. She was free of the old harridan—*free!* For the first time ever, she was mistress for herself! She savored the grown-up sense of freedom, but the joy she had expected to feel was tempered by the painful circumstances that had brought it about.

She watched until the cart was out of sight, then, realizing there was no one to say her nay, went for a walk by herself onto the hill overlooking Straffen. Freedom was no longer the ultimate fulfillment it had once seemed for her. She stopped under that great old tree where Jack had asked her to wed him. He rose in her mind, his expression tender, as it had been in private-most moments. As she watched, enrapt, his lips parted as though he would kiss her and her own parted to receive them. She froze, aching with expectation that would go unfilled.

Jack. His slow, tantalizing persuasions to loving had made her feel beautiful, adored. His tender caresses, his interest in her unthinkable questions, the freedom she'd felt in his presence, all had broadened her world, had somehow opened her to new possibilities that were slowly being realized in her life. She recalled the wondrous glow in his tawny eyes when he looked at her. Did he gaze upon all his vixens that way? Did he make them feel beautiful and adored? Did he make them love him, too?

Love him? She held her aching breast above her heart, and knew it was true. She loved Jack Huntington . . . Gentleman Jack. He'd made her love him with his natural charm, his easy indulgence of her quirks of mind, and his breathtaking sensuality. She'd given her heart and there was no calling it back.

Tears squeezed from between her lashes. It was too much to hope that she might have won a place in his heart, but had she never pleased him at all? Had there been nothing but a rake's beguiling skill in his fonden touch?

If she'd only had a bit more time. . . . But then, what chance would she have stood against beautiful, titled ladies who were accomplished in fleshly pleasures, and who craved his loving, too? Jack was a man to whom women's love came easily . . . and apparently meant little. She'd fallen in love with a true knave of hearts.

"Do give my regards to his lordship." Jack nodded as he tucked the lady's lacy petticoats into the sedan chair and drew the leather side-curtain past her crimson face. "Walk on!" he ordered the bearers and released a controlled breath as they lifted the enclosed chair and shuffled off into the cobbled Westminster street.

Seabury appeared at Jack's elbow, on the front step of their house. "I take it her ladyship was expecting

. . . better entertainment.'' He met Jack's look with an inquiring rise of brows.

''I'm . . . not in the mood.'' Jack turned and strode back into the house and back into his snug parlor, which was cluttered with papers and books. Seabury shook his head and followed. He couldn't count the number of times that strained little scene had been enacted on the front step in the last three weeks. Another nubile, overheated lady gone off in disappointment. Jack had taken to reading to them, often in Latin. They usually didn't stay long; he sounded too much like their priests when he began rattling on in the church's chosen tongue, and the last thing on their minds was confession.

An hour later, another guest appeared, the handsome Baron Bosworth. He'd apparently come to inspect Jack's circumstances and moved about the parlor, assessing the comfortable carved chairs, fine tables, and hanging tapestries with long, elegant fingers. He politely declined Jack's offer of a fencing bout, and Jack politely declined his offer to bring a party of ''choice young friends'' by that evening to liven up the place. When Jack tried to engage the rakish baron in discussion on a book he'd been reading, Bosworth's tolerance for such pursuits proved no greater than that of the ladies in Jack's life.

Seabury reentered the front hallway from seeing the baron off and found Jack leaning a shoulder on the parlor doorway, still scowling at the book in his hands. ''Lord, this Desiderius Erasmus is a piece of work. He's probably where old Overbeake got it—'' He raised a dark look to Seabury. ''He's very big on pinching.''

''I take it the baron wasn't enthralled with your resurgent scholarship?''

''You surely find out who your friends are when you start *reading* to them.'' Jack looked disgusted and took a seat on the nearby steps, closing the book. ''I tell you, Bosworth has no earthly idea what to do in the case of an outbreak of malt bugs in his wheat. And not the foggiest notion of the conditions of his grain storage and whether he has a proper partridge population in his hedgerows or not. It's a sorry comment on the state of England's landed manhood, that's what it is."

Seabury joined him on the steps and they both propped their chins in their palms. They were discontent personified, the pair of them.

"Are you aware you've spent near all your considerable winnings this last month on books?" Seabury asked. Jack seemed genuinely surprised and shook his head. "Well, you have. I've begun keeping a record of all our expenditures and your winnings in a bound ledger. I read a pamphlet on it. It was quite enlightening."

"Indeed?"

"In fact, I've discovered I quite like ciphering and numbers. Did I ever tell you my father was a banking clerk?"

"I don't believe so." Silence descended on them for a time. Each stared off into a private vision; Jack's was blue-eyed, Seabury's was brown-eyed.

"Lord, Jack," Seabury said, voicing their common worry, "look at us, doddering about, keeping hours with the chickens." It sounded even worse, spoken aloud, than when they'd just thought it. Jack drew himself up, scowling, and set his jaw.

"We've got to get out more. Tonight! Dammit—*every* night!" he declared forcefully.

A full week later, in the midst of Lady Antonia's gilt-and-satin pen of pleasure, the wine was running freely and the gaming was at full tilt all around Jack Huntington. He blinked, trying to concentrate on his handful of queens. Their inked faces kept fading to lovely satin tones and their regal coifs kept bursting into fiery, red-gold flame. He closed his eyes and emitted the hugely dissatisfied sigh that had become his habit of late.

"Whatever is the matter with you, Huntington?" Ferrar cocked an irritable look at him. "Antonia says that glum puss and damnable luck of yours is driving her trade clean away. We should all just hand over our purses at the start of the eve and save ourselves the humiliation of losing to you again!"

"Your estates, Ferrar . . . your farms . . ." Jack raised a distracted look that said he hadn't heard a word. "What do you know about grain storage? And markets . . . Where are the best markets for surplus gr—"

"This is the damned limit, Huntington!" Baron Bosworth snorted his final disgust, throwing his hand of cards on the table and stalking off to seek more diverting company. The others at the table followed his lead, casting looks at Jack that ranged from ripely annoyed to near bloodthirsty. After a full month of his abominable distraction, his phenomenal luck at gambling, and his sudden bizarre obsessions with the workings of provincial estates, they were ready to renounce him forever.

"God's Liver, Huntington, what do I look like—a damned bailiff?" Ferrar barked. "Get a copy of Tusser's *Five Hundred Points of Good Husbandry* and quit badgering me about my estates. First hedgerows, then the possible uses of hog offal—"

"Excellent notion." Jack raised a beguiling, lopsided grin, to Ferrar's indignation. "I've been meaning to ask you to recommend another bookseller. I've got a rough translation of Ovid, but I have desperate need of a copy in sound Latin."

"*Ovid*?" Ferrar's furrowed face suddenly smoothed with astonishment. Love poetry . . . Jack wanted Ovid! "By damn. It *is* a woman! Bosworth said it was!"

In spite of himself, Jack flushed. Ferrar bounded from his chair and bustled around the table to deposit himself next to Jack, his face filled with predatory glee. "I thought this monkishness of yours preposterous. God, Jack Huntington and a woman. . . ."

Jack was all too aware of just how absurd it sounded and of how pathetic a figure he must make to his fast-going companions. In all layers of London's worldly and fashionable society, nothing was considered more laughable than a besotted rake. There was a perverse and irresistible irony in the sight of a man who had flagrantly enjoyed countless women, now reduced to pining for one.

"How awful!" Excitement squeezed into Ferrar's whisper as he leaned close. "Who is she?"

It was galling in the extreme to suffer Ferrar's taunting condolence and curiosity, but Jack was in need of solace, any solace, just now. He took a deep pull from his goblet and turned a look on Ferrar that set the pudgy earl all aquiver with expectation. Jack opened his mouth, closed it, and took yet another pull of his wine.

"She's married," Ferrar guessed, logically.

Jack sighed quietly and made a nearly imperceptible nod. The pain collecting in his tawny eyes said they were beholding some inner vision of her, even now. And it spoke eloquently of his lady's inacessibility. Not in his wildest fancy could Ferrar have guessed that Jack's forbidden lady-love happened to be married to none other than Jack himself!

"God's Spleen! And she's *virtuous*." Ferrar said, hazarding yet another guess, holding his breath.

Jack nodded again, seeing Merrie in his mind and thinking that "virtuous" was a pale, lifeless word to apply to something so rare and vibrant as she. She was spirited and curious and wise beyond her years . . . and desirable and sensual and unpredictable . . . and good, so very good. All the noblest hallmarks of mankind seemed to have been compressed into her odd and delectable being. And when she turned those huge, searching eyes on him, and bestowed that generous, forgiving smile, he wanted desperately to believe she saw something good in him, too. As he thought of her, the heat that seeped into his eyes melted them to shimmering bronze.

"Poor bastard." Ferrar shook his head and clapped Jack on the shoulder. "Go home, Huntington."

Jack shoved to his feet, fully preoccupied with his mental vision, and headed for the main doors, forgetting the gold coins on the table and inured to the bevy of "naughtie nieces" bent on intercepting him.

Ferrar, beside himself with excitement, made a straight line for young Bosworth, who was leaning on the mantelpiece, tossing back strong brandy and fondling the wenches collected around him. Ferrar plucked him from them and jerked a nod toward Jack, who was now surrounded by four of Lady Antonia's loveliest.

"You're right, you clevershins. It *is* a woman." The earl fairly twinkled with anticipation as Bosworth straightened with interest. "I didn't get her name, but she's married," Ferrar supplied triumphantly, *"and* virtuous."

"God. I knew it!" Bosworth narrowed a wickedly competitive grin at the caresses and busses Jack was bribing the wenches with as he tried to leave. "Do you know, I went by his house in Westminster a few days ago and—Lud!—it's like a bloody schoolroom. Stacks of *books*. Found him engrossed in a volume on civil methods of *child rearing*. And he delivered me a heated lecture on the barbarity of some Dutch fellow named Erasmus, who apparently instructs parents and nurses that laughter and foot swinging and fidgets are signs of either empty-headedness or wickedness in the soul. Damned peculiar interest—children—for a rake like Huntington. There's only one thing that turns a man's mind in that direction . . . a *skirt.*"

They watched Jack pat buttocks and tweak rouged nipples as he snatched his hat from the boy at the door and made his exit. Only two months ago, they knew, he'd have swept the wenches up the stairs with him and left them all heavy-eyed and sated the following noon. They exchanged knowing grins.

"Poor bastard."

By the time Jack reached the street, he was feeling the first twinges of panic. He was desperate to escape the cloying scent of women that clung to him, and nearly as desperate to escape his own memories and desires. These last weeks he'd tried to keep thoughts of Merrie at bay, occupying his mind with reading and discussion and his body with the rigors of strenuous fencing and riding. He'd found himself worrying about Straffen's supply of bees and whether the orchard was being properly pruned, and went among his landed friends in search of answers. Then, by night, he tried to bury himself in the temptations of Antonia's and made the horrifying discovery the Antonia's held no temptations for him anymore. It was unnerving the way his body seemed to ignore all that delectable flesh and willingness. He might have worried about his lack of sexual interest, except for the hot visitations of desire he experienced in his solitary bed at night. It was achingly clear to him: his body answered to one master, and it certainly was not himself.

He flipped the fellow who held his horse a ha'penny and swung into the saddle, headed toward Westminster without a single thought of Seabury or even the hazards of the steamy London night. He kept seeing the amusement, the pity, and the promise of scandal in his companions' faces. By tomorrow night it would be all over London: Jack Huntington was besotted with somebody's wife.

Somebody's wife? His own wife, dammit! And what a horselaugh it would be if *that* got out: the woman who stirred his blood and wrecked his peace and made his life an agony of wanting was the one woman to whom he was legally entitled! A cold shiver of dread raced through his broad shoulders in the sultry night air. His mind and senses sprang to life, quivering, alarmed. *Legally entitled.* It echoed wildly off the hardening walls of his body.

She was his . . . his *wife*. He felt a long-tied knot uncoiling deep in his belly again and recognized it as the binding that held his most feared urge in check. His jaw clamped shut and his fists clenched on the reins as he grappled with it and his heels dug into his mount.

When he reached his house, he thudded to the cobbled street and crashed through the door, startling the aging footman awake and growling a tortured order to see to his horse. He took the stairs by twos and threes, fleeing the force that was freed and rising inside him. But by the time he blew into his stuffy, darkened chamber, the pressure had shoved upward into his chest, constricting his lungs, squeezing his heart. He could scarcely breathe! He staggered to the window, threw it open, and ripped the confining ruff from his neck.

His shoulders twitched; every muscle in his body strained against the storm that was surging through him. Sweat banded his forehead and trickled icily down his neck. The impulse overwhelmed his resistance, possessing him completely. His handsome features contorted into a grimace and he bit his lip savagely in a last, desperate attempt to hold it back. Then a final lightning surge of power erupted from the depths of his loins, tore through his belly and chest, and blasted free the clamped hinges of his jaws.

"W-w-wh—" he rasped, unable to breath or swallow against the force of the outrushing question. "W-wh— . . . *why?*" For one breathless moment, it hovered on the air amidst pure silence—scintillant, triumphant, supreme—a question dredged from the very depths of his being. "Why?" It rumbled through the chamber like approaching thunder as he repeated it in convulsive, cathartic volleys. "Why . . . why . . . dammit . . . *why?*"

He gripped the window ledge for support as wave after wave of long-suppressed questions welled in him, demanding expression. But there was only one why that mattered just now . . . the one that had waged war against the worldly complaisance of his nature and had won. *"Why did I have to leave her?"*

No sooner was it said than it began dividing and subdividing, ordering itself into a logical and relentless chain of inquiry that multiplied to fill the emptiness in him. Why him? it began. Why in God's Name would anybody choose *him* to wed an innocent . . . any innocent, much less a little jewel like Merrie Straffen?

He was lustful and opportunistic and jaded and self-centered . . . and probably greedy and materialistic and a host of other nasty things he hadn't even thought of yet. These last eight years he'd lived his life recklessly, for himself alone, his pleasures, his pride. Why would any grandfather, no matter how crotchet ridden or perverse, choose such a mate for his lovely granddaughter?

And why Merrie? Why did it have to be Merrie he was contracted to wed? Merrie with her caressing eyes and petal-soft lips. Merrie with her endless questions and ageless, wizened soul. Merrie with her curious mind and equally curious body. Merrie who hungered to be touched and who yielded to him as though he were part divine. What in his entire life had he ever done to deserve something like her?

Unseeing, unblinking, he surrendered to her conjured presence, letting the painful sweetness of it slice through him at will. Merrie. He couldn't drink without seeing the glisten of wine on her lips, couldn't eat without recalling the ravenous way she bit a honey bun . . . and let the wayward drops of honey slide erotically down her breasts. He couldn't button his shirt without feeling the whisper of her fingers across his chest. His senses transformed all perception into rememberance of her; candle flame became her hair, the sound of trickling water her laughter, and the fine burn of brandy became the heat of her kisses.

Why would they buy her a husband and then— He staggered from the window, feeling gut-punched, gripped the post of the bed for support. He had most certainly been bought; the realization sickened him.

But why would they go to the trouble of buying her a husband and then allow her only one night with him? What sense was there in a marriage where the partners never saw each other and from which no heirs were expected or even desired? His eyes widened in horror. The old man had apparently wanted her wedded and bedded, but had adamantly withheld all hope of children from her. Why?

Out of the recesses of memory crept a still, small voice, repeating the disturbing conclusion of his betrothal day: "The gell knows nothing at all about her own marriage." Lord, why hadn't he asked these questions then? He'd known things weren't right. One look at Merrie's enchanting face and lush body had told him that. And when he learned she didn't want to marry him . . . why hadn't he asked *then?*

He slumped onto the edge of the bed and buried his face in his hands. The pained confusion in Merrie's blue eyes and the sound of her calling his name as he left her dug into his heart like spurs.

What kind of man was he to seduce and wed and leave her? *Or was he any kind of man at all?*

For several hours, Jack wrestled with his private demons in that upper room. He'd lived all his life as though he had nothing to lose, for as the youngest of four sons, he'd *had* nothing to lose—no land, no money, no promise of a future. He'd rebelled and rejected his family's standards because they offered him nothing but a lifetime of strangling duty and penurious, galling obeisance. Now, for the first time in his life, he did have something to lose . . . someone. Merrie. His wife.

As the first gray steaks of dawn appeared in the sky, Seabury came bursting through the door, eyes wide, chest heaving. The sight of Jack in a chair by the window, his shoulders rounded and his head in his hands, stopped him in his tracks.

"Lord, Jack, I looked everywhere—" His voice dropped to a grave whisper. "What's happened?"

Jack lifted a shadowed face and fixed him with eyes that were haunted and intense. "God knows I can't undo it . . ." His voice was hoarse and strained. ". . . but I have to find out who really wanted this marriage . . . and why. Why did they want me to marry and leave her?" He rose and squared his broad shoulders, accepting the weight of genuine caring on them for the first time in a very long while. "And I have to be sure she's all right."

It took something powerful indeed to bring Jack Huntington to such a state, Seabury realized. It was the first real question he had heard Jack ask in all their years together.

"There's one place to start." Jack turned to Seabury with a decisive set to his jaw. "Bedford. We're going to see her guardian. What in hell was his name . . . Garwin? Granley? Gadfly?"

"Gannulf!" Seabury supplied, grinning. "Sir Edgar Gannulf."

Chapter Fourteen

As it happened, it was Sir *Edwin* Gannulf, and his home was just outside the town of Bedford. It was a large, tumbledown house of wattle and daub, shored up over the years by thick brick buttresses. It nestled, like the ill-kept fields around it, in an air of neglect, as though the house and its owner had both been forgotten. Exterior shutters hung askew and weeds had overwhelmed the gravel of the entry court.

Jack pulled down his woolen traveling doublet and set a gloved hand to the crusty door nail. After each volley of knocks, he shot a doubtful look at Seabury, who stood a few paces behind, holding their horses. He was about to cry off and look for another entry when he heard a scraping, like a bar being drawn.

The door screeched open on rusty hinges and a withered, sexless prune of a face appeared in the opening, scowling against the bright light. "Whaddaye wont?"

"I am John Huntington of Kent, here to see Sir Edwin on a matter of great importance."

"Wull . . . Sarr Edwin don' see nobudy." The old croat closed the door, though not quickly enough to prevent Jack's boot from wedging in it. "Hey—"

"Sir Edwin will see me." Jack pushed the door back against the surprised fellow's hold and stepped inside a darkened hall. It was better kept than the exterior, but still had an air of disuse about it. He removed his gloves and strolled audaciously past the aging houseman, claiming, "I am his nephew's wife's son by her second marriage and I've come to see my granduncle on the matter of my recent inheritance." He gave the fellow a lidded, impatient look and waited for the words "uncle" and "inheritance" to have an effect. In houses like this, part of the gentry's gaunt underbelly, such words usually worked magic . . . even if they were lies.

"Wull." The old fellow appeared confused, then seemed to recall something and grow more assured. "Sarr Edwin, he ain't feeling smartly this week. Ain't seein' nobudy." His watery eyes flicked toward the stairs as he spread and flapped his arms to sweep Jack and Seabury back out the door.

"Oh, I'm certain he'll want to see *me*." Jack barreled past the fellow, heading for the stairs. "You needn't fear, I shan't tax him. Just a few precious moments of dear Uncle's time . . ."

While Jack strode the empty gallery with Seabury, the old servant scuttled off into another part of the house as quickly as he could go. They peered into one dark room after another until they came to a partly open door that cast dim light on the worn gallery floor. They pushed back the door and stepped inside.

It was once a goodly chamber, generous in size and probably well furnished in its day. Now a massive old bed with faded hangings dominated the room and in the bed was the faded figure of a man, neatly capped and tucked within the covers. They approached warily and came to a halt by the bed, staring first at a side table filled with vials and jars and apothecaries, and then at the old man who required them. He had to be eighty if he was a day.

" 'Ain't feeling smartly this week,' " Jack muttered, gesturing to the display of medicaments. "Nor any week, from the looks of it." He leaned close to the old man. "Sir Edwin? Sir Edwin, can you hear me?"

The old fellow's eyes fluttered open and Jack let out the breath he'd been holding. "Eh? That you, Alfie?"

"No sir. It's John Huntington, Sir Edwin, and I do regret imposing upon your sickbed like this, but I'm desperate for a bit of information. I'm Lady Merrie Straffen's husband. You know, your ward Merrie Straffen, the Earl of Straffen's granddaughter? I wish to know the terms of the old earl's will and why I was selected for her husband.''

''Earl?'' The old man's time-dulled eyes dimmed with confusion. ''Where's Alfie? Who's Earl? Is 't time fer m' powders? An' broth . . . with salt . . .'' He laid a thin, blue-veined hand on Jack's sleeve with a puzzled, childlike expression. ''Who're you? Have 'e got my buttered bread?''

Jack glanced at Seabury and tried again. ''Please, Sir Edwin, try to think. Why did the old earl choose me to wed Merrie? Did he discuss it with you before he died?''

But it was no good. Old Sir Edwin was quite incapable of telling them anything they needed to know, or even of remembering that he'd been named Merrie's guardian. They bade him rest and withdrew to the door, then to the gallery, in puzzlement.

They were halfway down the stairs when there was a flurry at the rear of the hall and the old houseman reappeared, bringing someone with him that Jack and Seabury recognized. The very corpulent Master William Makepiece, Sir Edwin's solicitor, whom they'd met at the wedding made straight for them as fast as his hamlike gams would carry him. His step faltered when he drew close enough to recognize them, but then quickened to intercept them at the base of the stairs.

''Master Huntington! 'Pon my word, s-sir, I had no idea!'' His instant of distress was quickly cloaked beneath a broad, ingratiating smile. ''What a sh—. . . surprise you've given me, sir.''

''Master Makepiece, I believe.'' Jack nodded.

''When Alfred said there was someone here inquiring after an inheritance, I feared . . .'' Makepiece rattled on, flicking a sweaty glance at the stairs, then recovering enough to strike an artful pose. ''That is, I manage all Sir Edwin's affairs and I couldn't recall anyone that h-had—''

''Seabury and I were in the area with a hunting party.'' Jack paused, toying with his gloves while he invented a plausible reason for having come. The house-man had gone straight for the old fellow's solicitor, he realized. And the laywer must have been very close at hand. Protecting his interests in the old man's estate?

"I must confess, sir, that is not the full truth." There was no one in the world who knew how to use a sincere-eyed look to better advantage than Jack Huntington. Now he wielded it superbly. "I did come to Bedford intending to pay a call upon Sir Edwin—to beg a boon of him."

"A boon, sir?" Makepiece's smile was so oily it nearly slid from his face. "Sir Edwin is hardly in a position—"

"A monstrous great boon, sir." Jack filled with subtle drama. "I was given to know that when Sir Edwin negotiated the marriage contracts with my family—"

"He what?"

"Master Cramden told me how Sir Edwin was responsible for my marriage."

"He did?" Makepiece's beady eyes darted back and forth as he tried to decipher why Cramden would have told Jack such a thing and whether Jack's tone had hinted at credit or blame.

"Emphatically. And now that I think on it, I must say . . . there are some conditions of the agreements which are exceedingly odd."

"There are?" The risk of blame suddenly overwhelmed the possibility of credit.

"Oh, sir," Makepiece said, choosing the expedient path, "I must correct any such notion straightaway. Sir Edwin had naught to do with your marriage contracts." Once begun, his hasty denials kept tumbling forth. "Indeed, the good knight has been just as you have seen him for a very long time. Hasn't had a lucid moment in weeks . . . months! His guardianship of your lady-wife was surely considered a formality, an arrangement between old friends, nothing more. Your marriage was certainly the result of the old earl's wishes and last testament, sir."

Jack sighed, adopting a confidential air as he turned

wary Makepiece toward the front doors with him. "Such grievous news. You see, it is known, sir, that I have been estranged from my family for some time. I was hoping to beg Sir Edwin's aid in reestablishing ties with my brother Henry—Baron Huntington. Such a mischance. Well . . . I suppose I shall just have to brave it on my own."

Makepiece watched Jack and Seabury mount their horses and rein off. His mind buzzed now that imminent danger was past. They'd had a cozy arrangement for some years, he and Lawyer Richard Cramden, trading legal sleights of hand, notarizing and verifying dealings with one eye closed. He was loath to see their lucrative association end. Ever a man to tend both sides of his fences, Makepiece hurried off to send a warning to Cramden that this Huntington fellow was in the area . . . asking questions.

Once on the London road again, Jack and Seabury reined up, glancing uneasily at each other. "Sir Edwin had nothing to do with it; I'll credit that," Jack said.

"It must have been the old earl's will, then," Seabury supplied.

"But why?" Jack took a deep breath and stared searchingly at Seabury, who could only shrug. "Cramden knew about me. Then the old earl had to know. And still they chose me for Merrie's husband." He shook his head. It didn't make sense. "Do you suppose the old man was peculiar in matters of the flesh and wanted her to remain . . . ? But they gave her to me, insisted I consummate the vows. Then, what's the point in sending me away, in leaving Merrie alone?"

In spite of the warm evening, a broad chill coursed through him. She was alone. Alone in that rambling house. Alone in her marriage bed in the dark of night. . . . The sight of her as she slept on that morning after their marriage flooded his mind and overflowed into his hungry frame; her perfectly matched features and her exquisite body, tangled in covers and fiery, love-tousled hair. She was so warm and soft and eager . . . and vulnerable. So damned vulnerable.

"Dammit!" He started, trying unsuccessfully to shake off the potent, rousing effects of her image and the unholy sense of dread his own questions raised in him. His jaw set grimly. "I have to see her."

"Of course you do," Seabury agreed, watching the carnal struggle in Jack's roguish eyes and starting to grin.

"I have to make sure she's safe." Jack glowered at him.

"Oh, absolutely." Seabury's grin broadened wickedly, filled with the suggestion that it was not just her safety Jack sought.

"Dammit, she is my legal wife—"

"That she is."

Jack gave Seabury a murderous look and his mount the spur. It was some distance later that Seabury caught up with him, when he slowed his horse to a walk.

Jack looked at the knowing crinkle of Seabury's eyes and demanded, "What?"

"I was just thinking. This might prove a very expensive visit. Five hundred a year . . ."

Fully ten different emotions flickered through Jack's bronzed features before a tortured hunger settled over them to stay.

"It'll be worth every damned farthing."

Merrie bent low on her mount and raced headlong down the cart path toward the dim outline of Straffen's buildings. The pelting rain of the sudden downpour stung her cheeks, tore at her wired linen cap, and pounded through her sturdy woolen gown. Somewhere beside or behind her, Chester was struggling to keep pace on a leggy gelding that panicked and reared with each crash of lightning or boom of thunder. Suddenly the dim, wavery outlines sharpened through the sheets of rain and the stable loomed out of the mists.

The stableboys were watching for them and dashed out in the muddy yard to swing the doors open wide.

Merrie rode straight in and pulled to a halt, panting for breath. A heartbeat later, Chester and his skittish mount ducked into the alley beside her and the lads rode the doors shut behind them.

"I knowed it'd hit afore we got back, milady." Chester groaned, heaving his bulk down to the stone alley floor. He handed his horse off to a stableboy and came to give Merrie his knee for dismount. He paused, looking at her ruined cap and the way her sodden clothes were plastered to her. His square features twisted in a wince as he predicted: "Ye'll come down with th' snurle or th' ague, an' me ma'll murth—"

"She'll not *murther* you, Chester. It was my fault; I just wanted a few more minutes." She unhooked her leg and let him help her down. Now that she was mistress of herself, she made it a point to ride daily, in good weather or bad. And she wasn't about to have Chester blamed for her own single-mindedness. "I'll tell Goodwife Gert and she'll understand."

Chester straightened, looking utterly skeptical. "Ye don' know her, do ye?" The doom in his voice stopped Merrie in the midst of plucking soggy woolens from her skin.

"She's a reasonable woman, Chester."

"Yea." He scratched at the itchy wet wool around his neck and leveled a jaundiced eye at his mistress. "Reas'nable as a stone hammer."

Merrie couldn't help but smile at him; "stone hammer" wasn't too far off the mark in describing steeley Gert Lombard. Poor Chester seemed to come in for more than his share of her bruising brand of maternal correction. "I'll tell her." She bestowed a heartwarming smile. "And I promise not to get sick."

She turned to peer out the door and listen to the din of rain on the tiled roof. She really should get to the house and out of these wet clothes as quickly as possible. Summer rains could be positively bone-chilling. A moment later it seemed to be slackening and she began gathering up her sodden skirts, bundling them about her knees. She watched the house appear through the grayness and scarcely heard Chester's mumbling as he led her horse away.

"I'm going to make a run for it, before it pours again!" she called as she took a deep breath and dashed out into the rain. She ran, half blinded by the stinging, wind-driven drops, sometimes dodging the sucking mud and sometimes thrashing right through it.

Behind her, in the stable, Chester was holding her horse and staring at a stall which should have been empty, but which was filled with a great roan stallion. Chester Lombard never forgot a horse and he knew beyond a doubt who this one belonged to. "M'lady—" he turned to hurry back down the alley, calling, "Master Huntington's—"

Merrie blew through the rear door of the great hall, slammed it shut with her elbow, and collapsed on her shoulder against it. She was panting, blinking against the rivulets of water running down her face and grappling with the bundle of skirts that threatened to escape her. If Overbeake could only see her now, she thought, laughing. It was a long moment before she could regain her breath, wipe her face on her wet sleeve, and turn.

She stopped dead. The laughter died on her lips. In the center of the hall were three figures, three faces trained on her in varying stages of shock: Goodwife Gert and Manley . . . and Jack Huntington.

Jack took three long strides toward her and she watched him come, feeling frozen, suspended in disbelief. Jack—here? He'd come back? Her gaze was pinioned helplessly on the wide, muscular chest that was moving toward her like a velvet-clad wall. He paused a few steps away and her harried vision broadened to take in his dark hair and sultry tan-gold eyes and the angular perfection of his jaw. A tide of hot color rose from her middle up through her breasts and into her face.

Jack watched the smile on her face and the sparkle in her eyes dim as he came forward, but he was too busy searching her, allaying his nagging fears about her safety, to heed it just now. She was wet to the bone, holding her skirts in a droopy bundle about her knees, and her shoes and stockings were spattered with mud. When he stopped a few paces away, his eyes were drawn to the way drops of water slid down her glowing, healthy cheeks. She looked absurdly adorable, standing there, water dripping down her nose, staring at him with those great velvet eyes of her. It sent a crush of sweet pain through his chest and curled his mouth into a smile.

That smile somehow kicked her mind back into motion. That smile—that bold, sensual mouth . . . Was he—was he *laughing* at her? She stiffened as if stung and released her wad of skirts, brushing them frantically down over her muddy legs. She purpled and lifted her chin against the taunt of his amusement.

"You're . . . back."

"And you're . . . wet." His smile broadened to a roguish grin as his eyes drifted to the way her wet gown was clinging to her breasts. He'd have given his share of eternity to trade places with that bit of cloth just then.

Merrie saw where his eyes lingered and a sharp stab of pain shot through her. How dare he look at her like that . . . as if he wanted . . . Her heart began to beat erratically. Icy-hot currents of panic were curling through her, and her knees were turning to mush.

"I . . . I was caught out in the rain. I must change, straightaway." She lifted her heavy skirts to go, but he sidestepped straight into her path, bringing her up short. She tucked her chin and stepped back a step, both fearing and refusing to meet his eyes.

"Have you no word of welcome, my little Merrie?" His deep, memorable tones invaded her, sliddering along her nerves to collect and vibrate in her middle.

"Welcome . . . sir." Her voice sounded astonishingly calm as she hurried around him toward the stairs. "Goodwife, will you send hot water? I'm chilled through."

Jack watched her go, feeling utterly unmanned by her coolness. He'd expected some reluctance, some feminine pique at his absence. . . . then he closed his eyes. *You're wet?* He'd ached and burned, anticipating seeing her again, and he'd drafted forty different gallantries to woo her with in greeting, and all he could manage was *You're wet?* He groaned internally and when he opened his eyes, he found himself staring into the Lombards' hostile faces. The minute he'd dismounted, they descended on him, demanding he withdraw from Straffen. He'd refused, planting himself in the hall and demanding to see Merrie. Well, now he'd seen her, those looks said, and he'd better leave.

Jack flicked a glance at the stairs and was tempted to bolt up them after her, to sweep her into his arms and kiss her until . . . He squelched that heated impulse and strolled defiantly over to sink into a chair. Being an experienced amorous tactician, he knew better than to pursue a woman when she was embarrassed by her appearance. He vowed they'd start over when she dressed and came down. He raised his square chin to the Lombards' glares. He wasn't going anywhere.

Upstairs, Merrie trembled as Tess and Bevis pulled her wet clothes from her, replaced her shift with a dry one, and wrapped her in a blanket. But the cold summer rain was only partly to blame for her shivers. Even now, the heat of those probing eyes and the powerful aura of sensuality that radiated from him breathed hot anticipation against her skin. A look, a rakish smile, was all it took to make her feel him all through her susceptible body, to make her forget. . . .

She stiffened, clamped her chattering teeth, and shoved her feet into the small wooden tub that even now was being filled with hot water. As the heat traveled slowly up her quaking legs, it seemed to unknot her thinking as well.

He was home after more than six weeks. Six long, lonely weeks, without a word. And he had taken one look at her and laughed. Her throat tightened and her eyes burned before she took herself in hand. After a month and a half of his refined London ladies, he'd come home to a dripping wet "child." And he'd laughed.

Well, she wasn't a child anymore! How dare he even think such a thing! Because of him, she'd known a woman's pleasure and a woman's pain, and learned the pain sometimes outweighed the pleasure. Such lessons had propelled her fully into the realm of womanhood and forced her to begin deciding things for herself. And just now, she was deciding not to allow the knave anywhere near her . . . or her half-healed heart!

She took more than an hour to wash and dry and slip into fresh linen and a silk undergown. Tess watched her nervousness and her purposeful dawdlings and finally waved Bevis aside to take over the task of brushing her hair dry. Her new status as Merrie's "companion" meant such things should be beneath her. But, more than anyone, soft-hearted Tess knew Merrie's moods and the turmoil her mistress was suffering at that moment.

"Mebee he didn' have time for a letter." Tess finally spoke up.

"No doubt he had his hands too full of other things." Merrie's eyes closed against the sight of Jack with his hands full of vixens. The image was so real and depressing that she bit her lip to stifle a groan.

"Mister Seabury didn' come with 'im." Tess's tone quivered with disappointment.

Merrie stiffened at that news. "That means he probably won't be staying long. He'll be eager to get back to his business in London." Back to his vixens, back to his Deirdres, and back to spending her money. She sagged. She hadn't even known she *had* money until a fortnight ago. A wave of fresh and powerful hurt washed through her, taking her breath. How could she face him, knowing that every smile, every fonden touch, was merely a means to an end. Oh, Lord—she didn't want to see the glow in those eyes that could melt her into puddles or to feel her blood heating from the sight of his big, supple hands.

"You'll have to tell him I'm ill," Merrie choked out, whirling on her seat. She gripped the blanket tighter with one hand and Tess's arm with the other. With frantic mental apologies to Chester, she implored: "Tell him I've taken to my bed . . . with a terrible ague. I'm racked with fevers and chills and not at all well—"

The door swung open as she spoke and Jack filled the opening like a colossus, his shoulders braced and booted legs spread. He'd waited and watched the stairs in the hall, expecting, anticipating her return. As each minute passed, he had read disquieting new meanings into her frosty welcome and his uncertainty had mounted. Uncertainty about a woman was not a state Jack Huntington was accustomed to suffering. He fidgeted and squirmed and paced and suddenly found himself taking the stairs two and three at a time. He opened the door just in time to hear: ". . . fevers and chills . . ."

"What's this?" He stepped inside the chamber, his eyes fixed on the sight of her, huddled in a blanket and surrounded by a flaming shield of vibrant red-gold hair. One step and then another he advanced. "You're ailing?"

"I . . . am . . . not well, sir. The cold rain . . . I fear I've contracted an ill humor . . . the ague. . . ." He just stared at her with those penetrating eyes as she rattled on, bolstering her courage as she emroidered her excuse. "I . . . it was my own fault . . . not heeding the stormsigns. The bees went to ground and the leaves were all turned up and standing on end. It is proper punishment for my stubbornness. My joints are aching and I've signs of fever." Her pale hand went to her crimson cheek, and her eyes did seem fever-bright just then. "I fear I must take to my bed, sir."

That wrenching tone of regret, so gentle, so genuine. He suddenly realized he'd heard it before. St. Edgar's—she was obviously up to her old tricks; inventing snurles and humps and now fevers and agues to avoid him! She was more piqued than he'd expected, and perhaps a bit more vulnerable. His eyes glowed briefly, his face tightened with exaggerated concern.

"Merciful Heaven! This could be serious indeed!" He sprang at her and scooped her up into his arms, blanket and all. Over her gasps and squirms and sputters, he carried her to the bed and deposited her with a flourish. "I've had vast experience in just such matters." He shot a duplicitous look straight into her eyes. "You must put yourself in my hands, wife. Thank the heavens I've arrived in time to care for you myself!"

With that, he swept the horrified Tess and glowering Bevis out the door and closed it firmly behind them. He turned to find Merrie's eyes burning like beacons. His blood heated a degree as he stalked to the bed and stood gazing down at her blazing eyes and her white-knuckled grip on the blanket.

"You must tell me your ills, sweetest, if I'm to help you." He gave her his most noble and charitable look as he settled on the bed beside her. There was a telling silence. She didn't want his help, didn't want him anywhere near her!

"I-I'm c-cold . . . very c-cold." She managed to make her teeth clack convincingly while pulling the cover tighter under her chin and flicking a covert glance of longing at the door.

"Ummmm." He stroked his angular jaw thoughtfully. "Not like you at all . . . *cold*. Let me see." One by one he peeled her stiff, icy fingers from the cover. Then he raised them and applied his lips in gentle, rousing caresses, warming them with his breath and with shocking little swirls of his tongue over the pads of her fingertips.

Hot tingles radiated up her arm and she jerked it back beneath the cover with a shiver that was utterly genuine. His smile took on a knowing tenor.

"And this aching?" He leaned closer. His warmth and manly scent invaded her head, her lungs. "Tell me where it aches, sweetest, and I'll do my best to relieve you.''

''A-all over,'' she choked out, trying to be sufficiently vague, trying to make her soupy brain function.

''*All* over?'' He swept her body with a long, tactile look that came to rest on her bare toes, peeping out of blanket and skirts. He slid down by her feet and when his hands closed on them, he felt a pulse of excitement go through her muscles. ''Here?'' His voice was silky and caressing as his hands massaged her in slow, erotic circles. ''Do you ache here?''

She nodded, stiff with panic.

''And here?'' His hands covered her ankles and fingered them gently, then moved up her calves, pushing both her linen skirts and her panic higher. His touch was hot, undulating, like living flame on her icy limbs. ''Ah, I can feel how you're knotted up, my love. And I can fix it for you.'' Those long, wicked fingers claimed and kneaded . . . wandering, questing . . . up the insides of her knees.

''No—*please*—'' She wriggled abruptly, loosening his grip and pulling away a few meaningful inches. She was trembling, dark-eyed.

With fear or with wanting? Jack wondered.

''Why, you're quaking, sweetest!'' He fought the grin lurking at the corners of his mouth to declare solemnly, ''There's but one proven remedy for so grave a condition.'' He rose to his knees, straddling her lower legs, and began to tear at the buttons of his doublet. ''A pilaster of warm guts! And there's not a minute to lose.''

She watched in choked horror as he pulled open his doublet and tore at the fastenings of his breeches, eager to apply that age-old remedy for chills, a bit of belly heat. Lord knew he had plenty to share.

''N-n-no!'' She groaned, scrambling beneath him, frantic to escape. But he caught her as she tried to flee and levered himself above her. The heat of his chest and belly spread over her as he moved lower, trapping her on her back in the thick feather ticking. He was huge and hot and hard everywhere their bodies met and she had to struggle for breath against the swell of her own stormy emotions.

"No," she gasped, feeling in the helpless warming of her body that it was futile to resist. Anger, fear, and humiliation slithered up the back of her throat in succession, then seeped into her huge, expressive eyes. Every emotion she'd ever known seemed to be clamoring to be free—all at once!

The stilling of her body and the hard rise and fall of her breasts against him brought a wickedly triumphant grin to his face. Her gambit had provided him an opening to her bed within an hour of his arrival—it had to be some sort of record! He raked her tumbled hair and her peach-flushed skin as he lowered his head toward her quivering lips. But his gaze snagged on her darkly luminous eyes and he halted, a breath away from paradise.

Those eyes. Shimmering pools of raw feeling, wells of nameless, tangled emotion. Desire was there . . . but there was more, so much more that it stopped his breath and tightened his belly. He stared, drawn into those depthless, disturbed waters, glimpsing anger and mistrust and desire and hurt. Deep, aching hurt. There was no pleasure, no joy in those vulnerable eyes.

She strained her face away, feeling as though she'd been plundered. He had no right to see, no right to make her feel so small, so foolish.

Jack lay sprawled over her, his doublet and breeches loosed and pushed aside to bare his heat to her, to entice her to bare hers to him. He'd meant to seduce her with it, to tease her with it, to make her react to it. He'd meant to trade her tit for tat, flam for famble.

But this was no amorous game. She lay beneath him, stiff with strain, eyes luminous with gathering tears. He could make her want him physically, could undoubtedly rouse her reluctant desires. But she didn't want to want him. And the implications of that were painfully clear. Suddenly *his* chest was hurting, *his* feelings were tossing and roiling.

"Merrie . . ." There was a strange constriction in his voice and he stroked her burning cheek with one tentative finger. Her eyes closed. Her breath stopped. And he knew. Those swirlings of new, dark feeling in her eyes; he'd caused them.

When he raised above her, she didn't move, still didn't breathe. She felt the movement of the bed as he slid from it, then heard the whisper of fabric brushing fabric. Was he disrobing further? Leaving? For several agonizing seconds she strained to hear above the thumping of her heart. Then all was quiet and she felt the heat of his gaze searching her. He was standing at the edge of the bed when she opened her eyes. His mouth was canted in what appeared to be grim amusement, or a grimace of self-inflicted pain. And his doublet was properly buttoned.

"I trust your chill is gone, my lady."

Merrie rose shakily onto one arm, staring at the dark lights in his countenance. The tenuous look of relief in her face was painful for him to witness.

"Then I shall see you this evening . . . when we dine." He turned on his heel and was gone.

She was unable to drag her eyes from the door. The chill in her body had vanished; his passionate heat had dispelled it. But how was she to deal with the chill in her heart?

Chapter Fifteen

That evening Merrie descended the stairs to find Master Cramden newly arrived in the hall, his face unusually red and his expression uncommonly severe. He'd just been returning from Bedford—he cast Jack a look laden with meaning—and he'd decided to call and see how Lady Meredith was faring.

"And but imagine my surprise upon finding Master Huntington returned from his business in London already!" he declared dramatically. "Pure *fortune* that you were able to settle such grave and complex matters so quickly!" He wound an inquiring, uplifted hand at Jack, as though to elicit some desired response. "Or is it indeed settled? Mayhap you shall find yourself departing again . . . soon?"

"All is settled to my satisfaction," Jack answered, his smile tightening. "A pity you cannot abide for dinner, Master Cramden, but I know how compelling the thought of home and bed is after a journey. Do call another time." He reached for Merrie's hand and turned her toward the table. Cramden stiffened and blanched, taking on his lardlike look again, and when Merrie cast a glimpse back over her shoulder, he was squashing his hat onto his head and barreling out, mumbling to himself.

She stared at Jack, confounded by his rudeness to good Master Cramden and goaded by his remark about beds. That was obviously all the knave thought of . . . bedding and pleasures and fleshly indulgence. She lifted her head and felt her cheeks heating.

Jack complimented her gown, a violet-and-crimson brocade overdress that cast intriguing lights about her hair and in her eyes. "A very fetching Italian style," he observed gallantly. The overdress was made with an open winged collar that framed her face and breasts like caressing hands and made her seem older, more elegant. Or perhaps it was Merrie herself who had changed. . . .

"There have been changes in Straffen," he mused uncomfortably, and then raised a most obvious one. "I have not seen Mistress Overbeake. Will she join us for dinner?"

Merrie avoided his eyes and withdrew her hand from him to clasp it in her other. "Mistress Overbeake is no longer employed here. She was . . . discharged."

"Thank God for that. The old prune was a pure menace." He ushered her into her chair at the table with an impulsive brush of his lips against her daintily capped hair. He did not miss her equally impulsive flinch. With a tight breath, he settled on her left, in the master's chair at the head of the table. "It surely took Cramden long enough to send her packing."

"Master Cramden didn't." She raised a look to him. "I did."

"You?" He frowned.

Her beautiful eyes darkened a shade. "I am mistress here, after all . . . as you said." *I needed you, Jack.*

"So you are." Jack heard her clearly; both her words and her thoughts. Heaviness settled in the pit of his stomach. *I'm here now, Merrie.*

There was a long silence before she spoke again. "I have taken another companion." She was watching him through her lashes and when he looked up from his goblet, she glanced away quickly. "Tess Lombard. She is bright and eager to learn and very knowledge-able about the workings of the household." There seemed to be a question in her voice and Jack realized her sidelong gaze was filled with tension, as if she expected him to object. It puzzled him momentarily until he realized that, for all her hostility, she still consid-ered him the true master of Straffen.

"She has supped with me in your absence. I wonder if she might join us for meals?"

"Whatever suits you, Merrie. No doubt she will make a fine companion. I know Seabury thinks quite highly of her." The good-natured suggestion in his tone brought deeper pink to her cheeks.

"Where is Mister Seabury?" She had ceased eating altogether and her hands were folded tightly in her lap. "He did not come with you."

"He should arrive tomorrow with my things from London." He watched her rigid posture melt a few degrees and realized his reply had allayed one of her suspicions. In his eagerness to see her, arriving alone, ahead of Seabury, he had given the appearance of a "visit." The thought made him uneasy. His eyes drifted to the Lombards, stationed by the rear door and watching hawkishly.

They finished dining in silence, Merrie achingly aware of Jack's penetrating gaze on her and Jack agonizingly aware of the Lombards' on him. He finally sat back in the master's chair, toying with his goblet, and said, "I shall pay a call on Squire Millingham first thing tomorrow . . . about the hedgerows. Do you know, the wretched things have haunted—"

"It's been settled." She took a very controlled breath and watched as his handsome features set like mortar. "I asked Mister Lombard to speak with him and, jointly, a land surveyor was procured. They were Straffen's hedgerows, after all."

Where were you, Jack? Hurt surged and swirled in her sky-blue eyes. She let her gaze linger on him one instant too long; when she pulled it away, his image, his troubled look, came with it.

Dammit! He groaned silently. Every muscle in his body began a slow, defensive contraction. Those blessed hedgerows had haunted him for six weeks, had become a wretched obsession with him! He'd ached to do the right thing by those cursed bramblebushes. He'd wrangled and pestered and nagged every landed man he knew to learn every damned thing there was to know about hedgerows! And he was too bloody late to do *anything* about them. Why that should breed such a tempest inside him was beyond him for the moment, but he was suddenly strung tight as a bowstring and vibrating with frustration.

"Speaking of neighboring houses . . ." Merrie's voice brought him back to the present and he leaned forward to concentrate on her, trying to shake off this growing uneasiness. "Some of Straffen's more exhalted neighbors came to pay a call while you were gone. The Earl of Epping led the party . . . with his lovely wife, Countess Deirdre."

She watched him absorb the name and saw his face and his body stiffen. And his eyes, those irresistible eyes, darkened noticeably as he caught the implications of her news and of the steady, searching gaze that accompanied it. "Of course, I am unused to moving among the nobility, but I found their visit . . . enlightening."

"The earl is a charming man." She knew she trod thin ice, but her keening pride and her burning need to know pushed her on. "But he is somewhat older than his countess. And she is so beautiful and spirited and . . . She said she might be traveling to London, that she might pay you a call."

Did she come? Merrie's velvety eyes peered into him in that way they had of seeking, sorting, of seeing more than he wanted her to see. *Did you love your haughty vixen?*

God. It was a genuine prayer for help in that moment. Their gazes fused and Jack felt the ache in her heart migrating that visual bridge into his own chest. She knew about Deirdre, those true eyes said, and about him. And how much more? *Please God, don't let her know everything . . . don't let her see—*

It wasn't just his absence that had hurt her. It went deeper, much deeper than that. It went to the core of him . . . and the kind of man he was. She'd learned things about him; he could see the truth in those haunting eyes. They were filled with clouds of doubt about him. And in that moment, John Huntington of Kent wished with all his heart he were any man in the world other than the supremely carnal and irresponsible "Gentleman Jack."

Merrie tore her gaze from that painful, intimate union and pushed to her feet. She was reeling, unsure of what she'd seen in the tumult inside him and afraid to trust her own capricious emotions further. If he reached for her, touched her right now, she would simply crumble. She bade him good-night in a whisper and he was on his feet in a flash, watching her move to the stairs.

Jack strode from the house in the deepening twilight, walking hard out the rear yard and past the cottages, making straight for the quiet darkness of the cart path between Straffen's fields. His mind and heart were seeing nothing but the hurt and disappointment in Merrie's face. He wished with everything in him that he could somehow take it from her . . . restore the sparkle to her eyes and the smile to her lips and the desire for him in her heart.

He found himself standing against a low stone wall around the horse pasture, fists clenched, wishing he could have done battle for her. He should have been there to sack Overbeake himself, to see to the damnable hedgerows, to listen to her questions. And to hold her, safe and pleasure-sated, in his arms at night, every night. He should have been there when Epping arrived and Deirdre—Deirdre. That arrogant, conniving bitch. Jack's eyes hardened and his shoulders knotted. The witch's pride was obviously still sore from that night at the inn. And she'd chosen the cruelest, lowest means possible to get back at him. God knew what foul, hurtful things she'd said to Merrie. He should have been there to intercept her malicious comments.

But he hadn't been there. And Merrie had had to sack Overbeake and tend to Straffen's welfare and face Deirdre's vicious vanity by herself. And he couldn't help thinking that doing those things had changed her in some intangible way.

If only he could make her know how she'd been on his mind, day and night. How she'd made it impossible for him to pass a bookseller without going inside. How he'd lost interest in gambling and gone to bed with Pliny and Horace and Cicero instead of willing wenches. If only he could start over, make her forget the man he was . . . *was*. It brought him alert, alive. He'd changed, too, in these last weeks. He knew about hedgerows now, and he knew something about the economies and husbandry of middling estates. And he knew all about wanting a woman so much that every other need became secondary.

She had needed him and believed in him before . . . and she had wanted him. A breathtaking sensory impression of her wriggled into his mind: laughing, teasing, chiding in that wry and forgiving way of hers. Need heated his blood so that it scalded his veins. He had to have her, had to make it right between them, somehow. If she'd wanted him before, she could want him again. He was going to make her want him . . . even if he had to court and seduce her a second time.

An hour later, Jack strolled back into the house, intent on wooing his reluctant wife back into his arms. It was in her interest as much as his, he told himself, to put the past behind them and begin again. With each step he mounted, his grin broadened and his heart pounded harder. He paused before the door to the master chamber for a deep, preparatory breath, then lifted the latch.

The darkness confused him. He stepped inside and allowed his eyes to adjust. The outline of the great bed became visible and he stole forward, searching its shadows for her shape. His eyes found nothing and shortly his hands confirmed it; she was gone.

Gone! Where would she . . . ? He stalked out, down the gallery and nearby hall, to stand in front of the door to her old chamber. His hand paused on the latch as hot waves of confusion broke over him. She was there, he knew it. If he pushed open the door, he'd have to keep pushing—into her bed, into her arms, into her body. . . . But he knew it wasn't possible to *push* into her heart.

He turned away, more determined than ever to have her, to make her his mate in truth—even if he had to coax and charm and seduce her to achieve it!

Dawn broke bright, humming with an expectation that had been absent from Straffen in the past weeks. Everyone on Straffen knew the master had returned and it wasn't long before they saw him, dressed in his gentlemanly velvets and boots, striding from grainery to malt house to stable. One by one, they stood before him, answering his questions and assuring him all was prospering in their small part of Straffen.

The Lombards watched in muffled outrage. How dare the rake defy their agreement to invade the place and strut about like the cock o' the walk! They finally cornered him in the stable and demanded that he leave within the hour or find his stipend in certain jeopardy. They eased a bit when he turned to Chester calmly and ordered his horse saddled . . . and were jolted afresh when he ordered Lady Merrie's saddled as well.

"Ye can't do that." Gert glared daggers at him.

"Cannot what, Goodwife?" Jack raised one brow. "Cannot take my lawful wife for a morning ride?" Gert pulled back, sputtering, but with an odd tenor of relief. Were they worried he might take Merrie somewhere? He turned pointedly to Chester. "Bring the horses round to the front court so my lady won't have to soil her skirts again in the muddy yard."

He struck off for the house with a bold stride that narrowed the Lombards' eyes to mere slits as they trailed behind. "Wot does 'e want?" Manley groaned.

"Money. What else?" Gert sneered. "He's got the lay o' the place an' now figures t' take his share. Th' knave would pick th' worst time . . ."

''Jus' when our other irons is heatin' up, again.''
Manley groaned. ''We mus' tell Cramden, straightaway.''

Jack found Merrie in the hall, breaking fast on boiled
eggs and stewed apples and fresh-heated rolls. He
paused to watch her eat, savoring the curve of her waist
and the gentle swell of her bosom even as she enjoyed
the honey-drenched bread and tangy morning ale. So
many times, in memory, he'd seen her just like this.
''I've had Chester bring our horses around to the
front court,'' he announced in intimate tones, smiling
at the way she started. She turned to look up at him
through feathery amber lashes.
''Horses?'' She choked on her bite of bread and finally won her battle to swallow it. He loomed big and
dark above her chair, engulfing her, overwhelming her
senses. So many times, in memory, she'd seen him
above her like this.
''I was given to understand you ride daily now.''
''I think . . . not today.''
''Then I shall be content to stay by your side, sweet
Merrie.'' He knelt beside her and pried her hand from
the arm of her chair to toy with her fingers. ''I place
myself at your disposal. I'll assist your stitchery and
linen airing and herb tending . . . and be your arms
when you're too short to reach and be your voice when
you need call.''
This was to be her punishment for fleeing his bed?
Suffering his gallant and undivided attentions? The
belly knot of tension she'd awakened with that morning began loosening. She had expected him to be angry, to rave and rail—she'd counted on it! Her own
anger had blocked remembrance of the thorough gentleness of Jack Huntington's revenge, the seductive
quality of his taunting helpfulness. A horse or two between them suddenly seemed a very good notion indeed.
''Perhaps a ride would be good,'' she said.
They were soon mounted, and instead of turning

back across Straffen's lands, Jack led her off along the road away from the manor and into territory she had seen only on the day of her arrival at Straffen and on the fateful night of her abortive flight. The smaller Straffen Manor became over her shoulder, the greater her anxiety grew. Where was he taking her?

Jack smiled his mischievous best when she asked their destination, and refused to answer. In truth, he had none in mind, except perhaps neutral ground . . . a place untainted by the hurts and memories that lay between them. He began to talk—and such talk! It was gossip, every bit of it, from the latest *affairs de coeur* at court, to the arrests made over mere rumors of the queen's precarious health, to the feared financial collapse of certain prominent families. Whenever she gasped, he grinned and was spurred to greater outrageousness with his next tidbit.

They had left Straffen well behind them. When Merrie realized it and looked around her, she couldn't recognize a thing. Whatever he had in mind should begin any moment now.

As if reading her thoughts, he reined up, looking at her. She slowed her mount and paused a safe distance away, looking at him.

"Have you no questions for me, Merrie?"

In the morning sun, his raven hair framed his smooth, sculptured face and his crimson doublet threw odd, violet lights into his warm eyes. She'd never seen him so beguilingly beautiful, so utterly irresistible. Her throat tightened with shameful longing. *Questions* . . . He always answered her questions. She just managed to shake her head and reined off sharply. Lord, what had possessed her to come away with him alone?

"Perhaps we should take some shade." Jack had caught up with her and nudged her mount off the rutted road, pointing to a small stand of trees to the right.

Merrie looked down into his outstretched arms as he waited to help her dismount and knew exactly what had possessed her. She wanted to slide into those arms, to feel them wrap around her. When he set her

on the ground, it was dismay with her own wayward
thoughts that caused her to brush her overskirt as
though ridding it of his touch.

Jack sighed. "I think, Merrie Straffen Huntington,
you do have questions for me. But if you will not ask,
I cannot answer."

There was a long, disquieting silence. Ah, she could
be a stubborn little thing. He watched the determined
set of her spine and the protective tuck of her arms
about her waist and ached to melt that distrust, dispel
that hurt.

"While I was in London, I was reunited with several
old friends."

She stiffened furiously. Old "friends"? How dare
he—

"Plato and Cicero and Seneca," he continued, his
voice deepening, softening, dampening the flare of anger in her before it was vented. Smoky warmth remained to spread through her. "I'd forgotten them,
you see. And you reminded me. Do you know, they
all speak to goodness and evil and virtue and wickedness, the universal ponderings of mankind. I was
young and callow, I suppose, when I read them the
first time. I had little patience for such things. But this
time I found myself wondering too, wishing I could
ask questions." His voice dropped to an earnest whisper. "Wishing you were there to ask."

Merrie felt his eyes on her, touching her gently. She
didn't want to ask. She wouldn't ask! Did he honestly
expect her to believe he *read* his "friends" instead of
bedding them? What kind of fool did he take her for?
Did he think she had no inkling of the vixens he'd
dallied with in London . . . or so little pride that it
wouldn't matter as long as he'd returned?

But he had played his hand expertly, knowing her
curiosity. She strode this way and that in stubborn silence, growing agitated.

"All right. What questions?" She lost the battle and
turned on him, her eyes flashing, her chin at a hostile
angle. Her body was set to withstand his expected

pounce, but she found him sitting on a great, exposed root, leaning back against the tree. His arms were crossed over his chest and his expression was sober and searching. Her tone gentled in spite of her anger.

"What . . . questions would you have asked?"

He sat up straight, feeling her visual probing, knowing he had to ask the right questions and praying that he would do so.

"Which is the lesser evil . . . to break an agreement or to break a heart?" He watched her surprise turning to suspicion as it trailed through her face. He tried again. "Which is worse: to grow old penniless or to grow old unloved? And which is the wiser course: to make actions conform to ideals or to draw ideals from beneficial actions?" He paused to read her reaction and was heartened by the tremble of her hands as she clasped them before her. He was touching nerves, he could tell.

"You once asked: 'Where do ugly men come from? From ugly seeds inside or from others' ugly deeds?' " He pushed to his feet. "You see, I did remember. And your question has haunted me. Now I ask you: How is it decided whether a man is 'ugly' or not? Is it the glare of his own faults and flaws . . . or is it the harsh light in which others cast him?"

Did she object to what he'd done, or to what she'd heard he'd done? he wanted to know. She closed her eyes, confused, torn between the weight of wanting and of fear. When she opened them, he was coming closer. She stepped back and he stopped.

"These are great questions, sir. Surely among your fine London associations, there are minds wiser and truer than mine to answer you." The quiver of hurt in her voice was faint, but there.

"Not one your equal. I thought of you, Merrie."

"Did you?" She braced, fearing to breathe.

"So much that I was poor company indeed for my 'London associations.' "

Her heart thudded. She tried valiantly to suppress it

but the question shoved into her breast and crowded into her throat, demanding to be asked.

"Did she come?"

Her eyes raised to him, darkened, depthless sapphires, windows on the longing of her troubled heart.

"No."

It penetrated her, that single syllable, seeking the chill around her heart, sending warm tendrils of hope through it, dislodging it. Such a small word, and so softly spoken, to contain such power. If only it were true. She turned and found her horse, somehow, and made herself stand beside it, waiting for help in mounting. All she could see were two fiery points of light, the flames of desire that glowed in Jack Huntington's eyes.

When they returned to Straffen, a heavy-wheeled horse cart with a saddle mount tied behind it stood in the front court. Raised voices burst in volleys from just inside the arched doorway, and the cart driver stood glued to the sight, his simple felt hat clutched to his breast.

"Ye'll not be unloadin' that lot!" Gert Lombard waved a furious hand toward the cart that was visible through the doorway. "Ye'll be packin' it off t' London on th' morrow, by troth!"

Seabury's face was crimson and his fists were clenched under her unexpected tirade. And to make it worse, he could feel Tess's eyes on him urging him to do something. "I've strict orders from Master Huntington to see these things delivered safely and I intend to do just that, madam. They are his personal effects and his gifts to Lady Merrie—"

"Wull, he won' be needin' no pers'nal e-ffects!" Manley stepped toe to toe with him and stared him hard in the eye. "He shull be leavin' come sunrise. So ye jus' leave the lot of 'em in the—"

"There must be some mistake." Jack's voice boomed from the doorway, freezing every muscle in the hall. He stepped inside, pulling Merrie with him by the wrist. One glimpse of the suspicion-become-certainty in her eyes and he was ready to rip Manley Lombard's flapping tongue out by its roots! He pulled Merrie along beside him, ignoring her tugs as she tried to free her hand.

"I cannot imagine where you might have got the notion I would be leaving again so soon. Perhaps you misheard me. Well"—he waved a dismissing hand as his gaze narrowed meaningfully above Merrie's head—"it is no matter. If you would be so good as to have the servants help Seabury with the unpacking . . ."

He pulled Merrie along with him to a seat in the hall and it was all he could do to meet her distrustful look with a steady, confident smile. He called for a bit of sack to slake their thirst while the cart was being unloaded and she scarcely touched the cup. He would have sworn he had made progress with her earlier, but then they'd walked straight into Lombard's wretched blathering. When the last bit of baggage, a moderate-sized trunk, was trundled from the cart, Jack spotted it and directed the servants to halt at the bottom of the stairs.

"Come with me." He smiled dazzlingly and pulled Merrie from her seat and toward the bottom of the stairs and the trunk. "I'll need the key, Seabury." He knelt before a heavy ward lock, extending his hand to his companion. He opened the lid to reveal a clothlike cover, then pushed to his feet, putting the key into her hands. "It is a bit late"—his hand caressed hers briefly in the transfer—"but nonetheless heartfelt. My wedding gift to you."

He stepped aside, waving her to it, with a purposeful glint in his eye. Merrie stared at the cool, finely wrought key in her hand and was torn between pride and curiosity. Did he think he could purchase her opinion, her wifely cooperation, with a few baubles? Her skin was glowing where he'd touched it just now and she rubbed it irritably.

Soft chamois, a wrapping reserved for precious things, was tucked over . . . whatever he supposed her acceptance and wifely service were worth. Just what did he consider a fair exchange for them in his crass material terms? The desire to know seized her with a vengeance.

"Shall I help?" He read both doubt and temptation in her expressive face and knelt on one knee by the open trunk. He peeled back the covering to reveal numerous flat, rectangularly shaped objects, wrapped individually in that same gentle chamois. And he watched intently the widening of her eyes and the quickening rise and fall of her chest.

He reached for one of the objects and unwrapped it. A book slid from the soft skin, a volume bound in beautifully tooled leather. Her stunned gaze drifted from the book in his hands to the assorted stacks of them in the chest. Books? He'd brought her books?

"This is your Heraclitus . . . and a few fellows of similar turn, all done up in one binding." He stretched to put it in her hands and turned back for another to unwrap. "Ah, your Plato—the dialogues with Socrates. Lord, he asks even more questions than you do." Jack thumbed the pages and caught her gaze with a shameless and cajoling grin. "Rest assured, my love, your questions are far more interesting." His grin grew a trifle wicked as he thrust that volume into her hands as well. The third he retrieved was: "Dante . . . his *La Vita Nuova*, The New Life, written for love of his Beatrice. And his *Divine Comedy*." He held it out to her, searching her odd, wistful expression, and apparently pleased with what he saw.

She took it from him with trembling fingers and laid it gently on the others in her arms, cradling them against her breasts. She swallowed hard and came to kneel beside the trunk, staring at the veritable treasure he offered her. Books were luxuries, meant for those with education and leisure enough to indulge in them, and were priced accordingly. And books such as these, gilt-edged and likely hand-colored, must have been dear indeed. Laying the ones she held gently in her lap, she began to unwrap the others, one by one. Plays and a book titled *Proverbs* by a fellow named John Heywood. A solid rendering of old Chaucer, Sir Thomas More's *Utopia*, and slim volumes of sonnets in English and Italian.

Her fingers feathered lovingly over them, absorbing their reality, wondering at the riches waiting inside. Seneca in solid Latin . . . and translations of Aristotle. . . . Some were old friends and some beckoned to new adventures. *Old friends*. She stopped dead. Even her heart stilled in that moment of insight. The books and trunk suddenly swam before her eyes. She raised her head and found him watching her with a deep, unsettling hunger in his face.

"You *did* think of me," she whispered.

"Every day." The admission was painfully sweet. "Every night."

They faced each other on their knees, with a lap full of books between them. But their hearts met briefly in their eyes.

This was the man Merrie knew, the man she wanted. Perceptive, generous, scandalously permissive Jack. What other man would go to such expense for a bride already secured, a bride of . . . mere convenience? Her hurt and anger were dealt a mortal blow. She closed her eyes and pushed to her feet, feeling flushed and giddy and more than a bit frightened of the surrendering that had begun inside her.

"I thank you, John Huntington." When she looked at him again, she felt the burn of collecting tears and the pull of his mesmeric presence.

"You're most welcome, my little wife." He rose and loomed above her, dark and potently male. As he reached for her, intent on experiencing her gratitude in a more direct manner, she fell back a step. Then, to his aching disbelief, she wheeled and ran up the stairs, still clutching *Utopia* to her breast.

"But wait—you've not even unwrapped them all!" Jack jolted after her two steps, running smack into Seabury's frowning face. He sputtered irritably and wrested in Seabury's grip . . . until he caught his friend's frantic cast of eyes and looked around him to find that his earnest wooing had been witnessed by every housemaid and footman on the place. He pulled his doublet down sharply and exited, red-faced, to the front gardens to regroup.

Merrie kept to her chamber that afternoon, trying to sort her jumbled thoughts and steel her reeling pride against his maneuverings and charm. With his desirous and sincere-eyed looks and the disarming revelation of how much he'd held her in his thoughts, he was making her remember all the reasons she'd fallen in love with him. And not even the awful pain and humiliation she'd suffered on his account seemed capable of countering it.

Even as she paced above, Jack paced below, in the hall, the garden, the small parlor . . . eventually even the cart path again. He kept seeing the tears in her eyes as she turned away that noon. What in Hell's Blistered Hump did she have to cry about? Couldn't she see how much he wanted her, how much he cared for her? His ruffled rake's pride asserted itself and he began to plot in carnal earnest. He'd tantalized her curious mind. Now it was time to do something about that curious little body of hers.

When Merrie invited the Lombards to keep company with them in the hall that evening and entrenched herself between them and Tess and Seabury, Jack's eyes darkened determinedly. *Ah, Merrie.* He sighed, watching her absorption in helping Tess learn a difficult French stitch. *Do you honestly think you are safe from me there, amongst those thorns? How wonderfully green you are, sweeting.*

He smiled his most dazzling and dangerous smile when she finally paused and looked up. Then he rose and withdrew a small leather-bound volume from his doublet, rebuttoning casually. "My lady has often graced us with the glory of her music, and in gratitude I dare to offer her a diversion of my own. There was one volume in my gift to you, sweet wife, specially selected to answer a question you once asked of me. The writings of the poet Ovid . . . his *Amores* and *Ars Amatoria.''*

Merrie watched him open the elegant little book as the titles double-translated themselves in her mind. *Love* and *The Art of Love.* There was suddenly an alarming glint deep in his eye. He took a full breath and began to read in flawless Latin:

> I swear I do not ask too much of heaven:
> O make that thoughtless girl
> who yesterday made me her spoils of war
> either love me
> or let me share her bed to prove I love her.
> I ask too much too soon? Then I beg pardon. . . .

He read slowly, purposefully, in stentorian tones that filled the hall with noble scholarly sound . . . and filled Merrie with growing horror. He was reading such stuff to them here . . . now? She looked frantically about and found Seabury and Tess watching Jack with politely blank expressions and the Lombards regarding him with dull irritation. Nowhere was there the slightest hint of discomfort . . . or comprehension. Apparently none of them knew any Latin beyond *Pater Noster* and *Anno Domini.* Jack was reading for her ears alone, but in front of them all!

Her horror spread as his recitation continued with a far more wicked soliloquy concerning some ''banquet'' . . . and some fellow who desired—*lusted after*—another fellow's wife! His voice grew deeper, pliant and provocative, as the subject of his discourse heated it:

> . . . steer down beside him, innocent and cool,
> your naked foot on mine beneath the table.
> Gaze into my eyes,
> read what they have to say!

The round, elegant, seductive syllables; Ovid was not the only knave entreating with those words. Simmering in angry confusion, Merrie shot a look of furious indignation into Jack's tawny, long-lashed eyes . . . those warm, desirous eyes. And her last precarious defenses against him began to melt into warm, fluid streams that swirled through her tenderest places and awakened her body's response. His eyes held hers prisoner as he raised the book to keep them both in sight and continue.

Each move I make is yours to read, to follow.
Look, I incline my head,
I raise an eyebrow; these are words, my dear,
words without sounds—and when drinks are served
across the table
I'll write 'I love you' in spilled drops of wine.
Then answer me in kind: if you remember
how joyfully, how well we mount each other,
drunk with delights of Venus
in my bed,
then touch your glowing cheeks with
　one slow finger.

Merrie's fingers came up—all of them—to press against her burning cheek. ". . . if you remember . . ." She suffered quick, hot flashes of memory of the breathtaking pleasures of "mounting" with him. Oh Lord, how she remembered! She ought to be outraged by this disgrace, furious with his arrogance, or at least shamed by his flaunted wickedness. But her body was coming alive with a will of its own, growing warm and yielding and moist. She wriggled and fidgeted tellingly in her chair, trying to dislodge these insistent hungers, trying to counter the desire he was conjuring in her with his shameless words.

Jack paused, watching her flushed cheeks and bitten-cherry lips and the helpless way she squirmed. He had an electrifying vision of those very wriggles, naked under his hands, beneath his aching loins. His face bronzed and hardened and his eyes half closed to hide their telling glitter.

"In this next, I found the answer to your inquiry, my lady. I believe you did ask if there were writings on the subject. Recalling your request, I sought them out. May they prove instructive."

Each girl should know the pleasures of her body
And how to use them when she falls in love:
Your beauties guide your style: a pretty face
Always looks best if girls lie on their backs—
But if your back looks better, hide your face;
And show your pretty buttocks to your lover. . . .

On it went . . . shocking carnal instructions couched in classical allusions and mythic reference. It was wickedness distilled. It was also arousing, so disturbingly, intentionally erotic that it took her breath. She was glowing, trembling, aching for a taste of those tantalizing pleasures at his hands.

"Enough!" Her speech was strangely thick, almost slurred, as she managed to push to her feet. "Prithee, you must not tax yourself, sir, on my account. I must retire." She trembled, panicking, as Jack caught and held her gaze, filling her with the bold promise of pleasures beyond imagining. Somehow she managed to pull away and the others' puzzled stares followed her as she made her way to the steps.

Manley yawned and stretched indecorously and Gert wakened from some reverie, neither the wiser, as they rose to secure the hall for the night. Tess hurried after her mistress, unsure of what had just transpired, and Seabury settled back to study Jack's roused form through wondering eyes. He wasn't sure what Jack had been up to with all that Latin nonsense, but it certainly had had an effect on Lady Merrie. He shook his head with a wry smile; Jack knew women, all right.

Chapter Sixteen

The hall darkened and the house quieted. The Lombards had finally made themselves scarce and, at a nod from Jack, Seabury departed for his own bed. Jack sat alone in the hall, sipping a goblet of wine and waiting. He imagined her disrobing, brushing her hair. He wanted to give her time. He kept seeing her eyes darkening with pleasure, her long, luscious nipples tightening with desire. They would be his tonight . . . and every night from now on.

He mounted the stairs with urgency in his blood. And he found his bedchamber lit by one candle . . . and empty. His eyes searched the great bed with disbelief. Where in hell was she?

He'd underestimated her—again! He'd expected her to think with her loins, as *he* was wont to do! But she didn't. She thought with her stubborn little head and just possibly her heart, which was every bit as stubborn. Well, this time there would be no gentlemanly accommodation, no reprieve of reason!

He stalked furiously down the gallery to Merrie's old chamber and fairly ripped the oaken door from its hinges as he burst inside. She was in bed; he could see the glow of her bright hair as she sprang up in the dimness. He was around the bed in a trice, grabbing her, wrestling one arm beneath her bare knees and clamping the other around her waist. He flexed and dragged her, wriggling and sputtering, up into his arms. Over her earnest wails and flails, he managed to carry her—mother-naked!—out the door and around the darkened gallery to the master chamber.

He dumped her on the turned-down bedlinen and

strode back to slam the door so that it rattled half the house. She scrambled and snatched a sheet around her as he came to stand over her, his face glowing, angry.

"Your place is in this bed, woman!" He punched a commanding finger at her. "You belong here . . . at Straffen . . . and in this bed! If anyone's going to leave, it's going to be *me*"—he jerked a furious thumb at himself—"do you understand?" He finally focused on the sight of her through the raging blood in his head. She was flushed, tangled in the fiery fall of her hair and dark-eyed with confusion. She clutched the sheet to her lush body as though it were immortal salvation. Maybe it was. He groaned, shutting his eyes against the sight. He was certainly acting like the very devil. Lord!—carrying her through the house stark naked, dead set on ravishing her . . .

Merrie watched him turn away, saw the tension of his shoulders, and knew she'd driven him to it. She'd never seen him truly angry before—never! She half wondered if she ought to be frightened. Frustration screamed from every line, every angle of his tall, graceful frame. It settled, rough and smoky, in his voice as he spoke.

"I want you, Merrie Straffen Huntington. How much plainer do I have to make it?"

Merrie bit her lip, fighting the squeezing, the hurt of wanting in her chest. *I want you, Jack.* But not for just one night, or two. A lifetime of wanting was crowded into her very womanly heart. And to have him, to love him so much, knowing he didn't love her, knowing that sooner or later he would leave her again for his London ladies . . .

He turned with his eyes hot and his chest heaving, to search the sweet stubbornness of her face and naked shoulders. He had to win her head to have her heart and that would take words, the right words. "I didn't send word from London because I didn't know what to say. I was an idiot to have left at all. But I thought of you. God, how I thought of you. Every blessed day, every unending night." She swallowed hard and blinked to prevent tears from forming and he felt as if someone were turning an iron pike in his guts.

"I didn't see Deirdre. I don't know what she said to you to hurt you." But he could guess and he took a deep breath, preparing himself to speak the truth.

"There've been women. Many . . . women." He swallowed very hard. It was the most difficult thing he'd ever done, making himself meet her luminous, deep-seeing eyes. He could feel her reaching into him, gently sorting the precious honesty of his need from the dross of treacherous desire, which would say anything to have its way. It was purely painful. The muscles of his chest wall and belly were cramping and every nerve in his body was on fire.

It was the truth, Merrie knew. She'd always known. But she could see it in his eyes, which had become oddly clear and vulnerable, like a child's. He let her see, wanted her to see the kind of man he'd been. If she rejected him, that pained offering of self said, it should be for what he'd done, not for what she feared he had done. He didn't want his past to lay between them anymore. She could barely breathe.

"But there hasn't been any woman but you since the day I laid eyes on you, Merrie Straffen. I swear it." Lord, he wished the truth were more spectacular, that it would announce itself in the world with trumpet flares and a singular, dazzling radiance that would make it undisputable, undeniable. Why did truth have to be so meek a commodity, trussed and bound up in words which could be misconstrued or rejected . . . or ignored?

But Merrie didn't ignore it or misinterpret it. She gathered it gently into her heart and let it free the hope that was bound there. Her blood began to warm and flow again.

"Why did you marry me, Jack?"

It was the question he'd dreaded, the one for which he had no answer, except his own unworthiness. Ah, God, this *truth* was hard business indeed!

"It was arranged . . . according to your grandfather's wishes. I don't know why I was chosen." Lord knew that was the truth! He only wished the rest he was about to reveal didn't make him sound like such a heartless swine and feel like such a duplicitous rogue. How much of his fecklessness and perfidy did he have to reveal? "But I was in need of money. A fellow named Roscoe Swather was ready to make bread meal of my bones. I owed him gaming debts. I . . . gamble. My luck had been running thin. And when I was offered a chance for a marriage and a decent living, I took it, no questions asked. It was to be a marriage of convenience, I thought . . . until I saw you." His broad shoulders eased, his face softened, took on a breathtaking tenderness. "No one had told me anything about you," he said.

"You were the most *inconvenient* thing I'd ever encountered in my life." He stopped short of laying the entirety of his rake's pride at her feet, confessing how she'd aroused and mystified and utterly consumed him. "I'd never met a woman like you . . . you with your blessed questions and your big blue eyes and your innocence and your eagerness. And your hair. God, Merrie, how I love your hair. It's like the sun's own fire tamed to fit into a man's hands . . . my hands." He stumbled forward one step, the wanting a devastating pain in his chest, in his loins.

Time stretched so that it seemed to warp irretrievably. Neither heart beat.

"You really did want me?" she whispered, hope swelling recklessly within her. The question sliced to his very core.

"I did. Lord, I did. I *do*."

She stared at him, at the honest entreaty of his features, at the love shining in his eyes . . . and knew it was the truth. The sweet, inescapable truth. He wanted her as a woman, as his mate. A shiver of acceptance went through her shoulders and she closed her eyes, dislodging a tear down each cheek.

"Merrie?" He came to the edge of the bed, his arms

dangling emptily at his sides. "D-do you want me—
It sounded so pathetic he had to add, "To stay?"

Her luscious, cherry-ripe lips curved up in a womanly bow.

"Facta sunt potentiora verbis." And while the words
were still rumbling off the walls of his mind, she let
the sheet slide down her naked curves and translated
for him: "Deeds are more powerful than words."

She slid toward him on her knees, sank her fingers
into the slashings of the front of his doublet, and
pulled. His mouth closed over hers, ravening hot, fiery
sweet. His arms convulsed around her, clasping her
nakedness against his cinder-hot frame.

Joy erupted between them, sensual and consuming.
Merrie's arms slid around his neck and she opened her
mouth to him, her tongue circling, darting, dancing
over his as she pressed closer to his body. His hands
fed voraciously on the planes of her back, the taper of
her waist, and the ripeness of her buttocks.

They kissed and entwined, pressing, heated and
growing hotter. Merrie managed to loosen his embrace
and arch her body back, holding his mouth on hers
with a bold, erotic possession. Her fingers slipped between them to work feverishly at his buttons and his
hands soon joined them. Together they shucked off his
doublet and peeled off his shirt, but it was her eager
hands alone that attacked the ties of his breeches and
hose. His fingers were drawn to those long, velvety
nipples that jiggled and tickled against his ribs as she
worked. His hands closed over the cool globes of her
breasts and he caught those hard little spouts between
his fingers, rubbing them back and forth in a slow,
sinuous rhythm. She gasped against his mouth and
pressed hard against his hand, wanting more.

He moaned from deep in his chest and tore his hands
away to shed his boots and hose. Then with relentless
desire he pushed her back on the bed with his body
and down . . . down, beneath him. She welcomed his
weight on her, writhing with pure wanton pleasure

against his taut belly and hard, raspy chest. She was trapped . . . and soaring free.

"I want you, Jack Huntington."

He stared down into eyes that shimmered with a kind of triumphant desire he'd honestly never seen before. Her hips tilted and undulated against him, brushing her silky heat over him, and in his mind, her sweet little bottom was perched, mother-naked and wriggling, on the throne of his heart as well. He was a claimed man, a kingdom conquered.

"You have me, Merrie Huntington."

He took her mouth with his, nibbling, licking, toying luxuriantly with her lips. Then he kissed her chin, nuzzled her throat, and when she moaned and flexed her shoulders to encourage it, he captured one nipple gently between his teeth and flicked his tongue over and over it. She twitched with each stroke; pleasure radiated deep into her body, curling into her loins, releasing her moist woman's response.

"Oh Jack . . . love me . . . please. . . ."

He raised eyes black with need to her. Weeks of night cravings erupted in him, demanding satisfaction. "I will—every part of you."

He dropped his head to her other breast and growled as his mouth closed on it. "You have the longest, sleekest nipples I've ever seen. Ummmm. . . ."

"Is that good?" She sucked in a rapturous hiss as he suckled her.

"Delicious. Gourmands appreciate such things. And your skin . . ."

"It suits your tastes?"

"Perfectly . . . like sweet cream . . ."

Merrie sighed as he nibbled his way up her chest and down her arm to her elbow. He was devouring her, wild trills of sensation racked her heated body. It was scarcely bearable when he began to stroke her legs and hips and turned her over to nibble the backs of her knees. She began to tug and wriggle, turning on her side to return his nibbles and explore his body, that soft lacy hair on his chest, the hard mounds beneath. She kissed and licked, teasing him.

"You taste . . . salty . . . like salty wine." Her eyes and fingers feathered down that trickle of hair to the nesting swell of his manhood. Instinctively, her womanflesh tightened and she closed her eyes, touching him. His breath stopped when she slithered down his chest and belly, eyes still closed, nuzzling him, feeling him with her cheeks and nose and lips. And when her chin nudged his swollen shaft, she caught his eyes with hers and slowly, deliberately, rubbed his silken shaft with her face and her hair.

Pulling her up, sliding between her parting legs, he claimed her mouth and the aching center of her response in the same moment. He stroked and caressed her creamy heat, sending her higher and higher, on searing updrafts of pleasure. From cloud to cloud she soared, spread on hot winds of pleasure, open to him completely, surrendered to his power over her—trusting it. Then it came, that splintering release that seemed to dissolve the boundaries of her body. And in that quivering climactic state, her need for him was even wilder, deeper. Nothing would do but that she be joined to him, and in a breath she was.

He filled her with his hard length, filled her senses, filled her heart. She met his deep thrusts wildly, moaning his name, wrapping his legs with hers, taking him with her into those vast, steamy clouds of sensation. Together they rose until they burst the outer limits of those mists and soared above, flung into loving's brightest mansions of delight.

For a long time they lay together, spent and joined in some new, intangible way. Neither was willing to relinquish the other and when at last they made concession to comfort, it was only to turn onto their sides and adjust their embrace. She gazed into the sated glow of his face and smiled. He kissed the tip of her nose and closed his eyes, capturing the sensual luminance of her expression and the deep splendor of her eyes to hold inside him as he drifted to sleep.

* * *

Some time later, Merrie wakened to the sight of him watching her and the feel of his hard warmth around her. He smiled, a recklessly happy and tender smile that was utterly contagious. She smiled back and sent her fingers to trace his smile, thinking there never had been a man so handsome, so pleasureful. A trill of elation went through her; he belonged to her now . . . he wanted her. He raised onto his elbow and released her to roll onto her back and nestle in the crook of his body.

"It was the books, wasn't it?" He grinned.

Her laugh was pure intrigue, mystery and music combined.

"It was . . . say it was," he prodded. "You loved the books."

"I loved the books," she admitted. "But I loved what they meant even more. You did remember things I said. You did think of me."

"Every minute."

"And you really wanted me . . . as a woman." The awe in her voice sent a stab of sweet pain through his heart.

"That surprises you?" He laughed to counter the pain. "Sweeting, you're only the most desirable female I've known in my entire jaded and hopelessly hedonistic life."

"You don't think . . . I'm a little 'green'?"

He laughed, deeply and irresistibly, and she grinned with embarrassment for having been so candid. "God—" He wiped his eyes. "Yes, love, you're a little 'green' in places. In all the right places. You're 'green' enough to give without thinking of what you'll get in return, and to still forgive when others disappoint you . . . for which I am eternally grateful. But in every way a man needs a woman, you've all the experience a man could desire. You are a quick little thing, Merrie Huntington, and a curious minx in bed. What you don't know of loving probably isn't worth knowing."

"Oh." Merrie blushed deeply, utterly lost for how to respond. Every word spoke to one of her fears. Jack laughed again, seeing the wonder and relief in her face. He hugged her shoulders to him and felt one lush breast crush against his ribs. It sent a noticeable ripple of pleasure down his loins.

"Tell me, then." She got a very naughty glint in her eyes. "Do you think I should lie on my back . . . and show my face when we're making love? Or perhaps on my front—do you think Ovid would approve of my bottom?"

Jack almost blushed as he returned her grin. "I was a desperate man; you're a very stubborn woman. I did manage to hold your attention, I see."

"Or perhaps . . . that one where 'little gells should mount and ride like ponies' . . . that one had possibilities. You are much larger than I am."

"Merrie—" He watched the dance of seductive lights in her face and felt his blood stir mightily.

"Or perhaps that part where Milanion raised Atalanta's lovely legs upon his shoulders. Legs upon shoulders . . . hmmmm. How would that one go?" she mused, letting her tongue peep from the corner of her mouth. She raised one silky knee higher and higher along his rousing loins until it reached his stomach. "I suppose one would have to be awfully 'loose-boned' to manage—"

Jack growled and grabbed her and rolled onto his back, pulling her atop him. Her gasp and flush of embarrassment betrayed her sham of worldliness, but he gave her no quarter. "You wanted to learn, sweetest; you positively asked for it. More than once. Now open to me." He sent her his most beguilingly lustful look as he reached for the backs of her thighs and pulled them to his sides. "Come, sweeting, your *pony* is waiting."

She sat up slowly, testing this new position. She was a little shocked to be sitting, naked, astride a man's hot, naked belly. And he certainly was hot. His features had turned to bronze and his eyes glowed with the luster of polished Circassian amber. His hands came down to cup her breasts and to palm her nipples

in lazy, unending circles. She warmed under his sensual adorations and began to move, exploring parts of
him that had been hithèrto unreachable. She was fascinated by the way he twitched and writhed between
her thighs. Was this what it was like for him, this sense
of power?

Soon their play became earnest passion and she
stretched out on him to indulge in his kisses and to
feel his hard body as a cradling, rousing bed of sensation. Then he nudged her legs apart again and slid her
down onto his swollen shaft. He coaxed her to a sitting
position, to watch her rapturous wriggles as he stirred
inside her. Then at last, quivering with need, she
spread over him to meet his thrusts, grasping him possessively with her thighs.

They came together, arching, writhing, soaring . . .
then shattering the barriers of sense and separateness
in a blaze of light. Then, drifting warmly, they fashioned a comfortable niche in each other's body and
shared a steamy and exhausted glow.

"What a horsewoman you are, sweeting," Jack rumbled with a wry, endearing grin. Merrie giggled.

"Did I ever tell you how *loose-boned* I am?"

Tess had heard the muffled squeals of outrage and
the slamming of the door, and flew from her bed in a
half-fogged dither. Her first impulse had been to run
to her mistress's aid, but she stumbled back and forth
in her chamber, shaking her hands in anxiety. Something kept her from jolting down the hallway—and it
took a minute for her to realize that it was her own
nakedness. Groaning, she fumbled into her soft new
shift and ran into the dark hallway, colliding with Seabury and nearly toppling them both.

He managed to stay on his feet by the barest of mar-
gins and righted her on hers, then she tore away from
him to run into her mistress's chamber. She halted, her
hand over her mouth, at the foot of Merrie's empty
bed. Seabury's movement, behind her, startled her and
she turned, her eyes wide in the moonlight.

"I . . . saw 'er to bed here, tonight," she explained in a frantic whisper. "I heard a racket . . . an' now she's gone."

Instinctively they both suspended their breath to listen. There was silence. Terrifying silence to her ears; promising silence to his. He took a deep breath that dismissed Jack and Lady Merrie altogether, and let his eyes roam Tess's curvy, half-dressed form. Her hair was loosely plaited, hanging over the shoulder that her loose-hanging garment had bared.

"Oh, sir, I fear he's come an' . . . done somethin' to 'er."

Seabury's eyes glinted; undoubtedly Jack was doing something to her. Probably the selfsame thing Seabury was wishing he could do to desirable little Tess just now. His body heated precipitously at the thought.

"Ah, Mistress Tess, you do worry." He came closer, his voice warm and comforting. "Lady Merrie's in no danger; Master John is her husband."

"But I heard a cry—"

"A bit of a tiff, no doubt. She is unhappy about his absence. . . ." Seabury stood a pace away, remembering the feel of Tess's curvy body pressed against him in all innocence, wishing he had a greater share of Jack's smoothness with women. In truth, he had something far more effective: Tess's complete adoration.

"Why, Mistress Tess." His voice grew betrayingly husky, but it didn't seem to alarm her. He grinned at that piece of fortune. "You're trembling. Come, sit. . . ." He put a consoling arm around her to usher her to the bench at the foot of the bed. "You musn't worry for your mistress. He cares for her a very great deal. I'm sure they'll settle their differences quickly."

"Ye do think so?" Tess gazed up into his handsome face, her worries for her mistress evaporating in the warmth of his gaze. He nodded. She realized his arm was still around her when it tightened, pulling her closer to his side, turning her toward his chest. Her body was tingling strangely wherever it pressed his. He was so firm and gentle, so accessibly male. He never overwhelmed or frightened a gell, as Master John was wont to do.

"No one else calls me Mistress Tess," she managed to say, having to moisten her lips with her tongue. "Only you, Mister Seabury."

"Thomas, remember?" he admonished, aching to have that darting tongue moisten his as well. "Mistress Tess suits you. I was pleased to hear Lady Merrie made you her companion. And your new gowns are twice becoming." His mention of clothes made them both achingly aware of how little she was wearing just now. Her eyes dropped from his and she stiffened as if to pull away. He wouldn't let her. "But with all your new finery, sweet Tess, I much prefer you as you are now." It was a bold and seductive thing to say and it surprised sensible Seabury. They were both surprised when she answered in kind.

"I prefer it, too."

Bit by tantalizing bit, her body was melting against him, trusting, seeking. Seabury did the only reasonable thing. He lowered his head to hers and claimed the liquid treasure of her mouth, gently then with deepening passion. Tess nearly shattered in his arms. This was exactly what she'd dreamt of since that night weeks ago. . . .

Overwhelmed by powerful longings, she imitated the movements of his mouth and the delicious probing of his tongue. He pulled her tight against him, and through her loose linen garment she felt his hands moving on her waist, her back, her shoulders. Those possessing strokes made her bubbies tingle and burn so that she had to press them hard against him. It was the very sign he needed. He rose and scooped her into his arms and carried her around the post to the bed.

He cradled and stroked and teased her, letting her learn about kissing and lovemaking at her own pace. When she bared her nubile young breasts to him, he adored and excited them in every way possible. And when she would have bared the rest of her as well, he halted her hands with his.

"Are you sure?" he asked, shifting to search the dark pools of her eyes in the moonlight and feeling a bit unnerved by his protective impulse toward her.

"It's time," Tess whispered, feeling in his reluctance the assurance that he was the right one. "Most gells on Straffen 'ave by three-and-ten. I'm well along in sixteen." She reached up to touch his burning cheek. "M'lady says it be very nice." When he was silent, she withdrew her hand and a hint of anxiety entered her voice. "It is nice . . . isn't it?"

Seabury closed his eyes. "Yes, sweet Tess, it's . . . very nice."

"I want it to be you . . . Thomas."

"I want it to be me, too, sweet Tess." He claimed her love-swollen lips and began a slow, tantalizing assault on her senses. Soon he lay entwined with her softness, claiming that most precious of treasures and wishing tomorrow would never come.

Everyone could see a peace had been made between Lady Merrie and her husband. They appeared in the hall the next morning to breakfast, staring fondly, openly at each another. They had a ride, a long one, and returned to seek out Straffen's carpenter. Jack had a notion to build a special set of shelves in the small parlor to hold the books he'd brought Merrie. They spent considerable time with old Jud, the carpenter, measuring the books and the wall and deciding on the best placement. They were so absorbed in their task and in each other that they failed to notice the Lombards' meaningful scowls and attempts to draw Jack aside.

But when Master Cramden appeared in the hall, to pay his respects and insist on a private word with Master Huntington, they were forced to pay some heed to what transpired around them. Merrie pulled Jack down to kiss his cheek and declared she'd be upstairs with Tess, whom she hadn't seen all morning. He stroked her cheek and watched the sway of her bottom with wistful lust as she mounted the stairs.

"S-sir!" Cramden sputtered irritably, waving toward the small parlor for the interview Jack dreaded. Jack took a deep breath and set both his shoulders and his mind as he strolled into the room. Gert and Manley Lombard appeared miraculously, as before, and their overt hostility raised the air temperature noticeably.

"What on earth can you be thinking, sir, coming here like this?" Cramden demanded. "This is a bald violation of the marriage agreements!"

"They are *marriage* agreements, after all." Jack crossed his arms over his chest and spread his legs, seeming very large and determined. "I've come to visit my wife. I see nothing untoward or outrageous in that."

"Ye know the lay o' things! Ye mus' withdraw at once, sir—" Manley barged forward.

"And break my lady's heart anew?" Jack narrowed his eyes. "I'll do no such thing. Now that I'm here, it would be sheer folly to pack me off again so quickly. *Questions* would be raised, not to mention that it would cause Lady Merrie unhappiness." At the mention of "questions" the grim tribunal exchanged looks of alarm. Jack's handsome face took on an expression that was half threat, half smile. "I intend to have a proper stay this time. What possible difference could a few days here or there make?"

"It might make a baby—" Gert snarled, only to be cut short by a frantic Cramden.

"At least have the decency to spare the gell your . . . fleshly impositions," Cramden sputtered. "The whole house is awag with talk of how you forced her to your bed last night. Prithee, sir, let the gell return to her own bed."

"Damn you," Jack growled with such vehemence that their neck hairs stood on end. "She is my wife and where she sleeps and what passes between us is none of your affair!" He strode for the door, but turned back, raking them with a look of murderous contempt. "I was right; you *are* perverted . . . the lot of you!" And he stormed out.

Manley turned on Cramden and his turnip-faced wife. "Ye had to do it, didn' ye? Had to go pokin' about in 'is beddin' ar-rangements. Now we'll ne'er get him off!"

"Well, we can't 'ave him makin' a babe on the gell," Gert snapped. "He's got too big for his britches, the randy hound!" She turned on Cramden. "Ye mus' do somethin', Cramden."

"Me?" Cramden found them united in that prodding stare again. Why was it the dirty work always fell his way in this partnership? he wondered, moaning. "Look you, we must be cautious in our movements . . . prudent. And the prudent thing to do is to give him a few days to get the yearning for her out of his system. 'Tis the novelty, I trow. He'll soon be on to—"

"But we got anoth'r night visit," Gert replied, slashing a look around her and lowering her voice dramatically. "Things is hot in London. Whene'er the message comes, we mus' be ready. We cannot have Sir Daniel and 'is queen's men hearin' of Huntin'ton's presence an' comin' callin'—snoopin'—like before."

Sweat beaded on Cramden's fleshy face at Gert's reminder. The thought of what was at stake, his own corpulent neck included, forced him to reconsider. "Please, let us give him a few days. I shall stay, try to make him see reason. Th-then if he persists . . . " He looked a bit green about the gills, and Gert finished for him.

"Then we shall deal with him."

Each day Cramden found a fresh excuse to lengthen his stay at Straffen, resorting to a concocted gout attack, which required him to sit in the hall with his leg wrapped in a pilaster of vinegar and brown paper and propped upon a stool. His gambit, however, made it appallingly easy for Jack to escape him, by simply steering Merrie upstairs or outside. Merrie couldn't help but notice Jack's avoidance of the portly, affable solicitor and raised the subject as they picnicked one afternoon on their hill, beneath their tree.

"Master Cramden will think we've abandoned him altogether." She raised her head from his chest to look up at him. He sat with his back propped against the tree's trunk, holding Merrie in his arms.

"If he's going to intrude on our 'honeymoon,' he has to expect to feel like an outsider." Jack grinned, opening one eye to peer down at her. "He ought to hike up his gouty leg and hie himself home."

"Fiend." She gave his shoulder a good-natured swat, then frowned. "Honeymoon? What's that?"

"It's what John Heywood—he's amongst the books I brought you—calls the first month or so after marriage, when fleshly pleasures of marriage are new and unbridled. Think a minute. . . . Honey—luscious and sweet—and a month of moonlit nights."

Merrie's lashes lowered and her cheeks flushed. Jack knew exactly how to appeal to the hidden sensualist in her. She saw his eyes closing, his head bending.

"You know why Master Cramden's here, of course." *That* brought both of his eyes open and his head up instantly. He stared at her as the question registered. How could she know . . . ? "He's worried about me. I think he worries about what may happen to me in your . . . clutches. I've seen the looks he and the Lombards give you."

"Me? Me . . . do you harm?" He huffed a half-laugh at the irony of it. Bright little Merrie missed very little indeed. She'd caught the looks, the whispers, felt the covert clash of wills.

"I think they may fear you'll leave again soon. I was so unhappy before. They're very protective of me."

Protective. It rumbled about in his head as she snuggled her cheek against his soft shirt again. Somehow that word didn't quite describe Cramden's and the Lombards' behavior toward her. It was close, but they seemed more involved . . . more self-interested . . . more possessive. . . . It rumbled about in him for a minute, taking hold. *Possessive.* Impressions combined and linkages formed in his mind, whipping up vague apprehensions. They wanted him gone . . . and not just to satisfy some wretched will, he realized. They wanted her to themselves; she was *theirs!* The conclusion was so obvious and inescapable he was amazed he hadn't seen it before.

Their possessiveness extended to her time and presence and even into the realm of the flesh; they were purely horrified by the fact that he bedded *their* little mistress! What further proof could he need? Quick on the heels of that discovery came a question that was even more alarming: If they wanted her to themselves, what did they want her *for?* Even as he grappled with that unholy thought, Merrie's voice brought him back to the present and gave him a clue.

"Please don't be angry with them." She'd seen the turmoil in his face and now stroked his cheek. "They're just so used to taking care of us Straffens. They took care of my grandfather for years and years before me."

"Years and years?" He sounded a bit choked. For some reason, vivid impressions of old Sir Edwin's sickbed flashed into Jack's mind. Years and years . . . tended by the grasping Makepiece. . . . His mind churned like a windlass, pulling the truth closer, trying to make it come clear in his mind. Then Makepiece's porcine face was replaced by Cramden's, and old Sir Edwin became . . .

"Merrie." He sat up straight, taking her by the shoulders and trying to mask his agitation. "How much do you know about your grandfather?"

"Well, not much. Only things they've told me. He was sickly a long while. What is it, Jack?" She sensed the intensity in him and it puzzled her.

"How old was he, the old earl?" His eyes glinted as she frowned and thought.

"I don't know precisely. But quite ancient, I'm afraid. My own father, his son, was past two score and ten when I was sown. And he died almost seventeen years ago. Then my grandfather must have been . . . near ninety? Could that be?"

"It is possible. Then the Lombards must have taken excellent care of him indeed." He wondered why that thought didn't reassure him. He pulled her tightly into his arms and made himself relax. Merrie pushed back in his embrace, her thoughts set on another, very womanly course. Her cheeks pinked.

"It seems we Straffens have never been overly lusty . . . or prolific."

The concern in her eyes and her apologetic tone captured him utterly, and he shoved his own worries aside for the present. He smiled warmly into her upturned face. "Perhaps the fates were saving it all for you. You're a sensuous little delight, my love." She flushed deeply, glancing about to see if Seabury and Tess were still nearby. He caught her look and grinned, caressing her waist meaningfully. "Don't look for rescue, lovey. Seabury had orders to escort your Tess back to the house long ago."

The suggestion in his declaration escaped her as she was recaptured by her original worry. "Jack, what if . . . we have no children?"

The pensiveness of her expression sent that question drilling into the core of him. His chest was suddenly squeezing, his heart beating faster. She stared at him with those big velvety eyes that grew luminous with anxiety. *They* didn't want her to have children. *Damn them.*

"If you want babies, Merrie, you'll have them. I swear it." The raw intensity of his eyes and words unnerved her for one brief moment. Then the sun itself came out in his face, a dazzling, captivating light that made her forget all else. His lips crushed hers as his hands attacked the buttons at the throat of her long bodice. By the time she managed to surface from that mind-numbing kiss, her bodice lay open and her stitchet and shift were retreating. A heartbeat later, his hand closed on the aching flesh of her bared breast. Two heartbeats later, his mouth followed.

She gasped. "Jack . . . ohhh, Jack. . . . Here?" His only answer was to send one hand beneath her skirts to her silky hip. She quivered and began to wriggle helplessly against him. "Jack, surely not here."

"Why not here?" He raised a grin of pure lust to her. "I thought you wanted babies, my love. I'm doing my best to accommodate you. This *is* how they're gotten, you know."

Her eyes widened as his fingers began to move beneath her skirts, teasing, tantalizing. He kissed her deeply and her eyes closed. Her voice was noticeably huskier when she dragged her lips away to say, "But . . . how?"

"You're quite a horsewoman, love." His wicked, whispered laugh brought her eyes open. "And am I not your favorite pony?"

Chapter Seventeen

Merrie basked in the warmth of Jack's unwavering attention, treasuring their daily sharing of tasks and talk and their nightly sharing of sensual delights. It seemed he had made up for the six weeks of his absence with six gloriously intimate days and six long, liquid nights. And as she watched him, day by day, inserting himself into Straffen's routine, she was convinced that he meant what he said, that he had no desire for his London life or associations.

Each morning after they rode, Jack would spend some time in the stables, studying the riding stock, suggesting small improvements in harness or exercise, or putting a hand to a horse Chester was working. Chester always jerked a nod in acknowledgment of Jack's expertise with horses and set about what he was bidden. But he made it clear; there was never true willingness in his obedience. On the seventh morning after his return to Straffen, Jack asked if any of the saddle mounts had ever been raced, and Chester answered, "Nay, sarr," refusing to raise his head. Jack released a very controlled breath.

"You don't like me much, do you, Chester?" Jack stood scowling, his legs spread and arms crossed determinedly over his chest. There was a long, resentful silence in which Chester raised a beetled brow and drew back physically, as if wary of the question and the man who asked it.

"Don' much matter wot I like . . . an' not." Hulking Chester turned partway, lifting an accusing glance at Jack from the corner of his eye. "Ye won' be 'ere long . . . sarr." That disapproving glare blatantly recalled the circumstance of their first meeting—around a bed-chamber door—and conveyed Chester's flat estimate that Jack would soon be off, plying his pleasures elsewhere.

Jack watched Chester turn away and felt his chest constricting, his arms flexing, his fists clenching. He strode out of the stable, straight for the house. Dammit! Chester, doey-eyed little Tess, old Bevis—they all watched, expecting him to leave, to just up and abandon Merrie again! Well? his beleaguered conscience taunted snidely, if he wasn't going to leave, what *was* he going to do? He'd been stalling, putting it off for days now.

"Master Cramden!" Jack hailed the gimping solicitor the instant he set foot in the hall. "I would have a word with you, sir. Be so good as to join me. . . ." There was an unpleasant snap in his tone and a command in the way he swept his hand toward the parlor.

Cramden hoisted himself up from his chair with a look of alarm at Gert Lombard, who ran to fetch Manley. They arrived at the door of the small parlor just in time to hear Cramden declare: ". . . more than generous with you, sir, in light of your unthinkable obstinance. Withdraw from Straffen, forthwith, or be prepared to loose your stipend!"

Jack watched the ferret-brown pair of Lombards weasel through the door to stand behind Cramden, and his eyes glittered. "Take it then. *Take the damnable stipend!* I'm not leaving her. Not again . . . not ever."

"W-what?" "Noooo—" and "God's Almighty Teeth!" they exclaimed, recoiling in shock.

"B-but you cannot—" Cramden sent his fleshy paws frantically into his doublet, looking for his handkerchief; he was breaking into a raging sweat. "Have you no inkling of the tumult—"

"I'm staying, Cramden." Jack included the Lombards in his furious glare as he demanded: "Get used to it."

A hot, charged silence spread among them. "It be

th' money." Gert spat, discharging sparks of contention as she turned on her fellow conspirators. "I knowed he'd be wantin'—"

"Damn your eyes!" Jack swore in earnest and jolted forward to tower over her. "It's not the cursed money! I don't want the wretched stipend, or anything else from Straffen—except Merrie. I've married her . . . and I intend to live with her and make babies on her and grow old with her."

Gert stiffened, quivering with outrage at this fresh flaunting of his lusts for the gell. "Well, ye cannot!" she declared, lifting her tight-eyed fury straight into Jack's face. "Tell 'em, Cramden. Tell 'em 'bout the will!"

"God, yes, the will!" Cramden mopped himself furiously, thinking frantically. "You have violated its provisions, sir, and *in jure*—"

"That accursed will!" Jack spun on him. "Fine. Bring it on. I wish to see it myself—this *will* that supposedly bars me from living with my wife in all decency and harmony. Bring it on, and let us see just what perverted moonflaws a ninety-year-old man could have conjured to twist the lives of his own blood kin! Bring it on, and then prepare to answer how that ancient and infirm old cod could possibly have known I existed, much less chosen me to mate his unseen granddaughter. Or will you swear it was dauncy old Sir Edwin that put me forward, that frayed old cuff who has not had a lucid day in years?"

The Lombards' eyes were the size of goose eggs. He knew about Sir Edwin? They turned in horror to Cramden, who purpled and looked away guiltily. He'd received a message from Makepiece saying that Huntington had been to see the old chocker. He'd withheld that worrisome news from the Lombards, knowing their volatile natures and praying it signified nothing of importance. That now proved to have been a disastrous bit of discretion.

"What—no answer?" Jack thundered. Then his voice dropped to a dangerous rasp: "Bring on this *will* of yours. And be prepared to defend it and yourselves before the crown itself and the church's high courts. No doddering old croat, or scheming agents, or overfed lawyers can tamper with that which the Almighty Himself ordained—the true union of a man and woman in marriage. I'll take it to the queen herself, and hear what that good Catholic lady has to say!''

The queen. Good Lord. They were struck dumb.

Jack watched the shock deflect their outrage for the moment and seized the final word before stalking out.

''I'm staying.''

It was a full minute before they came to their senses. Cramden staggered, pale as pot cheese, into a chair, and Manley had to slide his feet farther apart to keep from toppling. Gert stood like a stony gray tower amidst their heaving panic. Her eyes darted furiously. Her mind raced.

''He knows . . . too much.'' Cramden groaned and bit his lip as though in pain.

''Whadda we do?'' Manley wrung his hands, scowling.

'' 'E's dang'rous. We mus' get rid of 'im,'' Gert declared flatly. ''Th' sooner, th' better. . . . Tonight.''

Their gazes came to rest on her and when the idea took hold, they nodded . . . even Cramden. This was no time for fishy-livered sentiment. Great things were at stake here, and they were not about to let Huntington's greed and his unbridled lust for their little charge imperil months—years!—of work.

''Tonight,'' they agreed.

Outside, Tess froze, flattened against the wall, hearing those awful words reverberating in her head. ''. . . get rid of 'im,'' her mother had said. Rid of Master John. Tess's brown eyes widened in horror, and her heart pounded like a doe's in flight. She hadn't meant to listen, truly. She'd just been passing. And she'd heard raised, angry voices, just enough to know that they were insisting Master John leave Straffen for some reason that had to do with the old earl's will . . . and that he refused to leave. And her mother called him "dang'rous."

Tess had known her parents and Master Cramden did not get on well with Master John for some reason. But she also knew Lady Merrie loved her handsome husband with all her heart, and that since his return he'd done everything in his power to make up for his hurtful absence at the start of their marriage. He must care for Lady Merrie—the way he looked at her and touched her and spoke of her. But why would her parents call him 'dang'rous' and insist he leave Straffen, if not for Lady Merrie's sake? It was all so fearful and confusing! What, who, to believe? She'd never been so conflicted in her life!

The sound of the parlor door creaking open jarred her back to the present and she slid back along the wall, praying she wouldn't be seen. Master Cramden and her mother and father exited the parlor in the other direction, looking grim and determined. They paused in the main hall and Gert and Manley exchanged nods before Manley strode purposefully out the door to the rear yard.

Tess clutched her heart and ran for the servant stairs at the far end of the passageway. Once upstairs, she ran smack into Lady Merrie, who had been hauling a trunk from her old chamber down the hallway toward Tess's chamber.

"Why, Tess, you're pale as a sheet," Merrie declared, feeling for her icy hands. "Are you all right?"

"F-fine m'lady. I jus' need a . . . rest." Tess shrank away and hurried into her chamber, shutting the door firmly.

Merrie watched her, frowning, wondering. Tess had been unholy distracted these last few days and Merrie had seen the potent, longing looks that passed between her and Thomas Seabury. It was clear as French window glass that the little maid was smitten. Had Seabury done something untoward? She thought of Seabury's sensible good looks and restrained, kindly manner. Surely not. She chewed the inner corner of her lip. But perhaps she should mention it to Jack . . . get his opinion. . . .

It was well past the witching hour. All shapes had become shadows and all shadows had taken on a sinister changeability. The darkened house was shrouded in quiet that was broken by the click of the latch on Tess's chamber door. Seabury's head appeared in the opening, listening, peering into the inky gloom of the windowless, unlit hallway. Then he pulled back a moment, closing the door partway.

"My little dove"—he pulled Tess's trembling, scantily clad form into his arms—"you musn't be afraid. You've done right, telling me; I'll not betray your trust." He searched her features in the dimness and collected one last, painfully sweet kiss before slipping into the hallway.

The light was better along the gallery, where moonlight came through the leaded windows. Seabury felt his way along to the door of the master chamber, took a deep breath, and slipped inside.

Jack was startled by the feel of a hand clamped over his mouth and an arm across his chest. An instant later he recognized Seabury's hiss of warning. "We've got to talk," Seabury whispered, pointing to Merrie's form, snuggled against Jack's side. His whisper became even fainter. "Not here."

Jack made out the jerk of Seabury's thumb toward the door and sat up, taking pains to disengage gently from Merrie's warm curves. As he reached for his long shirt and breeches, he saw Seabury slip outside. Moments later he stepped out onto the gallery, still tying the band of his breeches.

"Seabury?" he whispered, craning his neck and squinting, examining the shapes and shadows around him. None moved. None had human dimensions. He took a deep breath and inched along the gallery railing, senses alert, humming with expectation. Louder this time he repeated, "Seabury?"

A muffled cough came from below and Jack tensed. He moved around the gallery and down the stairs with painstaking stealth. It must be dire indeed, he realized, for Seabury to roust him in the dead of night. He paused at the bottom of the stairs, searching the dim shapes of the hall: table, chairs, candlestand, sideboard. No Seabury. He squinted, sweeping the hall again and this time located him by a perceived movement, near the blackened hallway that led toward the side parlor door.

"What in hell's going on, Seabury?" He reached the hallway. "What is—?"

Jagged lightning exploded in his head, in all his senses. And as he reeled and his knees crumpled beneath him, all faded to gray . . . then black.

There was a rustle, then another, and yet another. Then came the sound of a body being dragged from the dark hallway into the brighter main hall itself. Now three solemn forms stood over two silent ones.

"Obligin' of 'em . . . walkin' straight into it that a'way," Manley observed, his arms crossed so that he appeared to be hugging a cast-iron poker to his chest. "I thought we'd 'ave to clout 'em in their sleep."

It wasn't long before the insensible Jack and Seabury were trussed up like Christmas geese, heaved into the back of a horse cart, and covered with a blanket and a thin layer of hay. Their saddled horses were tied on behind and stolid Chester mounted onto the board seat of the cart.

"Remember"—Gert grabbed his arm with forbidding force "—don't stop 'til ye reach Morris's house. Ye give 'im this." She handed him a sealed letter and he stared at it, nodded, and tucked it inside his rough leather jerkin. "An' don't bungle it, ye great looby!" She gave him a stout warning swat on the shoulder and waved him off.

Chester scowled, rubbed his arm, and swapped the reins to set the horse in motion. Soon the creak of the wooden cart wheels was only a dim whisper and Straffen's three agents melted back into the house . . . to their respective chambers. And all was quiet once again.

Merrie wakened and stretched lazily the next morning, finding the bed beside her empty. She smiled at the hollow where his body had lain through the night and got up to call Bevis to dress her. Jack often rose before her and walked about the place, just at sunrise. She'd see him soon, downstairs, in the hall.

But he wasn't in the hall and she broke fast without him, expecting to see him at any minute. He was probably delayed, maybe in the stables. . . . She finished quickly and bade heavy-eyed Tess good-morning on her way out the door to join him.

But he wasn't in the stables. And when she looked for Chester to ask him if he'd seen Jack, she found him absent as well. She shrugged, puzzled, until she realized they could be out by one of the pastures together. As she turned to go, her eye caught on that stall at the far end, where Jack's big stallion was kept. It was empty and she studied it for a moment, enlarging it with the realization that Seabury's mount was gone as well. Ah, that explained it. They were out for a ride, then. She'd see him when he returned.

But the morning came and went as she fashioned patterns for clothing for Straffen's inhabitants, and still no Jack. It wasn't like him to leave for so long without telling her where he was bound, she thought. He'd been scrupulous about it since his return, as if constantly assuring her of his presence, his permanence. Tess seemed alarmed when Merrie asked if Jack or Seabury had mentioned where they were going and when they'd be back. She paled so that Merrie had to order her to hand over her shears to goodly Bevis and sit down a while.

Mid-afternoon, Merrie watched the Lombards and Master Cramden in earnest consultation at the rear of the hall and realized she'd not thought of asking them.

Indeed, she'd seen precious little of them this day. She put down her shears and left her pattern making.

"Goodwife, Mister Lombard, have you seen Master John this day? I've not seen him and . . ."

The threesome exchanged doleful looks and both Gert and Manley gave Cramden an elbow in the side, forcing him forward to deliver the bad news. He stuck a finger between his wattly cheek and his beleaguered ruff, as though it, or something he was about to say, choked him.

"He is . . . gone, dear sweet lady." There was such suffering, such pathos in his fleshy face that Merrie knew instantly he meant *gone indeed*. She stiffened, clasping her hands before her to control them.

"This is no jest, sir." She swallowed hard. The growing alarm of the morning now jangled furiously along her nerves. "No laughing matter a'tall. Now be so good as to tell me where he has gone."

"T-to London, I must suppose, m'lady. No doubt, this morn, a-at sunrise. And his man Seabury with him."

"It be true, m'lady." Manley stepped forward to confirm it. "He got a letter yest'rd'y frum London . . . an' their horses is gone. . . ."

"But he wouldn't have left without telling me. He wouldn't—" Merrie felt as though everything in her body was going liquid and draining to her knees. A cold, empty feeling was creeping, seeping into the void that was left. Not again. Please, not again. "A-and his trunk . . . his clothes—" She'd seen his doublet and boots on the floor in the chamber that morning; she grasped furiously for some footing in denial.

"Ah, likely he'll be sendin' fer 'em." Manley winced at the slip and looked pained. They had forgotten about the rake's clothes and such. They held their breaths, hoping she wouldn't ask any more questions.

Merrie wanted to scream it wasn't so, wanted to stomp and rage and make them quit this cruel hoax. But their dark avoidance of her gaze and the pained anxiety in the looks they exchanged validated their news. He was gone. He had left her, once again. No. She wouldn't believe it, couldn't believe it.

She made it to the stairs before Tess was there . . . and Bevis. They put their arms around her waist and helped her to her chamber. And as they assisted her to a chair, her eyes fixed on his tall, elegant boots . . . on the floor, just as she had remembered . . . and silent, choking tears began to roll.

"Dammitall to S-seventh Hell and back—Damn, damn, *damn!* Can you do nothing right? Keep hold of him, you thick-headed s-swad—" A foul litany of invectives coupled with rude jostling, hoisting, and thunking falls jarred Jack awake . . . or as awake as he might be with a bruised brain and after a full day of unconsciousness. His head was pounding, his eyes were grainy and thick, his mouth and throat were coated with burning dust—and he was close to retching from the pain in his head and the heaving lurches of his own body through the dark space about him.

"In there," said that snarling voice from somewhere near his feet. A pure demon, it flashed in Jack's beleaguered brain, and he writhed to escape it. Suddenly he was falling in blackness, bounced and thudding down against sharp edges and landing with the wind knocked from his lungs on something that half howled, half grunted . . . another human? "S-shit!" came that demon hiss from farther away. "It's a cellar, piss-head—*steps!* Did you kill him?"

Something—somebody—moaned and heaved from beneath Jack, rolling him onto a hard something—a floor? He was hoisted and dragged through a graying, unfocused fog, where distant lights danced and human shapes lumbered. It seemed as if a veil had fallen from his senses, and it took a few minutes of blinking and concentrated breathing to realize it was actually a blanket that had slipped. He managed to raise his head and look about. He was indeed on a stone floor, in a dank, cavernlike cellar—a truthful demon, after all—and on a pile of fetid straw. A dim tallow lantern set on a barrel shed a circle of sickly yellow light nearby. It was enough to make out human forms on the steps, laboring with something. . . .

Moments later Seabury was dumped on the pile of straw beside him, and Jack found himself squinting against the pain to behold Chester Lombard being verbally disemboweled by a slighter, exceedingly well dressed fellow with that hissing-demon voice and . . . Gert Lombard's face!

"Just who in sulphurous hell do they think they are, saddling me with this?" The demon shook a wadded paper in Chester's face. "I've done their legal tinkering—wills and guardianships—but I'll have naught to do with this! I don't want to even see this mess—or you, do you understand? Keep the bastards out of my sight or I swear I'll have your balls for olives!"

"B-but I cain't—" Chester pulled in his neck. His eyes blackened with old hatreds and fresh resentments. "I have ta—"

"You have to do exactly what I say, you bloody stupid lump of beef!" The demon punched a nasty finger into Chester's wide chest. "I won't play keeper to their stupidities! You'll stay and see to them yourself, or just kill them now and get it over with—I don't give a damn which! But I don't want to see hide nor hair of them or you." He cuffed Chester's ear viciously. "Do you hear?"

Chester's stolid frame quivered with suppressed rage as the dapper demon stormed up the crumbling stone steps and banged the heavy door behind him. It was a long moment before he calmed and came to examine his charges, rolling them over, testing their bonds, and staring into their eyes and mouths—as though checking his horses back on Straffen.

"Wh-ere are we?" Jack's parched voice cracked. "What are we doing here, and who is that sewer-mouthed wretch?"

"London." Chester stood up, his face as dark as the corners of that dank cellar. " 'E's me bruther, Marris.

E's . . . a law-yer." He turned and took the dingy light with him.

"The bastard certainly favors his mother in looks and temper," Jack snarled.

Out of the darkness came Seabury's parched rasp, reassuring Jack and unnerving him all at once.

"God, Jack. We're in trouble."

Merrie hardly slept that night in Straffen's great empty bed. She kept feeling Jack beside her, kept hearing his soft murmurs in her ear, kept feeling the warm caress of his breath moving her hair. His presence was all around her, all through her. Then why wasn't he there?

Nothing felt real the next morning; not her surroundings; not her thoughts that were trapped in hopeless circles; not the dull, throbbing pain in her middle. She walked about the hall, the gallery, and, later, the soggy, rain-beaten garden, in a fog. She'd trusted him . . . forgiven, forgotten . . . believed in him. Why would he betray all he'd seemed to work so hard at building between them these last days? *Where are you, Jack?*

The Lombards watched her with growing concern. Cramden looked to be near tears each time he set eyes on her.

"Stiffen up, Cramden," Gert admonished irritably. "We done what needs must be."

"For whom, Goodwife?" Cramden sighed wearily. "And what shall we do if the rake won't recant, won't stay in London and honor the agreement?"

"Morris'll make him see." Gert lifted her chin. "My boy's th' smart one—a lawyer, fully read. He'll know wot to do."

"How long will you keep us here?" Jack demanded repeatedly through that dark, harrowing night and well after gray wisps of light shoved through a crude glass window, set high in one wall. "For god's sake, Chester—"

No answer. Never an answer. Perhaps Chester didn't know.

"Then at least tell us what you're planning to do with us. Why are we here?" Seabury tried.

Still no answer. They were trussed up, hand and foot, kept on pallets of mangy straw in a dank cavern of a cellar, somewhere in the bowels of London . . . all because Jack refused to relinquish his husbandly rights to Merrie and his affections toward her. Jack's head throbbed, his throat was parched, and the fleas and nameless other vermin in the straw were making a feast of his bare shins. *Think, Jack—*

Just because Chester didn't talk didn't mean he wasn't listening, Jack reasoned desperately. He prayed that Chester's dislike of him was outbalanced by Chester's regard for his mistress. He began to work on Chester bit by bit. "What are their plans for Lady Merrie . . . your mother and father and Cramden?" he demanded several times. Chester lay on a pallet of straw exactly like theirs, across the cellar, and never answered. Jack tried again.

"What are they going to do to Merrie now that we're out of the way?" His own words jolted him; they had most certainly been removed for a purpose. Anxiety spread cold tendrils through him, like the fusty, seeping dampness of the cellar. "I swear, Chester, if they harm her in any way . . ." He saw Chester sit up and get to his knees in the dim lamplight. There was a twitch in the tight line of his mouth, and his coarse face was darkened with doubt.

"They won' hurt m'lady," Chester blurted out.

"Good God, Chester—" Jack drew tight as a strung bow. He'd finally struck a nerve in that great lump of humanflesh. "Look what they've done to her already! They've trumped up some bogus will, married her off to a known rake and gambler, hired that gorgon Overbeake to pinch her if she asked even the smallest question." Jack's aching head swam as the insight hit him. The pieces fell unerringly together: old Sir Edwin and the old earl . . . a governess to control her . . . a bridegroom who would take the money and ask no questions, leaving her . . . alone. It arrayed itself in his mind with fearsome clarity.

"They didn't want her to ask questions. They were afraid she'd learn how they were manipulating her and her holdings." Could it honestly be as simple as greed? "That has to be it," he answered himself. "The holdings. They made free with the old earl's accounts while he lived, and when he died they arranged to take care of his granddaughter the same way. Lord, Chester, you can't let them do this to her. She's the rightful Lady of Straffen! She has a right to a life of her own. With her rightful husband."

"Ye—ye jus' wont 'er yerself." Chester's dark eyes flashed.

"You're damned right I want her!" Jack's temper blazed as he wrestled against his bonds and made it to his knees. "She's my woman, my wife, my very heart! And you'll have to kill me to keep me from going back to her! Do it, then, just finish me off! Because if I live, I swear, I'm going straight back to Straffen for Merrie, and I'm going to get rid of those conniving vermin—"

Every muscle in Chester's body was flexed, swollen with a savage force that was a hairsbreadth away from unleashing mayhem. A growl rumbled from deep in his throat, and his hamlike fists came up to crash head-on against each other. The sound of bone smacking bone carried sickeningly through the cellar. He whirled, his face like bruised granite, and heaved himself up the steps and outside, slamming the heavy door behind him.

"That was close, Jack." Seabury exhaled, going limp on the moldy straw nearby. "The next time you're feeling a bit reckless with your lifeblood, do you think you could make it clear to him you're speaking only for yourself?"

Chapter Eighteen

Merrie couldn't eat. Not fresh-baked bread spread with herbed olive oil, nor the pepper-roasted pork Edythe Lombard had fixed specially, nor even her favorite fresh raspberry tarts. She sat in the small parlor, in a chair by the window, looking at the writing table where Jack had sat only three days earlier, scratching a fresh-shaved quill over creamy parchment. The sun was streaming in, just as it had been that day. His soft raven hair had shone in the sunlight and his handsome, angular features had glowed. When he felt her gaze on him, he had turned to her with eyes that shined like exotic, polished 'tiger's eye' and abandoned his writing to escort her upstairs to their chamber.

"M'lady." Tess touched her arm, startling her back from that wrenching idyll. "M'lady, ye can't go on . . ." Tess bit her lip and sank to her knees beside Merrie's chair. Tess couldn't go on this way, either, letting Merrie think Jack had abandoned her. "He wouldn'ta left ye wi'out a word . . . not if he could help it." She paused and clutched the chair arm, steadying herself. "I know he didn' leave ye of his own, no more'n Thomas left me."

Merrie's hands tightened over Tess's."

"Please don' hate me. Thomas—Mister Seabury—'e was to come to me that night." She flushed at the admission, but made herself go on. "Please don' be angry, m'lady. I've give him my heart, an' he's give me his. He woulda come to me, if he could. Oh, m'lady, I fear somethin' dreadful's happened to 'im." It was a small lie, a sin of omission mostly. A truth withheld for a plaintive truth revealed. She truly was afraid for Thomas Seabury and Master John.

Merrie stared at her, feeling that news soak into her sore heart like a healing balm. "He was to come to you . . . and he didn't?" A true lady, a proper mistress, would be affronted, shocked, or stern with reproof to hear her own dear companion had surrendered her precious virtue. But all Merrie could think was that young Tess was obviously in love with the sensible and gentlemanly Seabury, and was fearful that he might be in some danger.

"Tess! Ohhh, it's true—" Merrie exploded from her quagmire of sorrows, jumping up, grabbing Tess, and pulling her along. As they made the stairs, Merrie lifted her skirts and fairly flew up them to the master chamber. "His things—he left his things—" She stared at the boots and doublet still on the floor, as if expecting them to speak. "Go straightaway—see if Seabury's things are in his chamber."

As Tess ran down the narrow hallway that led to the personal servants' quarters, Merrie snatched up Jack's boots, squeezing them as though to make sure they were real. Still hugging them, she flew to the wardrobe and threw it open. Doublets, hats, and velvet breeches. . . . She hurried on to his trunk; there were shirts, ruff linen and collar wires and pegs, brushes, garters, handkerchiefs, a dressing gown, and shoes . . . four pair. Four pair . . . and his boots. If he left her of his own, he had likely done it in bare feet!

Among the neck linen she had felt a curious rattle and crackle, and now she delved and brought up three sheets of folded parchment, perhaps what he'd been writing that day in the parlor. She unfolded them to read: "To Carlton Ferrar, The Most Estimable Earl of Wolden, The Strand, Westminster. Good Ferrar. You will no doubt enjoy this immensely; I am in a terrible difficulty and in dire need of your help. . . ." Trouble! Her heart sang. Jack was in trouble!

"Exact whatever payment you will from me later, but I implore you to use your high connections to help me procure. . . ." There, the writing stopped. Procure what? Merrie groaned in frustration. What was it that Jack needed, that he would beg a friend—an *earl*, no less!—to help him obtain? She pushed up and began to pace, then stopped dead, her thoughts now finely tuned and seeking.

One question begat another. What trouble had pressed him before? Money. Gaming debts! A fellow had been looking to make bread meal from his very bones! She whooped with joy! Jack needed money— he was probably in trouble over money again!

Halfway down the stairs, Jack's unfinished letter in one hand and his boots in the other, she slowed and stopped. Her elation over realizing that Jack hadn't left her voluntarily had momentarily eclipsed his very real peril. Jack was in danger. Some of the hot color drained from her face. Someone had *abducted* him . . . *taken him by force*. . . .

"Goodwife Gert! Master Cramden!" She ran through the hall, nearly colliding with Jean and Bevis, who directed her into the small parlor. "He's not left me—" She broke in on them, her eyes bright, her face scarlet, her breast heaving. "He's been abducted— napped. I'm sure of it!"

"Who?" "What!" and "Siddown, m'lady, a'fore ye swoon agin—" they said in response to her stunning news.

"No!" She brushed Gert's hands away and took a firm stand. "He didn't leave. He was abducted! And I know why—"

"Ye do?" Manley expressed their collective shock.

"Debts!" She waved the letter at them, panting, trying to gather breath. "He gambles and there's a 'Roscoe' somebody who wants his bones for broth in lieu of payment—" They looked at each other in blank astonishment, and she took a better grip on herself. "He told me why he agreed to marry me."

"He did?" Cramden looked ready to topple from his chair.

She nodded. "He told me about his gambling and the debts."

"The knave!" Gert gasped.

"No, truly . . . he was honest with me, and thank the Almighty for it! He's been taken off by force and is in peril of life and limb—I'm sure of it! We've got to help him."

"Help 'im?" Manley flushed, shooting a panicky glance at his fellow conspirators. "How?"

"Money. I do have money, don't I? Somewhere?" Merrie looked from one to another, perceiving their reluctance to accept her explanation. She paused and dredged up her most mistresslike mien. "I know you don't approve of Jack. You think he's not very responsible and not a proper husband for me. But he is my husband, before God and all mankind, and I love him with all my heart. And I'll give my last farthing to see him safe." She advanced on Manley, her straight young shoulders regal with determination.

"My good Lombard, you must help me wring funds from Straffen's coffers." She saw his face pale. "We do *have* coffers?"

"B-but how c-can ye be sure he were carted off?"

"Did anyone see him leave? Where's Chester? Did Chester saddle their horses?"

"Ah . . . no. . . ." Manley's ears grew red.

"Well, by his own hand he's in trouble." Merrie lifted the letter in one hand and the boots in the other. "And he's left all his clothes and footgear behind." Her conviction was unshakable. "He did not leave me of his own will, and I'm going to find him if it's the last thing I do. I must have money to travel to London, Mister Lombard," Merrie insisted, growing perturbed by their reluctance. Never mind that they weren't convinced. It was her money, after all. Her inheritance . . . and her husband at stake!

"Faith! You cannot travel to London alone." Ashen and clammy-palmed, Cramden heaved to his feet and to Manley's support. "None of us know anything about the place."

Merrie groaned. Why were they being so obstinate? "Then I shall appeal to Sir Daniel Wycoff and the queen's authorities for help—perhaps to escort me." She missed the looks of genuine horror they exchanged while she suddenly wondered how she would find Jack in a place as large as London. Who would know where to look? "This 'Ferrar' fellow . . . we must find the Earl of Wolden. Jack was writing to him for help. He must know something about this 'Roscoe' person."

She swept the threesome with an impassioned look. "I must go. Fetch your strongbox, Mister Lombard; I shall return as soon as I've written a note to Sir Daniel and set Tess to packing." She lifted her skirts and rushed out, leaving the stunned threesome momentarily speechless.

"S-she means it." Manley sank into a chair in blank dread.

"What can we do?" Cramden groaned. "Tonight of all nights! If she calls on Sir Daniel there will certainly be a search. And if he catches us with Sir William here, all heads are forfeit—*great and small!*"

"There be only one thing for it." Gert's face twisted into a pained grimace as they looked to her. "Git rid o' th' gell herself!"

Get rid of Lady Merrie. The suggestion seared their midst like a lightning bolt, stunning, immobilizing them. And in its garish, merciless light, they were forced to confront the ugly depths of their own acquisitiveness and ambition. Would they—could they—actually kill Lady Merrie to save their own conniving necks?

Cramden fell into his chair with a fat-sounding smack. He began clawing at his standing ruff as though fighting for breath amidst the troubles rising around them like floodwaters.

Even flinty Gert's face paled at the spectre she'd raised. She staggered across the parlor to melt, boneless, into a chair. They sat in silence, each recalling the graceless child who had arrived; the frail young thing, so frightened of her worldly husband that she swooned; the earnest and dutiful heart that had withstood Overbeake's tyranny; the forgiving lamb whose very body had been sacrificed on the altar of their ambitious greed. Her every smile accused them. Her good-hearted trust convicted them.

"Ah, God. It has come to this." This time when Cramden pulled out his handkerchief, it was to mop tears. He buried his face in his hands and shuddered with broken sobs. "I cannot. I cannot see the little thing destroyed. It is not in me to be a . . . woman-killer."

Manley was quaking and Gert was not much steadier. They looked at each other and knew Cramden was right. They could never do it. They were many things short of perfect, the Lombards, but they had always served their lords, in serving themselves. And yet there was so much at stake here.

"Nor could we." Gert drew a heavy breath and straightened, dragging herself back through the ashes of regret to her resourceful self. "Then we mus' put her off, keep her from sendin' fer Sir Daniel. 'Tis the only way. We got the meetin'—tonight o' all times! We mus' get through that first. An' we mus' think of somethin' fer when Sir William be safe and gone."

"Owwww—dammit." Jack slumped back down the slimy wall he was using for support as he inched along on his rear and his feet. He curled momentarily, trying to ease his screaming shoulder and neck muscles while little white stars rushed through his head.

"What happened?" Seabury called anxiously, peering through the gloom toward the shadows where Jack had disappeared.

"Banged my noggin on something—never mind." Jack shook his head to clear it. "That barrel has to be somewhere near here. I saw it. The sprung hoop might be rusted enough to make an edge. . . ." He cast about with his feet, and a thud and wooden rattle said he'd located it. Gathering strength, he inched over, got to his knees, and began to grope for the loose piece of iron he had seen, with hands that were tied tightly behind him. Twice he located it, but it was too high to reach with his hand ropes. "If only I could see what I'm doing!" He groaned. "Wait . . . maybe I can get it with my feet." He gritted his teeth, rolling back down onto his bruised shoulders, then his back, to lift his feet into the air. If he could get his foot ropes over it and pull . . .

There was a topple and a crash, and it took a moment to realize that the old barrel had landed fortunate side up. Jack was able to flex and find that piece of iron, which was blessedly jagged. He heaved and contorted himself up and over it, sawing the ropes on his wrists back and forth.

"Is it working?"

"I can't tell." Jack moaned as the jagged metal bit into his wrist.

Just then, a ray of dull yellow light sliced through the gloom and widened as Morris Lombard shoved the tallow lantern through the door. He tromped down the stairs, scowling at the darkness, and Jack froze. One look at Chester's empty straw pallet and then at Jack's and Morris flew into a blind fury. He cursed vilely and rushed at Seabury, stopping just short of trampling him.

"Where the hell is he?" He kicked Seabury viciously in the belly to coerce an answer. "And where's that piss-wit, Chester? Where?"

Jack quickly slid from his knees to a sitting position and the scraping movement brought Morris lurching across the cellar with his lamp raised, searching the gloom. Jack had just enough time to slide onto his back and raise his legs defensively.

"Insolent bastard! What do you think you're doing— trying to escape?" Morris lashed out with a nasty kick. Jack rolled and flexed his legs to meet and deflect it. Infuriated by the resistance, Morris let fly a second boot before Jack had time to recover, this time connecting with Jack's ribs.

"Is that any way to show gratitude to your *benefactor*?" Morris sneered, openly enjoying Jack's pain. "*I'm* the one you have to thank for your advantageous marriage. It was me that searched out the biggest rakes in London and contacted you through 'mutual friends.' Your two playmates, Ferrar and Bosworth, were titled—and too astute, or too greedy, to agree to a marriage without a full disclosure of holdings and incomes. That left you, a most presentable piece of flesh, interested in nothing but rutting. And you had such convenient gaming debts. In short, Huntington, you had the perfect shape of a man, but none of the substance. Don't spoil it all by trying to act like a man now. Just take the money and leave.''

''You bastard,'' Jack growled, Morris's revelation searing through his chest, a worse pain than any kick could inflict. ''I'll see you rot in prison for this, the lot of you. If I live—''

''Yes—*if* you live, Huntington.'' Morris reddened and his eyes glittered dangerously. ''I fear that has become the issue.'' He drew back and let fly another vicious kick aimed at Jack's groin. Jack managed to roll just enough to take the brunt of it in his flank instead and Morris choked, now infuriated.

But the door above them was flung open and Chester, seeing the light below, hurried down the aged stairs. He halted two steps from the bottom, to witness his tankerous brother standing over Jack, who was doubled over in pain. Chester's broad face darkened, and his muscles coiled with dread. Morris was in one of his moods. . . .

''Where the hell have you been?'' Morris wheeled and laced into Chester before he reached the cellar floor. ''I told you these bastards were your responsibility. I just caught them trying something. They might have escaped, ass-head!''

''Had to 'ave food, Marris,'' Chester answered, gesturing with the bucket of ale and the great round of heavy bread he carried. ''We ain't eaten in more'n a day.'' He came down the rest of the steps, his face dark, his eyes wary.

''I told you not to leave here, dolt!'' Morris vented

his frustrations in long-standing tradition; he laced Chester's ear stoutly. Chester froze, muscles coiling. A second blow glanced from his head, making him stagger a step. "I'll send food down when I'm ready. You're not to go out again, not for anything. Not until I say so—"

"Just like a Lombard," Jack snarled, pushed beyond all reason. His shoulders bunched defiantly beneath his bonds. "You bash and bully—but only those who can't fight back, like Chester . . . and Merrie." Morris stalked back to him, eyes glittering viciously.

"Ah, yes, your little bride. A docile little thing, I understand. Was she docile in bed as well?" He laughed at Jack's angry lurch. "Wasn't the five hundred a year enough, Huntington? How foolish of you to think your own greed could outpace my mother's. Did no one ever teach you that greed is one of the seven deadly sins? No matter, you'll learn it soon enough."

Jack's eyes shimmered like molten bronze as he sought Chester's simmering scowl and charged: "You do intend to kill us, to add murder to your list of crimes. Is that what you intend for Merrie, too, when she learns of it? You'll kill her, too? Make no mistake, Lombard, she is a bright little thing. She will most certainly learn of it."

"If the necessity arises, my mother will deal with her," Morris snarled.

"Nay, Marris . . . they'd not murther m'lady Merrie." Chester stalked toward his older brother, trembling with angry confusion. He was thinking of sweet Lady Merrie, of what Jack had said about them hurting her. They wouldn't really hurt her. They would never kill the little mistress, would they? Lady Merrie . . . who touched people the way she touched his foals, gently, warmly. Lady Merrie . . . who smiled at him and listened to him and had even once hugged him. Would his steely-eyed mother really . . . ? More than anyone, Chester knew the depths of Gert Lombard's capacity for ruthlessness.

"Ye can' murther nobudy—"

"Don't you dare tell me what I can and cannot do, you bastard lump!" Morris snarled, heeling to face Chester. "Why do you think they sent them to me in the first place?"

"Nay—ye'll not murther nobudy." Chester's fists clenched and his neck pulled into his thick shoulders as he towered over his younger brother. "Ye won', Marris."

"Shut-up, ass-head!" Morris smacked Chester's ear with a bony fist. "I'll do what I have to . . . and *you'll* do what you're told!" Chester's head rang with the force of the blow, and when his eyes refocused through the pain, Morris's snarling face became Gert Lombard's—contorted, always angry with him, bashing, punishing . . .

"Nay!" Bottled anger and frustration welled up in him and he reached out with both hands and gave Morris a furious shove.

Morris stumbled back toward Jack, one step, then two. His face was dusky with ire and his eyes glittered with fury. "How dare you touch me, you . . . lout! Stupid, drooling ox—and a bastard ox at that!" He laughed harshly at the visible frisson of fury that raced through Chester. "Oh, you do hate that. Bastard . . . *bastard*—"

Behind Morris, Jack burned, watching Chester's pain and impotent fury. He managed to roll onto his back and lift his legs to give Morris a kick, shoving him straight toward Chester.

Years of abuse, long years of bearing his mother's bruising correction and his smarter brother's scorn, poured through Chester like blistering pitch. When Morris lurched forward, he lunged and lashed out with one hamlike fist and caught Morris a blow on the side of the head that sent him reeling, twisting and flailing onto the steps. Morris staggered up and turned, white-eyed with fury, beyond both reason and fear. He dove for Chester, swinging, intent on punishing Chester's audacity. Chester met him fully . . . and in Morris, he met his mother and every Lombard who had scorned and hurt him.

They fell onto the stone floor, grappling and snarling and gouging. And, for once, Chester had the advantage over his favored brother. He was soon on top, straddling Morris, overpowering him, bashing him.

Jack crawled to where Morris was pinned, shouting at Chester to stop before he killed his brother. His hoarse cries finally reached through the blood-surge of fury in Chester's head and the blows stopped.

A long, taut silence stretched out around them as Chester staggered to his feet, wiping his bloody nose on his sleeve and staring at Morris. He turned on Jack with dark, hollowed eyes filled with the smoke of damped fires of vengeance.

"He won' be murthering . . . nobudy."

Jack sagged against his bonds and met Chester's tortured look. His heart was pounding so that he could scarcely draw breath. "Chester, he was going to kill us. He would have had to, to keep me from going back to Straffen. Chester, you have to help us."

Chester staggered away, panting, rubbing his head, trying desperately to think. He turned to stare at Morris's inert form. It was too late to go back. He didn't want to go back—ever. He finally lifted a wrenching look to Jack, lit with a stubborn spark of humanity. "Pro-mise me . . . ye won' let 'em hurt Lady Merrie."

Jack had the most insane urge to hug battered Chester just then. He grinned from the pure pain of it. "I promise. I'll see Lady Merrie safe and her inheritance restored. And, I swear, I'll see to it Morris never hurts you or anybody else . . . ever again. Untie us, Chester. Please—we've got to hurry!"

Chester's gaze searched Jack's face and he nodded, accepting that promise. And when he knelt to cut Jack's bonds, it was a free act . . . wrought by a free man.

It was a bizarre threesome that burst through the door of Lady Antonia's late that night. Gentleman Jack and his man Seabury, bootless and barelegged, wearing filthy shirts and a coat of grime, in company with a square, gawking ox of a fellow in peasant garb. They found the Earl of Wolden at his usual place at the gaming tables, just ready to call it a night and toddle upstairs with his nubile companion.

"Gawd, Huntington—" Ferrar's reddened eyes widened and he came upright, dumping that "naughtie niece" right off his lap. "What in hell's happened to you?"

"Ferrar, I need your help, your connections in the courts," Jack declared, bracing himself urgently on the table and leaning toward him. "Where's Bosworth? I have to get hold of some documents, quickly and quietly. I have to have information—Ferrar, my lady's in danger." He saw Ferrar's gaze wander over him, still in shock. "Did you hear me, Ferrar? I need your help for my lady."

"That's not all you need, Huntington." Ferrar came alive, his nose curling even as his eyes danced with excitement. "You need a *bath!*"

The next morning, the trio of London's leading rakes barged into the offices of the library of Court of Wards, demanding to see the secretary. It was here that legal records of guardianships and bequeathed nobility were presented, recorded, and stored. The truth of Merrie's inheritance and marriage lay somewhere in the moldy tomes within these halls, and Ferrar charmed and bullied and wielded every privilege at his command to wrangle them an appointment. The secretary did agree to see them, but not just yet. They found themselves reduced to the fate of all supplicants to government since time immemorial . . . *waiting.*

Jack was wedged between a half-dozing Ferrar and a tight, hollow-eyed Bosworth, both snatched from the jaws of ripe debauchery in the wee hours of the night just past. Stuffed into clothes meant for Bosworth's sparser frame and boots sized for Bosworth's somewhat smaller foot, Jack fidgeted uncomfortably in his seat and watched the set of massive doors across from them, willing them to open. Bosworth inclined his head toward Jack with a nasty glint in his eye.

"I meant to ask . . . how are your *hedgerows*, Huntington?" Only pure boredom pulled Bosworth's claws out like this, Jack knew.

"Excellent. They're perfect, Bosworth. Couldn't be better." Jack sighed with deadly patience, sinking harder against his chair. Hedgerows. It gouged him in a very vulnerable place just now. He hadn't been there to rescue the damnable hedgerows, but he sure as hell intended to be there to fight for Merrie's freedom and her inheritance. Somebody had to stand up for her, defend and protect her. And by damn, Jack Huntington was going to be the one!

Soon after doors swung open to admit them to the Secretary of the Court, Jack found himself confronting a large writing table littered with papers and parchments, explaining his urgent request for the pertinent documents in front of both Ferrar and Bosworth, both of whom awaited the explanation like hungry owls.

"The last will and testament of the Earl of Straffen and supporting inventories . . . and the documents regarding the guardianship of Lady Meredith Straffen, of Hertford," Jack announced, trying not to meet his friends' surprised looks. They'd agreed to help, expecting to learn at last the identity of his mysterious lady-love.

"Rather irregular, sir." The graying, brown-garbed secretary glanced from the earl to the baron, then back to Jack. "I should have to know by what right you claim access to it."

"My wife, Lady Meredith, is named heir therein."

"Ahhh. And you wish to know if she has gained her full inheritance against some titleholder, perhaps," the secretary surmised.

"Titleholder?" Jack frowned briefly. He honestly hadn't thought of that. Who was titleholder now? Had the earldom lapsed for want of a male? Then a horrible thought struck him; if they'd conjured or jiggered the will, then was it possible Merrie wasn't even the true

heir of Straffen at all? The thought pierced him briefly
and he fought it back. Whatever she was, she was his
wife, and if it turned out that she was penniless, he'd
carry her from Straffen and all its wretched memories,
and he'd find some way to support and care for her
himself.

"I have come to inspect the will with regard to the
provisions of my marriage. But it would not hurt to
learn the right and true extent of my wife's holdings."

The secretary looked pensive for a moment, then
nodded. "This may take some time, sir. My secretary-
clerk, Morris Lombard, has not arrived today. I shall
have to find another clerk who knows the archives."
He rose with an air of gravity to begin the search for
the documents.

Morris Lombard, Jack was thinking, would not arrive for many years . . . from Newgate Prison.

Bosworth stared at Ferrar in puzzlement, then at
Jack. "I thought all this had to do with a *lady*, Huntington . . . your *love*."

"It does." Jack braced, giving Bosworth his most
scalding look. "And my love is no *lady*, sirrah. She is
my wife."

Bosworth glared at Ferrar for a moment as that tidbit
settled into place. Then his face lit with unholy glee.
Huntington's inaccessible lady-love was his *wife!*
Things had just gotten immeasurably juicier!

They stood and paced nervously as they waited,
Jack's jaw clamped tight against his companions' pro-
gressively more pointed inquiries. It was more than an
hour later that the secretary came bustling back into
the office with a cherry-red face and a clerk laden with
numerous documents and bound registers.

"Straffen"—the secretary nodded toward Jack with
fresh respect—"I knew it was an old name, not much
in evidence of late. Writ of Summons, don't you know
. . . unusual codicils . . . interesting stuff. . . ." He
rambled on a minute, waving aside the clerk, who was

arranging the documents on the desk. It finally registered on Jack's mind.

"Writ of summons?" Jack paled briefly, feeling Bosworth's and Ferrar's attention fastened on him like a shrinking shirt. The ramifications filtered through him slowly.

"Oh—" The secretary suddenly recalled his manners. "Please, Your Lordship, do be seated. It may take some time to uncover all the provisions of the old earl's will and your countess's inheritance."

"Countess?" Jack looked to Ferrar, who was grinning with a delight that only a devout gossip could experience. A moment later, it sank in that the secretary had been looking straight at Jack when he said "Your Lordship." "Merrie is a countess?"

"But, of course," the fellow intoned, growing toadier by the moment. "In her own right, and with the right of conferring a title upon her husband, should he be an untitled man, and of making the next Earl of Straffen through childbirth. As to the provisions of the charter and the will, there is quite a little stuff. It will take time."

Jack sat down with an unceremonious plop.

Even as Jack and Seabury were securing release from their prison, Merrie had found herself newly trapped in hers. Night had fallen and Manley Lombard still had produced neither casket nor coin, and Merrie's trunk still hadn't been packed and a cart and escort still hadn't been arranged. Twice that afternoon she'd been on the point of screaming at them. What were they doing, dawdling and twaddling about with Jack's safety at stake? Everyone moved as if they were immersed in pitch!

"Look for a reply on the morrow, at the *earliest*," Master Cramden had assured her when she'd given him the letter to ferry to Sir Daniel. When she suggested riding to Sir Daniel's estate instead, to hasten things along, he sputtered and produced a litany of narrowly passable excuses, ending with: "We cannot possibly be ready to leave any sooner than tomorrow noon in any case, Lady Merrie.'' Then he'd trundled her off to her chamber before sunset, like a troublesome child. She clearly was overwrought and needed rest, he said, and the Lombards had darkly nodded agreement.

It was now long past nightfall and Merrie refused to sleep, pacing her chamber and growing steadily more outraged by their behavior. How many times had she felt as though the Lombards indulged rather than obeyed her orders? How many times had she experienced that odd sense of infringing on their domain? How often had she realized she was appealing to their good graces instead of expecting their cooperation? And why did she have the unshakable conviction that of late they'd been exchanging glances of meaning over her head and behind her back? But it was their open animosity toward Jack that finally capped her indignation. They were blatantly dragging their heels, passively resisting her determination to help Jack. How dare they presume to judge and interfere in her married life! She couldn't allow their petty resentments to endanger Jack's safety!

Intent on confronting them, she drew on a loose overgown over her shift and snatched up the single candle to stride from the master chamber. The hall and gallery were lit only by the nascent moon; the house was settled under a dark, concealing blanket. She paused to consider her course and turned down the upper hallway toward Master Cramden's chambers; he usually seemed more sympathetic than the others. She knocked gently on his door, called, frowned, and poked her head inside. Darkness. Quiet. She inched farther inside and saw that his bed was empty.

The small parlor was empty, as well. Where could he be? The Lombards' chambers, she decided, screwing her courage to the sticking point and venturing down the inky hall. A cool draft blew from somewhere, snuffing her candle and sending a chill up her spine. She gripped the candlestand with colder fingers. Her steps foreshortened and her slippers whispered cautiously over the wooden floor. As she approached their door, she felt the draft increase and squinted to make out that the door stood open a piece. There was moonlight beyond . . . and it was apparent that the outer door, which led to the yard, stood ajar. Everything in the chamber was cast in gray smudges and looming black outlines . . . a table and wardrobe and Manley's steward's desk. She slipped inside and tiptoed to the bed-closet built into the far right wall. It was empty, also.

She chewed her bottom lip. Where would the three of them be at this hour? They were sometimes abroad at odd times; she'd seen them. . . .

While she stood, puzzling and deciding whether to wait, a knot of darkened figures was slinking toward the house, clinging to the moonshadows to avoid notice. They carried no lamp and their muffled voices, floating through the half-open door as they approached, jolted Merrie. Voices—out of the shadow-ridden darkness. She clutched her candlestand frantically, and at the last minute, she bolted onto the cupboard bed to flatten herself against the wall, behind the bed drape.

"Thank God. Has the signal been sent?" A hushed male voice carried a grave air about it. It came from inside the chamber and there was the sound of the door closing. Merrie's heart began to thud.

"Chester . . . ain't here. Manley'll be takin' it shortly." It was Gert's voice and there was a rustle and a scraping of chairs and a bloom of tallow light. "Can I get ye aught, sir?" Gert said, positively purring. "A dram o' claret, mebee?" Merrie imagined the stranger must have nodded, for there was self-satisfaction in Gert's response. "Fine. I shull be straight back, sir."

"I do not mean to press you, Sir William," came Cramden's voice, "but do tell the state of affairs in London. What of the queen?"

"Ill, Master Cramden. That is a certainty. The palace and Mary's council viciously guard all news of her straits, but I still have certain . . . private sources at Hampton Court Palace. She is barren and ill and they are desperate. And there is the frightening talk of frightened men. I pray that is all it is." He paused and his voice lowered. "Some say the council is pressing the queen to order Princess Elizabeth brought up on charges and beheaded, so the 'Protestant whore' will never succeed to the throne. They are panicky at the thought of what Elizabeth, as queen, would do to reprise the deaths of the Protestants Mary has burned and tortured. And, of course, they fear for their own necks."

"Saints!" Merrie heard Cramden mutter. "Death in the wind yet again. Is our precious Elizabeth's head truly in danger?"

"I pray not, but Elizabeth must be warned. There are some men of sound mind still left in government. Surely they see what a calamity it would be to remove the only clear heir. The country would be in chaos within the week!"

Gert returned just then, and there was a clink of metal and glass and a muffled "Delightful." Cramden delivered Gert a short version of what the fellow had just shared, and she gasped and clucked distress.

"They would have to trump a charge, some plot of treason," the man went on, "and they have nothing to knit one around. Elizabeth has been spotless in both conduct and connection." There was a disquieting pause. "Except for our little meetings. . . ."

Chapter Nineteen

*E*xcept for our little meetings? Merrie's mind staggered. Meetings . . . here . . . at Straffen? *Treasonous* meetings? The queen was ill and . . .

"You've risked much, good Lombards, Master Cramden," the fellow answered her unspoken question. "You peril your necks each time I come. But these meetings are necessary. Elizabeth cannot be caught unawares when Mary dies; she must have some alliances in place and be prepared to move. Most certainly, her enemies will be prepared to act against her."

Merrie could take in no more. The Lombards were involved in a plot with some fellow and the Princess Elizabeth that imperiled their necks? The impact of it hit in successively larger waves. They imperiled their necks . . . and likely the rest of Straffen as well!

The knaves! How dare they presume and contrive and intrigue? How dare they take it upon themselves to hazard her life and her home? Her heart stopped for a long, harrowing moment. *Jack.* Was that why they were so loathe to have her stir things up with—with *Sir Daniel, Queen Mary's local authority?*

If she hadn't been sitting on her knees, they'd have given way beneath her just then. They *had* dragged their feet in helping her send for Sir Daniel . . . a purpose . . . because they had this intrigue planned! And imagine Sir Daniel charging in, searching, looking for Jack, uncovering this nest of conspirators. She shuddered. The magnitude of their arrogance and assumption was staggering.

A bolt of fury shot up her spine, so hot and virulent that she could not fully contain it. It escaped her in a low growl that froze every muscle in the chamber's inhabitants. The secret of her presence now forfeit, she clambered from the bed to stand in the light, hair swirling and eyes blazing.

"M-m'lady!"

"God's Teeth!"

They stared at her in shock. Then, as she lunged for the door, they were there to meet her, snatching her back by the arms.

"No! Let me go—" She struggled briefly between Gert and Manley Lombard before her eyes fell on their mysterious visitor. Under her lightning blue glare, he rose, looking pained in the extreme. "How dare you come here to place Straffen and my husband in danger?" Then she turned on the Lombards and Cramden with her body braced to resist. "And you! How dare you sneak and skulk and contrive to involve us all in such dealings."

"Regrettably so." The slender gentleman, garbed in unadorned but expensive black, sighed and stepped from the table to stand before her. He took in the fiery hair and equally fiery spirit of the little lady of Straffen and smiled wryly. "I suppose introductions are in order, though I feel I already know you, Lady Meredith. I fear I have been your unseen guest on more than one occasion now. William Cecil"—he made a gallant leg—"at your service, madam."

"As I am apparently at yours, sir." She turned her head to watch him from the corner of a furious eye. Her mind was frantically collecting impressions and searching the annals of memory for traces of that name. Then it came. "Sir William Cecil? Once councilor to King Edward?"

"The same, madam. God willing . . . perhaps advisor to a queen, soon. You have heard part, and a little knowledge is a dangerous thing. You must hear more if you are to judge us fairly. Will you hear us out, Lady Merrie?"

Caught in the Lombards' tenacious grasp, unable to move, Merrie evaluated Cecil. He was taller than middling, had regular, serious features with a prominent nose and an elegantly trimmed beard, and possessed a commanding carriage. But it was his eyes that drew her; they were ageless, wizened, alive with wit and learning in a way Merrie found irresistible and alarming. This man had been advisor to a king, her king . . . and apparently was now involved with their future queen. These were grave matters indeed.

The memory of the princess talking with a distraught maid in the forest, counseling her, consoling her, rose strongly in Merrie's mind. Her heart began to calm and her thoughts began to settle into reassuringly logical patterns. They had said something about a threat to the princess's life. If Elizabeth were in true danger, then she must listen to their story. She felt Gert Lombard's hand tighten on her arm and glanced down. In any case, what choice did she have?

She expelled her held breath when she finally jerked a nod. She was seated at the rough table, across from Sir William and beside the pale, pasty-looking Master Cramden. Gert and Manley positioned themselves pointedly at each side of her chair, and were thoughtful enough to pour her a drop of her own claret.

"You put us in jeopardy, sir, by your presence here," she declared, welcoming the heat of the wine into her blood. The silvery glint of anger in her great blue eyes held Cecil bound for a moment.

"It is not lightly done, madam. It is the gravest of circumstances which necessitates this . . . visit. Queen Mary is ill, dying slowly despite the palace's continued denials. And the Princess Elizabeth is rightful heir to England's throne. She cannot wait until the announcement of Mary's death to speak with England's nobles and to draft men of ability to help her govern; her enemies will overwhelm her if she is caught unprepared.

"She is forbidden guests and right channels of news; her home and staff are riddled with Marian agents, eager to claim a reward for uncovering a plot against the queen, whether real or imagined. Even I, who am and have been surveyor of her several holdings, am denied proper access to her." His face darkened and he paused to master the deep anger in his tone. "That Wycoff is a tenacious hound. I have tangled with him on the matter already, and the mere sight of me so close to Hatfield would convince him treason was in the works."

Somehow, the mention of "Wycoff" and "hound" in the same breath seemed altogether appropriate to Merrie. The adulterous knight did have a droopy, bloodhound look to his eyes, she thought vengefully. And as Sir William verbally sketched perils and plots and intrigues, Merrie's vivid imagination became his ally, providing the oils and pigments to bring those pictures to life.

Cecil had come every few months, more often of late, alone and under cover of darkness. He brought Elizabeth information: secret words and nods of acknowledgment from men of substance, intelligence of the royal household, and assessments of the intentions and opinions of foreign powers. And at times he carried a word away with him for another. Nothing was written. All depended on one man's memory and integrity. If their meetings were discovered and exposed, two of the heads that would roll, Elizabeth's and Cecil's, would take those devastating secrets with them.

These realm-shaping events had transpired through the cunning auspices of the Lombards of Straffen. They possessed some murky family connection to Cecil himself, were situated in a house that bordered a conveniently wooded part of Elizabeth's Hatfield, and were of a mind to assist England's glorious future . . . and likely their own.

Stung by how far she'd let her rightful anger slip, Merrie looked from "stone hammer" Gert to the deceptive Manley, then to gentlemanly and "sensitive" Master Cramden, who didn't seem to be overly distressed by little things like risking a charge of treason. She was seeing them with entirely new eyes. Apparently Jack wasn't the only knave about. The place was thick with them.

"Jack!" She rose abruptly, jostling Gert and Manley back a pace and glaring fiercely. "You deliberately delayed, knowing Jack was in danger, so you could ply this intrigue—didn't you? How dare you? Even now my husband's life may be in peril."

"N-nay, my lady, please—" Cramden rocked to his feet, his face a convincing twist of anguished conscience. With a pained look at the Lombards, he divulged, "We knew of his debts, his gambling, my lady. But I swear to you, they are not cause for fear of his life. His creditors, if indeed they hold him against his will, would never kill him. Never that. They would want their money, foremost." He shot a sweaty look at Gert Lombard; Jack's captors did indeed want their money. "One more night in their hands will hardly break him . . . and shall make England's future more secure. Forgive us. We chose the latter, never meaning to see you so distressed."

"We shull see to Master John, I swear," Manley pleaded. "Soon as Sir William's heel quits Straffen lands."

"It were jus' bad luck they come all at once," Gert tossed in, with a dram of contrition in her face.

Cecil rose, frowning. "I know naught of your husband's difficulties, Lady Meredith. I can only beg your silence, even your help, for England and her future queen. And I shall pray that God is as merciful to you as you have already been to us, this night."

Merrie stared at the grave and dignified face before her and had the eerie sensation of glimpsing something timeless, some part of England's future in it. She bit her lip to quell its trembles and looked to Cramden and the Lombards. She had mislaid trust on them before, but at least now she knew the truth, the whole truth. And their manipulations had been for a greater cause.

"I must not stand in England's way. I owe the princess a debt and am grateful for the chance to pay." Her voice caught and hung, quivering, and she whispered, "Then we must pray for Master John . . . that he is kept safe and whole until this business is done. And the minute it is finished, we are off to London— no excuses!"

"God be a merciful man, m'lady," Gert uttered and took a long, relieved breath. She glanced at Manley and Cramden with a satisfied gleam in her eyes. "He shall certainly keep your husband in safe hands whilst we do His work fer England."

Merrie's discovery of them had prevented the proper signal from being sent in time to arrange the meeting between Cecil and the princess that same night. An entire day must pass before the signal could be posted in a particular tree, under cover of darkness, and discovered by a certain game warden on rounds from Hatfield, who would carry it back to his mistress. Sir William was secretively installed in a guest chamber for what remained of the night, and the rest dispersed to their chambers. None slept much that night and the next day seemed endless; going forward with the business of packing and preparing for a journey while waiting for the cover of darkness to arrange the meeting.

Tension collected with the day heat in Straffen House and as the sun began to sink in the sky, Merrie checked and rechecked the arrangements with the Lombards. They exchanged uneasy glances at the determination in her manner and the new skepticism in the way she regarded whatever they said. It boded ill, this change in their charge, and they began to dread what might be revealed after Sir William's mission was accomplished.

All was in readiness as the sun lowered behind the knolls and hillocks. Merrie's trunk at last stood packed, a modest sum in coinage had been wrested from Steward Lombard's protective custody, and she and Cramden were agreed to depart for London by the following noon. She stood at the edge of the weedy, woodlike gardens, watching the flaming orange ball of sun sinking to the earth's cool breast. She wished with all her heart Jack were with her now and she prayed that wherever he was, he would be safe.

* * *

By the light of that same tumultuous sunset, five horsemen were charging toward Hertfordshire out of London. Their lathered mounts churned dust and sent clods and rocks flying at those unfortunate enough to share the London road with them. Driven separately by anger, comradeship, and raw curiosity, they were united in urgency, possessed of a single sense of mission. Jack rode at their head, flanked by Ferrar and Bosworth, Seabury and Chester Lombard close behind.

Darkness crept timidly over their course and in their wake as they rode, not for Straffen proper but for another estate not far from it. Night closed firmly and they passed the road that led toward Straffen, slowing to read the darkened landmarks thereabouts. Soon they crested a rise and reined up, panting, staring at the dim outline of a manor house planted at the edge of the village below.

"What if he's not home?" Ferrar asked, watching Jack with something akin to awe. He'd never seen the amiable rake like this—so intense, so coldly furious.

"Then I'll find him . . . wherever the hell he is."

A quarter of an hour later, they rumbled into the courtyard of Sir Daniel Wycoff's modest, well-kept manor house, dismounted in a flurry, and ignored the knocker to assault the door with a hail of fists. They shoved past the housemaid who answered and then past the house steward who came at a run.

"We have no time for niceties, man!" Something in the steward's anxiety hinted that they had come at a bad time for his master, a very bad time indeed. A cool smile spread over Jack's dusty face. "No need to announce us. We'll see ourselves into his presence. Chester, see to the good steward here."

Jack drew the short sword at his side and headed for the stairs. Bosworth and Ferrar followed suit, leaving the steward shrinking in Chester's brawny clutches. The master chamber was not difficult to find, nor was the door any obstacle.

They threw back the portal and surged inside, startling Sir Daniel up from a low couch beside the cold hearth. His shirt was undone, his loosened codpiece flapped ignominiously, and he staggered slightly, passion dazed. ''G-good God!'' he finally swore, casting a frantic look at his paramour, sprawled in scandalous, erotic splendor on the couch pillows.

''W-what is the m-meaning of this outrage—this disgrace!'' Wycoff managed to snarl, his eyes fixed on their swords and his mind fixed by the thought that the lady's husband had resorted to the extremes—

''I don't think we should discuss *disgrace* just now, Wycoff. You're hardly in a position for it,'' Jack declared coolly, letting his eyes slide over the queen's upstanding agent, then transferring them to the dark-haired creature on the couch who was correcting her exposed state with notable lack of haste. ''Good evening, Deirdre.''

''You bastard.'' The countess's eyes blazed. Shock accounted for only part of her delay in cloaking her seductively bared charms. Haughty Deirdre had a perfect passion for being admired. And behind Jack, Bosworth and Ferrar were certainly in a position to . . . admire.

''Have you met Deirdre, Ferrar? Or you, Bosworth? This is Epping's *adventuresome* countess.'' Jack's eyes warmed vengefully as he watched her bristle and burn. Scores were being settled this night; how satisfying that this was one of them. ''Not acquainted? No matter; I'm sure you'll recognize her when you see her in future.''

Deirdre sputtered, looking daggers at Jack . . . briefly. Ever a creature to take opportunity where she found it, the haughty vixen quickly began assessing the price of the earl's and baron's silence in their warming eyes.

''Dress and send for your captain, Wycoff. You've duty to perform.'' Jack dismissed Deirdre and turned on the compromised knight. ''You're the queen's agent and I've brought a queen's warrant against the Lombards of Straffen Manor and Richard Cramden. You're to arrest them all and help me secure Straffen and its mistress, Countess Meredith, against all perils."

"God's Teeth!" Wycoff swore. "Steward Lombard and Lawyer Cramden? You're mad—"

"Hardly, Wycoff." Ferrar had pulled his eyes reluctantly from Deirdre's bare shoulders. "If anything, Huntington understates the situation. This very moment the Countess Straffen may be in grave peril. Baron Bosworth and I are here to attest to the seriousness of the charges and to lend the queen's justice whatever aid we can. Carlton Ferrar," he added, introducing himself with perfect condescension, "Earl of Wolden. Now be so good as to button yourself up, man, and take your duty in hand instead of this lady."

Jack could scarcely enjoy Wycoff's impotent fury as the sense of Ferrar's words struck him. It was true. Even now the fiends might be implementing some heinous plot against his vulnerable little Merrie. Long-blunted dread began swelling in his gut. He pulled from his doublet a parchment, stamped with Queen Mary's seal, and thrust it at Wycoff.

"Do your duty, Wycoff. Enforce queen's justice," he uttered in a chilling growl. "And earn the queen's gratitude . . . and my silence."

It was late, but candles dispelled the darkness of the small parlor where the Lombards, Cramden, Cecil, and Merrie waited for the appointed hour. The rest of the house had been sent on to sleep and in the quiet, each minute dragged its feet as though dreading its fated oblivion. Only a little longer and Manley would slip out to the stables, travel stealthily along the hedgerows, and trace the dim path through the forest to raise the signal. Then, near the stroke of midnight, Cecil and Manley would slip through the woods to meet the princess and her trusted warden at the appointed place.

Only a few more hours, Merrie thought, her heart twisting dully in her breast. She prayed that Jack was not in pain, not hurt or maltreated. Lord! There were so many terrible things to fear for him. Sir William read her anxiety for her husband plainly and leaned close to clasp her icy hands with his.

"He will be well, Lady Merrie. The depth of your loving devotion cannot help but reach across the miles to him. It will be his comfort and his stay." She nodded wordlessly. Cecil watched the aching of her heart in her luminous eyes and even the worldly and determined politician in him sighed with regret.

Cecil's words were utterly prophetic. At that very moment, Jack was heartened by thoughts of Merrie . . . though the miles her devotion had to cross were startlingly fewer than Cecil could have imagined. Just then, Jack and his companions were leading Wycoff and a dozen armed guards over the last rise . . . and straight for Straffen's throat.

A dull rumble sounded through the hall, into the parlor. The occupants snapped to attention, listening, eyes widening. The rumble increased . . . now volatile, thundering vibrations! Something approached Straffen like a howling storm. . . .

Gert and Manley ran out of the parlor to see what was afoot, and a lightning bolt of recognition seared the air of the hall: horses . . . lots of horses! With Merrie and Cramden close behind, they ran toward the front door of the hall, where Gert stopped Manley just short of pulling it open.

"No—the window above—" She ran for the stairs instead. They watched her race around the gallery and throw open one leaded window. Light from outside flickered eerily over her frantic features. "Horses—riders with torches," she called in a rasping whisper. There was an edge of panic to her voice that caused the same terror to bloom in the faces watching her from the hall below.

"Merciful God—" Gert half choked, half squealed as the horsemen reined up in Straffen's front court. By the dancing flames of torchlight, faces were all too visible as they dismounted. *Jack Huntington*—the shock immobilized her tongue—and *Chester* and— "Ohhh, God—Sir Daniel! He's upon us!"

That strangled name sent a galvanic shock through everyone in the darkened hall, robbing them of thought, of motion. Only the banging of fists and sword hilts on the door, the harsh shouts and demands for admission, penetrated their trance of horror.

Merrie shot a panicky look around and caught sight of a deathly pale Sir William, lagging behind, standing near the parlor door. She had to do something—*now!* She bolted for the princess's surveyor and grabbed him by the sleeve, tugging mightily. "Come with me, Sir William!" When he stumbled and held back, she yelled above the din of banging and threats, "For God's sake, *come*—you've got to hide!"

Merrie's impetuous action ignited the others; they threw themselves against the door and its beleaguered bar while she dragged Sir William upstairs. Merrie paused in the gallery, then jolted instinctively toward the master chamber, the lordly sanctum of Straffen. Here, if nowhere else, there might be refuge from search and seizure.

"Now where . . . ?" She halted in the dim light, swallowing her heart back into place. Sir William finally realized what she was about and lurched along beside her. She scurried, dragging him from trunk to bed to servants' hallway, investigating every possible niche of concealment. She finally pulled the window hangings aside. Sir William winced.

"That's the first place they shall look," he protested. Merrie slumped, biting her lip. Then her eyes fell on the small wardrobe and inspiration lit her determined features. She'd made use of one once—

"Here!" She pulled him to it, visually measuring both him and the wooden chest that was set on squat, turned legs.

"In there?" Sir William choked out, pulling back.

"It's small, but I trow you'll fit. We have to make you fit!" Merrie opened the wardrobe and began yanking Jack's doublets from it. She paused with one in her hand, seeing his disbelief and hearing the splintering of wood in the hall below that signaled the breaching of the front doors. "Would you rather lose your head? Take off your doublet—quickly!"

Sir William swallowed hard and began tearing at the buttons of his elegant padded doublet, stripping it quickly from his shoulders. Then he climbed into the cramped space in a half-reclining position, folding his legs in after him. Merrie rolled her eyes at the close fit and closed the doors on him.

"Whatever happens, whatever you hear, don't make a sound!" she hissed. She snatched up the doublets, Sir William's included, and stuffed them into one or another of the trunks. She heard shouting in the hall, furious wrangling and unintelligible protests. "Please— don't let them come up here," she prayed feverishly. Were the shouts growing closer?

Then she heard it, her name shouted above the din of confusion. "Merrie! *Merrie!*" Her knees buckled. It sounded like Jack!

Each mile from London, each pace of the way from Wycoff's house, had both fired Jack's anger and tempered it. His loathing was for himself as much as for those wretched, scheming bastards who had used Merrie so foully, prostituted her on every level to satisfy their hideous lust for mammon. He was little better, he'd come to believe; he'd used her body and taken advantage of her sweet, curious nature and accepted her money and even her forgiveness without regard for anything but his own needs and desires. He had wanted her . . . and he'd charmed and seduced and wormed his way into her confidence, into her passions, perhaps into her very heart. That was the worst . . . Merrie's heart. God, what blind, overwhelming conceit—to imagine he deserved something as wonderful as a place in Merrie's heart. . . .

By the time they reached Straffen, he was roiling inside, tortured by the magnitude of the scheme and by thoughts of how far the Lombards and Cramden would go to protect it. He pounded to the ground and battered his way through Straffen's ominously barred doors, burning for release, for someone to bash and punish, and he was punishing himself. Then he charged in and had them in his clutches, shaking Manley like a dog does a bone, demanding, "Where is she? What have you done with her?"

At Wycoff's order, above the Lombards' benumbed protests, the guardsmen struggled with the confused house servants who had roused and come running to provide late resistance. In the chaos, Jack could get no response and tossed Manley into the guardsman's arms and raised his deep voice to thunder her name as he shoved through the mass of jostling bodies.

"Merrie! *Merrie, where are you?*"

"*Jack!*" Her voice came above the confusion, shrill with disbelief. She ran from the chamber into the eerie orange torchlight on the gallery. "Jack—" She searched the swarm of bodies below as she heard her name called again. She found him—at the bottom of the stairs, his raven hair, his broad shoulders, his beloved features seeking her. "It *is* you!" she cried, pushing off from the railing in a wild lunge for the stairs. "Jack—Jack!"

The frantic motion in the hall slowed as Merrie crested the stairs and started down. Jack raced up them, two at a time, to meet her halfway. He swept her from her feet and into a crushing, frantic embrace that momentarily smothered all response. "Merrie. Thank God! Are you all right?"

Lesser conflicts and struggles faded slowly as Wycoff's armed men quickly gained the upper hand over Straffen's servants. Awareness of what was happening on the stairs now permeated the hall. Gradually all heads turned toward that reunion, some in curiosity, some in horror, some in teary relief. After the searing current of release subsided in Jack, he allowed her to push back in his viselike embrace.

"Jack, is it really you?" She struggled against the swell of emotion in her chest and relinquished her savage grip on his doublet to feather her hands frantically over his face, his chest. "You're all right?" A litany of breathless questions came pouring forth. "They didn't harm you? How did you get free? Lord! I was so worried. Where were you and what did—"

"Merrie, they didn't harm you in any way?" Jack's questions came in counterpoint to hers. "Did they lay a hand on you? Did they threaten you? Lord! What you must have been through—"

They finally stammered to a halt, staring at each other, each realizing the other's concern and confused by it. Into that abrupt silence came a jarring awareness of the stares of the straining, contentious figures below.

"Jack, what happened to you?" She pushed back in his arms, sweeping the hall with widening eyes and genuine bewilderment. "And what are you doing here with Sir Daniel . . . and all these *men?*"

The questions themselves told Jack a great deal. She was unharmed and still had no inkling of the treachery of those in whom she'd had such trust. He turned a vengeful gaze toward the Lombards and Cramden, who were safely restrained in Ferrar's, Bosworth's, and Wycoff's clutches, and pointed.

"He's here to help me protect you, Merrie. To arrest those foul wretches for their crimes against you."

"Against *me?*" Merrie's head spun as he dragged her down the stairs to where Straffen's scheming agents were even now being bound. *Jack* had brought Wycoff? And his presence had nothing at all to do with Sir William and treason? What in Heaven's Name was going on? Jack halted a few paces away and turned her to face him, holding her shoulders in a fierce grip.

"Merrie, I didn't leave you. I wouldn't have left you—"

"B-but . . . you were abducted," she said. "I puzzled out that much."

"Yes, I was." His bright, inquisitive little Merrie. Lord, how he wanted to hold her! "But it was those three wretches who knocked me unconscious, bound me hand and foot, and carted me off to London." He lifted a murderous glare to Gert Lombard and the quivering Cramden.

"Them? They did it?" Merrie followed his stare to their crimson faces, shocked that they didn't deny it. "Why? Why would they do such a thing?"

"I refused to leave Straffen and go back to London as they demanded. I intended to stay with you, make my home here, and they wouldn't countenance it. They bashed me over the head—Seabury as well—and had Chester cart us off to London, where they intended to keep us prisoner . . . or worse."

Merrie looked around frantically and located Chester, who scowled and nodded pained agreement. She gasped and searched for Seabury. He was nearby, holding Tess, whose face was buried in her hands, and his dark nod confirmed Jack's story. Merrie pushed out of Jack's hold to confront the conniving threesome.

"You did this? *You* had Jack abducted?" She read their answer in the way they hung their heads. And still she had to convince herself they were capable of such callousness: "You knew where he was all along? You let me go on and on, frantic about rescuing Jack, *pleading* for your help—" The pain of betrayal crept into her voice and she swayed. "That's why you were in no hurry, why you were so certain Jack was in no danger— All the while you knew where he was! It was *you* who had him taken! Why? Just so you could ply—"

"So they could remain in charge of Straffen," Jack charged, pulling her against his side to support her. "It's a long and twisted tale, Merrie. They milked the estate of a small fortune over the last twenty years, especially while your grandfather lay ill and incapable of deciding anything. They got him to sign things—papers taking you from the Hales and setting Overbeake over you, documents naming Sir Edwin guardian, codicils to the earl's will requiring your marriage and forbidding you to truly live with your husband." He felt more than heard Merrie's shock and turned her to face him. His countenance bore the bleakness of his soul.

"They selected me for your husband, Merrie, intending to wed us and then see that we never had more than one night together. Do you understand what I am saying? I was never meant to truly be your husband." There was more, so much more to say, but a flash of movement nearby brought his head up . . . straight into Ferrar's avid stare. Not here . . . he couldn't say those things to her here.

"You . . . did this?" Merrie turned toward the Lombards and Cramden, anguish in her sweet face. "You took Jack away? You let me marry and love him . . . then snatched him away? Why?" Her hurt was slowly turning to anger. "What could make you do such things to me? I never did anything to you. I even tried to understand, to help when I learned about—"

"Greed, Merrie." Jack pulled her back to him. "You have numerous holdings, as best I could learn."

"Most of which *we* acquired for Straffen," Gert snapped.

"Only so you could steal it later," Jack declared. "Merrie, if you truly married, and assumed your rightful role at Straffen, someday either you or your husband would have asked questions about the holdings and the incomes and the accounts. Sooner or later you would have learned the truth about your inheritance and how they'd appropriated and misused it . . . and misused you. Merrie . . ." His voice dropped, hoarse with tension. "You're a *countess*. In your own right."

Not a breath was taken or let in the hall for the full moment it took for the statement to register in her mind.

"A c-countess? I'm a . . . a . . ."

"Countess," Jack supplied, his expression as grave as his tone. "You've inherited the old earl's title as well as his estates. And they kept it from you, Merrie . . . to keep both you and Straffen in their control."

Chapter Twenty

ountess. It rumbled through her head like a cannonade. *Greed*, *abducted*, and *never meant to be your husband.* . . . Her knees gave and Jack caught her against him. She clung to his broad shoulders, reeling, grappling with his revelation. It was so plausible and settled so familiarly in her mind; it was as though she'd somehow known . . . at least in part. It explained the way she'd been restricted and deprived, and her feelings of being a "guest" at Straffen, and their reluctance to have her become involved in manor affairs. They had wanted the money . . . wanted Straffen . . . so much that they'd come to think of it as their own. And to protect their possession of it, they had controlled her and everything around her . . . her fosterage, her education, her isolation, her enslavement to Overbeake's cult of seemliness, even her marriage. Had any part of her life ever been her own?

She turned to look at them and new anger spread through her. Their audacity knew no limits! Even while holding her husband prisoner, they'd finagled and drawn her into a treasonous scheme that imperiled her neck . . . and all of Straffen! The cosmic gall! The monstrous guile!

"You foul, despicable rogues." Her whisper was raw with loathing. "I trusted you, believed you, *helped* you. And all along you—"

"B-but my lady—" Cramden sputtered, dragging the guardsmen who held him forward as he struggled closer to Merrie. His fleshy face was wet with tears and crimson with shame as he fell onto one fleshy knee before her. "I—we never meant to h-hurt you. We meant to take care of you, to see to your welfare—"

"You took my heart, my love, from me," Merrie whispered harshly. Not even Cramden's genuine tears could soften her toward them now.

"We ne'er expected a green young gell'd set her heart on the likes o' him!" Gert tussled forward, jerking her head contemptuously at Jack. "It were all Cramden's fault . . . sayin' he had to be handsome an' smooth wi' the women, to make yer first night bearable. Too soft-hearted by half, Cramden. He were alwus goin' fishy-livered on us!"

Merrie looked directly into Gert's unrepetant face. "Take them out of here," she ordered. "Lock them up. Get them out of my sight."

"Yes, my la—*Countess*." Sir Daniel, who had watched it all, bowed curtly to Merrie, then ripped the keys of office from steward and housekeeper and surrendered them to Ferrar, the ranking nobleman. A moment later, Sir Daniel ordered Cramden and the Lombards locked in the deepest cellar and posted his men to secure the hall and servants, to be sure none escaped in the night. As Cramden and the Lombards were summarily dragged out the rear door, Gert's snarls of blame and recrimination drifted back over the silent hall.

Merrie turned to Jack, her face filled with a sense of betrayal and loss. Words failed her. For once in her life, she could not muster a single question. All her energy, her being, her desire, now focused on the comfort of Jack's embrace, of his love. "Jack. . . ."

He enveloped her, pulling her against his chest. Then, oblivious to the stares of both noblemen and servants, he lifted her into his arms and climbed the stairs with her, leaving things to sort themselves out in the hall. Ferrar and Bosworth watched Jack Huntington's fierce tenderness with his stunning little bride and couldn't seem to muster any indignation that he'd not bothered to thank, or even introduce, them.

* * *

Jack carried Merrie into the master chamber and kicked the door shut behind them. He deposited her gently on the bench at the foot of the bed and before he straightened fully, she was on her feet with her arms wound tight around his neck. She smothered the parts of him she could reach with desperately exuberant kisses. "Oh, Jack, I was frantic—I was so worried—"

He let her go on for a minute, struggling mightily against the urge to clamp his arms around her, to plunge physically into her joy with her. She was so warm and soft and pliant against him . . . and he was so relieved she was safe and whole. He took a deep breath and allowed himself a fleeting embrace before setting her back.

"There is more."

His voice and face were so somber that a new trill of anxiety ran through her. She tried to dive into his arms again, but he held her away. "I don't want to hear any more. I don't even want to think about them or what they did. It's over and you're home."

"Merrie," he persisted, "there's more. I would have you know it all."

Something in his tone made her cease resisting the distance he put between them and she allowed herself to be pushed down onto the bench again. He knelt beside her on one knee and tried not to look at the dread in those depthless blue eyes.

"They contrived it all . . . your upbringing with Mistress Overbeake, the provisions of your grandfather's will, your marriage to me." He swallowed hard. Truth was a pitiless master. "Merrie, there was an understanding from the first: I was to bed you one night, the wedding night, and then I was to go back to London to live. And I agreed to it."

"One night?" She frowned, confused, and sought the comfort of Jack's hands with hers. He winced at her tender touch and raised her hands to kiss them before setting them back in her lap. Fear began to curl through her at that telling gesture. "But you stayed . . . two."

Two. It sounded so paltry. He could see from the way she briefly lowered her eyes that she was realizing that too. "You must see, Merrie, they chose me for your husband because of the kind of man I was. They needed someone who was practiced and smooth at pleasuring women, someone to dazzle and seduce the innocent gell they'd guarded so jealously. And they needed someone who would take the yearly stipend they offered and would . . . ask no questions." His throat tightened and his voice thickened miserably.

"That man was me, Merrie. I was cut loose by my family years ago for my irresponsible and dissolute ways. I lived by gambling, mostly, and by helping my noble friends from time to time with their stables. No ties, no obligations . . . and no questions asked. I came to Straffen fully intending to wed and bed you in only two days, then to live out the rest of my life on your money." The muscles in his face tightened abruptly and hot liquid welled in his eyes. "They bought me for you, Merrie, body and soul."

The stunned look on her face was too much. He pushed to his feet and paced away to collect himself. He had to finish; he owed her the whole truth. "I never expected you, Merrie, with your curiosity and your delectable body and your questions. I didn't mean to find you irresistible, didn't want to want you more than anything in my life. I didn't want to care for you, to feel responsible for you. It scared me to death. So, when Cramden and the Lombards demanded I leave, I . . . left."

He turned away, braced his legs apart and laid his head back, surrendering to the pain.

"It was the hardest thing I'd ever done in my life, leaving you."

Merrie watched him through the tears in her eyes, biting her lip.

"But you came back."

He saw the stubborn yet fragile set of her jaw and smiled involuntarily, painfully. "You did things to me, made me see things and feel things differently. I began to ask questions for the first time in years. I wanted you and worried about you and I yearned to make it up to you . . . wanted to be the kind of man you deserve.'' The pain overtook the smile. It was best she didn't know just how hard he'd worked to try to become worthy of her, or how vehemently he'd renounced the agreement and defied the Lombards to remain with her. It had all gone for naught anyway and would only make it harder to do what he knew he had to do.

''Merrie, don't you see?'' He came closer on stiff legs. ''The knaves stole your gellhood and your money and your land . . . and God knows what else that will be revealed when Bosworth goes through the estate accounts.'' His eyes darkened with anguish. ''Through me, they stole your innocence—and worse, they stole your future. I helped them. I just closed my eyes and took every bit of you I could reach.''

The pull of her, sitting there with tears rolling down her cheeks, was too much to resist. He stumbled forward and went down on one knee beside her, knowing he had no right to touch her and straining to keep his hands at his sides.

''They stole your freedom and your future . . . and . . . I mean to give them back to you.'' He dipped his head and lifted her gaze on his. ''I shall petition for an annulment for you. Our marriage was predicated on false conditions and intents. No court in Christendom would hold you to such a contract.''

Annulment? Merrie sat in shock while he rattled on about properties and titles and things that had nothing to do with anything that mattered to her. Her marriage, the one thing in her life that had given her joy and made her feel worthwhile and free and wanted— he was saying it was all wrong because the Lombards had arranged it for their own benefit. How could he believe such claptrap?

''No. . . . *No!*'' She shook her head and wiped her wet face with her palms.

"Listen to me, Merrie. They stole—*I* stole—things from you that can never be replaced, but—"

"No! They *haven't* stolen anything from me. Straffen is well and prospering and the wealth you say they pilfered, how can I grieve its loss when I never knew it existed? I didn't earn it, I never acquired or managed it. It was more theirs than mine." A bold new fury was racing through her veins, rousing something feral and female and possessive in her. "And now the one thing that *was* mine—truly mine, all mine—you're trying to take from me!"

"Merrie, you're a *countess*." He groaned.

She flinched and stiffened as if slapped. That was it? The damnable title? He'd spent his whole life in pursuit of his desires and pleasures; why in Heaven's Name did he have to start acting unselfishly now? And how dare the handsome wretch get all noble and self-sacrificing for something as empty and undeserving as a *title*?

"No! I'm a woman . . . and I'm your wife. You *asked* me to marry you and I agreed, of my own free will. I'm the same woman you married, the same woman you teased and touched and listened to and loved through long, pleasurable nights. Have you forgotten those nights, Jack?" She watched the blood crashing against his dusky skin and saw the spark that was struck in his eyes. He was remembering. "I'm the one you bought books and studied up on Latin for and read Ovid to. . . ."

"M-Merrie." He swallowed hard, fighting both her anger and his need in order to speak. "You don't understand—"

"I understand *plenty*." She growled and bashed both of her doubled fists into his shoulders as hard as she could, sending him sprawling back on the floor on his rear. He flailed and sputtered and sat up to find her on her feet above him, hands at her waist and eyes crackling. "It's you who doesn't understand! I don't give a moldy fig about being a countess. That's what this is about, isn't it—me being a countess?"

He made to rise, but she pinned him to the floor with visual daggers. ''Yes, dammit, that's part of it!'' he declared defensively. ''In decent society, in the hands of straight-fingered executors, you would *never* have been mated with a rogue like me. You'd have been recognized, a full countess and heiress, and they'd have found you a proper husband, a titled noble of some sort with a fine, upstanding name and a sound estate. You deserve that, Merrie, and I pray it's not too late. You deserve better than a feckless, irresponsible whoremonger for a husband.''

There it was . . . the rawest, barest truth Jack Huntington had ever faced. His eyes burned strangely, his heart twisted in his chest, and his guts were tying themselves in knots. That was what he was: rebellious, licentious, unreliable, self-centered . . . and arrogant, so damned arrogant. The devastating impact of his self-assessment was written plainly in his face.

''Well, Cramden *wasn't* straight-fingered,'' Merrie declared furiously. ''And I wasn't tutored and cosseted and brought up a fancy heiress. I was pinched and bullied and forbidden all the things I loved. I couldn't ride nor read nor ask questions nor keep a friend nor even leave the house! I was as green and ignorant of life as they could possibly keep me. And then you came. . . .''

She halted, seeing him and her love for him with new eyes. Jack had brought fresh breath to her airless life. He brought her strength on his broad shoulders, mirth in his irreverent laugh, and pleasure in his generous hands. He brought her a spirit unbound by convention and expectation and all the rules that had tortured and contorted her life. Jack Huntington's bold relishment of her quirks and his loving and scandalously permissive nature had been exactly what she needed, what her very being craved. How could she help but love him?

She sank to the floor on her knees, near him, clasping her hands desperately to keep from reaching out to him. His handsome jaw was set with self-loathing and his recklessly sensual eyes were dark with self-doubt. As Jack had once given her acceptance and love and hope, he now needed her to give them to him. And the fate of her love, her precious marriage, hung in the balance.

"Princess Elizabeth once told me a woman must find her heart's desire in marriage, somehow, else life would be too difficult to be borne." She collected his gaze in hers. "Freedom was my heart's desire, the thing I'd never had . . . and I found it in you, Gentleman Jack. You took the outrageous things I did to you in stride and accepted my quirks and shams and fambles. Around you I was free to read and think and ask questions. Can you imagine how precious that was to me? You were enough of a scholar and a rebel not to care that it was a mere gell who asked you questions you couldn't answer. You let me be me . . . whoever, whatever I was. And you wanted me anyway."

She inched closer on her knees, watching the turmoil in his face. "I needed you, Jack Huntington, like barley needs rain. You held me and touched me in wonderful, pleasureful ways, and you let me touch you. Do you know how long it had been since anyone had touched me except in anger? I was so frightened and green, and you were so patient and gentle with me . . . and persistent. . . ."

"I left you, Merrie," he said, reeling from her disarming defense of him. How could she really want him after . . . "I married you and loved you and left you."

"Even that brought some benefit," she declared, determined to outbalance his guilt with the truth she'd come to see. "Don't you understand? I had to grow up, Jack. I had to begin doing things for myself. I had to face Overbeake and seize some control over my own life. And you came back to stay . . . for the same reason you're going to stay this time. You're a better man than you'll ever know, Jack Huntington, and *you love me!*"

It hit both of them with gale force, battering his resolve to relinquish her and solidifying her resolve to keep him. He *did* love her; it sank into her very bones. Her heart took flight, delirious with joy. He loved her a very great deal indeed! But while her feelings were scaling heady new heights, her feet were planted firmly on the ground. She wasn't about to let his wretched noble instincts interfere further with her love and marriage. And if she had to use everything he'd taught her against him . . .

"L-love?" His tongue stumbled, thick and clumsy, over the word. "B-but, I . . ." He halted, looking shaken to the core.

"What surprises you, Jack?" Her blue eyes sparkled with confident challenge. "That you love me . . . or that I know about it?" Her lips bowed in a fonden smile that dared him to deny it. "You've often said what a 'quick little thing' I am."

"God." He swallowed hard and tried to drag his eyes from her fiery hair and the rising heat in her bold look. It was true, every word of it. His senses were opened wide, focusing, drinking her lush, vibrant sensuality into his hungry core. Merrie watched the wanting growing in him, that craving that had always been a bit outside his control. She knew just what it felt like. It was the counterpart and complement of her need for him. And she was determined to satisfy both that wanting and her own heart's desire.

"You love me with every part of you," she charged silkily, her voice and lashes lowering. "With your heart and your mind and your big, hard body. You ache all through whenever you see me."

"That has nothing to do with wh—what's good for you. . . ." His voice cracked ignominiously. He knew exactly what she was doing with that sultry, steamy look that was seeping into her eyes . . . and he was appalled to find it so utterly effective. He was beginning to vibrate with raw carnal excitement, and his "big, hard body" was getting bigger and harder by the syllable!

"Your fingertips tingle sometimes with the urge to touch me. And your lips—" She licked her upper lip slowly, inducing the same motion in him. "Your lips thicken and burn, wanting mine."

"Now, Meredith. . . ."

"Are you sure you want to give me to another man?" A seductive curl appeared at one corner of her mouth and she rose onto her knees, dragging her hands slowly up her hips and waist, along her boned ribs and up over her corsetted breasts in a slow, sinuous stroke that held his eyes captive.

"You've taught me to relish the delights of the body, John Huntington. Would my next husband be shocked by the things you've taught me to crave?" The tiny, mother-of-pearl buttons down her bodice front spun and gave, one by one by one. He couldn't swallow. His eyes were hostage to the sight of her emerging skin.

"Can you promise that my new 'noble' lord, with his respectable family and his sound estate, will be as marvelously upstanding as you? Will he feel as hard and lean and pleasurable between my thighs? Will he be my pony when I've a mind to ride?" In the hot, quivering silence, her body swayed and her shoulders flexed as she pushed her bodice from her. Her voice grew thick and honeyed, alluring.

"Will he be outraged to learn that I like whispers . . . naughty whispers . . . in my ear as we make love? Will he know how to start fires in my bubbies with his tongue the way you do?" The ties of her skirtwaist now dangled and her trembling fingers worked the lacings of her small corset. From its stern confines two creamy globes emerged, long-nippled, lush, divinely erotic. His mouth watered abruptly, shocking him.

"Would my respectable husband be willing to shave his beard so that I might feel his brambled chin on my breasts at night? I've always loved the feel of your roughened chin, Jack, rubbing me. . . ." Her fingertips brushed brazenly over those taut, rosy spouts that held him in thrall. A visible frisson of pleasure coursed through her and a wild tide of desire roared through him.

"Would he ask your advice on where I might like the feel of his teeth? Would he enjoy the slide of my hair across his bare belly, as you do?" Her gown and petticoat slid as she rose, clad in a thin shift that she pushed aside to bare her breasts. She swished her hair about her shoulders and he could have sworn he felt it slither across the burning skin of his belly.

"Will he let me nuzzle and lick and taste him . . . adoring his body however I want? Will he love me only once a night . . . once a week . . . or once a month? Will he make me breathless and hot, wet and sliddery inside . . . with only a look, as you do?"

Jack's breath was a choked rattle in his throat. His ears, his face, his loins were ablaze from her blatant verbal seduction. Every shocking question was meant to conjure memories to mingle with the thick, molten streams of desire she was generating in him. She was boldly asserting her queenly sovereignty in his heart and in his blood.

"No answers? But you said you'd always answer my questions, Jack." She pulled her long shift up, baring her stockinged legs, offering and turning one seductively for his inspection. A womanly awareness of sensual power told her he was coiled on the brink of an explosion. "Do you think he'll like my legs . . . on his shoulders? Will you tell him how I squirm when you nibble the backs of my knees?"

She came forward inch by tantalizing inch, hips swaying, eyes silvery with erotic heat. Then she turned, presenting him the sensitive part she'd just named, and glancing seductively over her shoulder. Her tone was pure temptation.

"Nibble me, Jack."

He exploded with a primal male growl of possession, engulfing her, lifting her, claiming her as no other would ever have the right to do. She squealed terrified delight as he bore her to the bed and dropped her on it. His body fell over hers, a great, burning instrument of conquest, bent on pure, maddened pillage. And she threw her arms around him and welcomed that breathtaking plunder. She opened hungrily to his rapacious kiss and sent greedy fingers curling up his neck and through his soft hair. He clasped her fiercely, plunging into her mouth, devouring her, inhaling her, feeling her soft flesh yielding and seeking beneath him.

Their mouths merged and moved in stunning counterpoint as raw possession was tempered by passion's refinements. Powerful currents of need pulsed through their glowing, straining bodies; the urge to join filled their throats and veiled their eyes. All was pure, unalloyed feeling . . . desire that turned their blood to fire and their bones to ash.

Her hands clasped and conquered every part of him, while he inflicted on her all the tortures of passion she'd verbally subjected him to. His bristled chin rasped her burning nipples and his wet tongue absorbed the flame. His hands traced her shoulders and the curve of her waist and the heated satin of her inner thigh . . . and his teeth followed, dragging across her skin, pausing to fasten deliciously on an especially succulent morsel.

"Jack! Oh, Jack—love me," she cried, wriggling, gasping and feverish with need. "Fill me . . . let me feel you inside. . . ." Her body arched to follow his as he rose above her, only to drop back when he went out of range. Her eyes fluttered open to focus on him as he braced, ripping at his doublet and shirt and breeches. Half blind with desire, quaking with need, he fumbled clumsily—no trace of the rake's cool grace left in him. He was a genuine lover, as wildly eager as though it were his first taste of pleasure.

When he finally kicked his breeches aside, ripped at the ties of his hose, and rolled to pull at his boots, she tugged him back with a groan.

"Forget your wretched boots. Just come and love me!"

He did just that, pouring over her and into her receptive body with a sheer animal joy that matched her driving feminine need for completion, for union. He filled her body and her heart with furious adoration, as he lifted her on drafts of searing, breath-stealing passion. Over and over he carried her just to the brink, pushing her cries and her pleasure ever higher. Writhing in a delicious agony of arousal, she cried his name and begged for more . . . still more.

Their groans and cries echoed wildly about the chamber as they abandoned all but the consummate joy of their new joining . . . loved and loving, together in bold revelation of self and in joyful embracing of other. All boundaries dissolved, all limits faded as their soaring ended in an explosion that shattered body and soul into a million dazzling, ever-burning embers. And as their wild torrent of passions crested, in the wardrobe nearby, Sir William Cecil clamped his hands harder over his ears and tried very hard not to smother.

Chapter Twenty-one

It was some time later that the world began to spin again and their hearts went back to merely beating. The volatile force of their joining left them deliciously consumed, charred to the ends of their toes, and smoky with satisfaction. Jack flexed and shifted, bearing his weight to one side and turning her with him so as to preserve that precious connection between them.

Merrie opened her eyes into his sated, long-lashed gaze and smiled, the most earthy and replete expression he had ever witnessed.

"I think you were right," he murmured. "I do love you, my sweet little hoyden." The satisfaction in her smile deepened.

"And?"

"And I don't think I could ever allow another man to do what I just did to you . . . no matter how damned noble and deserving he was."

"And?"

"You need more? Troth! You are a greedy vixen." He looked away and took a steadying breath. "I'm a hopeless rogue and a whoremonger—" She clamped a hand over his mouth and gave him a blistering glare. When she drew her hand away, he sighed and gave her her way. "Actually I'm a marginally respectable, possibly redeemable—" Again her hand stopped his words and her eyes narrowed dangerously. He knew better than to cross her a third time. "I'm a damned saint!" he declared to the world. "I'm a splendid piece of manhood; generous and patient and loving and . . . well-read. Is that enough?"

She took a deep, happy breath and let the sun shine

in her eyes for him. "It's a very nice start. You were saying?"

He grinned, a bit dazzled. She was a very determined little thing. "I was saying . . . I don't believe an annulment is going to be possible. I think you're saddled with me 'till death do us part.' " He sobered. "Any objections?"

Her love-darkened eyes grew luminous with tears. "Not one. I love you, Jack Huntington. With all my heart." She sniffed and wiggled against him. "And with a few other parts of me."

He laughed and kissed her softly, wrapping her in his arms. He reveled in the calm floating through them, the peace that lay between them. There was no hurry, no peril, no complications. Only love. I love you, she had said, and it was as though those words were recreated, just for them.

"Jack?" Her voice rippled through the calm waters of his reverie minutes later. "If I'm a countess, what does that make you?"

"A lucky man," he rumbled with sleepy charm.

"No—" She wriggled onto her elbow to look at him. "I mean . . . does that make you titled somehow, too?"

"Not necessarily." His eyes remained shut . . . adamantly so.

"Jack Huntington, tell me the truth. Does marrying me make you an earl or something?" She shook his shoulder and made him open his eyes. The look on her face said she'd brook no further evasions.

"A baron. It may make me . . . baron of something. According to the old records I may be granted the old earl's lesser title. But there may be conditions attached along the way. It's not all sorted out yet."

"You were going to give up the chance for a title . . . for me?" There was a trace of awe in her voice that made him feel very uncomfortable.

"Well, I was going to try. Seeing the way things turned out, and knowing my raging weakness for your sweet flesh, I probably didn't stand a chance."

Merrie got a glint in her eye. "Well, if I'm a countess, and you're a baron, what will that make our children?''

''Besides lucky to have you for a mother, you mean?'' He laughed. ''I think our eldest son inherits through you . . . becomes Earl of Straffen.'' He winced. ''The little cuff will outrank me someday.''

Merrie's throaty laugh was temptation distilled. ''Oh, that won't do a'tall. Then you'll have to make me daughters, Jack, lots of lovely daughters.''

He was over her in a trice, rolling her onto her back and absorbing her laughter with his mouth. He loved kissing Merrie while she laughed. They cuddled and snuggled and whispered like joyful children until a muffled cough finally penetrated their glowing, sensual haze.

Jack heard it first; his senses were attuned to just such things. He started and pushed up onto his elbow, frowning, searching the dimly lit chamber as he listened. Again it came . . . a cough, muffled but unmistakable. And this time Merrie heard it too.

She frowned and sat up, listening . . . hearing again . . . finally comprehending. She looked at Jack in pure horror. ''Oh, Jack! Oh, Lord!'' She scrambled from the bed, searching for her shift. ''Jack, get up—now!'' She raced around the bed, snatching up her petticoats and tossing his discarded breeches at him.

''What in hell is going on?'' he demanded, bounding from the bed.

''Put some clothes on . . . *please!*'' she whispered desperately, remembering *everything* and looking more sickly by the instant. ''Oh, please, *please* don't be angry—''

Her panicky plea sounded a little strangled at the end. She reached for her gown and burrowed into it as best she could, trembling at the laces and misbuttoning everything. Running a hasty hand through her tousled hair, she hurried to the wardrobe, looking at it as though it contained the Devil himself. Another cough sounded and Jack bolted across the chamber to her side.

"It's . . . Sir William. He's in the . . . wardrobe . . ." She gestured lamely to the large chest, then pulled open both doors.

Sir William was curled into an improbable ball with his knees under his chin and his boots lofted and braced against the side of the wardrobe. He was drenched with sweat and gasping for decent air . . . and red-faced, very red-faced. When he turned a beleaguered gaze on Jack's shocked face, he knew for certain what was dawning on the handsome rake's mind.

"Oh, sir, are you all right?" Merrie started for him, but caught sight of Jack's deepening outrage and stopped, leaving the princess's surveyor to uncoil himself from his hiding place. "Jack, this is Sir William Cecil, once counselor to King Ed—Oh, Jack—"

Cecil staggered to his feet and arched to relieve the crook in his back, expecting to find himself trounced bodily at any second. But when the heartbeats labored by and his hide remained intact, he lifted a pained expression to Lady Merrie's big, virile husband, then to the scarlet-faced lady herself.

The three exchanged crimson-faced looks, then fled each other's eyes . . . all with the same humiliating thought in mind. He'd heard *everything*.

Merrie moaned silently. Jack had every right to think the worst, to bash and trounce and denounce them both. It took every scrap of audacity she owned to turn a crimson-faced plea to him.

But Jack Huntington was every bit the man Merrie believed in. He looked at the clear, guileless entreaty in Merrie's eyes and knew she would never have betrayed him. But the wretch had invaded the sanctity of his bedchamber. . . .

In a flash of pure diplomatic brilliance, Sir William forced a convincing yawn and stretched his arms wide, blinking as though having just wakened from a heavy sleep. "I trow—I must have been plum exhausted. Snuffed like a wick, I was. What hour is it, my lady? Are we safely through?"

It was a thin conceit, but a face-saving one. Merrie pulled the shaky Sir William to a chair and, even as Jack demanded it, launched into a furious explanation about the Lombards' intrigue and the queen's illness and Sir William's covert mission to meet with Princess Elizabeth.

Every word deepened the look of horror on Jack's face. Cecil took over the narrative, expanding on Merrie's story: the Lombards agreed to arrange Cecil's rendezvous with the future queen of England and Merrie caught them the night of the assignation. She'd been recruited into the scheme to help Elizabeth, despite her frantic worries about Jack's safety. When Sir Daniel came riding in with a force of men, they had naturally expected they had been discovered. Merrie had hidden Cecil in the wardrobe . . . and in the ensuing turmoil, had forgotten all about him.

Jack listened, appalled, then angry, then furious at the vaulting ambitions of Straffen's larcenous agents. They hadn't been content with stealing Merrie blind and wrecking her life and her happiness; they'd insisted on imperiling her neck as well! He stalked and ranted and snarled until both Merrie and Cecil were white as Dover chalk.

"Good God!" He finished in a whispered shout. "I've insisted Wycoff, as the queen's agent, secure Merrie's properties until the coil of her inheritance can be untangled. The hall is full of his guardsmen, even now!"

"If he sees me here, this close to Hatfield, he'll know instantly that I've come to see Elizabeth." Sir William winced, looking a bit gray. "They look for an excuse to move against her and it shall be the very thing to make into evidence of a conspiracy against the queen."

"Because it *is* a conspiracy!" Jack charged irritably.

"But not against the queen!" Merrie swallowed her heart back into place and stiffened her shoulders to face him with all her love and trust in him shining in her eyes. "Jack, we must help Sir William. England needs Princess Elizabeth. She's a very wise woman and will make a wonderful queen. And Princess Elizabeth needs Sir William . . . and Sir William needs us. If he tries to slip out of the house on his own, he'll be found out. They'll call it a plot and his neck will be forfeit.''

''And if we help him, *our* necks may be forfeit as well!'' Jack thundered. ''This is madness, another twisted contrivance of those cursed Lombards—''

''No. It has nothing to do with Master Cramden and the Lombards.'' She grasped his sleeves and met his handsome eyes. ''It has to do with me. I owe it to the princess. She helped me once when I needed guidance badly. She's a fine lady . . . a worthy lady, Jack. . . .'' Her voice carried the potent lull of reason and the irresistible seduction of her faith in him. He growled frustration and stalked away, feeling tense and irritable, with his husbandly prerogative melting shamelessly under Merrie's entreaty.

He stopped. His shoulders rounded, his head dropped in surrender. Behind him, Merrie read that gesture like an Italian sonnet and turned to Sir William with her face alight. She ran to Jack and threw her arms about his waist, hugging him fiercely.

''Oh, Jack! We'll manage it somehow . . . you'll see.''

With no possibility of arranging a meeting until the following night and with a houseful of strangers which included Sir Daniel and his queen's men, the awkward threesome was forced to pass the rest of the night together in the master chamber. Jack and Merrie retired in some embarrassment to the bed, fully clothed, while Sir William, emphasizing that he'd had *abundant* sleep already, sat up in a chair. None of them truly slept; they kept listening for the tred of heavy boots on the stairs, shouts of discovery, and the rattle of swords.

But the uneasy peace of the hall continued, uninterrupted, through the night. The next morning, Jack and Merrie broke fast in their chamber, so as to provide covertly for Sir William, then reluctantly descended the stairs to make a show of seeing to their guests and taking charge of their home and holding.

The first face to greet them was the very one they dreaded to see: Sir Daniel Wycoff's. He had bad news . . . which implied good news. The Lombards and Cramden hadn't revealed anything about the extent or manipulation of Merrie's inheritance, but they apparently hadn't yet divulged Sir William's presence in the house, either. Sir Daniel's eyes glowed menacingly as he assured Jack and Merrie: "You needn't trouble yourselves over their stubbornness. I know quite a little number of ways to loosen tight tongues."

Merrie cast a wilting look at Jack. If the Lombards' tongues loosened too much, all of their heads might be forfeit. They had to do something.

"Of the three knaves, only Master Cramden showed any remorse," Merrie said, her mind racing. "If he were separated from the Lombards' influence, might he be persuaded to reveal more of their dealings? Perhaps I could speak with him . . ."

"Nay, Countess." Sir Daniel shook his head. "I'd not subject you to such unpleasantness. But I shall heed your suggestion and question Cramden separately. You are right in thinking him weaker than the others; he moaned and blubbered the whole night long." He bowed and purposefully exited the hall through the rear door, heading for the cellars where Cramden and the Lombards were held.

Merrie glanced nervously at the staircase leading to Sir William's hiding place. Jack's gaze followed hers and his anxieties rose apace. A moment later he straightened. Ferrar and Bosworth were arriving on the stairs at that very moment, expressions bright with curiosity and undisguised appreciation for Merrie's enchanting face and form.

Jack was forced to introduce the pudgy, endearing Earl of Wolden and the arrogantly handsome Baron Bosworth, and then to endure the way they scrutinized his glowing jewel of a bride and fawned and outgallanted each other shamelessly with her. Within minutes, he was ready to give them both a swift boot. This was no time and he was in no mood to defend his wife and marriage against his old partners in debauchery. They were rescued only by Seabury's announcement that he had finally located Manley Lombard's ledgers and what appeared to be a cache of deeds and documents, which had been hidden beneath the steward's bed closet. The pressing concerns of Merrie's estate required the noble rakes and Jack to turn to less volatile matters.

While Sir Daniel harried Cramden, Jack and Merrie tried to maintain an appropriate guise of concern by questioning the chief servants and Chester and Tess. They were soon convinced that Gert and Manley had jealously limited involvement in their lucrative scheme. The numerous other Lombards on Straffen, to a body, claimed ignorance of and expressed horror at the revelation of the former steward's and housekeeper's perfidy. They were quick to vow loyalty to the master and their mistress, and Jack and Merrie wisely decided to let it go at that. Time would prove which Lombards were fair and which were foul.

By midday, Jack's and Merrie's nerves were taut with strain. They joined Bosworth in the hall, where he was ensconced examining the ledgers and records of the accounts and business dealings of Straffen. He had a gifted eye for numbers and a knowledge of legal transactions, having studied at the Inns of Court in former days. With Seabury acting as clerk, and under Sir Daniel's intense, periodic scrutiny, the handsome baron perused and read and tallied and questioned. Whenever the record of transactions became too puzzling, Sir Daniel withdrew to the cellars and returned with a grimly satisfied expression and an answer. Cramden, unaccustomed to discomfort and ill-constituted to withstand duress, had apparently begun to talk. And as Bosworth began to undo the stubborn knot of Straffen's financial affairs, Jack and Merrie exchanged subtle, speaking looks and glanced anxiously at the stairs.

They could only pray that the cracking Cramden didn't spill too much information.

Seeking escape from the tension, Merrie made her way upstairs that afternoon and found Tess in her chambers, packing, preparing to leave Straffen. "But you can't go," Merrie insisted, grabbing the girl's hands. "I need you, Tess."

"I be so shamed, m'lady. I can't stay 'ere." Tess lowered teary eyes and tried to pull away.

"I would never hold you responsible for what your parents did, Tess." Merrie hoped an appeal to Tess's sense of duty might work. "And I've desperate need of you now. You know so much more than I do about the hall and its workings. Please stay, Tess, and help me set things right. I couldn't bear it if you left. Nor, I think, could Seabury. Did you know, Jack is thinking of making him Steward of Straffen."

Tess's wet face brightened. "He is? Oh, he'll find no finer man than Mister Seabury, m'lady."

"And I'll need a new housekeeper," Merrie mused pointedly. "Someone Seabury respects and works well with."

Tess's eyes grew to the size of goose eggs. "Oh, m'lady. I alwus dreamt of orderin' a house. Do ye th-think . . ." She stammered to a red-faced halt.

"Of course." Merrie's eyes twinkled. "I'd be losing a *companion* . . ." Merrie had always known Tess found her role of companion a bit uncomfortable. "But I can think of none more loyal or deserving. Stay with us, Tess." And in her last official act as Merrie's companion, Tess gave her lady a great hug.

Night fell slowly over Straffen. When the moon rose and the house nestled in slumber, dark, shifting forms again appeared in Straffen's great hall. They slipped from shadow to shadow, stealthily invading the stables and emerging into the hedgerows beyond. When the moon briefly escaped a cloud's grasp, the forms took the shapes of two men and a woman, leading mounts, aiming for the cart path leading back through the woods.

The evening had seemed endless for the three conspirators. Cecil was still cooped up in the master chamber, listening to every creak and moan of the house timbers and every hint of a human voice. Downstairs, through supper and afterward, Jack and Merrie had to suffer Sir Daniel's constant scrutiny and to listen, on pins and needles, to his zeal for uncovering the extent of the Lombards' plot. And when not plagued by Sir Daniel's menacing efficiency, they were saddled with Ferrar's gleeful curiosity about them and Bosworth's envy-spawned leering. They were reduced to exchanging a few glazed, potent looks of longing and fleeting touches of reassurance that were usually witnessed by Ferrar . . . who resonated with a gossip's joy and added each look to the enlarging epic he was fashioning about their scandalous love.

It was almost a relief to them to don black and actually begin to slink and skulk, instead of suffering tortured imaginings of all the things that could go wrong in such a venture. Loyal Chester had placed the signal in the tree earlier that evening to alert the princess and now Sir William led the way, while the master and mistress of Straffen followed at a distance, watching and mentally marking the course for future reference.

The Lombards had always accompanied Sir William to serve as lookouts and, in the dire event they were detected, to distract their pursuers while Sir William and the princess escaped. Jack and Merrie now took their places. Jack had objected to risking Merrie's safety, but she refused to be left behind, reminding him pointedly of just how "distracting" she could be when she put her mind to it.

Once into the cover of woods and mounted on horseback, their blood pumped faster and their senses and bodies came alive with expectation. Jack glanced at Merrie and found her eyes glistening with excitement in the moonlight. And Merrie watched Jack's features sharpen and his nostrils flare the way they did in

the throes of loving. Clearly, a bit of danger had unexpected effects on them.

Dismounting, they led their horses the last bit of the
way to a clearing that looked surprisingly familiar. It
was the same secluded spot where Jack had caught and
confronted his "sickly" little bride nearly two months
earlier . . . and where, together, they'd subsequently
encountered Elizabeth.

The moon drifted in and out of clouds, illuminating
the small clearing as they watched from hiding. As tension mounted, Cecil stepped to the center of the clearing, shedding his cloak hood to stand bareheaded and
recognizable. And as Jack and Merrie held their breath
and watched, a shadow stirred among the trees on the
far side and came forward. Another cloak hood slid
and a flash of fiery hair identified the form as Elizabeth.
The two approached each other and Cecil went down
on his knee before his mistress. Merrie sagged with
relief against Jack and he took a deep, cleansing breath.
The first half of the venture was done.

Elizabeth and Cecil removed to the far side of the
clearing. There was nothing to do now but wait. Jack
pulled Merrie back into the edge of the trees and found
them a seat on a patch of moss behind a large fallen
log. From such a vantage point, they could survey the
entire area and the shadows beneath the trees that circled it. At first they watched Elizabeth and her trusted
surveyor talking and pacing and gesturing, sometimes
angrily, sometimes in exasperation, sometimes in perfect quietude. But gradually their anxieties subsided
and Jack and Merrie turned their attentions on each
other, snuggling together under Merrie's cloak, giving
hands and passions scandalously free rein. It was the
first time they'd been alone since their recovery of Cecil
from the wardrobe.

"Never," Jack whispered hotly into Merrie's tingling ear, "not in all my loose-living days, was I ever
so close to the headsman's block." His fingers found
the lacings of her front-closing gown and nimbly loosened them.

"I promise you . . ." She gasped outraged delight as his hand slid over her aching bubbie and tantalized its eager tip. "Oh, Jack . . . ummmm. . . ."

"You were promising me?" He suckled her earlobe maddeningly.

"Respectability will not always be so . . . hazardous. Just a few more . . ."

"Ummmm . . . yes . . . more . . ."

"Meetings . . ." she whispered.

He kissed her deeply, and as his knowing hands extended their claim on her passions, he stopped her throaty moan with his mouth on hers. Soon her hands were moving, exploring, returning him pleasure for pleasure.

Across the clearing, after more weighty confidences had been exchanged, Elizabeth flicked a glance toward the Huntingtons' bower, locating them only by the dim glow of Merrie's hair. She scowled.

"And what of Lady Merrie and this Huntington fellow?" she inquired.

"Ahhh . . ." Cecil flushed in spite of himself and, as always, measured his words carefully. "Utterly trustworthy, Your Grace. They've been . . . immeasurably helpful, considering the foul circumstances under which they were drawn to our aid. I never imagined the Lombards were so ambitious."

"Ambitious servants are ever a plague. They shall always find a place. They are like cats who with the Devil's aid always land on their feet. It would be unwise, I think, to allow these ambitious Lombards to languish long in Sir Daniel's hands. They know quite a bit with which to bargain their own freedom." She turned a steady look on Cecil and he understood.

"I shall see to it. Lady Merrie can likely persuade her husband to be . . . forbearing, if not forgiving, in their regard. She is a remarkably levelheaded and insightful young woman."

"Is she now?" Elizabeth turned that piercing gaze back across the clearing, wondering if they were truly engaged in . . . what they seemed to be engaged in. Bundled close, kissing, perhaps. Fondling, undoubtedly. She tapped her foot with a certain annoyance. "Even so, I cannot imagine the gell is properly equipped to cope with such a rake," she declared regally. Inbred diplomacy tempered Cecil's response. He had followed both her gaze and the jealous tinge of her thoughts.

"I am not so sure, Your Grace. From what I have seen and *heard*"—he smiled with judicious mischief—"methinks she handles him . . . exceeding well."

Thus Cecil made an earnest plea
to Jack and Merrie to set the knaves free.
Jack wouldn't allow it; he ranted and railed.
But Cecil and Merrie and wisdom prevailed . . .
  Cramden and the Lombards were released.

Poor Cramden was stripped of his duties and wealth
And banished from Hertford with only his health.
Thereafter he lived on the grace of his daughters,
An example to all of the fate of bad lawyers . . .
  who betray the trust of their patrons and wards.

Penniless and chastised, the foul Lombards went
In search of another infirm, rich old gent.
Cecil found them in London, quite ragged and sore,
And got them positions tending privies and floors
  . . . at the queen's Hampton Court Palace.

Such is the fate of vaulting ambitions
And servants who callously scheme for positions.
Such is the fate of knaves who connive
And scheme and famble and try to deprive . . .
  true hearts of their freedom and love.

Epilogue

I t was well more than a year before Elizabeth's crowning. A new age in England was said to be dawning. The new baron and the countess of Straffen were there to pledge faith and fealty to Old Harry's heir.

One of Merrie's hands held her stiff, brocade under-skirt as she hurried along the rush-strewn palace corridor. The other was secure in Jack's grip as he led her too quickly along. She wished with all her heart for a third hand, to bear her clove-scented pomander nearer her nose to ward off the barage of odors. Panting, growing dizzy, she finally pulled them to a staggering halt in the dimming light. Jack was around in a trice, catching her by the waist, supporting her.

"I—I have—I—" She panted, leaning gratefully against his hard body. Sandalwood and spicy brandy . . . he smelled better than any pomander. "I have to . . . catch my breath!"

"You're flushed." Jack turned her face up to his and searched its moist glow with true concern. "Are you sure you're all right?"

She nodded, swallowing and forcing her heart to calm. "It's just this wretched boning . . . makes me short of breath."

"I shouldn't have let you wear it," he said with a glower, pulling her protectively against him.

"I'll not have the court saying Jack Huntington has married a shapeless squab—"

"Who is six months gone with child," Jack hissed in a furious whisper. She could be so stubborn. And right now she was giving him that through-the-lashes look that always harbingered her getting her way with him.

Well, not this time! He released her, dipped, and swept her off her feet and up into his arms.

"Ja-ack—" she squealed, flinging her arms about his neck. "Put me down!" She cast a panicky glance about them and found several widened eyes following their hasty progress. "You'll make us a spectacle—"

"We're already a spectacle," Jack muttered. "Ferrar and his blessed ballad . . . I could hardly do your repute further harm if I was caught bedding you on the chancel floor of Westminster Cathedral!"

Merrie chewed her lip to keep back a laugh and relaxed in his arms. Jack was still furious at his old friend Ferrar for composing and publishing a ballad celebrating the more notorious details of their unusual courtship and marriage. The song had long since preceded them at court and when they arrived for Elizabeth's coronation, curiosity about them had created a small sensation, even in the greater glow of Elizabeth's consuming glory.

Merrie's mode of arrival at the queen's Hall of Presence was noted with raised brows, shocked whispers, and not a few secretive smiles. The countess was breeding, it was said, and her reformed rake of a husband, the once notorious Gentleman Jack, cossetted her flagrantly, shamelessly. Numerous ladies watched with unguarded envy as he lowered her to her feet and steadied her as she righted her laces and smoothed her undergown. Too well, they recalled the mesmerizing pleasure of his gentlemanly attentions.

Merrie caught their covertly desirous looks and as they stood outside the great chamber in the ranks of nobles yet to be presented, she looked up into Jack's handsome face and whispered, "I wish we could just go home . . . to Straffen." Her voice and lashes lowered. "I miss our comfortable bed . . . and our privacy."

Jack nodded with a rueful, understanding grin. He was all too aware of the bold male glances searching his delectable wife. Even pregnancy was no protection against wayward passions and indecent propositions in the jaded halls of court.

Moments later they were announced, and they entered the grand chamber, floating through a sea of be-satined and brocaded nobility. Merrie's strongest impression was of light; banks of beeswax tapers had been set strategically, illuminating the throne and the stunning young queen who sat in red-gold splendor upon it. Numbly, Merrie felt her body moving and heard herself proclaimed "Countess of Straffen" and heard Jack announced as the Baron Estenwerth, her grandfather's lesser title. Jack's hard arm was her stay as she knelt and repeated her well-practiced oath of fealty to Elizabeth. And from one step behind, Jack went down on one knee, repeating the same phrases.

All attention was riveted on the sight of the stunning couple, clad in matching wine-colored velvets. All eyes fell inescapably on Merrie's hair, which flowed from beneath her delicate French cap like a river of flame, then they flew to the new queen's memorable red-gold tresses, which had been left in artful, maidenly display to accept her weighty crown.

A wave of whispering went through the court as Elizabeth bade the countess rise and the baron remain in place, on his knees. She turned to her secretary, Sir William Cecil, for a word, then called to the Duke of Norfolk, demanding use of his sword. The onlooking crowds of peers strained closer with fevered anticipation.

"In recognition of your service to the crown, in former days"—she lowered the blade to touch each of his shoulders in turn—"and in anticipation of your continued loyalty and service . . . rise the Earl of Straffen. And may God be with you." Jack managed to rise, to kiss Elizabeth's ring, and, ever gallant, to murmur a rather dazed soliloquy of gratitude. Elizabeth beamed, accepting his tribute with a twinkle of queenly mischief. "It would never do"—her eyes fell on Merrie's radiant form—"for the coming child to outrank his father."

The chamberlain tapped his staff and announced the new earl to the court, as Elizabeth stepped down to take Merrie's hand and present them. A rousing cheer went up around the hall, all but drowning Elizabeth's further words to them.

"You have my leave, Straffen, to take your countess home. Court is no place to birth a child in peace. And I would have this one born in all joy and serenity. You have been good and faithful servants; enjoy your reward."

Merrie curtseyed and kissed the queen's hands, through jubilant tears, then hugged her husband with shocking enthusiasm. The Earl and Countess of Straffen exited into an engulfing tide of congratulations.

Elizabeth resumed her seat, watching them go with an enigmatic smile. Sir William Cecil leaned to her ear.

"A magnanimous gesture, Your Grace. Queenly in generosity."

"Yes," Elizabeth agreed, "it was." Her hand came up to resettle her stunning red-gold tresses on her shoulder. "Is her hair really so much like mine, do you think? Perhaps a bit thinner . . . lacking a bit of the fire?"

Cecil sighed. Elizabeth had the makings of a great queen. If only she weren't quite so much a woman. . . .

Later, in a far-flung, half-lit corridor, Jack carried Merrie to a secluded window nook and managed to collapse on the seat, pulling her firmly onto his lap. His joy could find release only in her and he kissed her over and over, stealing her breath and then giving it back in hot, sensual billows. She finally pushed back in his fierce embrace to wipe her damp, glowing face and bask in his love.

"An earl . . ." He sounded a bit awed, shaking his head. His eyes were rimmed with moisture.

"You'll be a wonderful earl," she said, beaming. Then the babe inside her seemed to react to the excitement, moving strongly, and she pulled his hand around to the front of her waist. "And a wonderful father."

His face melted into a mischievous grin and his hand closed possessively on the growing mound of her belly. "Do you suppose it's too late to request a boy?"

Merrie laughed, adoring his strong face with her fingertips. "Perhaps next time." Then her lips spoke against his. "Take me home, my lord earl . . . please."

In joy and in peace, Jack and Merrie retired
To Straffen with the Seaburys, whom they had since hired.
They raised horses, babies, and each other's passions,
Asked questions and loved in the noisiest fashion . . .
    always after first checking the wardrobe.

True love has a way of setting things right,
Of balancing forces of darkness with light.
The scheming and plotting, when they were all ended,
Left two hearts and two lives beautifully blended . . .
    in secula seculorum.

Author's Note

I hope you enjoyed the story of Merrie Straffen and her "Gentleman Jack." I have always been intrigued by the color and liveliness of Elizabethan language. In my childhood, some of my elders in isolated pockets of the Appalachian hills still used words I later learned were Elizabethan in origin: *dauncy, dasn't, shan't,* and *frenent.* It has been a pure pleasure to create characters who use such language.

Be assured, the speech, the customs, and the attitudes of the people of the mythical Straffen Manor are authentic. *To fonden* is to tempt to enjoyment and a *fonden look* is a desirous and tempting one. *The snurle* was the Elizabethan equivalent of "a virus" (respiratory symptoms, fever, perhaps with intestinal complaint); *the ague* was similar, concentrating on aches and chills. To *chouse* or to *famble* someone was to cheat or trick him, and to *mousle* someone was to mouth and nibble them in either a lewd or desirous manner. And a *tankerous* or *tanglesome* fellow was the Elizabethan forerunner of our "cantankerous" one.

The Elizabethans must have indulged frequently in using derisive names and epithets, for many of them have come down to us in their writings. An old fellow could be an old *cod, croat,* or *chocker,* depending on the mood of the moment, and a disagreeable old woman could be an old *trot, bloat,* or *harridan.* An immoral female could be a *sloy, hoyden,* or *trull;* a fat person could be *soss-bellied* or have a *pussley gut;* and a wizened, thin-faced person would be called *chitty-faced.* A dull or slow-witted fellow enjoyed a full range of abusive possibilities: *dolt, buffle-head, beef-brain, addlepate, ass-head, booby,* and *dunderhead* . . . to name a few of the more respectable ones.

Cursing had a particularly colorful flavor in those days. A fascinating array of bodily parts and clothing accoutrements were invented for the Almighty . . . and sworn by. But it was certainly only the noble or wealthy classes that swore with impunity. Everyone else did penance.

As to customs: table manners were considered the mark of noble breeding and proper rearing and were enforced vehemently upon the well-born young. Those who *scarfled* and *slorped* ate greedily and with gutteral noise. Licking fingers or wiping them on garments or tablecloths was considered a grievous offense, which may seem surprising for an era when people ate primarily with knives and fingers and are thought of as tossing bones to dogs milling beneath their tables. Thus, Merrie's crude, gluttonous behavior rightly appalled her gentle companions.

Further, the Elizabethans had no tender regard for children. They thought childhood (they did not even use the term) a messy, troublesome period to be gotten through as quickly as possible. They strongly believed that to spare the rod was to spoil the child and were almost universally physically and verbally abusive to their children. By *their* standards, Overbeake's pinches would have been mild indeed, and it is a mark of the rebel in Jack Huntington that he resents such treatment of Merrie. Apologies to the Dutch humanist Desiderius Erasmus; Jack found his writings on the discipline of children offensive, but everyone else in England at that time found them quite enlightened. He was indeed a "humanist" and a great thinker in his day; it's just that our definition of what it is to be "human" has changed quite a bit in the past four hundred years.

Lastly, I wish to credit the delightful translation of Ovid and *The Art of Love* to Horace Gregory. The lines Jack reads from Ovid are from *Love Poems of Ovid,* translated by Horace Gregory (© 1963 by Horace Gregory). Reprinted by arrangement with New American

Library, a division of Penguin Books USA, Inc., New York, New York.) It is a modern English translation that captures the wit, irreverence, and timeless sensuality of Ovid's verse. I recommend it to you.

And the Lombards? Well . . .
Very like cats, as Elizabeth had said;
They did land on their feet instead of their heads.
Where better to traffic in scheming and malice
Than in the ripe halls of a decadent palace?
A gossip, a secret, an indiscreet passion,
The seamiest morsels became their possession . . .
   and were bartered for advancement.

You may see the Lombards again in the story of Jack and Merrie's daughter, Corinna, coming next.

The Timeless Romances
of *New York Times* Bestselling Author
JOHANNA LINDSEY